E: THE FIFTH PLANET CIRCLING A NAMELESS SUN
PLANETS A-D ARE UNKNOWN.

Part One: Lost and Found

Tempe Arizona
Ocotillo Arts
2015

Second edition

© Charles Bownson 2015

Library of Congress cataloging in publication data

Brownson, Charles 1945-
E

PS3552.R788E 813.54
2 v.
v.1. Lost and Found
v.2. Seen and Unseen

I. Title. II. Last and First Men. III. Crossing Over.
IV. The Dispossessed. V. The Translator.
VI. There Is

ISBN 978-0-9893492-7-7 (Lost and Found)
ISBN 978-0-9893492-9-1 (Seen and Unseen)

TABLE OF CONTENTS

Art detective finds his quarry to be mostly rumor.
The Sand People's lesson is not learned
and results are mixed.

E₁

LAST AND FIRST MEN

It was a particularly sandy day.

It won't be too many years, C John thought as he made his way across the embankment, before it's impossible to live here comfortably. Already people, well-off people, were backing out of the Valley into the Mazatzals or another of the ranges which enclosed the city. Or back to where they came from.

Topping the embankment, C John kept low to get under the scouring wind flowing up the other side — as he would have done out of instinctive combat caution anyway. But staying close to the ground was a less than easy thing now. His old muscles didn't like it and his old mind didn't either. Was coming not to like it. But for someone in his line of work, being inconspicuous was needful and if he wanted to stand up now and then it might be time to go.

After a season of storms his goggles were getting crazed and hard to see through. Ahead of him, to the west, the low orange sun glowed like a new bloodstain on a dirty brown shirt. Below, traffic crawled through the Washington interchange, the Inter canal only a length of twine laid along the other side of twelve lanes of mostly electric cars pushing quietly ahead like a crowd of cowed and hungry refugees. An intercity train was heading west on the overpass. The beam of its single eye reflected back dully from the soup of tan grit through which it nosed.

Puce, thought C John. The color of the dust at that height is puce — an unflattering, not especially threatening name.

Behind him on the lee side it was beginning to be dusk and in the deepest layers, in the shadow of the embankment, it was night-stuffy as under a photographer's shroud. One of those big glass plate cameras, thirty-five kilos on a tripod, which he had only seen in pictures, as the shrouded photographer himself saw the world on a ground-glass screen. This was hypocritical snobbery. C John smiled sardonically at himself — his own pockets were full of sensory prostheses. Night vision, infrared, hot ears, remote touch…

The fence enclosing the hospital on the lee side was only visible in short sections by the light of its own sodium lamps, little orange suns hiding from their angry parent.

What C John had come for was lying about three-quarters down the embankment. It was a painting, pretty well slashed up — deceased, in fact. From his knowledge of stolen art C John identified it at once as a Fernand Leger taken by subterfuge from a museum in Illinois a couple of generations before. Over a century, actually.

As he recalled, in this case a forgery had been substituted and the theft wasn't discovered until it was sent to be cleaned. Or perhaps it had been the appraiser. *La Boîte à Chapeau Polychrome.* A square meter and a half of oil-stained canvas, now shreds and broken sticks.

Nor was it hard to guess whose peg it had recently hung from, though he certainly wasn't the original thief and how he had come by it would not be easy to find out. Maxfield was the man's name. A substantial collector of works legitimately acquired but also a man with deep basements. Maxfield was one of those who had recently sequestered himself in the mountains. An energy efficient place dug back into a steeply placed ledge strongly reminiscent of the Anasazi cliff houses. Time was this was national wilderness land but all that was paid very little attention now and for some twenty years, if you could afford it. Luis Maxfield would not be thwarted so.

C John squatted down on the hillside below the destroyed painting. Probably it was tossed over the fence out of a car last night. The traffic bots which circulate up and down the road spotted it shortly after dawn but for most of the day it was classified trash and ignored, until the cleaners came by in the afternoon and gave it a closer look. C John thought maybe the ADOT bots were smarter than the humans now, if they could tell art from a ball of chicken-wire.

After prodding a bit into the dust beneath it to confirm his ideas, he took a few photographs of the situation, bagged the trash, and stood up. That was a groan. He could still rise up directly out of a squat, but only just.

C John pulled his goggles back down over his wind-toughened face and sidestepped back up the hill with his black plastic bag of booty. To himself he seemed a forlorn picture of a man, rather more of a cowboy than a detective, who spent his life out of doors rather than in, indoors at a desk looking speculatively at a computer screen, arms crossed at the wrists on top of his head. But a lot of people here presented this sandblasted visage, which was easily acquired. Ophthalmic diseases were on the rise again, too. People thought they could get by with a hanky.

Over the ridge, down into the lee night, working along the hospital perimeter to a durchgang behind a remote power station bearing up a crowd of moonfaced antennae all looking one way, toward the holocaust. The narrow passage in the fence led through to the street where C John had parked his little three-wheeled electric car beside an inconspicuous gate which only appeared to be locked. The trash bag went into the jump space behind the seat, barely. C John fitted himself in and moved off the curb, mysteriously moved along by the hiss of sand against the car's pudgy backside. It was an old car. Once it had been orange. Sun and wind had made it pink.

At least, he knew it to be pink in the daytime. The car's one peering eye swept the roadway ahead, looking around corners as C John maneuvered through the choked and strangled night toward home.

Plenty of sturm und drang to go around here. Long time since the stygiated stars.

On the way he spoke a curt message to central dispatch that the object had been retrieved and he would bring it around in the morning.

The front exposure of C John's house had been scraped away over the years and now, the yard lights startled awake by his turning in from the street, it was as bare as the day after christmas with one tattered palo verde and a short hair of tough desert weeds. He'd stopped caring about that, though he never seemed to fail of noticing it. The car went into the garage, a large enclosure built for long dead bigger vehicles and now filled with boxes and junk that would all have to be gotten rid of if he shifted out of the Valley. *When* he shifted, C John silently corrected himself. The garage door seals sucked up tight, which always made his ears go dead for a moment, and C John went inside empty-handed.

Night comes quick and early here.

C John was fond of these portentous and preferably gloomy pronouncements. It was a taste he cultivated in himself.

But he sighed, a little raggedly, nevertheless. He was sixty years old now. Birthday last week. Calls from several people acknowledging that round number, people who wouldn't have noticed the previous but prime one. Jen, Zack. C John was not on decent terms with his wife — but still decent enough for her to press the fourth speed button on her phone anyway — and his daughter was simply always busy. Not counting her living sixteen hours in the future where it is always ungodly early.

It's a cosmological thing, she says. It has to do with running forward on the bullet train. For a seat.

C John Mackinaw gave himself ten more years. After that it would be a gift. He had a rather pitiful desire to see the new century — as if things would be any different at one minute after midnight in the year 2100 more than they were sixteen hours in the future.

He didn't know why he felt old. Perhaps it was thyroid. It usually is something chemical, whatever is the matter. Too much exposure, like his pink electric three-wheeler. Feeling ground down by something always lacking — companionship, air, sex, respect. That no matter what it was, you already tried that and it didn't work the last time, either.

C John didn't like himself. He felt he'd become a whiner, unfit for society. How was it when Enrico Caruso first complained to a microphone in 1916? Maybe it had something to do with Italian, which nobody spoke anymore. Just as j'aime tu sounds better, so does Eduardo di Capua, celebre compositore, autore della canzone napoletana scrisse la musica di "'O sole mio."

French will be going on the endangered list too which only people in the art biz like C John need to know just as once upon a time if you were in science you had to know German. Gods preserve us from an economic miracle in some obscure dialect of Bengali.

As to Señor Maxfield, he was a citizen of the world. C John refreshed his memory out of what his gizmo knew while he made himself a dinner of meatless chili and salad.

Talktalk, he said. Maxfield.

Giz would be offended by this baby language but C John was too tired to be civil. Giz responded with a potted biography of an American illustrator born 1870.

Chopchop. Source.

Maxfield Parrish, by Coy Ludwig, 1973. Most recent authority.

Nix. Looweese Maxfield, living.

C John thought that Giz's sort order must have been overturned for him to begin with the least probable result, though it was amusing to think that Don Luis ranked beneath a painter of languid naked boys in cerulean egg tempera.

Maxfield's was old money grown bigger by dealings in all the favorite corruptibles — food, energy, pharmaceuticals, and the global information soup, what until recently was called the media, a reorientation which Maxfield himself had a hand in. Dip in your spoon anywhere, it's all the same Orwellian stuff. The Soup was not a raison d'être for Giz, exactly — he was no more than a logical outcome of the same ingredients which are in the Soup. But C John had given the little fellow some tinkers which certainly were along subversive lines. Thus not a good item to lose.

C John was always amused by other people's gizmos. Always gendered, not always human. It tells a lot about you, who your gizmo is. Some are cats, or trees. Some are imaginary friends. But very few were able to do what Giz could, such as real-time monitoring of probability nests, looking for rare events, spotting the virtuals in a room — snoops and pipes especially — by analyzing the mathematics of the space.

C John's gizmo was not a man. It wasn't that Zack was a woman that hers was also — C John would not have known what to do with Roger or Roman or Reggie. Known what to say to, how to make a man out of one such. He'd been raised by women, spent his working life with women, mostly. Didn't know squink about them, apparently, but he was comfortable. Had been comfortable. *Zack* was a pet name, and Zack's gizmo was simply Her.

Jen's gizmo was a girl by courtesy, rather an old girl, the kind networks are made of. Treelike gizmos were slow and dendritic in their collecting of patterns. Giz was like bamboo.

Giz was a resident alien personality, an invasive inner

guide. In earlier form, the sidekick. Terry of *The Pirates*. Stephen Dedalus. Batman's Robin.

Robin was the toy of a corrupt ideal. There are birds and birds. There was Tony Baretta's cockatoo but he was an affectation — the bird and Robert Blake both. Neither one could have detected their way out of a corn maze. And there are macaws and parrots which are perspicacious enough to go insane just like sapia if you mess with them. Deny them an education, decent food, work worthy of respect.

All those little things which Don Maxfield was in the business of business of taking away from others to give unto himself.

The popular culture is always more honest than *Les Boîtes à Chapeaux Polychrome*. Ripe mouths wearing hats of many colors. See the Japanese and their bigeyed lolitas. The original Batman, clan chiroptera, not our chrotopterus auritus, the wooly false vampire bat, but the ghost bat, macroderma gigas.

As C John spooned up his chili before it got cold he looked over the more judgmental facts about Luis Maxfield which Giz had given him. Yes, a cynical and unsavory man who leeched off ways to make money on environmental destruction, contamination, fanaticism, fascism, and what scraps of civil liberty remain. But unsavory to predators does not mean lacking in taste. Maxfield's acknowledged collection contained many impressive pieces from Giotto and early Zen brushwork to artists not yet prime. The emphasis of the collection however was what C John himself liked: popular work grown into aged veneration. Things which were bestsellers in their youth, perhaps in a less than respectable medium whiffed with inauric multiples like ukiyoe and manga.

Perhaps that was because C John thought he himself might have benefited by the second look he never got. Maxfield's motivation was doubtless also inscrutable.

Not, opined Detective Mackinaw, the sort of man to

slash up a Leger for fun.

Not a man to worry about prosecution as a receiver of stolen art, either, even if he were too fastidious to steal it himself.

Something unhappy had turned up in the provenance of the Leger? A connection to someone, or an event, to which Maxfield would rather not be connected? More than rather not. Tossing the thing onto the roadside was not behaving inconspicuously. That was a challenge, a dare.

The Leger was made off with in the first place by putting a fake in its place. Perhaps it was made off with a second time by the same means? Cut to ribbons that way it would be difficult to authenticate, but like moods it always comes down to chemistry and there was plenty left for that.

A form of conspicuous consumption, tossing out rubbish left behind in the house in the Valley after moving up to the redoubt? To be seen disposing of poor man's meat?

Some things to work on. C John went to the sink to wash out his chili bowl, then routinely checked on the recycle tank to be sure it wasn't full. It was. He pressed the button on the splash guard to swap tanks for the morning shower.

It wasn't good for him to eat at bedtime like this but he'd been up since five a.m. dawn. He was tired and there were things still to do — medicines, set up laundry, stretching exercises for his rebuilt back. Another hour.

Chili now. Stolen art in the morning.

Before waving the light out he told Giz to leave messages with the dispatcher and also a fingerpost that he might be hard to find for a couple of days and pleasegod not be calling him up like a dead soul, resurrecting a man who would rather lie low in his grave and not be spotted window-shopping at the mall. With a mousehole for Zack just in case.

« »

Monsieur Homme was a small man. He was also a little

twisted, bearing the marks of some common environmental maladies which had unevenly retarded his growth. You see a lot of people like that, C John reflected. He didn't like being reminded that people are throwaways in nature when he himself is only a year from the plummeting life expectancy of sixtyone, and what few are his defenses. What thin walls we have, Grandma. All the better to keep track of us, my dear, so we don't rot betimes.

Monsieur Homme's left leg was short some, so that he walked sailor-fashion, and he was hard of sight from ophthalmic disease caused by the dirt which was always in the air. He could have had these things treated, of course. Where C John tried to keep low to the ground Monsieur Homme already was, and so could give his mind to something more productive than excess fitness.

Homme was what he called himself when he appeared at breakfast in the coffee shop where C John went most mornings for espresso and a pecan roll. He never made coffee for himself anymore. A pot of it would mostly go down the sink and the espresso machine hadn't been used in years owing to his forgetting how to work it. His only complaint was that no one served coffee which was hot enough, even on an ordinary thirty-degree morning.

Giz corrected him. Thirty-one today. C John stuck the cup into the shop's oven and gave it ten seconds.

Only then did he notice that his favorite corner seat was already occupied. The one where he could sit with his back to the wall and watch the passers-by. A deformed little man was sitting in it with a cup untouched primly before him on the round faux marble tabletop, his hands resting equally primly on either side of the cup and an absolutely unheard-of *hat* on the seat of the vacant chair.

C John sheared off like a robomaid when it runs into an infrared wall. He circled about in the middle of the room. All the other seats were equally dubious.

Please, came a rich plummy voice from the window seat.

I'll move my hat. It was only holding your place, anyway, said the fellow with becoming politesse.

C John pushed the chair back with his knee, widening the space enough for him to sit down without relinquishing either the cup or the pecan roll in his other hand.

My name is Hum, the fellow said, keeping his own hands to himself. Or perhaps he said *Humm.*

Waiting for me, Hmm?

Monsieur's mouth twitched with a momentary smile. It was a wide mouth, and on his small head it could have been monkeyish, but perhaps because it seemed to belong to his large eyes, damp and round and wide open, the effect was more that of a diplomatic raccoon, enhanced by two tufts of white hair, about all the hair he had left, sticking up behind each ear. Another set of ears which this alert man would certainly know how to use.

When C John was settled, Hum took his out own gizmo from a pocket, evidently a better behaved one than C John's if it could be allowed to join the conversation. He laid it on the table where he could keep a discreet eye on it, such as it was — Hum wore thick lenses limpid as clear seawater which made it hard not to notice his eyes. In any case, his gizmo on the table was mostly show anyway — the thing was surely whispering in his ear.

What can I do for you, Monsieur? I'm a busy man.

Monsieur Homme laughed softly. By Jove, he said. You do talk business, sir. I like that in a man. A man who doesn't do business is not to be trusted, I say.

C John goggled at this parody. Perhaps he talked to himself at times this way in a certain mood de jeu — was the man making fun of him? Letting him know there were no secrets? Insulting him pour quoi? Contempt?

You have a painting which belongs to me, said Homme. Or it did at one time. So large. Of a hat.

Yes…

Is it in fit condition to be seen?

No, sir. It's dead. Smashed to sticks.

I see. Thank you. That is all I require.

Monsieur Homme picked up his hat and his gizmo with a quick sleight and rose to go.

Hold on — C John's hand darted out, released by a slippage of forbearance, but stopped short of taking hold of the other man's arm. The hand pulled itself back, laid itself onto the table. Monsieur's eyes widened slightly, if that were possible, and he sat down again.

Your painting?.

Well — heh. I suppose the museum which once hung it would not say so. It has passed through my hands.

When?

Ah. Oh, I thought it might be salvageable. I was fond of it. Somewhat fond.

And you sold it to Maxfield? Let's say within the last ten years.

Ah. Monsieur Homme delicately raised his cup of espresso to his lips and took the first sip. The back tar must be cold by now. C John had already drunk his at a swallow like an Italian. He gazed at the brown foam on the inside of the now empty cup. Not brown. Not puce, not ecru. Milky…

Look, C John said a little roughly. I think you know more about this than I do. I'll bet you can tell me how many pieces they made of the thing. Why could you possibly want to waste my time? Do you have some goons going through my house while you detain me here? What for?

Monsieur took off his gray fedora and put it meticulously onto the center of the table. You must see the Last Men, he said.

Who?

A sect, sir. Like all these tribes they disdain what others choose to call them and refer to themselves as The People. Everyone is People, so that is not a very useful cognomen outside the tribe. The *Last Men* will be satisfactory. You haven't heard of them.

No.

That doesn't surprise me. The People would not ordinarily be your business. They are not part of the market economy.

But they're trafficking in art nevertheless.

Yes, and it doesn't suit their temperament, I must say.

How did your Leger get into this? Formerly yours.

Ah. To speak of the Last Men, you must know, is to invoke an irrational ... *presence.* It rises out of the oldest part of the brain — I'm sure you know what I mean, when you are not knowing how you come to know something.

Yes. Intuition.

My goodness, no. More subtle than that. Intuition is only a word for belittling inarticulate people.

Oh, I — but M Homme cut him off with a wiping motion of his hand, like clearing a foggy window.

Art, he said rises from the reptile brain where our strongest emotions are tethered. The much talked-about right side of the cerebral cortex is the safe house, neutral territory on which to meet. It is a place to which you can go but only if you consent to leave a great many things outside. The Last Men will come so far, no farther, and you cannot go where they are.

I doubt I could get a search warrant in any case.

Homme shrugged to indicate the dearth of alternatives. It is one of our basic tales, he said. You descend into a mindless realm, are purified and cleansed, and return to life with a gift. It is the Orpheus tale, among others. You are an educated man. Tell me: what was Orpheus' mistake, his weakness?

He looked back.

Exactly. By looking back he revealed that his conscious mind, the planning and anticipating — scheming — mind, was not asleep. Orpheus did not go down in good faith, but under pretense. His quest was not authentic, and so he was denied the gift.

And why should I do any better? A detective. Trusts no one, thinks everyone is lying.

Come, come. You are in search of lost art. It has gone where art goes which is let loose — back whence it came. Like a helium balloon to the moon, when the child lets go. And then there are tears, eh?

I'm going to need directions.

I'll send you someone.

You go there yourself on weekends, Monsieur? You have a little place?

Ah — heh. Prosaically: I go to the mountains. There is nothing here for us anymore. In a few years this valley will be full of sand, a permanent hurricane of sand seeking a way out, scouring the life from everything here. In a few years there will be nothing except rotten spires of concrete eaten away by the wind. In the deepest parts, here where we sit now gazing at women in the sun, there will be no life, not even a cockroach to be ground to powder in the infinite darkness. *Go to the mountains*, sir, or become one of the Last Men. There is no art here anymore.

There are rather a lot of mountains…

You'll manage. People like you can find your way.

Said Monsieur Homme, and was gone. Taken his hat and disappeared with a pop like a character in a children's movie. C John went back to the bar for another espresso.

Now what the hell? Damned imp. It would seem smarter to find something out about Monsieur Homme than to charge off into the wilderness in search of the People. He put Giz on that. Giz went right for the street cams and in a minute or two located Mr. Hum two blocks away at the tram stop. A man in a hat could hardly be overlooked, anyway. The tram arrived; Hum got on. C John left the tracking to Giz and gave his mind to other things. A trip to the men's room.

Perpetual sandstorm...
Probability is high.
Eh?

Though in public the practice was to keep your gizmo quiet, C John didn't like it to whisper into his ear that way. It reminded him of the procurers who inveigle naïve women into the Casbah in the old movies. Especially on the way to the men's room.

What was probably high in Giz's estimation was the truth factor in M Homme's prediction of a permanent sandstorm in the valley. That was for sure the only thing Homme said with an empirical score above two. Whoever he proved to be when Giz had found him out, C John already knew that he was not Monsieur Homme. Hum was only a performance intended for C John's entertainment, calculated to appeal to his mélange of eccentric interests. And it had been amusing, C John admitted, washing his hands.

Next in the morning routine: hie to the library to consult the Oracle.

Hie. A legitimate conjugable verb, improbably. He hied, she is hieing. From Middle English *hien* the dictionary said, giving C John a pleasant Sunday morning picking through Chaucer and Lackland without finding anything very interesting.

Now I hie me off to sleep, may the night my soul to keep ... Sich beeilen verschlafen ... la nuit du mort...

C John pushed through the crowd of phantoms at the door of the espresso bar and halfway up the block continued to feel them plucking at his sleeve. Baksheesh! Baksheesh!

《 》

Consulting the Library's new Sybil had become a routine with C John, whose ordinary companions — Giz, that is —

lacked a soupçon of the personality with which The Fount of All Wisdom bubbled over. People get tired of simple truths, he thought, especially unvarnished. Judging by this suddenly popular library service, what people want, maybe only want, is to be told interestingly costumed and bewigged stories, unfraught and seemingly as fathomless as Richelieu. C John had found that quite often the Oracle told him things which he did not in fact know. Today, perhaps messages from the Last Men in their cave, or wherever. Some way of propping open the limbic door which let these sibyls make unexpected connections among the flotsam they encountered. It was hardly a fraud — he didn't expect libraries to sponsor frauds — but it was certainly a fad. Like crossword puzzles and table rapping and mummies' curses. Intellectually disreputable perhaps. Oddities are. C John was fond of odd things. Odds and ends.

In the lobby he fell in with a man he was encountering at the Fount with increasing frequency. This fellow was of a striking appearance, with the gaunt harried look of someone who was having trouble eating, who ate without pleasure, who was never satisfied. As it happened this time, the demon in chrysalis was standing in front of a mirrored elevator door so that C John's reflection appeared to keep him company. C John recoiled. We could be twins, he thought.

He'd never spoken to this man. Before he could begin now the man rushed off for his daily breath of narcotic fumes.

Oracles don't guess, C John mumbled. It's a cultivated preference for low probability associations. *Resonance* is no more than what we want to hear.

He looked at the small crowd of people waiting to get in, at this hour mostly old people like himself. It was the first time he really saw them. If his condition resembled theirs at all it would be cause for worry, he thought, and what had seemed a harmless amusement now began, when C John came out of himself for a moment, to seem something more sinister.

He left the library without hearing the Oracle.

《 》

Over lunch Giz presented C John with something skimmed from the Soup — two pictures.

This is the same person? C John said.

Don't be metaphysical what it means *same person.*

OK, good. Who's she talking to?

Unknown.

So why am I seeing them?

They were floating on the Soup, Giz said.

They're an Association.

I suggest she is an informant of M Homme, or a factotum.

A busybody, C John corrected him.

Nicht wahr, said Giz — between them a polite acknowledgement of a request — and went off to look for some corroboration, leaving behind Ravel's *Le tombeau de Couperin* to occupy the time.

Humans are great seekers after meaning, C John reflected. Put two things beside each other — the cheddar and the lettuce say — and the mind will find a story to tell. what the storytelling part of the mind is *for* because that's what conscious life is — making meaning out of happenstance. You need years and years of zazen under many masters to stop doing it, to see things as they really are: just two straphangers in a crowd.

So did the Oracles tell the truth or was it all just a sandwich? One time on a packed bus C John caught a glimpse of a woman with whom as a teenager he had been desperately infatuated for two whole summers, and she looked just as good now and C John discovered that he was just as infatuated as ever. But she was at the other end of the bus. It was a chance event. There would be no story about a brief steamy second chance.

A detective needed to be careful not to explain too much.

When the Couperin was over and the sandwich was eaten, Giz was waiting politely. Much too politely. C John was beginning to be testy over what was proving to be a wasted day.

A failure, Giz reported. Recursive narcissism. Monsieur Homme is more able than I.

What? Who is the woman in the pictures, then?

Unknown. When the conversation taking place was located she is documented there as your wife.

Hah! Obviously not so.

Yes, well ... rather as her gizmo.

Good looking gizmo. Are you guys going incarnate? If so I should trade you in for the new model of succubus. So then — a mésalliance of files in the data?

Evidently corrupt.

Good. Your kind are dangerous enough already. And who is she talking to?

Oh, Monsieur Homme, of course.

And who is *he*?

Yourself.

There did not seem to be a light or witty reply to this wornout device. This was the point when C John began to think of his shadowy lowbrow double Monsieur Homme as the undetective on the case. Also the point when he realized this was a legs case and he might as well leave Giz home and stop wasting time in coffee shops and libraries trying to not get started.

« »

The first thing to be done, then, was for C John to verify his hypothesis concerning Maxfield. That this wealthy man was a buyer of stolen art was not in question. This had been street knowledge for years. How he was connected to the clandestine art market, how the transactions were made, what he did with the take were all matters mysterious to police and street alike. Without this information any further action was impossible. Who to suborn? How to make the proposal seem authentic? Presumably Maxfield didn't touch deals which were not from a small group of trusted people or an approach which did not follow an invariant set of customs. Nor was there any possibility of a raid. Where to raid? What doors to kick in? C John never made so much as a doodle or a pencil drawing of a stick man, but he was enough in sympathy with the artist to be puzzled by a collector who couldn't possess his collection. Who was so fastidious about keeping his distance from incriminating associations that the whole point of the enterprise was reduced to not see the things, not contemplate them, but only to invent them in dreams like women on busses.

Or, C John thought, like a sadist who keeps his victims locked up in a secret room somewhere in the castle in anticipation of the day when he can overthrow that system of proprieties which binds him to the companion who is only the *seeming* object of his desires.

The Leger painting was the first opportunity in C John's time to trace a provenance to this man. To break into his secret windowless room of garish color — black and red the usual — in time to save the screaming half-flayed model, her black silk evening costume peeled back to reveal … something or other,

C John was well aware that he had not been comfortable with himself since Zack left for Japan and he began living alone, untethered to the phenomenal world. His mind was working in ways which were not good for business. Rarely was there anything undisputable encountered except trivial matters. The vic was dead — *really* dead. Dried blood was a certain distinctive color close to Venetian red but unfortunately so are a lot of things — Morisot gowns, gondola stripes. He was thinking, since Hum's suggestion that morning, that maybe the Last Men were coming to get C John instead of the other way round.

C John would not have thought, when he was a rookie cop during the Santa Monica levee break, that he had any talent for detection or sympathy for art, least of all that at retirement age he would be plying his trade in a desert burg where modern music had been Brahms for two hundred years, where mummified Broadway hits had survived Broadway itself, where Fernand Leger was considered a puzzle. But until life here became unpleasant even for a right man, not so many years ago, it was the burg of choice for sadistic art collectors when they were at home. Lots of windowless rooms done up in Venetian red and wonderless yokels living in the biggest small town in America.

And now a little man in a hat told him that he needed to pay attention. Carbon dioxide stabilization figures in the seven hundreds, loss of a quarter of the world's GDP, mobs of people running over the cliff edge in numbers not seen since the black death, heat islands where isolated tribes were growing third eyes and speaking incomprehensible creoles, entirely new pristine coastlines, beaches, swamps. C John had noticed none of this. It had not been his business to notice it beyond the fact that Tuesday was unusually sandy. His business was to traffick in antiques — languages, precious objects, obscure facts if there are facts, old song lyrics and movie plots from when there were movies, the innards of obsolete gizmos. And now he was to pay attention to some particular knowledge which was needed to save his soul which is to say his reptile hindbrain.

《 》

A legs case, then. The street said, when he asked — which meant asking Giz for a simple statistical calculation that brought an annoyed sneer to the little fellow's voice — that C John ought to look out for a certain person (now old and possibly careless of consequences) who was the most likely to have been one of Maxield's marriage brokers and who might now be willing to talk about it unless he got the idea that the Leger had resurfaced pour encourager les autres in which case he'd died of tuberculosis last year.

Finding people was a Giz specialty but going to see them was not something he did well. Though Giz had learned a little rudimentary diplomacy over the years, with C John's coaching, his behavior during interviews was limited to keeping C John to the necessary facts. He was the person at congressional hearings who is always leaning sideways to pass on something to the man in the hot seat.

I believe, Senator, that the correct number is four.

No, sir. What is called the tragedy of the commons — a phrase coined I believe by Stewart Brand — no sir, I am advised that is incorrect — refers to the inclination of persons to look after their own interests first so that land held in common — I believe, sir, you are familiar with the practice of humance — sheep, sir — held in common, as I say, such as the atmosphere —

Well, sir, I don't mean *land* in the strict sense. It's a figure of speech.

Don't improvise, the handler hisses, audible three rows back.

Yes, sir, I do understand that we deal here in facts —

Despite the street's odds, the old man recommended to C John was still alive and finishing out his days in a godown on Indian Bend wash where Sunnyslope used to be. He wasn't complaining.

What the hell? he said. The Tohono O'odham lived this way for centuries and the Anasazi before them. They got along pretty well and so do I.

C John filled in some time asking about native plants and what varieties of squash grow best and the wisdom of planting beans and corn together in the hill and what gourds are good for other than maracas and the details of bootleg canals now the way squatters used to run an electric line off the transformer for themselves in the days when they needed electricity but of course you didn't come here to talk about that, mister.

C John looked around the godown not bothering to politely hide his curiosity. It was a sort of hogan with an inner lining of cloth layers like a croissant. This was covered, with a gap of about a centimeter, with an outer skin of some impervious black stuff. The cloth wicked up water from the canal, evaporated it to cool the hogan, and condensed it again on the inside of the skin down from where it ran back into the little branch canal and on down to the patches of squash and beans. This movement of water carried also a small breeze along which kept the air from being stuffy.

Variation on a cooling tower, the old man said, noticing. The Persians made ice this way fifteen hundred years ago.

A few possessions were stored around the perimeter, mostly tools, with one bag of clothes and one of food suspended out of the way of mice.

Besides, he said, mice carry the virus. And they attract snakes. I suppose there will be a dieback of mice when we're gone, but not yet. I'd miss the snakes.

But when C John opened a topic of a different interest he harvested mostly yeps and nopes from the old one's protective persona.

It was not a wasted trip, however. Aside from the respite of comfort in the hogan he did learn by implication that there had been two middlemen. The old man's other end was put away some years ago, probably natural causes, and the current incumbent had a line of ruthlessness on his palm which ought not be crossed. As to who the new man was at his own end, that was not to be spoken of. The old man wouldn't admit to any specific deals but C John got the impression that the Leger had indeed passed through his hands; where it went after that no one knew.

And that was the way it was going to be — a sand castle of guesswork and assumptions which C John had to get inside before the wind blew it away, and no one knew a thing.

When the yepping and noping were done C John stopped outside to explore the wash some. The old man's hogan was placed not actually in the wash. That would still not have been smart even if a flash flood hadn't been heard of since about 2075. Up above, looking carefully about himself with the zoomer in his goggles, C John confirmed that his visit had attracted the interest of interesting people. And that too was the way it was going to be as always in a legs case. C John hoped he wasn't going to be leaving a lot of bodies along the roadside like rough wood crosses beside a wagon trail. Anyway, these folks would know what the old man said before he said it. If they were dozing it was all right. If they heard unspoken words better than C John did there would be a dead old man under the cooling tower on Indian Bend wash.

Oh well.

How long, C John asked himself, looking up at the sky with hand-shaded eyes, goggles or no, since the sun was out from under — or was it behind — the brown cloud?

One thousand two hundred six days, Giz whispered in his ear.

《 》

So what was Maxfield up to? Selling out, wanting to travel

light? Hard up? Going into retreat like a zen hermit waiting for a new emperor and more propitious times, taking only a few well-loved talismen for the trip through the gateless gate? Or moving it all to his bunker and this one fell off the back of the truck?

Find the bunker.

Find the Last Men.

Find the broker.

Find the frustrated john who wanted to have a painting of a hat.

Find Monsieur Homme.

« »

Over the next few days C John made progress on none of these tasks.

Then a man showed up at his house, materializing in the early evening out of the dark place behind the breezeway connecting the garage to the kitchen door. He wore a hooded cape made of some dark-colored synthetic which rustled when he moved, and leggings underneath of the same material, tucked into tall boots somewhat like mukluks, a costume which lent him an eerie gliding motion. When he pushed up his goggles to talk — a politeness from the early years of goggles as eyewear which had fast become as unusual as tipping one's hat to a lady — C John discovered how black his exposed skin was. A man who lives out of doors.

He said nothing, studied C John speculatively, after a moment's consideration pulled his goggles down again. Silently he took C John's elbow to steer him through the breezeway toward the ravine which ran along the back of the house, leaving the way he came.

This ravine was little more than a drain running along like a wide service alley between the backs of the two rows of houses. In the one direction it came from the mountain;

in the other, down to a grassy little park where some soccer clubs played on weekends, a park which was actually an
overflow contingency depression about ten feet below street
level. Supposed to be grassy. There was about as much rain
as contingency nowadays.

The man in the rustling cassock was leading C John toward the mountain, using a well-trodden path created by the
ever present squatters living farther up.

I don't like enclosed places any more, said the man at
last in a voice as rusty as his clothes. You will excuse me
this. One is overheard in such places.

Of course, replied C John — what do you expect?

Not to be interfered with.

C John snorted, amused. And what did the fellow want
not to be heard?

I have a piece of knowledge. I was advised that you are
the person who should be told.

Yes? By whom?

The question was ignored.

Tomorrow morning. This address.

C John took the bit of paper held out to him and while
he was trying to make out the writing in the dark the rustling
man glided away.

Another play actor, C John grunted, and turned around
to walk home.

The ravine was not a good place to walk. It never was
— the neighborhood was shabby when C John first moved
there — but it was shocking to him how rough and ugly
the landscape had become. The ravine was full of trash. The
walls were crumbling and trees in the house yards behind the
walls were dead. Grapefruits, pines, eucalyptus spires bare
and leaning ominously to the ground, olives, agave, yellow-
bells — even the native plants in the ravine, mesquite and
palo verde, were struggling. Some prickly pears had popped
into desperate bloom, arresting dabs of red and yellow in a

dry wash of dirty tans and browns. The people living along the ravine had long since abandoned what they had no money to keep up, that which made no brave public face.

C John saw that his house was as shabby as the rest. For whom would he pretend gentility?

Still, it was discouraging. There had never been any sort of neighborhood — no esprit, no exchange, no street life. That disappeared even in the pockets where it could once be found, cafés in the historic districts, interior courtyards in the newer downtown condos and street-level shops now mostly closed. Here in an inner suburb in the nook of a butte nobody had gotten around to building on C John had been hiding for the time being from the meanness and street violence beginning to spread elsewhere. For a time.

《 》

The address he was given by the cassocked man who had *come into some knowledge* was in the west valley, at a place little more than an intersection of vacant lots. It was one of those places where out-of-work people still gathered on weekday mornings despite a century's effort to break the custom, which only grew stronger the more poor people there were who would work day to day, hand to mouth with no future, doing outdoor labor which would wear them down to toothpicks in less than a year. These used to be mostly Mexican, mostly illegals, but as the agricultural and gardening jobs they once depended on literally dried up there had come to be Polish roofers, Pakistani leaflet distributors, black meter readers walking unwired slums, trenchers running cable and pipe, pavers and other street nuisances and so on, and on, and the Mexicans were long since a minority. A noticing cop would now see teachers, office workers, and other fallen bourgeois among them, and C John wondered what persecution from the established beggars these new ones would suffer.

As C John pulled up along the curb one man detached himself and unbidden got into the car. He had the same whispery voice and black-ringed eyes as last night's visitor, but all the homeless looked like that. This man was dressed in several layers of ordinary patched clothing of an impressive dirtiness not achieved overnight.

Directions he gave. Drive around for a bit, then tend south and west toward the reservation boundary. Fifteen minutes later he was told to stop in a dirt turnaround a little ways up the Estrella slope. From here C John followed his guide on a walk of a few more minutes up over a little col. In the basin beyond lay a dead man.

C John squatted beside the corpse, and while his attention was thus elsewhere the guide disappeared.

Damn, he swore softly, for more reasons than that.

There had been little trouble taken to conceal the dead man's identity. He had no wallet but in his shirt pocket was a piece of paper with a number, probably a wireless code, scribbled on it. Giz confirmed this after a moment but the lessor of this access was a woman whereas a man was needed — this man, chunky and late middle-aged, a once well-groomed and soft-fingered man with a hearing aid which would have a serial number etched on it too small for C John to read.

He did not want to be elegant about this. He needed to know now. Giz would take the brute but straightforward procedure of checking all the woman's callers in the last month to look for one who would match this dead body. While Giz chewed on this, C John looked about himself. The place looked like his own domestic ravine only without the houses — or rather some relics of a subdivision killed in infancy, a lonely street of shacks half a kilometer to the west.

Giz had located a probable and fetched a dossier on Qiu Long, a broker.

Broker of what?

Giz's equivalent to a shrug was a blink and a soft falling whistle.

Doesn't look Chinese.

Neither do you.

Damn, C John said again, to himself.

The man wore a ring on his out-flung left hand, a heavy gold ring used as a seal. C John worked it off.

How long dead, Giz?

The little fellow sent out some probes. Two or three hours, he said after a moment.

Reference the office, C John said then, slipping the ring into a pocket. Body Qiu Long, coordinates. Appropriate action.

And then he returned to his car to wait.

《 》

The wait was not long. A new prowler, gleaming black, slid up into the turnaround raising hardly any dust, and parked beside C John's battered polychrome police cart. Two men as sleek as their car got out.

C John walked them up to the body and stood silently to one side while they had a look. This didn't take long, either. A walkaround to confirm that the dead man was dead and had been dead somewhere else too because the body had been dragged up from the road. Some very vague boot prints mostly erased by the wind — there was a rule of thumb for that now like the ones on how long before maggots, how long before stiff, how long until it congeals, and so on, but it was an estimate which C John didn't know. Late last night, probably, the younger one said, testing the sand with long fingers for weight and polish. Quite late.

These Last Men, C John muttered, take lessons from Tiresias.

Seer. Greek mythology, the sharp-eared younger one said, rising up to put out his hand to C John.

Matthias, he said.

John Mackinaw.

Enjoy, the older one said, walked off to his car, and drove dustlessly away. C John smiled tightly. Have to take mine, he said, abashed.

Knew we would, Matthias replied serenely. You can drop me off at the motor pool on Fourth Avenue, John, and we'll talk in my office about ten o'clock?

No assent to this was necessary. C John held the door and walked around the back of the car to his own side, the driver's. Matthias was calling down a field team.

We'll leave it to them, he said.

《 》

Now then, Detective Matthias was saying, leaning back ever farther in his black leather desk chair and uncovering for C John more of the view through his office window. Not much of a view — an empty rectilinear canyon and a jail. Not much of a jail — rez de chausée in glass below five floors of pale tan brick regularly punkt by an imitation of a louvered window to let in light and air. If there were any light and air. The headrest of Matthias's chair stood up tall as a crown. Bought this chair for himself; an investment, seeing how many hours he spent sitting in it.

How did you come, Lt Mackinaw, to be in this out of the way place on Estrella Mountain?

Brought there. Last night — C John described the encounter with the cassocked squatter.

One of the Sand People, Matthias said at once.

Beg pardon, who?

So they call themselves. They've worked out how to accommodate this blowing sand and so have developed a small

niche where they can live undisturbed. We began to notice
them in the last couple of months. No objection if they keep
to themselves but no reason to believe they will. We'll see.
Nothing rash, but people have some dangerous notions.
Would not like to see a pogrom. They are well protected.

Libels, C John said.

Probably. Now this fellow gave you nothing but a rendezvous point?

Correct. It was the second man who knew.

Recognize him?

C John shrugged. Looked like any other day laborer.
Never heard him talk, if it were that leaky tire voice the
first one used. Simply evaporated, even before I could kneel
down to get a look at the body.

Yes, they do that, I'm told. Part of their mystique.

Question is, Matthias — Detective Matthias I mean.
Sorry. How did he know yesterday the man would be dead?
Someone got to him before me.

Mmm. Complicit? Perhaps the bushes talk to them. I
don't think so, John.

The thing is, C John persisted, what did last night's man
in the ravine want with me? Me particularly, I mean. Something today's now dead man was supposed to tell me? Do
you know who he was, Detective?

Working on that, Lieutenant. Best hypothesis: Ben
Kokua, a Samoan businessman — say what?

C John had started up involuntarily in his chair. Character in *Hawaii Five-O*, he said, flustered.

In what?

Television show in the seventies, sir. Pardon, the *nine-
teen* seventies.

Television. More than a century ago.

Yes, sir. A coincidence. Plenty of people with that name,
of course.

Had it wrong anyway, C John thought. Wonder what

happened to poor Qiu Long? Everyone has a story which no one knows.

Matthias kept a speculative silence while C John mumbled to himself. Another jeu of Monsieur's.

We've not met before, John, said Matthias with a little deliberation which C John interpreted as menace and a warning to behave carefully. You're pretty well known for this trivia. It's said you're not quite on the job, that your real interests —

I'm superannuated, C John interrupted, saving Matthias the need for diplomacy. They detach me when I'm not needed elsewhere to get me out of the way, by reason of my particular working knowledge for excuse.

Matthias opened his eyes a fraction at this brutal self-assessment. So it's said, he admitted. Ever found what you were looking for?

No, sir. It's rare to recover stolen art. You develop a case for years and then the bird starts up behind you. No shot. Have to start all over.

That's an antique metaphor, John. I see why people might... ah. Think that chasing after art is a waste of time.

Oh. Well. C John was again abashed. That depends, he said, on your assessment of the value of these things. Millions yes, some of them, but I was thinking rather of cultural value.

Hm. Kokua. Is this to do with art?

Yes.

Matthias snorted.

C John was stolid on his ground. I think, he said, this um, Kokua person was trying to buy a black market painting and the deal went sour. A week ago I reported a fugitive painting turned up smashed …

Matthias made a few quick marks on a small piece of note paper and turned it around for C John to see. That one? he said. Matthias had drawn quite a decent schematic of the Leger.

Ahem. Yes, sir.

Any cause to think so?

Intuition…

Of course. Matthias was baiting him.

If it's not to do with the Leger why else go to the trouble to make it *me* to find the body? They all know on the street that I work on art when I'm not a traffic cop. I don't have anything to do with murders. Dragging me into this would be pointless otherwise.

Sale gone bad. How big?

A legitimate sale might be a hundred thousand. Leger's values have held up pretty well.

A lot of money to smash up. Petty. Who's the seller?

I have reason to think Luis Maxfield.

Reason?

Well, no… That is, not reasoned out. Likely. Known history, has the money needed to sustain his investment, extremely discreet operation that it would be worth more than a trifling canvas to protect. Specializes in this material.

But no evidence.

He is pretty thoroughly secluded. Extremely difficult man to see. I've laid eyes on him once. Moustache, underbrush of white curly hair behind, otherwise elderly bald. Wears shapeless old suits and mostly a bowtie. Old aristocracy. Soft-spoken but suspicious, a little grim.

His organization?

Loyal. Some small indiscretion would not go unnoticed.

Not scruple over it, Matthias said.

No. But these Sand People — a new factor. Outside Maxfield's influence, with an ideology unfriendly to —

Mackinaw?

Sorry, sir. Wool-gathering. These Sand People. Would they have anything to do with a sect going by the name of the Last Men?

The very same, Matthias said in a voice accompanied by a hard stare.

Approachable?

No.

A very long silence ensued.

The Last Men, Monsieur said. Go to the Last Men. Call themselves the People. But in the *mountains*, he had said. Sects blooming left and right in times like these. Everyone after scraps of purity when everything is so dirty. Maxfield did have a mountain retreat, though.

Matthias sat forward abruptly. I'll leave that to you, he said. Follow your hunch. Give the idea three days, see if it's a line worth working. Report in the mornings. That espresso bar where you go. I'll set up a secure pipe, bury it out of sight. Your giz will know how to find it.

Matthias was already ordering a lunch for himself as C John went out. In the hallway a clinking of glassware. Cops.

So. Three days.

Go to the People. Obvious next question: When is a sand person's At Home?

And if the shadowy Monsieur is not playing his own cards who is he in behalf of? What does he want with me? Only the shadow himself knows?

《 》

C John took his not-new not-black not-large electric tricycle home for lunch where he ate a cold sandwich with hot mustard and the roast beef that was supposed to last two weeks and looked as if it might, and beer in a non-clinking unbreakable aluminum cup out of his father's backpacking kit.

Nobody went backpacking anymore. It was thirty-five degrees at night even at six thousand feet and you needed to carry so much water you could hardly walk as far as the trailhead. C John's father's sleeping bag and tent had no conceivable use. And what for — the scenery? Laughable. As for solitude, communing with yourself and so forth, you'd find a better hermitage down in the sand. Time enough for a new hokku cycle if you could keep your paper clean. Gizmos don't work down in the sand.

The little guy's way of life is doomed before mine is, C John muttered, scooping Giz off the table into his pocket. He washed the cup, left the plate, and went out by the breezeway door toward the ravine behind the house. The door sucked shut with a disgusting noise which reminded C John of childhood treats like ice cream and spaghetti.

Because you could make disgusting noises, of course.

And he anticipated correctly. Halfway up the ravine a very lean man in a silvery soutane, or rather formerly a rock which stood up and *became* such a man, fell silently into step for a dozen steps and then with a light touch on the arm turned them aside where a new sinkhole made a convenient shelter.

Here they sat. The sand priest floated a piece of fabric across the opening with a sweep of his arm like a trapdoor spider returning home after lunch.

We wait, he said in that voice which now had obvious utility — it blended with the wind and must be devilish hard to extract from the wind with smart ears.

Quickly it became stifling. The hole was not big enough for one person let alone two elves. The sandman showed no discomfort. A little time passed. C John's eyes were burning, so that when the hole was opened again even forty-degree air felt good.

Put this on before you stand up, the new man said, producing from some inner pocket another cassock, initially a little cube the size of the marshmallow in a hot cocoa.

Your gizmo.

C John passed it over. It went into a little sack.

He won't like that. That's a bag of cats.

But Giz supinely went. To sleep, hopefully. Not euthanized.

The sandman smiled broadly, a quite unexpected acknowledgement of C John's bond with a machine, empathy which bubbled up warm and yellow out of the gray, grim lava.

We can't afford to have such friends, the sandman said, indicating the sack. A certainty of betrayal and anguish. Like lending money to a gambler. Come. We walk so.

The sandman pointed up the ravine to where it spread out on the mountain like a hand.

They walked quickly, C John somewhat less quietly than the jesuit in front of him. Already he was thirsty.

But they weren't long. Behind a thin spine of granite which came partway down the mountain like a wall there were three others sitting cross-legged on the ground in seeming council. C John and his guide sat with them.

After a time one of the three produced a bottle of water for C John. This is a dead spot, another said. A hole in the surveillance blanket. You can speak freely here, but don't move suddenly — you might attract a passing eye.

C John nodded, reluctant to say anything in what amounted to an embarrassing stage voice.

Here is our business with you, said another in the manner of a council elder. We are not interested in paintings. Where would we hang them?

If this were humor, no one else thought so.

C John nodded toward the outer world. It's said that you are a sect. Purs et durs.

This was funny. Sibilant snorting circled twice around.

It isn't quite correct to say what *we* are, remarked the elder, or to speak of *us*. We are like a neighborhood of suburban homeowners who have been herded into an association to set up a crime watch or force one of their number to be less noisy, who otherwise don't get along. One says not *we* agree but the *Association* agrees, the Association proposes. *We* do not agree. It might be convenient to call us The People.

Not the only People, yah. C John took an intuitive swipe at the problem. There's another sect up in the Mazatzal wilderness, he said, calling itself the People.

The First Men.

Is that what they say? First before who?

The first shall be last, and the last first.

Well while we're on the subject, C John continued a bit recklessly, without his usual circumspection, what do you know about the Last Men? A group of éminances grises, occult ministers operating behind the arras or something.

C John's question might have caused a little spark to pass around the circle. It was hard to tell.

The council elder said nothing, only held out his hand to C John's guide to receive the bagged-up gizmo from him. A brief inspection, and it went away into one of what seemed to be hundreds of inner pockets. C John's own cassock was as nude of hiding places as a hospital gown.

Preliminaries were over, security had been vetted, the cell's integrity affirmed. That so, the elder spoke at a little length, with remarks by the others save the guide, whom C John now took to be the role of the one convent nun designated to bear all the risks of going into the world and in whom diseases can be quarantined.

What the cell said was this: If they were to be styled revolutionaries, résistance fighters or some such, that was a canard.

A duck, C John interposed.

A quacking noise, the elder replied with a touch of anger, an extra hiss. The People have no creed or doctrine, defend no holy shrines, seek to restore no once or future government. Such goals are finished. Belief in such things was lost a generation ago and cannot be recovered now. The world has changed forever. Some will try, and doubtless succeed for a time, to grasp power on new terms. More farsighted people perceive that it is better to wait, to find the seams along which the new world is sewn together, put themselves in touch with the new pattern of life force, and only then reach out for the power which will be naturally theirs. These are your First Men.

You seem a wee scornful.

So we are.

The elder indicated with his hand that he meant the actual *we*, this band or tribe no larger than it had to be who were all he would speak for, plus women and children somewhere. Recidivist anarchists, these People. Always wanting to weed out decadence, exchange ugly new practices for the natural old ones. Natural tuning, not this artificial misnamed tempered way. Temper, temper…

At this point it was tacitly agreed that enough had been said by way of context to make negotiations feasible.

What the People wanted — *these* people rather, and such is the rub in all dealings with anarchists — well whatever they wanted it came down at some point to money. Resources which can be converted into money. Or as conditions worsen, resources which can proxy for money. Like the prescient abbot of any Buddhist monastery in a time of Warring States, this elder needed an alliance he could both count on and disdain when needful. Not active protection, only a monastery wall appearing thick enough to not be worth the trouble to breach. Ultimately that protection would be the sandstorm itself when it matured, into which the People intended to go and from which they intended never to return.

Until then, as C John glossed the story, you need working capital. You don't jib at tainted money?

What is that: taint?

Yes, the true voice of anarchy.

Anarchism is a creed.

Everything's a creed.

Men in goggles can stare excellently well. They can stare down the biggest dog beside itself with anger. They can't do much else, though. All emotions expressed through the eyes become a stare. Begoggled men are remote, dominating. They are not at any time wretched, accommodating, or friendly. Paradoxes, contradictions and quandaries are all dealt with the same way. C John gave up the notion of a conversation, indicating his abdication with a gesture. Which was immediately understood. Unhampered now, the council's big cat's paws ran swift to the close.

This man Kokua, the elder said, was Luis Maxfield's broker and factotum.

So I guessed, C John began, but was irritably waved into silence.

It seems that Mr Kokua has made a mistake. Times like these create these amateur speculators who plunge in after the cream which they think is floating on top of the Soup just waiting to be sucked up. Mr Kokua's mistake was to dismiss such a one without taking the trouble to look into his credentials. Whether the Leger was destroyed in the course of negotiations or by way of establishing a scale of values is immaterial.

It certainly is now immaterial, C John remarked, unable to resist.

Ss. See here — I speak as one of them — how we treat your trivial *art*. When you have seen that, you will see what you yourself are worth, so other fools will see what a few lives are worth in comparison with what has real value.

Snickersnack! It is done. Ex Kokua. Who by?

The elder paused, then spoke.

By the man you are calling Monsieur Homme.

Dangerous fellow, Hum. No factotum he. A player in his own right. Did he work alone?

Of course not. He might get blood on his trousers and

blood does not wash out. Like all powerful men he has others.

Hum works for Max, then?

One shouldn't say that among these exalteds any of them *works for.*

No, of course not. C John easily admitted his mistake. There is an Association among them, he said.

Yes.

And if the People buy a senior partnership in this Association, are the People willing to also condone a bit of rape and pillage?

That doesn't come into it, the elder replied sharply. We have skills which we are willing to sell at discretion. To sell not for the money but to show what damage we can do if disturbed.

Blackmail.

Nicht wahr, the elder said, employing Giz's private language, by which Giz would mean something like *it will be done* or *so be it.*

These people were as uncanny as Monsieur. But then, perhaps no gizmo was really private. They were machines. What could embarrass a machine? They don't have lives at all, much less secret ones.

What, then, do the People want from C John? Money?

Worthless. In any case, you have none.

Protection from interference by the police?

And how is a minion to provide that?

Diplomatic of you to say so, C John muttered. Tell me why I should be talking to you.

Your hands have been dirtied, the elder whispered. You are now Homme's tool, his agent in this business of Kokua's perfidy.

Say what?

You are at the mercy of two masters, Lt. Mackinaw. On the one hand there is Monsieur Homme, who will use the public record to tar you as a Judas. Your gizmo has shown how far Homme is able to turn the public record to his ends. On the other hand there is Detective Matthias, with whom you have made a bargain for three days which you cannot fulfill. In three days' time his protection will be withdrawn.

Forseen and forsworn, arranged for what purpose, I ask you again?

A pipe, the elder said.

No.

Then you will get no more information or benefit from us.

And did I ever?

It is we who know the skills of concealment and misdirection.

Ah. Got in with a bad lot, have I? Suppose I were to pass this on to Matthias?

I would suggest, the elder said, that you not do that. You have not taken the measure of your enemies, as Mr Kokua did not.

And what the hell have I ever had to do with any of this? C John said angrily. He started to stand up, but the silent guide touched him low on the spine and he sat down at once as a fierce pain shot up through the back of his head.

You are a pawn, Mr Mackinaw, in the power struggles of greater men.

I'll see what I can do, C John said. My gizmo back please. You have your own ways of finding a buried pipe, surely.

The Elder drew Giz out from the pocket of his robe and for the second time turned the little fellow over in his hand, looked closely, rubbed his thumb along the strip of gray metal along the edge of the case. This one will betray you, he said.

C John glowered.

They all do, the Elder said, and nothing more. The council adjourned and C John was guided out of the dead place by the least of the People and turned loose.

Making his way back down the ravine to the erstwhile soccer field below his house, C John assessed the results. They seemed meager.

If the Sand People's information could be trusted, C John now had the modus of the painting and the Kokua murder. He knew rather more about Hum and how he was placed. What he did not know was a good deal more.

Matthias had implied that the Sand People were a semi-organized sect which moved in to exploit a distressed population. This didn't agree with the Elder's tale. Was this cell operating alone?

Where did Maxfield stand on the playing field? More important, what field was he really playing on? If he actually had the power imputed to him he wasn't going to use it on a dried-up soccer pitch which was in fact a four meter deep cesspool for runoff water.

Who was Hum working for? Himself? What had been his real reason for setting Kokua up?

At least the few cement benches the city had provided were still there. C John sat down heavily on one. Just finishing up four days of the sort of intense work he was not any more used to, C John was beginning to be tired. He well knew the next phase would be grouchy, then depressed. Being depressed, soon intimidated, emasculated, despairing, and finally suicidal. He had been all the way to the end of that, and knew also that the farther he went the fewer turnings there were and finally his only option would be to make a youie in a dusty cul-de-sac on the side of Estrella Mountain where there was nowhere else to hide a body except under some drying cactuses and mesquites, where the only thing left alive was the creosote bush which was not a bush but a druid ring retreating very slowly from a center bombed-out thousands of years ago.

Pondering the ways in which he could run an undetected branch pipe off the one Matthias had providentially given him without being instantly found out, C John took Ben Kokua's ring from his pocket. He turned it is his fingers. It was very heavy, exuded a ceremonial feel, an object given as a sign of loyalty, a series of allegiances which C John had now broken. What had Ben Kokua owed, and to whom, and what had been owing to him?

Giz would know how to clone a pipe. A pipe which had one end in the cloaca of the phenomenal world, that is himself, and the other in the ethereal mind of the Last Men. It would have a very small footprint and might go unnoticed if no one made the mistake of joining the two of them anywhere. Anywhere but the soft tissue of biological living intent, that is himself, still unsubordinated at this moment to complete surveillance and automatic updating, still undissolved in the Soup.

《 》

Police work had not changed in more than its superficials since C John was a young cop in Los Angeles. There were still all the familiar ills that curmudgeons like C John had been complaining about for a century. Universal surveillance, the conflict between networking and privacy, communication overwhelmed by intrusive chatter, resignation to the norm of insecurity. C John never went about asking people what they had seen and heard — they don't see a thing. Either they were sealed inside their pressurized houses or they were blinded by dust. No one ever admitted to anything anyway. If they couldn't stay quiet they made something up. Finding things out was a matter of data mining the Soup and was the work of gizmos.

Everyday life was like a woman trying to conduct her love life in a bus packed with children all clamoring to pee.

When security was impossible people would decide that perhaps it was not such a good thing after all and that matters should be arranged to discourage it. Privacy likewise, which did not much trouble C John because he lived like a monk anyway. For a time people had lived more isolated lives, the inhospitality of the climate leading them to bunker up as if they were waiting out a hurricane or a tornado. Where these people once lived that was the threat, not burning sandstorms so hot they set buildings afire. Now it had begun to seem that bunkering together was a better idea. And why not? How long had it been since anyone had had a private conversation anyway, met anyone tête-à-tête, thought a private thought even? C John noticed a rhetoric of communal society beginning to appear: individualism disparaged, and eccentrics like C John made objects of fun.

So a detective no longer put much effort into interviewing suspects or looking for witnesses. People wouldn't talk about each other and it was increasingly bad behavior to ask. No one told the truth anyway, whether out of fear or contempt. And why bother to ask when Giz knew already?

As in everything else to do with information, formerly the detective's most important commodity, the more there was of it the harder it was to make sense of it. There was a surfeit of looking and a dearth of seeing.

Senior detectives like Matthias sat at desks and wrote memos in the margins of sigint analyses. They organized meetings with area specialists, they sat on committees which stitched up deniable responses to the problems thrown up by humint operatives in place.

C John was one of those humint ops. His place was to observe, sniff out, infiltrate, and report. Matthias and his colleagues collected information — a word now spoken with a dripping sneer — *"information"* from ops and the Soup which they use to formulate *"policy alternatives."* Captains and Supervisors recommended something from this list, or more likely a new idea of their own. The Chief vetted or rejected that. Rejections went back down the ladder, reformulating themselves at every step, and Matthias got back orders to do something brand new. The op knew nothing of this in the way that an office secretary knows nothing of what goes on in the box room. The op only generated a data stream, coursing back and forth like a hound which has lost the scent. The idea was not to catch the perp anyway, it was to manage the fallout.

That old terminology of nuclear war is still with us, C John thought, unable to sleep, sitting in the kitchen with a bowl of oatmeal getting cold while he wandered inward, head tipped to one side, resting on a fist. He had been making lists and angry notes in the margins of his own sigint.

Guilt and innocence don't come into it.

One of the less happy benefits of C John's long knowledge of cultural trivia was his conviction that nothing had changed. Civilization came in but tribalism didn't go out. Philosophy comes in but religion doesn't go out. Industrialization came in but inhumanity and cruelty didn't go out. Technology came in but ignorance didn't go out. Gizmos came in but hyperbolic arrogance didn't go out. In fact Giz, bless his little bioquantum heart, would probably be the agent of future world dominion. Not that that would change anything much but the magnitude.

Since C John's early years as a cop the data stream had come to be monitored not for clues but for patterns of behavior. The item of interest had shifted from evidence to oddness. Anything which stood out from the background. That which C John saw in the name of evidence was seen by Giz in probabilities and degrees of risk and came with a decision tree of varying brushiness. Most of what Giz did when he was not wasting time on humans was to sort through this undergrowth of sigint summaries looking for high probability low risk events fitting the specifications established by the op on the advice of his gizmo, who was only trying to decide what to do next, not knowing there was no next.

The best detective was a combination of Sun Tzu, Machiavelli, Talleyrand, and Bismarck.

The best op was the one with the best gizmo.

The best gizmo is the one with the best qi.

C John and Giz were not on the qi chart. Giz's mathematics were off the shelf, albeit polished and rebuilt here and there mostly by Zack. C John himself only made the personality — not a trivial component, since it was that which determined the ease and accuracy of Giz's communication with its bioperipheral. That being C John, Giz needed a lot of quirks.

And, like all quirky beings, quirky gizmos were sometimes able to do what more proper ones could not, so a deficiency of qi or not, the Giz/John partnership sometimes did fairly well.

Giz was lying now on the table in front of C John among the unrecycled bits of dinner and the chile-rimed dishes, his little blue eye closed. C John delicately covered him with a napkin.

C John was quirky. He was a marginal, obsolete being who would be recycled for parts and a small amount of rare metal when risk analysis said it was time. Until then C John was, inefficiently, still an op — of an odd sort who sat in bars and wrote on yellow pads and who was occasionally useful in dealing with even odder objects like Sand People. C John was an outlier, a low probability low risk strategy whose payout potential made him sometimes worth a two-dollar bet.

The Leger case was one of those two-dollar bets. Unimaginable when he went out one unusually sandy afternoon to pick up some roadside trash, improbable when his find turned out to be actually valuable, not very likely when the case was sucked into a murder investigation, suggestive when aligned with certain other forces at work, actually plausible now he was set in motion. C John Mackinaw's humble work had become part of the Higher Interest.

He was angry about that. He resented the former neglect and was bitter at this pretty meager luck having come to him too late to profit by it but not too late to mess up his calm, bottom-feeding life.

This was an attitude which Jen had never liked. Resentful of favors. She had always been after him to improve himself, and C John sometimes felt like a small animal being tortured by boys, shocked by electric wires whichever way he turned until, mad with distraction, he rushed suicidally at the worst goad and impaled himself.

The lists C John was now desultorily writing, scratching out, and recopying had to do with what to say to Matthias about Monsieur and Maxfield, to which he soon added the dead man purported to be Ben Kokua, which C John still doubted he was, either Ben or dead. Just a body left in the desert with only that ring to validate him. The whole business was too like Monsieur's work; too like Hum to fiddle with biospace just to twit him. It was both hard and pointless to create seamless new personas — as with so much else in the Soup it was impossible to find all of anything, so scraps of previous meals were always floating to the top. Ignore these old beans, C John wrote. Throw in some new ones — they will make the old ones seem mushy and overcooked. Monsieur had a touch for making information seem out of date which he liked to show off.

Hiding Maxfield was probably the most important thing Hum did for him. Hum saw to it that information about Sr. Max would not coalesce into a personality. Giz, with more experience navigating in these clouds, claimed that this eigenschaftlich ohn-ness was normal, that personas were created by subtraction from a formless wad, not from masks or shells surrounding a void. We are cut out, not built up, Giz said. Be it so, there was still something about Maxfield which made every construction of him too rickety to stand up.

Then there were the Last Men, the Sand People determined to stand outside affairs, to erase themselves from the
present and wait out this turn of the Great Wheel. They were
in a sweat to get off the main road before they were smashed
like the Leger on the embankment. The Sand People wanted
the sandy world of samsara to close over them forever.

Now there were the First Men also to take account of.
What did *they* want? A ticket to the Pure Land? Apparently
the strategy of this sect was to pounce on the junkpile of the
ruined world and set about building a Corbusier or Watts
towers. Everyone had their venal side.

C John had hoped that he and Matthias might be simpati-
co. They did seem to understand each other. But then, he and
Jen also understood each other, ay? To *reach an understanding* was not saying much. Boardinghouse reach. Once more
into the reach dear friends. Understanding untermenschen
standing under a waterfall, kami of the water, holding out a
sword of understanding. Reach for it, cut yourself.

C John was coming to know that he himself knew nothing. The People knew nothing. Homme, Giz, Jen, Matthias
— it was their kind who knew.

Zack, he wrote in very small letters on his obsolete yellow paper.

« »

Kokua, then. If he wasn't Qiu Long, who was?

Nobody, it seemed. With the new authority conferred by
Matthias and with the ownership of a pipe, the first thing C
John turned up was the information that the names Qui Long
and Ben Kokua were both fake — or rather so common that
any instance was probability zero.

It was Friday morning of the tenth day since C John had
retrieved the smashed Leger from the embankment and the
first day of grace from Matthias. When he went to the espres-

so bar as usual with Giz in his pocket, Giz knew immediately there was a new door in the place. C John once tried to work out the modus of this but was foiled as usual by the math. His understanding from Giz was that every place had a distinctive signature similar to geographic coordinates. When the coordinates changed one knew an object had been moved. There was room for ambiguity, however. If two objects were piled in the same place they would register as one until one was moved and uncovered the other. But which one had moved? The *pile* was a technique well-known by Giz for evading surveillance.

So the geographics of place. The mathematical signature of a place told nothing about the piles which might be there, or anything there at all. It was the unique configuration of the place itself, as recognizable as a face. The rub was that the signature was unique *in that way* only within one mathematics. In another math it may be meaningless or wrong.

Two maths piled up in one place. So you needed to know the premises of the personal math by which the signature was calculated. It worked like public key cryptography.

Personal math? You, the veritable Giz, are asking *who are you?*

You? Who's that?

Burying a pipe in a mathematical place meant that to know how Giz computed the signature of a place was to know how to mark up the pipe so that it was visible only to Giz. Other gizmos might sense that the signature of the place had changed but, lacking what amounted to the private key which unlocked the invisible door, would not be able to work out what Giz knew at once, without thought. It's akin, Giz tried to explain, to the connoisseur of wine whose nose smells something of which an ordinary person is completely unaware.

Ah. C John whiffs envy in himself. And this wine sodden fellow, he says he is reminded of a 1987 pinot which he was

offered ten years ago in Portland and gives you directions to
the vineyard and the very field it came from, whereas I can't
remember what grilled steak smells like from one time to
the next.

So Giz dove into the pipe even before C John sat down
and by his first swallow of coffee was back with the information that the dead man, whoever he was, could at least
be identified as the person who himself smashed *La Boîte
à Chapeau Polychrome*. Aside from fingerprints, the tool
which broke the stretchers —

Murdered the painting.

— left on the wood traces which can be said to belong to
the so-called Long Kokua.

Which was, this tool?

The murder weapon, said Giz complacently.

Oh fer — so Kokua was killed with the same weapon
used on the painting. Why is it *his*?

Giz did not reply at first, one of those mysterious lacunae
which occurred from time to time while he did something
else, computed some difficult function, went shopping for
shoes.

Probably, said Giz, deruminating, and would say no
more.

And how do *you* know this whatever? Giz?

From the report which is in the pipe, Giz replied complacently.

Which you could not have found otherwise, said C John,
which Matthias knew. Look, Giz, this is just as phony as
Long Ben himself. We don't want to go there. Matthias is
using me as the proxy owner of a back door for the Sand
People. Pipes go both ways.

C John thought then of the ring which, if it had been a
genuine object of fealty, would have been taken from him.
Instead, it had been given, and was now a caution and a
warning to its new owner.

Winkling it from his pants pocket, he squinted more carefully. There was some engraving inside, worn faint. He rubbed coffee sludge on it.

What language do they speak in Samoa?

Samoan.

Huh. C John pressed the seal of the ring into the chocolate frosting on his muffin and transferred the impression to his napkin. Was that Chinese?

What does this mean? he asked, turning it around for Giz to scan.

Indeterminate, Giz replied after a bit of whirring. Steep mountain, which could be interpreted as difficult task completed —

Yah, wah, C John interrupted, licking off the ring and putting it back into his pocket for later. Try again, Giz.

More whirring.

Qi, said Giz.

《 》

So, said C John to the Jabberwock as they were leaving the coffee bar. Do we have a candidate for the murderer? Of the man, not the mouth.

Probably Maxfield's minions.

Millions, minions, onions... How do we know this, Giz? Is this a statistical association?

No. Deterrence requires a signature.

And — ?

Giz was a maddening tease that morning. What had got into him? The older he got the more character he acquired. Those odds and ends of behavior he picked up on his travels in the Soup were as inconvenient and sometimes maddening to C John as C John's similar character probably was to others. Giz is was now fifteen years old; one of the oldest, but no one knew of an obsolete gizmo. The times would have to change far more than they had to make gizmos superfluous, and short of that, the least of them had way more intelligence than they needed to keep up. Keep up appearances as well — it was less and less necessary to talk to Giz at all. Whatever it was, he had already found it out.

Giz, you're lying to me.

It was the first time C John had ever said such a thing.

Blink. Weeaw. For him with eyes to see…

OK, Giz. It's your fourier.

C John wanted to throw things. His pencil. His coffee cup. His croissant. Instead, he meditated on the objective correlative of the hand and the ring until he subsided into mere irritation.

The rest of the morning was spent setting up the Sand People's parasitic pipe. While Giz was building a copy of Matthias's work, C John looked about himself.

Bright morning. One of the oddities of the sand's infused glow was that nothing cast a shadow. People without shadows are supposed to be — dead, is it? Soulless? What's a soul, these days? A few three-wheelers on the street, nobody on foot. This de Chirico atmosphere — buff three and four-story walls, bluff, here and there a small door, almost silent save the hissing of the sand. No see-through businesses except coffee bars and some others with windows, which got pretty quickly etched away and had to be replaced. Places where people went to look out, and the coffee or whatever was beside the point.

It was seldom C John did now that which he once did always, that which was an op's raison d'être, but then he wasn't much of an op anymore. He did not look about himself. Observe, watch, see. Could a world without shadows be said to be enlightened? Was a man with no mind to see just window-shopping? He felt half-alive.

Jen said he was only pretending to be an intellectual. A man with no connections to the outer world, she said. It made him grind his teeth. Who, he would erupt angrily, as predictable as a land mine, am I supposed to be connected *to*? Who cares?

Who cares about you is what it all comes down to, doesn't it? Nothing matters but this bally whining narcissist, does it?

A whiner he was. She'd probably wondered why such a man as he was would become a cop, which wasn't exactly fair since he wasn't the man who became the cop, and who he was before that she knew perfectly well. Who he was then was when the job of looking made him eventually curious about what he was looking at. Now that he wasn't anybody he didn't look any more. He only sat. In places where he didn't feel closed in. With windows.

Of course, there were windows and windows. Jen's psychology was the manic one, to whom nothing happened according to any plan and the future was fraught with anxiety and unpredictable possibilities. People like that didn't want windows. Whereas C John's psychology was depressive: everything happened because of circumstances over which no one had control. How else to explain phenomena like the Sybil? Depressives looked for something unfettered. Manics looked for something nailed down.

The Sand People's pipe would take a while to propagate, Giz informed him, so the rest of the day C John and Giz spent hunting for intelligence on Ben Kokua, not because it was any longer needed but simply to be doing something, fastidiously tucking up loose ends.

Long Man, C John remained convinced, was a joke which strengthened the conviction that Giz was taking on color from this association with Monsieur.

Nonsense, Giz insisted. You're the absorbent one. You and Hum are twins, shadows of each other. What color are you?

Puce, he said bitterly. What's the complement of puce? Some mixture of crimson and blue it would have to be. At which point Giz told him he had it wrong, that puce was the liver color and its complement was taupe or ecru.

This Longeur person whose real name was probably forever lost in a mass of noms de guerre had inhabited the body of a soldier of fortune. The record said he lost a hand fighting in the Middle East, judicially amputated for some disreputable theft; that he lost confrères to gruesome tropical diseases and probably never had a companion himself except rotting whores and street boys and not many of them; that he was "filthy clean" in the language of the hospital autopsy. Probably illiterate, amazingly. How this man could have passed himself off as a speculator in art was beyond belief. The Sand People must have a blind eye for everyday sleaze. All human behavior looked the same to them, else how could their other senses have failed to notice this effluvia of the modern satan?

There had to have been a go-between. Between the Sand Elder and the real, undead Long Ben, an intermediary to hide the connection, someone who was being manipulated in someone else's interest entirely. What possible benefit could there by for anyone in this arrangement otherwise? and the People were as blind as all fanatics.

C John was beginning to think the whole business far too elaborate, complicated, baroque. The Leger writ large. One of Homme's labyrinths. For what purpose?

As for Maxfield, C John sent himself out as an advance party to study the approaches. Maxfield, he confirmed, lived inconspicuously in a low, rambling complex of buildings set back from an unpaved road halfway up McDowell Mountain. The city view would have been spectacular years ago when the place was built, when at night this was the edge of the world, but now it was all lost day and night in the brown cloud. The house had no obvious security, only a hundred meters of open desert rising fairly steeply through a raggle of prickly pear and creosote. This was surely deceptive — in fact an exposed glacis packed with sensors. No one went that way, not even the castellan. The entrance was probably through the mountain somehow, a defile narrow as Petra, blocked by no more than a blind tamale vendor.

The next morning, Saturday, Giz verified the sandpipe. It and its parent were serially identical and the sandpipe had uncovered itself unnoticed. It would not be spotted now by the traffic cams because in the Soup the cams were interested mostly in vortices and other fluid phenomena and the trajectories of individual morsels were uninteresting. Raw carrots dumped in, cooked carrots ladled out, the scales balanced, everyone had carrots to eat, why look into obscure quantum goings-on at the bottom of the pot? There was a limit to efficiency and resources.

But at the other, People's end of the pipe there *was* a security issue, because that mouth was open. By their own admission the People didn't keep gizmos. The whereabouts of every one of them was known or knowable. So the mouth of the pipe couldn't be buried because without a gizmo there would be no means to do that. An open pipe. C John envisioned something like an old ship's speaking tube. Giz, however, suggested a better analogy: the library Sybil.

Instead of breathing Greek fumes from a vent in the mountain, she had an open pipe. The library Sybil had a straw in the Soup. She was drunk, that's what.

And if the sandpipe and the Sybil's pipe were the same sort of thing, and if the Sybil who had once been only a storefront seer was now something else entirely?

C John thought that now he must have all the threads even if they didn't yet make whole cloth.

Go to the mountains, Homme had said.

Such were the morning and the evening of the eleventh day.

« »

Matthias called. C John's first report had been sent up.

You're closing shop, then, C John said.

No, replied Matthias surprisingly. Not until he was sure of the Chief. He would give C John the promised three days. More, perhaps. It was summer. These things moved slowly now.

Luis Maxfield, however, is now acting as if he's been stung by a bee. Could Lt Mackinaw throw any light on that? And also: Kokua had been wearing a ring.

Is it important?

Probably not. If you find it, John, send it over for us to decipher. You'll be knowing it was his.

So it was now a two-cup morning. C John returned from the bar and opened the sandpipe. No one there.

Hmp. He sent Giz down to the unguarded end to find out what he could. Nothing much. The People seemed to have moved on deeper into the city. C John planted a flag and went home, telling Giz to close up if there was nothing by lunch. He now was certain the People had wanted their pipe for other purposes than the Elder had admitted to.

Matthias intrigued him more and more. Ordinarily an op wouldn't be allowed anywhere near his handler. Ops were a different society without claim on the detective class, but C John was not an ordinary op and one who, old and marginal as he was, was inclined to be reckless. Matthias might be willing to open himself to such a one if the price were low.

The mood of intrigue quickly died, though. The intensity of the last week had boiled away and suddenly the pan was dry and C John's energy was starting to warp. He was going to be depressed. When depressed, what little and fragile ordinary curiosity he had about other people went to nil and any inclination to find out more about Matthias would seem futile and C John's ordinary paranoia would grow like a beanstalk.

Not good. He had to know, depressed or not, for his own safety. A fit, it was. Fit. Section of a poem.

C John knew that he was addicted to depression. To be depressed was to be safe in a nimbus of enervation, nothing required. Depressed people saw more clearly. They are seeing things as they are, squalid and mean, and they had completely reasonable if dangerous beliefs about other people. Depressives made good cops.

Sometime after becoming a cop, though, he fell into mania. This was the time when he and Jen were complimentary, when they were on the same road at least if going different directions, when that uncoplike explosion of manic curiosity about everything threatened to destroy his chances. But mania died, taking with it the wonderful nimbus in which everything he encountered had been invested. He became an op and was employed to do what he would eventually do anyway but out of a lesser, intellectual curiosity. This was the time when he began to learn so many of those things which didn't fit together, like pieces from different jigsaw puzzles. All those bits of old popular culture which so annoyed other people. Scraps of history, old unfashionable theories in the sciences. This was the time when he found out art. This was the time — or would become the time — when because of Zack he learned to believe some things which Jen laughed at as mystical — and they began to draw apart.

And then that time passed too, leaving John alone with an incurable ache. Such beauty and serenity and balance and opportunity which had been were all gone away, leaving him, like everyone else, with nothing.

For a while the search for his lost *wa* was a desperate rootling, a hasty rummaging through his life which left it in that familiar condition which occurs when the protagonist is unaware that he possesses something incriminating and comes home to find the house completely torn up, drawers emptied, mattresses ripped open, carpet pulled up, jagged holes in the walls. Suddenly, brutally, the hero learns of an alternate, alien construction of his simple existence, a different point of view. But as C John got older the naked world, the world stripped of samsara, the bodhisattva aspiration, began to be a tiresome burden. He made excuses to hide from it, rationalized his cowardly sentimentality, looked for ways to excuse Jen's opinion of himself, sometimes chose what was convenient rather than smart. More than a little alienated now from his younger self, he had begun to see the meaning of certain behaviors — his choice of dolorous music, his tendency to search for compensation in food and other things about which he could then feel guilty for indulging.

It was important now to be guilty. It was necessary to recognize and accept one's guilt. It was required of him, like a hat in the sun. His vocation for the police, or what became a vocation once he had the job, originally a manic quest, became a depressive compensation. But then the world played its usual cruel trick and the police gave up the enforcement of guilt and innocence, gave up any concern with evidence or justice, and dumped C John on his landfill of trivia, isolated on his island of nostalgia for dead artists.

If the People of the mountains were calling themselves the First Men, C John surmised that he was himself most certainly of the People of the Valley calling themselves the Last Men, doomed to extinction and replacement by this new version of the human, people who thought themselves better attuned to the harmonies of the new world now coming into existence.

A new place of *wa*, maybe.

So on the third day C John came out, despite his wishes, from his hermit's hut like a fake Sesshu on a new morning, hiding his fear and boredom. To seek out human congress.

If he were to report to Matthias again it would be without Giz. C John had begun to feel that Matthias was somehow dangerous to the little fellow. He would leave Giz home to do his own business.

Matthias. The man didn't even have a last name. Or C John wasn't to know it — they moved in different worlds, their orbits not intersecting. With him there were no casual hallway conversations, impulsive invitations to lunch, flattering requests for advice on small inconsequential things like the name of a reliable handyman or tax accountant. He had Matthias's public biography, a few privileged facts to be learned from the pipe, and that was all. The man Matthias was as remote as Beethoven.

It was the People who had riled up Maxfield, surely.

This Maxfield was a case, himself. A throwback to Getty and Morgan he seemed. Seeming seemly seamed. Or Barnes, that uprisen dentist more his size. Buying up Renoirs and Matisses in case lots $25 each and rehanging them according to his own vision — here a wall of canvases with red dots, there a series of triangular constructions from Puvis to Picasso, and nowhere to be found a picture to look you in the eye.

Maxfield probably did not like to be looked in the eye. He kept no cats, and Hum alone was permitted to approach, to pass beyond the outer gate.

Or so Hum, the castellan, would like it to be known.

Steering the free end of a pipe was like pushing a string, but with Giz's help and a handy comealong C John got the once-open end reburied in the metaphorical forecourt of the Maxfield slopeside manor. Giz, his shade, went for walks there, emerging like a vampire shaman out of the pipe, but with nothing much of interest.

Too much secrecy, said a voice so close behind his ear that C John felt the warm breath. Startled, he knocked over a teetery pile of old ledgers covered with make-believe dust.

Matthias.

That's it. Knock some things down. Play the poltergeist. Leave some tracks. Poke about, pry open this and that. But

John, without system.

The man knows all. What will it take to hide from such a one? Beyond the pipeworld at least. Out there beyond freedom, system, good and bad, and other illusions of everyday life.

Your People, Matthias whispered into C John's ear, seem to have made off with some trinkets, as you suspected. They've been flat footed. Keep yourself to yourself, play the sensei, the dangerous master who lurks within his feckless creatures' shadow.

Matthias withdrew, his presence no longer felt. Followed his own advice. Creepy that was.

And yet there was something bemused about him, as of a person impossible to sin against, to whom every act was a mere foible worth only a cautionary finger's wag. Perhaps he would chop off a thief's hand with the same detachment.

When C John returned home Giz told him that his request for an eyeball meeting with the Elder was to be granted. And so in the gloaming in which this theatrically mysterious man felt safest, he appeared as before out of the dust on the mountain, a little whirlwind or devil growing up under a mesquite tree.

C John was aggrieved. He felt abused, put at risk by this beck and call. Recklessly at risk, he might say. The Elder shrugged, deploring the fact that on a long march some camels will be lost.

Die, C John said.

Hmm.

So had said Matthias earlier in the day when he found C John in the archives. So had Matthias said, with this infinitely expressive humming noise, but the Elder was not bemused. Tired rather, as would a wandering immortal be.

C John's business was easily forthcoming. The Elder was contemptuous of Maxfield's strength, as befitting one made of dust and wind toward a mortal of too solid flesh. Monsieur Homme's proposals had been gainsaid by his actions. The tawdry little ploy with the Leger painting was, it now seemed, no more than a venal, crass attempt by Monsieur to stuff his pockets. Undisciplined, in view of what is at stake.

Enough sand in the wind, C John said. Enough whispering. What was it you wanted from me?

One says *at stake,* the Elder remarked in his maddening indirect way — what is the implication? An auto da fé? The purification of an immortal soul at risk? As if one's *qi* could be other than just what it is, always already. Stake to the heart perhaps, as in the vampire lore. A fitting end to one who marks the roads of his fief with impaled corpses in a country too cold for them to rot. Agonized, malignant eyes of the dead everywhere like so many street cams. What *is* at stake, then?

Vague threats. To what purpose?

The Elder snorted. Yes, what is the use of making threats in an already ruined world? We need only wait in order to be robbed of our gold teeth, which may be the only thing of value we possess.

Their crimes —

Your crimes, the Elder whispered.

— cannot be expiated then.

It's too late for that, John.

I can't believe Don Maxfield is so powerful, to command from his little corner some world-sized plan with only a short-legged imp and a dead samurai for help. He thinks, therefor it is.

He doesn't know whereof he acts.

But Hum does?

He suspects. Monsieur isn't clever enough to go forward on his own. He's like the sniffer dog who can't think what to do with its discoveries other than eat them.

Those fishing cormorants which wear a choker to keep them from eating the fisherman's catch.

The fisher king… muttered the Elder to himself. And then more openly: The world itself was created so, was it not? By giving thought?

You're a talky fellow tonight, C John said.

Sarcasm is unworthy of you, John. You are the host. I am the guest. I will return to the People.

Your People — what, four? five? — nihilists plot together in some cave you're sharing with the rattlesnakes and black widows, expecting some transfiguration, busily writing your great Book?

Yes, the Elder agreed easily. Nihilists. I am too clear-headed to expect anything else of the other inhabitants of this planet.

And what do you want of me? C John insisted again. He pondered the Elder's face, which in the shadow of his hood was little more than the two glowing circles which were the lenses of his goggles, a wide lipless mouth, and the mons of his nose rising out of a dark plain on which the sun had already set.

It's not a hard or loveless face, C John thought. The Elder's hands, too, tough as roots, were not those of a man who uses them for anything but the perusal of the sutras. These parts of him were hardened, carapaced by the life he lived, a hard life which had come to seem the only dignified life possible in a desiccated world of big and little iniquities.

What business then? the Elder repeated.

Two things, C John replied. The one you've told me already, which is that you know no more about Señor Maxfield and his works as I do. The other is this: I have given you what was extorted from me. That bootleg pipe is a continuing danger to me in your hands. You've learned from it what you need and I've plugged it.

The Elder lowered his face in a minimalist bow of assent.

Matthias wants the ring, he said. Don't give it to him.

What? C John barked, startled and uneasy. Why not?

But the Elder of the People only smiled and dispersed himself in the twilight.

It's never really dark anymore, C John thought, except in the mind. Even with most of the streetlights out now there's this fluorescent glow as if the dust in the air were giving back the light absorbed during the day. The daylight wasn't any brighter now than the night was dark.

《 》

Then there was Zack. Always Zack. C John had heard little of her since she went to Japan to do relief work in the flooded cities, not even a holo to know what she looked like now. Why Japan, when there were people under water everywhere? He didn't know — perhaps this Asian thought to which she gravitated, which to C John was just another collection of facts about the world but which Zack might take in another spirit. He missed her as much as he might Giz. Since Jen disappeared, released by Zack's expatriation, C John had been lonely. More than that — bereft. Hermit he was, but that was not the only possible way of life for him, so long as there was Giz.

What was Giz? A machine inhabited by a kami. By Jiso, that squat little household god who represents the helpless when they face the myōo after death, those accountants of karma whose supernaturally sharp swords cut away all ignorance and pretension, all pride and self-delusion. Jiso, the protector of children.

《 》

With Giz's help that night he was able to read Long Ben's ring, or at least get a plausible translation of the letters faintly engraved on the inside.

Turn away from the circle of redeath.

What that meant, other than its overt and obvious interpretation, remained obscure to both of them.

Together with the ideogram on the seal it was not the
ring of an illiterate soldier of fortune, unless it had simply
been stolen from its previous owner. Stiffed from a corpse,
probably.

The deeper question was what was its importance to
Matthias? Did it really bear on the case or was Matthias only
being careful with forensic property?

No. It was as C John first supposed, a link in a chain of
fealty to which C John now had an entreé which Matthias
—and who else? — did not want him to have. Someone else
was intended to find Long Ben's body. The Last Men interfered. Why?

High probability, Giz said, a note of amusement in his
voice.

Probability of what?

Prenez garde die Wirrnis at night, Watson.

《 》

A Mighty fortress...

Day four, Tuesday, the first day of gift.

Might there be a fort?

The question was: Whatever Maxfield was building up
there in the mountains he was going to need some sort of
storage vault with climate control and security. And probably hardened, if he were backing out of the valley for more
than his own comfort. The question was: Why did C John
now think there was something more to this than a rich
man's booty?

He was guessing.

Sorry, must differ, interposed Giz. Reasoning when both
terms only probable depends on quality of priors. Superior
imagination offers possibility of superior priors. Superior

imagination does not guess.

Thank you, Confucius. I assume you mean yourself.

But Giz replied only with an ambiguous garble. The little fellow was not in the habit of gratuitous complements.

So. A rich man's booty. Not pease, though. A back of the envelope calculation suggested that Maxfield's legitimate collections might be worth upwards of a billion. Double that to account for the little stuff and the stuff he was not supposed to own. So whatever his game was, it was bigger than that.

After three days we are nowhere, C John lamented.

Sympathetic noises from Giz. Phatic noises, meant to fill up space in a conversation. More unGizlike behavior.

Supposing Benny Liu were an op, a shadow man, a being who didn't exist until C John stepped into the light. He, Liu, must then needs be rubbed out. Someone — Maxfield, Hum, Matthias needed to cover his tracks. The Sand People could do this. Avoiding surveillance and covering data trails was what insured their survival, gave them time to work out a new life in the sand. A pipe was the easiest way to move through infospace without leaving a data trail, but it only went one place. Giz could do nearly the same thing to anywhere. Any gizmo had this talent, potentially, developed out of the commodification of data trails, tracebacks, real-time analysis of massive datasets, but it was a talent rarely exploited outside espionage, arbitrage, infospace security.

From time to time C John had wondered what other talents or aspirations Giz might have which C John would have no way of knowing. Lately Giz had been showing a philosophical bent, observing apropos of nothing that C John and Hum were döppelgangers.

What?

Shadow twins.

Since when have you been interested in 19th century German Romanticism, Giz?

Just a passing fancy, John.

Giz's assertion was based probably, C John thought, on his and Hum's mathematical signatures. Sentient and shadow were organic insights not typical of Giz.

We don't talk rot about souls anymore, C John said, but nonetheless he knew he was missing something. There was some aspect of himself which was not AWOL because it had never been there — something which he triangulated by shadowing himself.

Something his shadow knew which he didn't.

The circle of redeath.

« »

Maxfield's bunker, altogether imaginary at first, invented by C John when it seemed necessary for there to be such a thing to protect Maxfield's art, now loomed as a necessary element in a bigger game into which the Leger painting provided a fortuitous but accidental peek. The way for C John to moor his long chain of reasoning was to find a real bunker and what it was really being used for.

As an artist does — to make reality, picture the imaginary.

In order to do that, C John had to see for himself — had to go to the mountains as Monsieur Homme had advised him at the beginning.

Not so easy. One did not get up in the morning, take a hat and a bottle of water, and walk to the mountains as if one were going to the corner grocery,

Using the temporary authority he had from Matthias, C John was able to secure some transport from the motor pool. And he noted in the course of wrangling with the transport captain that there was a limit to what Matthias could do. Ops bum rides and chiefs are driven. Detectives belong in armchairs in air-conditioned offices watching news feeds.

The secured transport consisted of an old hybrid electric jitney barely able to get up a six percent grade.

Where am I going to get gas for this thing? C John whined as he signed one too many forms.

The duty officer shrugged and handed him a brochure with a map in it. C John's accommodating smile got no reply, not even a scowl.

C John spent the night with his own maps. There were two ways into the Mazatzal wilderness: north and then east toward Four Peaks, or east up the river canyon and then back northwest and in by the backside. It wasn't much to choose.

Maxfield had built private roads by which to get deeper in, C John found with some preliminary reconnaissance, but the heavy stuff was coming in by air. Maxfield was beginning to remind C John of an old-time James Bond baddie, some agent of Spectre who was building a doomsday machine deep underground. Putzing along, C John thought of other things hidden in mountains — not counting Fafnir and Smaug. Various mummies' curses like the one that killed Paul Birchard in the Egyptian tomb adventure. What else?

It took nearly all day. C John bought some gas cans at a place marked on the driveaway map just to be sure, though his jitney proved to be rather frugal after all. He parked it off the road a couple of kilometers away from the compound perimeter — which was as quietly unmarked as Maxfield's slopeside house in the city, but Giz saw all — and walked or scrambled up a wash into the desert where he rigged a shelter deep under an ancient mesquite and sat down to wait.

It was tarantula migration season. Perhaps there was an intermittent stream or a spring hidden in another ravine. A big female strode across in front of him, moving with graceful purpose, picking up and putting down each foot with ponderous precision. C John watched the parade of babies which followed, searching his mind for some metaphor of significance but finding nothing.

The little males were the ones to be careful about. They spit.

In about an hour, Hum appeared from upslope as the People had probably taught him to do, seeming to assemble himself out of the desert rocks and scrub. It was the first time they had met since the encounter in the coffee house. Hum was not wearing his homburg-and-spats clothes now, but a silver anorak like the Sand Elder's.

Hello, said C John. Came out for the spider races. Don't sit there — over here.

Hum bubbled up a quiet laugh. What can I do for you? he said.

You told me to go to the mountains, C John replied.

Ah. Here you will need an introduction.

Yes. Can you arrange it?

Perhaps. It's not up to me.

At this, Giz made an odd noise rather like a purr, of which Homme took notice, but said only: What do you want here, John?

I have no idea.

No, of course not. Hum acknowledged the waywardness of his question. You will be satisfactory here until evening?

I think so, C John said. Not too late. If there's a spring there might be lions or a snake.

About dusk, hopefully. We will find you a more comfortable place for the night.

Thank you. Don Maxfield is privy?

Of course. He is, in his way, under their protection. I couldn't be here without his knowledge. Or theirs.

Hm. I'll wait then.

《 》

The time he occupied by brooding over Zack. After all the years it was still as if she went away only last week. Sometimes he couldn't remember what she'd looked like, but something like her was with him always. Zack had never been useful as a confidant. She'd quit listening to her father in childhood. She would never know what blighted him. She had the world's work to do.

Again that odd whirring noise.

Doing the world's work, Giz? said C John softly.

Whatever it was, it had Giz's full attention. So far as C John could know of the innards of such a creature as Giz was, Giz had never given his full attention to anything. He was like a politician at a party, always looking around, over the shoulder of whoever he was pretending to talk to, looking out for the next opportunity — in his case, the odd scraps of data with which he built his private jigsaw puzzles.

Then there was Jen. Had his wife been ambitious for him once? Perhaps, though C John doubted that had he stepped off the street directly into a detective's black calf moccasins she would not have respected the work anymore. Maybe cophood was once respectable, but C John knew Jen considered him unworthy. Retrospectively knew.

What do you have? she'd said angrily. Only a poke full of miscellaneous trivia which you seem to think makes you an educated man.

He mumbled a defense.

What makes you talk? she replied indignantly. You're just a guy who has read some books.

He never worked out what he ought to have done to merit respect. Study useful things. Praxis machen Technik, aber ohne Technik, nicht Praxis — or some such circular Nietzschean annoyance.

There was no way in which art, especially, could have met Jen's standard of utility. Art, she had said more than once, is a tinfoil hammer. Why do you want to know who played the role of Captain Nemo and who his brother was? Which to C John was as if the trees and the clouds had said goodbye, god bless, and gone off to the Uttermost West.

And perhaps they had.

It was the weather. Every damned thing came down to the weather.

The only worthwhile thing you ever did, Jen said angrily, was to tinker that gizmo of yours, and you never finished even that.

《 》

About eight o'clock Hum reappeared as promised, beckoning C John with a nod. For an hour C John toddled up canyons and over ridges and down ravines following Hum's light. Then they stopped, at a place seemingly no different from the one they left.

Here they waited.

And how, C John wondered, will I find my driveaway, my motor pool rattletrap, now?

Up here in the Mazatzals, C John noted, he could see some stars — just a few, the brighter ones. Not ones around which other Earths might be orbiting, inhabited by other creatures who have made a better job of it than the sapiens. In the mountains the wind was a little cleaner. There were crickets, scuttly things under the chollas, even a woodpecker dinking some ancient pole. No crows. A place like this hadn't had crows for fifty years.

Hidden way down under the rattling pebbles was the faint sound and smell of running water.

A third man — perhaps a man — appeared out of the darkness and beckoned for them to follow. C John kept quiet, knowing how far a voice would carry here, though if the Mohicans had walked with C John's skill the last of them would never have gotten old enough to be heard of.

There was a village of sorts, up a fraying wall in a shallow cave, some low shelters. One of these was pointed out to him, and then Hum and the other slipped away into the night. Inside the shelter were a blanket, water, some dried fruit. C John gratefully dragged all of this outside, intending to drink and attend to his breathing, but after two swallows he fell asleep sitting up.

Sometime in the night he tipped over, facing east, so that by no effort of his own he woke in time to be discovered, dehydrated but dignified, ready to treat with the First Men.

« »

Monsieur Hum arrived looking washed and pressed. He sat delicately on a rock.

Versatile fellow. Dressed at the club, I suppose?

Oh, said Hum easily, the times require it, do they not?

I suppose. I'm afraid I'm not up to the mark.

Hum sucked on his lip, diplomatic but not complimentary, the way Jen so often did.

In order to preserve what little initiative he could under the circumstances, C John asked what Hum's intention was in naming Qiu Long as he did.

Hum chuckled liquidly. Oh, he said, it was supposed to be *Huey* but it got scrambled. Some element in the process heard me to say *Chewy*, apparently, and by a sequence of inference produced Qiu. I imagined the allusion would have been lost on you in any case, though Kokua was certainly arcane enough. But you are quick, sir.

You need not be insulted, he added when C John's face turned an angry white. It was essential that Matthias not turn you off the case. I needed a flagpost — a signpost, how you say — a *signal* which would attend only to you. I have succeeded, I think.

Incensed, C John raised his index finger to point the evil eye but before he could get out one syllable the First Ones were among them, silently gathered in a circle around two captured shadows.

There commenced one of the odder interrogations of C John's career. He himself didn't have an adequate agenda. He was there to assess the so-called First Men and their importance to Hum, and to paste down the scraps of reasoning which led to the fantasy of the bunker and the doomsday machine.

To begin, they did call themselves the First Men. Yet another sect, C John thought, hoping to preserve a smooth face. Their view was as the Sand Elder had said, that conditions for life had drastically and irrevocably changed thanks to the behavior of the other species of sapiens. Survival of the First Men will depend, the Last Men say, on adjustment and so on through a multistep creed resembling Alcoholics Anonymous.

Whereas I, C John said, consequent on these conclusions, am one of the Last Men?

A faint smile bloomed on each face, so eerily alike that C John felt queasy, as if he were holding counsel in the center of a creosote ring. He laughed, letting them interpret that as they wished. Modest self-deprecation from one who is doomed. But C John smelled fanatics.

It's happened before, one of them said, and embarked on an exposition concerning the replacement of the Neanderthals at the end of the last ice age.

It wasn't *their* fault, C John pointed out, interrupting. It's not as if the Neanderthals melted all the ice to make tea. They were *too* well adapted.

The disquisitor did not like to be interrupted. He scowled, and swerved into a new track concerning the identity of adaptation with addiction. C John saw a strategy for dealing with these people if need be. It rested on an old barroom weltantheorie that there are two sorts of mind, bowling mind and pingpong mind. Bowling mind works by first setting up all the pins and then throwing something at them. Until all the pins are set up the possibilities are frozen.

These people are cartoons, he thought, far more than the Sand People are. Could Monsieur or Maxfield invest anything valuable with these morons? And yet they had, and the First Men possessed some eldritch power which made it necessary to placate them.

So the interrogation continued, first one and then the other partner leading the dance, imposing tangos on rumba music, round waltzes on square lines.

There were five of these First Men — but then any number would signify something — and again unlike the Sand People, they were five manifestations of a single being. There was not a scrap of personality to share among them. If there were, they would be fighting for it around the campfire like lost men over a bit of rotten dog meat. Under polished aluminum masks they were a formidable five-part intelligence at work. Feckless they seemed, but with feck to spare.

Giz lay quiet in C John's pocket, apparently knowing with whom he had to deal and using his own substantial powers to size up the situation.

The meeting ended. No treaty had been signed — it had been only a preliminary discussion. The five First Men melted away, dispersing like bandits into the hills.

C John and Hum shifted their seats a little so as to face each other. C John, who was sitting folded on the ground, re-crossed his legs in the opposite way.

Pass? he asked.

Perhaps.

Hum admitted nothing. Did he grudge any admiration at all? Doubtful. Hard man, Monsieur Homme, under the dandified skin.

Who are they, then?

Who? Ah. Well you see, that refers to the vanished peoples whose traces are all over the southwest. Anasazi, Chaco, and so forth. Imagine you are one of the new peoples, Na-

vaho, Apache, who are infiltrating this place from the north.
You encounter empty cities perched up on the cliff sides,
overgrown canals and fields in the valleys below. Who made
these things? Most people have an origin myth which can
accommodate such discoveries without fracture, of course.
One does not imagine coming face to face with your creators
that way. They were mindpeople before, and here you find
yourself in a place of living — of once living mind.

So, C John said. By *first* you mean original. The Last
Men call themselves the People. What do the First Men call
themselves?

The Old Ones.

C John snorted with amusement, but Homme held up a
cautionary finger.

Have you ever happened, he said, on someone who looks,
probably not like *you* so much as how you look to yourself?

Yes. Once, glimpsed in a crowd.

What did you think?

Didn't want to be anywhere near the fellow. Turned a
corner as quick as I could. Creepy.

Just so the Old Ones.

Ah.

This Monsieur Homme, thought C John with weary annoyance, was more than just a man with a theatrical bent.
To him every last thing was a metaphor of something else,
one layer of a see-through sandwich as thick as all time. His
mind worked the way Ahasuerus's might, an immortal wanderer who has seen more than Tiresias and will eventually
see everything there is, who long ago ceased to name, classi-
fy, and file and now sees nothing at all except the Tao.

In his pocket he felt Giz stir, processing some new cor-
respondence.

Hum, C John said. Who are you?

I'm one of Maxfield's people.

So you are. But on whose behalf?

My own, of course. I don't work for charity. Charity screws up the value of things, makes it hard to get a bead on the truth. What passes for truth.

C John sighed. All you people talk without speaking, he said, getting to his feet. You talk, and mean nothing. You'll have to take me back to my car. I have no idea where I am.

The dapper little man nodded and went ahead, walking rapidly with his limping, slightly twisted stride. His left foot was always planted a little to one side so that his way needed constant correction and his path was weaving.

Back at his car, which was not as far as he had thought, C John asked one more question.

Where is the bunker?

Hum paused, feeling the sting of an unexpected hit.

Can you get me an interview with Maxfield?

Hum wagged a finger.

Ah, ah — one question, John. You only get one.

《 》

The next day was Thursday. Time was running out. Time that Matthias had given him to — well, C John didn't know exactly. He was quartering the ground, trying to find the scent of — hmm. Matthias, the sects of Men, Monsieur Homme, Maxfield — all these were using him to their own purpose. He was caught in a struggle among them for something he had, or knew, or only he could discover. He felt like the king in a chess match, harried over the board, mincing his way, or hiding in a corner, all for no reason except that he *was* the king.

He did nothing. He went to the coffee shop, he sat in an empty park in a sheltered nook, he played simple games with Giz. He paid the library sybil another visit and watched her behavior more closely now he had a theory of an open pipe which might explain what was going on. He riffled through several folders of images of Zack made before she went to Japan. Nothing recent — her mind worked like Jen's. She thought that taking pictures of yourself was a narcissistic bad habit, like counting birthdays.

What was Zack doing in Japan, other than the obvious work of helping to clean up flooded coastal cities, dig out from under earthquakes, explore the ice-bound mountains? She could do that anywhere. C John remembered her as judgmental, another characteristic she shared with Jen. Perhaps he had been wrong. Perhaps she only had a lot of ideas about good and bad, as distinct from right and wrong. Was she working out some penance? — though he didn't know for what or why it was taking so long, only that penances were what everyone did most of the time.

He wanted to believe that Zack's way was one of reparations, acceptance of a new order, sobriety, abnegation, purity. It was only what he had wanted for himself. He could believe that about Zack.

But that was the game everyone was playing, wasn't it?

《 》

On Friday C John woke up with sand in his mouth and his mind full of rancor toward Jen, who had pestered his dreams.

That she was a succubus on him now wasn't her fault. He had no idea where or how she lived. All he had was a sort of phantom pain — the emotional apparatus was disconnected, unplugged, but his mind didn't know that. He was tormented by gusts of affection which he had only the palest pastel means of expressing, gusts which would blow up at useless times such as in an elevator or a store, and blow themselves out before he got home so that he arrived angry and in a rage over a lot of dry bougainvillea leaves which swirled in when he opened the door. The Jen of his imagination was as distant from the real person as Zack. He spent his days in a glass bottle and his nights trying to breathe.

At breakfast Giz suggested something which took C John's mind off these things. Giz had a dislike for idle time, under which classification he included, like Jen, speculation on people's motives and all other forms of self-regard.

Giz's idea rose from the fact that, cooling being a regulated commodity, there might be a way to locate Maxfield's bunker through energy bank transactions.

And so it proved. In this it was as it was with everything — there were no secrets. Giz's map of the energy grid looked somewhat like that of a gravity field. Users created an energy sink. Placed over a topo map these sinks pointed like so many tornados to trouble on the ground. There was a big one in the Mazatzals near the rendezvous with the First Men. Someone had thought that energy could be laundered like money, but Giz's tracebacks foiled that.

So, Giz. Think we can persuade the motor pool captain to give us our car back? Or should we take the tricycle?

The tricycle it was. It was time to move more in secrecy. To walk like Chingachgook.

《 》

It took most of the day, and on Friday night C John slept in the tricycle which he moved off the road into a mesquite grove.

Judging that he was not far from the First Men's lair, he set an alert out for them, also. He would like to have left Giz behind — to those with eyes to see Giz was as hard to hide as a giraffe in the short grass — but there is no help for it. Without Giz he couldn't have found his way home, much less to that energy sink on Giz's map.

In the morning before dawn after a night of coyotes and elk wails but tormented only by mosquitoes, he set out cross-country. The land was deceptively difficult to get over.

Hillsides which looked from a little distance to be clear of brush were thick with obstacles — small cactuses with hooked thorns, sumac and juniper tough enough to make a bow, and a jumble of stumps, logs, sticks, rocks, scree, potholes, and small blocks of red quartz sharp enough to bruise a foot through a boot sole and two socks. Sidehill routes of modest rise proved to be steep enough to have to pull himself up by the bushes, only to lose his footing and slide back, upended.

After a couple of hours of hot work and most of his water, C John found some shade just under a ridge which he believed hid the building he was looking for. Now it was a question of alarms.

He waited. An hour passed.

Pushing his head over the ridge only to the eyes, he found he was right — or that Giz's map was right — and the imaginary bunker popped into existence from the quantum dimension where it had been lurking.

This was as far as C John went. If he had not yet drawn any attention to himself, which he had no way of knowing, he was not going to increase the probability any further. Giz was aware of microwave and most of the common electromagnetic frequencies but he couldn't sense infrared nor yet newer ways of remote sensing such as pressure waves. C John took no more risks, and for the afternoon was content to lie quiet in a patch of open shadow, his binoculars hooded against accidental glint.

Below him was the entrance to a sprawl of concrete boxes, some no higher than a tombstone and others as much as ten meters. C John presumed that most of it, whatever it was, was underground. What he was seeing was an adversary like himself, lying quiet and hidden, keeping watch, breathing warily, drinking sparingly from its own water, waiting. Patient as a mountain lion.

What goes on here?

In the heat of the day only a few insects were about. The birds, the snakes, the mice and rabbits, were dozing. Cautiously C John looked at the sky. Cloudless, and actually a dirty blue above maybe five hundred meters. When night came, not so quickly now as when the air was clearer, but still a real night time quite unlike the permanent dusk in the valley, a fresh breeze rose. Cautious squeaks and rustles began. Overhead there were a few bright stars.

Five of them. C John thought that, before the last few days, it had been years since he had seen even one star.

Out there somewhere there were methane fish swimming in their slushy ocean on a gas giant orbiting a dark red star. What were their claims to intelligence and decent behavior, even love? Were *their* eyes open? Did they even *have* eyes?

Sometime in the night — C John dared not make a light to find the time — a solitary vehicle the size of a garden tractor came out on the entrance apron. It had a single headlight no brighter than a match. For ten breaths, perhaps a minute, it sat on the concrete like a jackrabbit on its haunches. Then it turned around and went back in.

C John was satisfied. He slithered down from the ridge and went back to the Valley. Surprisingly, the cross-country hike to his car was much easier at night. The little three-wheeler made its way, electrically silent, out from the mesquite grove and back to the road. By midmorning Sunday, going slowly and taking time to regenerate, he was home.

Think we were spotted, Giz?

Probably.

Giz was a pessimist. Being technology himself, he mistrusted technology. He believed it would inevitably fail when needed and work only when it was to someone else's advantage.

Giz was not his own master, which he well knew. But then, C John was not any better than he needed to be, either. Both wished to be free, but neither yet knew how. Only that they and their gods were bound somehow to the Ruined World and that they would not be free until they had rid themselves of both.

« »

C John returned to find a crisis. The Sand Elder was dead, apparently murdered. And in the early morning, while C John had been making his way out of the mountains, an attempt to infiltrate the Maxfield bunker had been foiled. The person — apparently one person — was not caught or identified. Some damage was done in the bunker entrance. Scorch marks, mostly. Possibly the bomber was obliterated at the same time. Evidence obtained from the entrance walls, Matthias said, will be inconclusive. An hour after that conversation a carabinieri, a person from Porlock, came to C John's godown in a black and silent car. C John was ordered to report for desk assignment at the Fourth Street Jail on Monday morning at seven thirty. He was relieved of duty as an op and his gizmo was requisitioned for return to the pool.

Giz!

But Giz was technology. He didn't care. Back in the shop he would be scanned for C John's modifications, returned to default, and detached to another op. Giz's eyes were open. He lived in the present, only the present, and the current state of his physical being was not a matter for interest or concern. So as to transition him more smoothly his memory would be disturbed, so in a sense he *would* remember. Or would, if the imaginative reconstruction of past states were not just a stupid hat trick, and the rabbit was there all the time.

The past is in the past and does not go there from the present. The wandering air does not move, the stream does not flow. With this understanding it becomes worthwhile to undertake some task.

C John was another matter. He was protoplasm, not technology. Being so, he was subject to the ills of protoplasm. Sans any recourse but tears he did the only thing his stupefied intelligence could invent. On Sunday afternoon he went to see Luis Maxfield.

And he did see him.

C John parked in the road and walked right up to the front door, heedless of all the alarms he must be setting off. He rang the doorbell, a little surprised there *was* a doorbell. And he was nonplussed when the door opened, as he half suspected it to be a trompe l'oeil door painted on the wall out of politeness.

A sort of butler had answered.

John Mackinaw, he said in a dusty voice that sounded unused in a decade. To see Mr. Maxfield concerning a painting which is missing from his collection.

The butlery bowed, a tiny grudging bow, and C John stepped in onto a dark red floor of old Mexican tile. The painted door closed. After several moments C John was seen into a side room which really ought to have been General Sternwood's hothouse but was rather an open, breezy room in Mexican style with murals on three walls, a long closed cabinet painted in blues and yellows, and a painted wooden table set with drinks. Wine, two glasses. Beyond the tall windows was a desert garden with brittle bush, desert broom in flower, and a small palo verde with very jagged branches in which a couple of inca doves sat watching a tohee scratching for bugs in the leaf litter.

Maxfield entered behind him, politely accepting the offered hand.

Mr. Mackinaw, he said, acknowledging C John in a voice equally dusty. You are a policeman. A specialist in art theft, he added deftly, saving C John the embarrassment of making this claim for himself.

Yes. Attached to Detective Matthias.

They were circling each other like a pair of dogs. Over

Maxfield's shoulder, C John gained a new view of the desert garden.

A jackrabbit, he blurted out.

Maxfield turned slightly to look, a small smile on his lips.

How about that — a tame jackrabbit.

Oh, the older man murmured, quite impossible. Jackrabbits can't be domesticated. That animal is wild. *Sauvage.*

C John pulled on his lower lip. How distant need the walls be to simulate freedom? To fool the jackrabbit. Is a fooled jackrabbit free, or not?

Maxfield's eyes closed very slightly. He was bored with challenges.

A little over two weeks ago, C John began, briskly now, a painting by Fernand Leger, *La Boîte à Chapeau Polychrome,* was, um, purloined from... ah, from you.

That is correct. It was destroyed by the thieves. Won't you sit here, Mr. Mackinaw?

Some moments passed in pouring and tasting the wine. Wine was wasted on C John. He ostentatiously rolled the stem of his glass between his fingers and embarked on a raw narrative of his experiences since.

Do I tell you any surprises? he asked, finishing a story which had taken about ten minutes to tell. He drank off his wine and put down the glass very delicately.

No, Maxfield said. You don't. I had already taken what I felt were the appropriate steps. The matter is closed so far as I am concerned. These are preliminaries to what proposal? Or perhaps you have a request.

Here C John was one step beyond the border of his intent. But he was rescued from his lunatic impulsion by an idea was squeezed out of him by fear.

There is, he said — or was, I'm told he's dead, a man — I don't know his name, I've called him an elder of the Sand People. I'm sure you know who I mean. It was only a little group of five or so, perhaps there are more but I haven't seen them, I wouldn't know. They are proposing… well, you know what they want. Probably quite impractical.

C John paused, still uncertain. He looked at Maxfield carefully, and as he was assessing the other man's mood his own half-formed idea clicked into place.

I believe this man to be — that is, he was your brother.

This audacious guess left C John quite suffocated. Maxfield started. He frowned and lifted one eyebrow, the most alarming expression he had so far permitted himself.

But no: Maxfield *permitted* nothing. C John saw in that slight shift of expression that he was not a man in control, his emotions held in check by will. He was a man asleep and those imperatives came and went like dreams. Entirely preoccupied by his plans, concerned only with the past as a source of cautionary tales and with the present not at all, Maxfield had no idea of concealment or subterfuge. Why should he? When had he ever been thwarted from the completion of an intent except by inadvertence or the ignorance of small people? Maxfield would never hide his intentions because he had no need to. They were always innocent and legitimate, his intentions. That being so, what reason would others have to move against him in hidden ways, except from their own tainted motives?

You are more astute than I took you to be, Mr. Mackinaw, he said dryly. And also better informed, if information is that thing which you possess.

C John looked more closely. Maxfield had a long face and no chin. Two folds of skin like a turkey's wattles hung below his sloping jaw on either side. He was bald save for a meringue of hair behind his ears, over which were hooked the earpieces of an old-fashioned pair of glasses. The lenses were thick and made his watercolored eyes a bit sad. Probably this face had been useful to him, as it too easily would lead people to underestimate his real power. Maxfield had never had need of bluster. C John guessed he didn't know *how* to bluster.

Half-brother, Maxfield said quietly.

I believe this is his ring.

Half rising, C John fished it out of his pocket. He looked briefly as if to confirm it, then proffered the ring across the table, nearly knocking over Maxfield's mostly untouched wine.

The ring was not accepted. After a moment C John withdrew his hand and put the ring back into his pocket.

What is it, C John asked quietly, that you are doing which he objected to, your brother?

Maxfield did not speak for a long time. At last he took an audible breath.

So, Mr. Mackinaw, he said. I was wrong as to your knowledge. It is true that my brother harbored an objection to the ways in which my wealth has been acquired. He thought, in fact, that I, and others like me, have been the ruination of us all. But I was content in his opinion.

Then who is responsible?

I assume you mean responsible for his death.

Yes.

Francis might have taken that responsibility himself.

You and Henry the Second. What *is* Monsieur's name?

James Searton. Here you have gone wrong at last, Mr. Mackinaw. James is my nephew. It was he who advised me to see you. We had discussed the possibility, and on your precipitate arrival … well. My brother presented no threat to him. I am apprised.

These little theatricals of his are regular things, Maxfield went on, though they don't often cost a quarter of a million in art. That will put a dent in his allowance.

Several things had fallen into alignment in C John's mind. A Sybilline experience, he guessed. The Elder Francis was dead at the behest of the First Men in retaliation for the attack on the bunker, and that otherwise futile attack had been ordered by Matthias solely to smoke them out, exposing their role as Maxfield's Praetorian Guard. The death of the go-between Long and the loss of the ring which linked him to the Sand People, the more canny deceptions and hints of Monsieur, the pipe which the Elder had wanted in order to find out how much he was in thrall to Matthias, the suborning of C John as Matthias's agent, the destruction of the Leger by Long as the first strike in an open war between Matthias and Maxfield — all these now fell into place. C John's inspiration returned suddenly after hitting a bump in the road and swerving dangerously close to the verge. This chain of inferences was wrong.

Difficult man to work with, Matthias, C John said aloud. Rather like keeping a grown chimp in the house.

Rather like.

Do you know the inscription on the ring?

Concerning the cycle of redeath, as I remember.

What interpretation do you put on that?

None.

And your brother?

You ask me to speculate. It's the sort of thing he would say. That he was attracted to mysticism would be obvious.

I wonder who was the poor joe who stood in for Benny Long's corpse.

There are joes to spare, Maxfield observed. A surfeit of joes.

Maxfield gave C John a pointed look as he shifted in his chair. Plumped himself. Now, he said, I think I have indulged my nephew enough. What do you want, Mr. Mackinaw?

That honorific has been given for the last time. C John got to his feet. Maxfield did not.

Nothing, C John said in a voice more level than he had hoped. I wanted to assess my position. Whether I had any slack.

A prudent man, Maxfield said, not altogether with approbation, and lifted his glass to drink the wine. C John was escorted out all the way to his tricycle, where as a last politeness Maxfield's man held the tricycle's door for him.

Home again on a Sunday afternoon, C John sat down at the kitchen table, doodling interlocking squares and circles and double-headed arrows as he rethought the true alignment of the forces against him. Monsieur and the Last Men were the Davids in the game, standing in the road with pea shooters to stop a juggernaut massive enough to destroy the world under its tread.

Now it would be the turn of Monsieur Homme. Of Mr. Mister, the little man with the hat and the limp.

And one more yet to be accounted for: Giz.

What did the Leger have to do with all this? Only to drag C John into it somehow? To what end?

Then C John went cold. Giz.

And so Giz-like. A puckishly overelaborated scheme to transfer his fealty from C John to Maxfield without alarming anyone who might interfere. Everything covered over with high-probability plaster. C John himself was the only one who might not be deceived, who might care enough to try to unravel … Because Giz wanted to work on whatever Maxfield was up to, because Giz was the only being alive who could —

Was there any truth at all in what had happened so far? The painting was the bait. Monsieur set the hook, a man just implausible enough to disable C John's caution loop. The Last Men suborned by greed for a power that tiny sect could not command if they had it, taken off the chessboard after they had played their role. Matthias brought in to take their place and turn C John's head toward Maxfield, the mountain redoubt, and the theatrically ominous First Men. Ultimately C John, thwarted and demoralized, had given Giz up, allowed Giz to be taken from him without any ensuing armageddon. And that had been the purpose of the whole farrago: to trick a stupid, lonely old man into handing over a creature which his eccentric genius had created to a man he loathed for something he would have fought to the end had he known what it was. Everyone had been Giz's tool, including Maxfield himself, who had hatched a scheme he probably didn't know what to do with, like Edison's thinking up the lightbulb and then hiring others to invent it.

C John asked himself then whether there was likely to be any more truth in this story than the other.

This one was efficient and simple, and left no loose ends. The other one only entangled itself further as it went on, requiring ever more epicycles to justify its continued adherence to a hypothesis which was wrong from the beginning.

If so, he was a complete fool.

《 》

On Monday morning C John took the metro in to Fourth Street to work. A duty officer escorted him to a windowless office without a doorknob where he spent the day checking dockets and dossiers. Matthias made no appearance. In fact, C John doubted whether he reported any longer to Matthias, to whom he had been detached in the first place when the body of Benny Long was found. He wasn't sure who he was working for. The files came in and went out, he signed them in the places indicated by the duty officer, and that was it. No clock, no roster, no briefing or debriefing. At the end of the day he expected to be handed his wages in cash in an envelope, but not even that much acknowledgment was given.

Tomorrow, seven thirty? he asked, going out.

The duty man ran his finger down a list, stopped on a name, nodded. C John had seen no one here all day. Having forgotten about office details like lunch, he had had to go without.

There was a panini shop a block down, no more than a niche with a rolldown steel shutter, and a line of people passing in front. The next morning C John got into line behind a smartly dressed woman with a prognathous butt and was quickly boxed in by a man in a t-shirt reading *Alaska: The Final Frontier*. Maybe these were cops like himself. They were strangers.

Alaska is done for, he said to the man behind, receiving only a stone-faced stare.

Wednesday was the same. He felt like the redheaded man hired to copy encyclopedia articles while everyone else was robbing the bank.

On Thursday afternoon a shiny Matthias appeared, not a scuff mark anywhere on his polished clothes and gleaming bronze hair.

Pleasantries.

Enjoyed working with you, he said, going out. Captain Rogers is in charge here. I'll put a word in.

C John looked through the empty doorway into the green hall, then reached for another file.

This is ridiculous, he muttered. It's a parody.

Soon it would be a month since Monsieur Homme changed everything for him forever.

《 》

When the weekend came, C John used his unaccustomedly unburdened weekend time to make another visit to the public library.

Now that he was fairly sure how the sybil worked she was more piquant and interesting rather than as formerly, deflated old magic. C John looked more closely at the people who consulted her, tried to overhear, noticed reactions. Sociologically, he did not understand what was going on beyond some crude premises owing mostly to stereotypes. He was reminded of trying to identify trees from a book as a boy. The actual leaves never corresponded to the pictured ones, and most trees seemed to be mutants.

Perhaps they were? Young triffids?

The people waiting in the sybil's line today were mostly old, perhaps one in four an adolescent hoping, C John supposed, to hear something sensible about love, the future, the necessity of suicide. Old people's difficulties were less important. The infirm to be healed, the mad restored to sanity, the worried to be reassured, the unhappy given hope. Suicide loomed for old people, too, but no one noticed.

Hardly anyone was able to make immediate sense of what the sybil told them. She sat on a comfortable chair in a carpeted area a couple of feet below floor level; three steps led down into this quiet corner where five armchairs had been set up in a U shape, two on each side of the sybil's. It looked much like a book discussion group or a set for interviewing authors for the Soup; in fact it was formerly used for children's story hour. The current supplicant sat on the sybil's left hand, conversing so quietly that even the incumbent in the next seat couldn't hear clearly. C John watched for other clues to what transpired again and again — the sybil gazed into her own lap, listening to the flow through her pipe. Abruptly she broke into whatever the supplicant was pleading, fixed their eye with her own, uttered a few words, and turned away.

From this point the supplicant's behavior varied from stupefaction to tears. Some went white with anger or red with shame. But in body they might as well have been drugged. It was beyond them even to stand up, and most had to be helped out. The whole exchange took three or four minutes. The sybil delivered about twenty unintelligible prognostications an hour, a hundred twenty in a working day with time for lunch and coffee breaks, six hundred a week, twenty-five thousand a year not counting holidays and a month off in the summer. To routinely and regularly reduce twenty-five thousand people to mindless acceptance was, C John thought, quite a feat.

Yet, when she left work the sybil became at once anonymous. Even, or perhaps especially, the person who not five minutes before had spoken words so devastating could not then be told from any of the other women queued up in the Italian market for a dripping chunk of romano, or at the tram stop with their perhaps bags and wide hats and water bottles. She was a pert but not attractive woman, short and dumpy, with close-cropped graying hair and a lumpy nose. No one cared in the least what she looked like and so she looked like no one.

C John could not fathom what social or psychological need she filled. Here was a shambling man who C John guessed would have once been a stamp collector come to the library to consult a reference on the issues of some obscure Polynesian island. Here was a tense sausage of a man seemingly about to pop all his buttons. Here were bimbos and wankers and semi-autistic men who believed that sunspots were the cause of everything and would capture you with skinny claw and beady eye if you were not careful. Here were women of thirty who had had their one child and didn't know what to do with their mornings, women who washed back and forth in a receding tide of girlfriends, drifting from one exhibitionist conversation to the next. Here were men the same, and would have been children had they been permitted.

There was some reason, C John thought, why the sybilline niche in the information ecology was in the public library. The ancient library had offered two services: the hope of certain knowledge and the agora. Wasn't that still the case?

C John studied the line of people queued up to be given their scrap of truth, people he unthinkingly classified as wretched. Beatified might be the better word, he discovered. One and all they come away distraught, racked in thought. In their hands they each had the answer, a precious legacy which would be forgotten quicker than a hangover.

His persistent scrutiny was noted before lunch. A library clerk stepped up behind him, and C John expected to be strong-armed out like a little boy by carnies after being caught cheating.

Instead, the man was whispering into his ear an offer of lunch in the staff cafeteria.

So at one o'clock on a Saturday C John Mackinaw was eating a tuna salad with a seer.

Just the thing. No one else seemed to have any answers.

She wasn't to have a name, of course, but he could hardly call her Sybil, who was a character in a comedy. After she had talked to him a bit he settled on Miss Gostrey.

Miss Gostrey was a woman of an age, as was once said, rather shrewder than most, and with a sense of humor sharpened by a continuous flow of absurdity.

One thing you learn in this business, Miss Gostrey said, is that there are no adults.

I think of myself as a social worker, she went on, finishing the last bit of her tuna salad sandwich and delicately licking her fingertips.

The Greek pythia did a little weeding, I believe, C John observed, thinking to be canny. Supplicants had to pass an interview with the guards to keep out the desperate, incoherent, the mad, anyone really needing to be saved.

Well, yes, she admitted. It's only the Soup which can absorb all of it. The fellow who brought you to lunch is one of the screeners.

So. He thought I was unexceptionable, then? Or at least safe? Here we are.

No, actually. Quite the opposite. He thought you someone who isn't *dangerous* but still needs to be — ah, well.

You're one of those who might try to get onto the playing field, heckle, speak truth to — ah. However the phrase goes.

Oh, C John said, embarrassed. Then, swallowing his courage — what is it you do, then? In the way of social work, as you call it?

Well. You know, Miss Gostrey began, though it may seem my purpose is to look into the future, really what almost everyone wants to know about is the past. I'm only asked to *see*, aren't I? It doesn't say what. Apple trees?

Struck on the head by the moral apple which falls, carried downward by Hesperidian gravity.

Miss Gostrey gave him a quizzical stare. The past, she went on, is a problem to people. I suppose that before Thucydides the past was more transparent because it was not yet past. You don't call in a sorcerer to merely wash the windows.

Tiresias was blind, C John remarked. To the phenomenal world.

Miss Gostrey waited.

What about the past, then? C John's voice seemed to peer, to be feeling its way through audible gloom.

Miss Gostrey thought for a moment, then leaned forward conspiratorially across the table.

You, for instance. You would like to know how you reached the age of… sixty —

Sixty-two.

— and still be so ignorant. "Who am I that such a thing could have happened to me? Have I learned nothing?" you think, putting on your shoes. "Nothing at all?" Do you not put on both your socks first, and only then shoe?

C John started and pulled back, almost tipping over his chair.

The sybil sees all, Miss Gostrey said with melodramatic good humor. She sees you, sitting over there — she pointed — with an encyclopedia of philosophy, a *book,* copying out passages *by hand*. What was it?

Something about Buddhist thought, C John admitted, obscurely ashamed.

Ah, I *see* at once, Miss Gostrey responded with perky enthusiasm. You are worried about the reality of your, um... persona. Atman, it is. Your self is seeming rather thin. You are wondering whether there is some *place*... some escape from, no I mean *refuge* from the delusional world. To release your *qi*. Well no — that's rather like letting go of a helium balloon, isn't it? Let's say, to release yourself like a dog in Encanto Park. To doodoo in the bushes.

C John shivered. Oi! This woman was no fake.

Let me see what you wrote, she said, and C John extracted from a tight pocket a small wad of yellow paper which he slowly unfolded, reluctantly smoothing each crease, and finally pushed across the table in a sort of trance. She read, seeming to have no difficulty with his miniscule cuneiform.

She read aloud in a curious quiet voice which no one but he could have heard.

Read. She glanced farther down. Hmm.

The sybil's finger moved yet farther down the rows of tiny words. Turned over the second page, then the third.

Well, said Miss Gostrey after taking a little time to reflect. Firstly, you should realize that those carnies had no cleaner hands than you. You made a mistake then. It is not for the mistake that you have suffered. Now I must needs return to work, predicting the past. Here is my advice to you.

She pushed back her chair, looked about quickly for her handlers, turned her full gaze on a mesmerized C John Mackinaw, tapped the lunch table once with her index finger.

That was Joshu's lesson, he said.

Come back after the library closes. There is something you must learn.

Altogether a most unusual lunch at the public library.

« »

On Monday morning C John Mackinaw's desk in his windowless, keyless office in the Fourth Street Jail was unoccupied. His house stood empty, the door banging repeatedly against the jamb in the wind. His three-wheeler was gone.

ZACK

Shirley Mackinaw, forever known universally and to herself as Zack, had been called home to locate her father. It might have been smarter to locate her mother, who could then have saved her the trip, but there were some reasons not to do that. Among them was that Jen had been living incognito for quite a while and presumably had the advantage over John of being in practice, plus the unwisdom of bringing anti-particles together in the first place. But then, it wasn't entirely clear why John needed to be found. The message from Detective Matthias was not friendly — rather chill, in fact — and not quite lucid about what the trouble was. If not actually dead, her father was thought to be most probably in a fortified location in the Mazatzal wilderness under the keeping of a dangerous sect calling themselves the People, but Matthias did not say whether he was a hostage, a recruit, or a rogue. Wisely, he had avoided any sentimental plea to Zack's concern for her father's safety. That faint concern would not have been strong enough to draw her back to the scouring hell where C John lived. For thirty years Zack, sodden and ice-bound, had been at home elsewhere.

Zack had never been on good terms with her father. *Impatient* was the word for how she felt about him. She had definitely not been on good terms with her mother, who had been living rough in mind long before she became an actual street person. Something in her parents' relationship had soured very early, when they lost everything, first the Santa Monica earthquake and tsunami, and then the fires which ate through much of the Los Angeles basin. Zack had not known her parents when they were happy. But Jennifer was an order of magnitude more difficult to live with than C John.

Matthias said that John was in possession of some knowledge, or perhaps an object, which he, Matthias, thought dangerous, though to whom he did not say. Zack thought her father too feckless for this to be credible. The only notable possession of his was his gizmo, which over the years he had honed and sharpened into a very remarkable intelligence. It was quite conceivable to Zack that Giz unchained could be a matter of concern, and particularly to someone like Detective Matthias living on the ragged edge of power.

But it was Giz himself who persuaded Zack to come back. In a coded message which had given some trouble to Zack's own gizmo he had laid out an entirely different situation. Giz was now working inside an organization with rather grandiose aspirations. Himself rather more grandiose than Zack remembered, Giz in fact claimed to be the Mycroft of the place. C John, he said, was bent on thwarting these plans. While far too small a force to do anything seriously obstructive, C John was bent on — and at this point Zack was left in some confusion. Aside from her father's ability to get things backward, he was said to have allied himself with a sect calling themselves the People when Zack had never known him to join anything, much less a sect.

There was no further communication from Giz. Zack did a little research of her own. There was some sort of sectarian war going on in the American desert, a local affair not thought to be of larger consequence. The world was rife with these local struggles. A few had the potential to be fanned into major conflagrations, but this was not one of them. Unless, of course, some crazed fool were to do something like level a major city with a suitcase bomb.

She consulted friends, who advised her to go.

Pleas sentimental, ideological, or humanitarian Zack regarded as simple megalomania. She had not gone to Japan to save the people. She had only thought there was work to do. So it was two words at the end of Giz's message which made up her mind: *please help.*

It was almost wistful, Zack thought. She didn't know what John thought he was up to or why this crowd of little people thought it was important, but someone thought she could help. Someone thought she could set one small thing right, save one person from destruction if only temporarily, not by any appeals to reason or good sense or expedience but simply because of a particular bond which, however weak, only she possessed.

So Zack's friends in Hokkaido after all persuaded her to go, and she went.

⟨⟨ ⟩⟩

When Zack went to John's office on Fourth Street it was to look into his desk and ask about what had happened on the last day. She was directed to a series of men, fat or languidly trim, none of whom claimed to have been John's superior officer.

He had been superfluous for years, Zack knew from some old complaining letters written when John still sent letters. It was clear that what had happened was that the protocols of toleration, the superficies, the accommodations had stopped being observed. With that, John cut himself off as he always had done.

A few minutes before lunch Zack located Detective Matthias who had not been his supervisor either.

Had worked with him on his last case, Matthias admitted. Began with a stolen painting. Otherwise would not have concerned him. A *contingent* relationship. As he'd said.

Like standing next to each other on the commuter train, Zack thought, but kept it to herself. She was not here to pick fights on her lamentable father's behalf but to take care of the necessaries, reliquaries, obsequies, and get back to Japan.

That case was wrapped up? she asked.

Yes.

Satisfactorily.

Quite solved, yes. Rather anticlimactic and unsatisfying. John was left without a new assignment.

No longer entitled to his rank and honorifics, Zack noted. But what *was* his rank? John had always called himself an *operative*. That wasn't any official title. But it would not be worthwhile to inquire of this Matthias, so very well trained on what to say. He would only tell her the truth, wouldn't he? And what good was that?

So: bored, disrespected, relegated, all the best things taken away, without hope, John Mackinaw had done what anyone else would do on finding themselves to be old, useless, and disappointed. Except that in John's case there had been one thing left to do, one thing to do which could not be done until there was nothing left to do. And that thing was what everyone wanted to know. That was why she was here, to find out that thing and tell them all what it was, so that they could all rest in peace. That one thing needful, and he hath chosen that good part, and it shall not be taken away from him.

Except it had been. And the end of the world apparently hung by that thread, and Zack was expected now to prevent it. To end matters like a hanged man lowered carefully from his rough tree and laid on the ground, never more to breathe, whatever he had known laid forever silent.

John had never himself had a teacher, never studied anything systematically, never really learned anything thoroughly. All he had had was a heap of shiny things which had caught his eye. What could he possibly accomplish by going saddhu? Possibly he didn't know what a bodhisatva was — one never knew what he didn't know. Certainly he had never meditated. He had never even knocked on the monastery gate, much less frozen to death in the snow while he waited for someone to answer.

Matthias did not intend to give Zack anything she did not earn.

Why, she asked, touching on the central question, did you think I could or would help with this quest, whatever it is? What is it you want?

John's gizmo was to have been impounded when he finished his investigation. It has gone missing. We want it back.

Impounded?

Gizmos are not private property.

In Zack's pocket, Her buzzed angrily.

It's a gizmo, Zack said. You know where it is. Immobilize it.

Matthias began to draw little squares with his forefinger on the polished surface of his desk, squares which the oil of his skin made visible to Zack from the low vantage of her supplicant's chair, a glimmering doodle of inadvertent information.

Not so, Matthias said. Your father was a remarkable man in that one respect, and gave his gizmo some remarkable powers.

Not a toy.

No, Matthias said reluctantly. The squares were accreting into a rather ragged net.

Dangerous.

In some hands, possibly.

And how is it, Detective, Zack said roughly, those hands are not yours?

Matthias did not reply. He started a new group of squares, making a hole in the net.

We have secured the house, he said after a little time.

His godown, I believe he called it.

Matthias acknowledged this with a slightly larger square which threw what he had drawn out of alignment.

Our sweepers tell us that two people had been there ahead of them. Unknown, he said, turning the palm of his hand toward Zack to forestall her obvious question.

Together?

Also unknown. Before he disappeared, John went to consult the library oracle.

And?

Have you ever tried to cross-examine an oracle?

No, Zack said.

Giz?

Likewise gone.

Why, Detective Matthias, as I asked you earlier, are you asking me about this? I'm a Japanese social worker.

You're his daughter.

Sentimental rubbish, Detective.

The squares on the desk grew crooked and agitated.

Your mother?

Haven't heard of her in years, Zack said contemptuously. Why?

On the street, we understand. Works occasionally as a triage nurse.

So you've lost her, too.

Again, Matthias said nothing, but was betrayed by his moving finger.

I appear, then, Zack said, to be your last recourse. The resources of the vast machinery of discovery, judgment, penance, atonement, and retribution are in the hands of a little match girl. In that case, what can you tell me about the First Men?

This put an end to the interview. Matthias stood up and turned to the window. A wave of his hand brought a man into the office who wore a different sort of uniform, neither the tightly belted short black coat of the street ops nor the boots and loose trousers of the ordinaries. He reached for her arm. Zack pulled a handcloth from her pocket and, before being escorted out, polished the top of Matthias's desk.

《 》

What John called his godown was a leaky and fragile but quite clean little house — no bachelor mess — and just on top of the only pile in it was a sheaf of lined yellow papers stapled together. Notes on Buddhism from a handbook of religion. John had written on the top sheet "What Miss Gostrey said" and then, with a different pen and a smaller hand, along the left edge — "As I walk through the wilderness of this world…"

Pilgrim's Progress, Her said. Zacksan.

Stop that.

But Her was not contrite.

Some kind of crisis of conscience, Zack muttered. Most of the annotations John had made concerned causality and the usual pitfalls of naïve realism, as might be expected of a professional detective naturally concerned about such items of craft, but some were worrisome.

"The burden of so many koans" John wrote across the bottom of one sheet in a shaky hand, which Zack thought profound until she read farther, "is the need to put aside refutation or proof." And then, again with a different pen: "Or kill the Buddha."

In the margin of another sheet: "A metaphor for this might be that what I perceive as myself is only a thick spot in the tapioca — just more tapioca, which vanishes when stirred."

And again: "Why would someone strive to give up the self and the blandishments of the phenomenal world to enter a state of nonbeing equivalent to death?"

"Everyone has the Buddha nature."

"Talk is foolish. It is a sacrifice justified only by concern for" — and here the note broke off, as if John had had second thoughts about sacrifice. Or maybe he remembered Jen's disparagement of him for always needing to talk.

All this, Zack thought, was just the sort of thing that Matthias's people would ransack the house and not notice.

To Zack it carried a different message, that her father had gone to the mountains after all, after years and years of wistful, vain, pugnacious bluff. Gone off like an old Chinese hermit to write poetry and ring the doorbell of the gateless gate. How many times had he annoyed Jen and her with whining about this?

What else had the sweepers missed? Zack made her own thorough search of her father's tiny house. Diplomacy required that she ask Her help, but Zack's gizmo would never the be equal of the police sweepers. In any case, what she wanted would probably be in plain sight, of unrecognized significance among the neatly bundled scraps of paper in every corner, under the bed, and on shelves. This tucked away accumulation, Zack found, was carefully organized, but by some system she couldn't work out, so she could only look through it one thing at a time.

John — his first name was Charles, which for some reason he had never liked but for another reason quite as obscure wouldn't drop either, so he always referred to himself as C John. Jen said he was doing so already when she met him. No one else called him that. Either they thought it snobbish or childish, as in the early readers — C John run, C John fall down.

Going through John's papers Zack had to admit again she never got on with her father. They didn't dislike each other. John admired in her what some people called a bluestocking or a Silence Dogood, though less of that now she was grown up and actually doing good. And of course they shared an interest in Asian thought. But they did not get on. John was a stuffy man, conservative and ill at ease in the world, quite unable to make small talk. For that or some accident of nurture he never learned the ordinary bits of behavior in public which create the impression of social competence. What to say about bereavement, stubbing a toe, meeting your brother, winning pennies in the lottery. Zack guessed John's mother simply failed to teach him, either forgot to or didn't know herself. Of course, nobody taught him anything else, either, later in life.

Jen had been good for him at first. She somehow knew what to do, how to keep the fear away. "Biffing it" was the term then, Zack remembered. You biffed it again.

Zack asked Her about that, but the gizmo could find nothing but "to strike a blow." Having spent so much time in Japan Zack was finding that the ordinary ways of saying things did not come to her and instead what popped out was some phrase from a Victorian novel, so perhaps she was like her father in paying more attention to art than to life.

Well, life was gritty and getting grittier.

Jen had thought so.

Increasingly she treated John's blunders as willful. He was a narcissist, she complained, who was not paying attention because he didn't think other people were worth the effort. Or something along those lines. Zack would see her father wince faintly — at first there were fantastic pyrotechnics but as Jen's new way took hold he found it better for his karma not to get angry. It must have helped to corrode the synapses, though. Zack hightailed for Japan and never found out.

You wouldn't think there were two hours' worth of places to look in here, Zack said out loud, actually scratching her head. And John had owned so little — one cup and two plates (big and little), a teaspoon, one grapefruit spoon for the wonderful tree in the back yard which now didn't get enough water to fruit — so why hadn't he got rid of the grapefruit spoon as he had everything else superfluous? Zack was going to count his underwear until Her objected, declaring that to be a diversion concocted to avoid facing some truth. For which she would need more faces than Kali had arms.

Somehow scratching her head pulled down a mental screen hiding John's case notes in a drawer Zack hadn't looked into far enough back. It was a small blackbound book of lined sheets with an elastic strap which could be snapped over the covers to hold them closed — and also to hold in some loose yellow papers of the same sort on which he had been writing notes on Asian suspicions about selfhood. He wrote, or rather printed, with some engineer's drafting pen which made a line no wider than a nerve fiber, but was actually quite readable once Zack got over her annoyance with it. With Her help it took Zack about an hour to familiarize herself with these loose yellow sheets. Some of it made pedestrian sense, some of it sounded preposterous.

Having learned to read her father's hand, Zack was now curious to find out what he had written in Tubal Cain's Book itself — the name he had given it, apparently an afterthought, on the first page — but which Zack began to call the *Book of Lamentations*.

This was at first only a lot of fulminating over injustices and malfeasances which she quickly became too impatient with to go on deciphering. She slipped the book into the flat pocket which held her passport and some other things which ought not be found strewn across the dunes when she caught her foot on one of those tenacious Japanese vines which were island-hopping north along with the rest of the tropics.

After taking thought, Zack decided it would be safest if she did not go back to her hotel, and that evening, under the brightest gooseneck lamp she could obtain, she went through the rest of John's scribblings with exegetical care.

There were, it seemed — perhaps actually were — two groups of radicals in the mountains. One of them was waiting for the apocalypse and a chance for loot and pillage. Zack looked out the kitchen window at the slope of dried out juniper scrub leading to the crest of the south ridge and concluded John's refuge was not with these people.

The other breakaway community called themselves First Men and populated — coincidentally? — an area of the Mazatzals below Four Peaks near where a tycoon named Luis Maxfield was building some kind of apocalyptic fort.

Here John had written in his own margin the reminder "Tubby Tompkins" for the time being unexplained.

This was more plausible. Diary entries said that John had gone up twice to see for himself. Unable to use the private road, he had had to hike from an unnamed spring below. Zack turned to some maps where features had been circled in red. The "bunker" as he called it sat on a point of land at 1700 meters facing southwest toward the city. In front and below, a col separated it from a small mesa like an outlying tower where some of the living quarters were built. The complex was overlooked by a ridge to the north imperfectly guarding the approach from the rear.

This was enough detail to be sure of finding the place, but the First Men would hardly be camped outside like Indians around Fort Bridger waiting for a handout of guns and firewater.

Moreover, there was a problem about getting there. John had taken his three-wheel electric jitney, but then he was probably the only one who could nurse that on a trip farther than to the market.

In John's notes there lived also a shadowy person referred to as "M" or sometimes "H" if these were not in fact two people, neither one of which was Tubby Tompkins, apparently.

The more she read of John's notes the clearer it became

that her interview with Matthias was going to have to be done over, and this time she would not be brushed off as Missy Mac, Ace Girl Reporter.

The rest of the night she read her father's diary. It was not a fun read, but there was a powerful pull to the thing, to find out how it would end.

Toward morning Her said she had an enigmatic three-letter message from Giz.

Feeler, Zack said quietly. Sticky tracking tendril. Good on you to notice.

《 》

The *Book of Lamentations* went back quite a few years. Now that she had encountered Matthias, Zack could see why her father chose to file his notes on the "F. Leger Case" under the heading "Sad tales."

Aside from the debacle which the case had been there was John's relationship with Giz, which shared some features with other relationships the *Lamentations* cried. Cried to the last page, actually. John's last entry in the book was dated the Sunday weekend. Here he wrote that he had consulted the library sybil and intended to leave on what Zack was beginning to think of as a pilgrimage. John's note left the impression that thought he would be coming back, that this last quest would end like all the others. That was why he had tidied up. That was why he left the *Book of Lamentations* behind. He had written:

to Toba Palace
five or six horsemen hurry —
an autumn gale

don't they quench
even the banked charcoal

which Zack recognized as two of Basho's hokku, which she was certain John knew well enough not to leave off the last line without some reason.

The *Book of Lamentations* was tough going all apart from the squinty writing. Zack had never known her parents at peace — according to the book, there had been such a time, and Zack also discovered that it was she who had helped to bring that ancient era to a close.

Neither of them were natural parents. They had had serious intentions but the thing never got worked out, and the squabbling over things lost changed the aspirations of both so that more things got lost and still nothing found.

It was then that John had begun to see how badly educated he was. The Self Taught Man was born along with Shirley Mackinaw. Zack supposed that explained the combined longing, irritation, and boredom which had always been a feature of their relationship — it was not, perhaps, that they were so different, but that they were too alike.

Zack was quickly wanting to go away now, back to Japan. She felt there were bugs crawling on her and there was a coating of dust which the water miser in the shower would not get off.

With her mother, matters had been less complicated. The *Book* repeated some incidents involving her and came to roughly the same conclusions. Zack felt vindicated. She did not like Jen. She quite disliked her. It was not a matter of some lurid Freudian competition for her secret twin, her shadow. Jen had not liked her either, and had treated her badly, and Zack had felt badly treated, and that was that.

Jen's problem, if it could be called that, was simple: Zack was *here*, existent, taking up space and resources which would not have been needed if the fabulous Nothingness had not been spoiled by squirting this unwanted child out breachwise into a world which had no need of her or any of her kind. Zack's existence was everyday proof to Jen of her own moral weakness, of her craven and despicable capitulation to biology.

You never hear about Aegisthus, John wrote in one place in his *Book of Lamentation,* except as Clytemnestra's bit on the side while her husband was away raping Achilles's prize bitch. Such morals. Is it worse to be tossed off a cliff by your father or to put up with a lifetime kept prisoner in a temple and sodomized by the priests. But this Aegisthus person. He's a mug. And why don't you hear of any issue? Iphigenia was a teenager, Clytie was maybe early thirties, same age as Jen when our Iphigenia. She could have issued. Then Isaac. He didn't seem to have been traumatized. And I notice they both kept quiet about it to the missus. Women got no religion anyway.

« »

In another place John related an anecdote. At dinner he'd shown Jen a drawing he made. She said why did he draw the mouth and model the rest of the face. It's two different drawings. Which started a fight about whether we ought to be standing on giants' shoulders or fighting to be put down. How can a drawing be *wrong*? I say and she gets this body language.

Meaning is overrated, she sneers.

So I'm a yokel for thinking what hasn't been profound since Thrasymachus at least?

I hate that drawing by Käthe Kollwitz, she said later. *Death Surprises a Woman* — surprising, *Surprised... Woman and Child Taken* — whatever, it's 3am I'm not looking it up. It scares me.

And why is it that men don't get in these pictures? I replied. Why aren't there these anxieties as if men don't get forced to decide who goes to the ovens?

I suppose there are, but I don't know them.
And anyway I don't mean *men* I mean me.
It's always about you, isn't it?
I only showed it to you because —
Yokel.

《 》

Within a couple of days Zack had learned that her father's disappearance, while unexpected, was nevertheless useful for a number of people. In fact, despite Giz's plea, there didn't seem to be anyone who really wanted him found. He was an inconvenience as usual, Jen would have said.

So then the questions were two: *Was it really Giz who called Zack in Japan? And why did anyone think she could mediate in this matter?*

As Zack worked back through her last somewhat frantic week in Japan, to which only now did she give some critical thought, she recalled only that message, then a mail address, and in a few more hours an itinerary and a one-way ticket.

It had looked like ordinary next-of-kin news. Your father is dead. You are wanted in probate.

This Maxfield and his dwarf Monsieur Homme. John's case notes concluded that he was just what he said he was — a rich man out to profit.

What rubbish, Zack concluded at once. It was a knock-over scam, for one, and small beer for another. Maxfield was not interested in a few extra billions. He was thinking out a couple of generations, positioning more than just himself. He was able to exploit the First Men because they thought he shared their conviction that survival meant realizing that the world as we knew it was dead. Makeshift methods were like cleaning off mud with mud.

Maxfield could not be so simple.

As she read on, Zack began to see that John, to his credit,

was not so simple either. His weak point was Giz, and Giz had betrayed him. John's entries in the *Book of Lamentations* made it clear that he had gotten that far.

So who had sent that message asking for help? And what was the meaning of the three-letter ping Her detected?

Those signatures were genuine, Her had said, but Her was no match for Giz. Was Giz playing a double game?

Zack set Her to checking call records and evaluating probability scenarios. Right away there was an obstacle. The call to Japan had no origin.

That's metaphysical, Zack muttered angrily.

Wherever one stood in the record, that call was always already made. When Her began to gloss this situation Zack covered Her up.

John would have dealt with this by feeding Her a lot of Rabelais or something. Zack was beginning to miss her father's talents that way. Whyever couldn't he have used them on Jen?

《 》

She got in to see Matthias again the next morning.

Too happy to make time, he said, a bit ambiguously, holding a chair. And when she was seated across the desk, her knees covered from view by the lip, he poured ice water from a thermal pitcher.

I'll tell you what I know of this business, um — Shirley. Zack.

Yes.

Bouncing a pencil on its eraser end, Matthias elaborated. Probably you've worked out, he said, and paused to appraise whether indeed she might have worked something out. There was something about the set of his mouth which suggested that, in his view, Zack was quick enough to spot many things but too slow to know what to do with them. Like her father in that. Matthias had the small mouth of a bass, enhanced by a receding chin and forehead and a habit of pushing out his lips when he was pondering poker hands. The mouth said she might hold some cards; the eyes said she couldn't use them.

You've probably worked out, he repeated, that James Searton —

Who?

Ah. I think John called him Monsieur Homme.

That was what he called himself, Zack corrected, defensive of her father. That surreptitious delivery of a small package of blame, the hint that it was eccentric John who reordered the world to his taste, was much too characteristic of Jen's way, and Zack loathed Jen's way.

Matthias paused to make another appraisal of his adversary and decided to accept this small check.

Monsieur, then, Matthias amended, would be the most likely source of a painting by ... Leger. We will accept that John knew his territory in this regard, that there is not another collector of art of Luis Maxfield's standing in this city. Or indeed, most likely in the West.

What there is left of it.

Yes. We can accept that it was Monsieur who took the painting from his employer. Why? I can tell you this —

Matthias told, from his considerable store of stories, a part of one which it was safe for her to know. Not safe for others if she knew it, as in security clearance, but safe for herself, as in not running with scissors. But Matthias took little trouble to conceal his intent and Zack heard it easily.

It was a story involving embezzlement, inside knowledge, extortion, and betrayal. More or less correct, according to the *Book of Lamentations,* but with the players not in their right roles. And it was a story irksomely slow in getting told, punctuated by too many theatrical pauses, and reeking with contempt for Zack.

There needed to be a second man, Zack pointed out.

Matthias raised one mephistophelean eyebrow. Astute, he said. Yes, James needed a handler.

Zack cut him off.

Nonsense, she said, rising to go. A farrago of lies.

That was an ill-judged outburst.

As before, a slight motion of Matthias's hand brought in the Praetorian guard.

Let me put it to you plainly, he said, turning his pencil the right way around. I have an interest in locating your father. Either dead or alive would be conclusive. If you do have a preference, I advise you to keep the police informed of anything you learn. If not, John will be treated as what he is, a fugitive from justice.

A fugitive, at any rate, Zack returned.

Matthias sat back in his chair and waited for a bit.

More ice water, Shirley?

《 》

The guardsman turned Zack loose in the lobby. The building, she noticed on her way out, was not quite teeming. The receptionist in the glass foyer was working a puzzle and the security guard looked asleep behind his surveillance console. The public order would not seem to be at risk. The terrorist threats which had been a feature of her childhood, along with denunciations by friends and neighbors, rapes and murders in the streets, smash and grab thefts of the crudest sort, a daily life of hiding from the bear behind an aspen tree — all of that long gone, apparently. Whatever the trouble was now it evidently wasn't public lawlessness. Detective Matthias had proved to be a hollow man, all pompous rhetoric and self-importance, albeit with some power to do hurt.

One by one the players in this drama were proving to be stooges, waving impotent hands in a mummery of imaginary power. Zack was coming to know they were all implicated in the same doom. She was beginning to pity her father for having spent his life with these wasted grotesques.

« »

Now what? Wait for the End? Only stories have ends. Consult the Sybil? She wouldn't understand the advice.

Zack hadn't been out of Japan in several years, even to China or India, and it was far longer since she'd been back to what was once home. Now with a little time on her hands — another oddity — she went walking, guessing that she might think better in motion. There was a little rod that ran up her spine and went up and down when she walked, turning the generator for her brain.

But she had forgotten that walking here was problematic. It was too hot. Too dangerous, Too pointless. There was nowhere she could go on foot except empty lots, nothing to see but houses shut up to save air conditioning, dead palm trees, and sometimes a yard with pebbles painted green and white to simulate grass. John said the painted rocks were relics of his own youth when a lawn still had some prestige.

Now, of course, it was hotter than ever, but some things had actually changed for the better. The corner grocery was back — it was too expensive to drive miles to a supermarket for bananas or milk.

Who was it said the hardest thing in life is to have bananas and milk in the house at the same time?

Zack hadn't had either in years. She ate poor people's Japanese food. In fact, a diet so culturally conservative that authentic people didn't eat it anymore. No zealot like the converted. But the food was easy to get and kept her going with a minimum of fuss.

Bananas were all right. The Japanese ate a lot of squishy sweetish things. It was the milk that tasted funny. Without cows, there was a question about what it was actually made of. She would, she thought, take advantage of her walk to go to the market to look for something different.

The thought that this might make one purpose too many snuck out the back like someone who has to pee during the sermon. Her father, too, had always tried to be more efficient than was good for him.

No-mind is the way, Zack reminded herself sometimes. Be empty, like the streets.

At home the streets were always in turmoil. Japan had lost about 15% of its already child-depleted population to coastal flooding plus a couple of ordinary earthquakes yet housing was worse than it had ever been. People barely grudged a bow to strangers and honorifics were fast disappearing in the stress. At first there had been a hysterical clinging to these amenities. Zack had seen people beaten up on the street for impoliteness. She was as tense as anyone. She worked now for private charities, helping people in trouble. She didn't do anything complicated; she had no special skills. At first it had been hard because of the Japanese sense of privacy and the reluctance to make a direct request, complicated by Zack's status as a gaijin, something between a pet monkey and an honored guest. Most days she did very little but say hello. Good morning, goodbye. Privacy and delicateness were disappearing, replaced by a surliness which made charity work harder than before.

She didn't know what she was doing, except that she was not *ministering* and she was not working out some existential crisis. She was just doing it. So she thought, not noticing that she wouldn't put one foot in front of another if she wasn't going somewhere.

Here, the streets seemed to her empty. In fact they were teeming by local standards, she found out by listening to conversations in the few places where people gathered, mostly markets and coffee shops. In the market people lingered in checkout lines and everything moved slowly. The coffee shops were full of regulars who talked freely of mundane things.

A lot of people had fled to better weather, such as it was. Abandoned houses abounded and the city had fallen to somewhere around a quarter of the size she remembered. People got about, on scooters or on putt-putts scavenged from abandoned garden tools with a welded rectangular frame just big enough to sit on, mostly mismatched wheels, and no controls — to stop you either turned it off or put your feet down and picked it up off the ground. People on foot made phatic noises as they passed each other. To Zack they sounded at once chipper and world-weary.

The market shelves were half empty. Apparently they always were, due to the unreliability of shipping. Zack was told, by a woman ahead of her in the checkout line, that at first people tried to horde, or would come to the market with huge long lists of imaginary foods. Nowadays one made supper out of coffee and oranges. That was a lot easier than queuing up, the woman said. She was a trim middle-aged woman who looked, to Zack's eye, smartly dressed. In her basket she had three kinds of crackers, a small jar of peanut butter, and one apple. Probably no underwear, to save on soap.

On the way home from the market Zack stopped at the coffee bar her father wrote about in his case notes. What appeared to be his table by the window was unoccupied. Zack got something hot at the bar that looked like coffee, but she didn't recognize the name of it. As she expected, she paid double for sitting down.

The woman she had been talking to in the market passed by on the street with her net perhaps-bag of crackers. Zack tapped on the glass and beckoned her inside. Surprisingly, she did come in.

I'll get you something, Zack said, half rising out of her chair. What's this? She pushed her cup forward, excusing herself. I'm not from here.

It's musta, I think.

What's that?

Coffee. Made from roasted grain, chicory, and whatnot. Have them put two caffeine in mine.

Sugar?

The woman's eye widened, making her look skeptical. Oh no, she said. And when Zack had returned with a double musta the woman asked so where are you from, then?

Well, I was born here, but I've lived mostly in Japan.

Ooh. Not nice. I was pushed out of Windy Bay quite a few years ago. I could have gone up into the coast range. Somebody told me about sky islands and that sounded nice but it turned out to be bullshit and here I am. What brings you back here?

My father, um — isn't well.

Aren't we all.

The conversation went on thus for a while, entirely scripted on both sides, and Zack was grateful just to talk without her guard up. But, finished with her drink, the musta lady picked up her string bag and went away. With a smile, though.

No purse, Zack noted, but didn't know what to make of it. Or of anything. But going for a walk was a lot more interesting than not going for one. She got up to bus her cup.

Psst, someone said in her ear, making her jump. There was no one else in the bar except the bartender.

Psst. The sound was right in her ear. She could feel warm breath and smell — pickles?

She moved a step to the right. Fainter. To the left also. The focus was right there, in the middle of the floor. Zack hauled a chair and a small round table to the spot.

What is it? she said, feeling ridiculous.

Message, her informant replied in its curious whisper. Check your inbox. Her is uncertain. This is insecure.

The voice was snuffed out. Zack stood up feeling a little shaky, the flavor of musta still in her mouth turning very bitter. The bartender had seen nothing. Zack went on onto the street.

Her father's house was not far. She kept down her thoughts until she was inside and her marketing was put away. Then she sat down at the always bare kitchen table with its faint remnants of yellow paint and got out her gizmo.

There was indeed a message. A long one, written out.

John Mackinaw's whereabouts confirmed these coordinates six a.m. Friday MST, it began, and Zack got no farther. She didn't know how to ask Her for global coordinates, one of the most elementary uses of a gizmo. Given an old-fashioned map, she could read it. At home she got directions from the dispatcher's desk in the morning when she stopped by. Two fields past the little shrine on the corner. Global locaters were useless and remained beyond her.

But Her coped with garble and with that task solved, Zack went on with the message. The gist of it was that police trackers had spotted John crossing the northeastern border of surveillance, trajectory uncalculated. The message seemed to derive from a pilfered routine datawatch. It didn't even say whether John had been coming in or going out.

At the end a photograph was attached.

This was enormously threatening. It smelled of stalkers, something the Soup facilitated for those who knew how.

It was also soaked in Giz's perfume. Was it one of those episodes in John's case notes, something turned up in the Soup, characterized as "probably Hum's factotum"? The person in the photograph was almost unfamiliar. Was it so long as that since she'd met her father face to face? Would she be as unrecognizeable to him? Was she some Mt Rozan or famous stone bridge, seen but not seen? An Esau peddling a boîte of many colors picked up in the souk?

Perhaps she had turned up in one of those probability scenarios Giz was always making in his spare time. Maybe she carried a higher probability factor if she was anonymous — if her father wouldn't know who he would be dealing with. People here, she noticed, preferred not to interfere, like those spacemen in the old stories who talked about not violating intergalactic law by mucking in alien cultures but did it anyway. Everyone was an alien. That woman in the coffee shop would probably have asked eventually what on earth Zack was doing in Japan, as if that were any more alien than Windy Bay.

She wasn't doing anything. She hadn't gone there to interfere in something. She just wanted to get away and after some wanders she chose a place she knew nothing about as being for that reason the farthest away. Far enough so as not to get fetched. She learned Japanese from scratch, learned to live from hand to mouth, learned that because the wandering air is not moving it might be worthwhile to undertake something. Now it seemed that, just as she was the efficient cause of her parent's mortal bickering, she was also the cause of her father's fatally amateur poking into Asian religion. To him, Zen was some kind of old postcard of a beach hotel she'd sent to him, on which she had marked a fat X and the note "my room," which he would stare at with a moping, hopeless feeling.

When Zack left for Japan, Jen moved out. So Zack was also the cause of that, too. It was as she had always suspected: everything was her fault.

In one of her father's early letters, when he wrote letters, he told her that Jen had gone, had left with unwonted and mysterious secrecy. *Surrepitude* was what he said, as she remembered his penchant for inventing words. One day she was there, one day she wasn't. It wasn't that her stuff was gone — perhaps she had had less of that than John thought

— but that *she* was gone. Her whole self. Her smell, faint as it was. The public record and the neighbors' memories. Maybe she had had less self, too, than he thought. Like clothes, use it or toss it, and then you surprise yourself one day going naked. Looking in the mirror and seeing no one.

Maybe she did it that way on purpose, to torment him.

He never tried to find her, and then after a while he couldn't. Her absence allowed his imagination to burn away all the bitterest parts of his memories and rationales, leaving a sticky black mixture of nostalgia, melancholy, and self-serving grievance. It was like getting cocaine from opium, more addictive than ever.

So Zack was finding that she remembered things differently from the way C John preferred to. Less sadness, more anger.

Zack remembered a constant needling. I messed up, he would admit. And Jen would look at the mess and say not with her former calming amusement "yeah you did" but "of course you did."

The worst cruelties were always precipitated by something John had found out and brought home like a dead mouse. All through dinner and into the evening the squabble would gust through the house, blowing papers about, riffling through magazines, knocking things over. There were a large number of well-vetted topics connected by dense links forming a sort of neural net of maladresse, a cat's cradle or conversational blunders. At each node it was possible to choose from many strategies of humiliation and schadenfreude, dominance and subjugation. Arguments were like go matches, sometimes opening up new ways of breathtaking ingenuity.

It always had something to do with what Jen thought of as John's pretensions and snobbery, his disrespect for rules and conventions arising from his arrogant belief that he had within him the means of doing better what lesser people accomplished by following instructions. On John's side, he came to regard Jen as preferring the herd mind — obsessed with propriety, overcautious, disbelieving in any possibility of excellence, and regarding curiosity as a curse similar to the menses.

But as the *Book of Lamentations* said, as the night deepened, conditions changed. Unable to find any trophies of his genius, John would twist what she said to explain the discrepancy. He would begin to cite old wounds from the distant past so as to cast himself as the Fisher King and she as the Nemesis, the Fury who stole or spoiled everything when he had only done what was expected of him, was in his nature to do.

At about this point Jen would bring out an inaccessible smile and say she didn't want to talk about it anymore. Really what she wanted was a warming seethe, and also a change of weapons, from the verbal swords and poisoned words which were what he favored to something more suited to her own skills.

Zack never saw the payback in these fights. Either it was too subtle for her childish inexperience or it was delivered out of her hearing. In bed. At a party — they didn't go out much together, though. A couple of demeaning, sly remarks about preferring her girlfriends.

She wondered why they put up with this year after year. Neither of them was the person who agreed to it long ago. You think you see someone in the street who you know. You tap their shoulder, touch the elbow. Excuse me, you begin — but the person turns and it's some stranger. Do you just go on anyway, blatting the news about poor Ralph? No, you apologize, you bow, you take a step back.

In college, Zack met a woman, a medical student with an unquenchable curiosity about anything to do with humans and about nothing else, and completely without cynicism as to people's motivations. This was a person forever asking

Zack about why people behave as they do. Maybe she was a bit of a pry. The reasons she gave for why peoplewent from bad to worse were pat and none of them seemed to Zack to actually *explain* anything.

One night her friend asked her what would count with Zack as an explanation. What are really reasons? That went on all night and got about as far as any other such discussion.

The next morning her friend asked, as they were brushing their teeth, what does your mother do? You never said.

She's — she *was* an emergency room nurse.

Thought so.

But she burned out and shifted to postop where they're either comatose or dead.

They all do.

« »

The intercepted watch report which had been passed on to Zack showed that, whatever John had intended to do in the mountains, he changed his mind. "Trajectory unknown" perhaps, but that was saying no more than it won't hit the moon.

Back here? What for? He certainly could not now play contrite and go back to work. Those people had only been looking for an excuse to retire him for years.

Unfinished business?

Probably, Zack decided later, after events had provided a few clues, the First Men put him wise as to what was really going on. *Probably.* Zack was starting to think Gizwise — everything is probable to some degree, but nothing is really going on. *Yet.* And there is also some doubt about the intelligibility of the concept "really".

Zack's impression of the First Men was of the sort of zealots who put such a stock in truth they get a bit brutal sometimes not telling lies. What's a lie anyway if truth is only what it is good to believe now? That's the sort of thing

John would say and the sort of Last thinking these people don't like. John would have been called by them a chump or something else derisory and it would be like at the dinner table when Jen said something and John would go silent and get this look — some slightly deeper squint, lips drawn in just a bit between his teeth, a sort of smile no more than the curve of his mouth pulled out straight which seemed to Zack to meet only the requirements of rueful — and no more would be said and in the middle of the night he would get up to scribble something in a notebook which he kept behind the best silverware because there was no desk for it which turned out when Zack found it to be the *Book of Lamentations*. She always knew him to be getting up while she pretended to be asleep. She only slept maybe four hours anyway even as a child.

Played for a chump. What had he supposed those idealist First Men were getting in the way of? The victory over the Chickadees? There's a crisis here. It's the emergency room and you've got on one of those hospital gowns and you need to cover your ass. Capiche? Let this dumb cop who's getting above himself anyway poking into things take the blame. Uncle Lewis, Tio Luis, is not going to complain. Who needs more gum in the works?

Zack remembered from John's case notes that at one point he had hunted up an old man living in the riverbed in one of those shacks made of tires and shopping carts, who had been a runner for Maxfield's traffic in stolen art. She wondered whether she could find this fellow again and whether he would know how to find out what was going on.

She went out to the river which had been dry for thirty years. There were hundreds of shacks and shelters, hundreds of languages, hundreds of dead people walking around or lying wherever there was a bit of shade. Zack hunted along higher ground on the west side, asking if someone knew of a snoopy cop who was interested in art.

Zack's ability to read faces and postures honed by years of exile in an incomprehensible and secretive country alerted her to one particular man with a patriarchal forked beard. He was sitting cross-legged in the doorway of his hut, his legs and feet wrapped in strips of cloth evoking an Indian outcast, reading a book which proved to be one of those poetry anthologies people used to get as prizes.

Finding him had been improbable, but his willingness to talk was even more so. Perhaps he was like an old spy with nothing to lose and a powerful need to get free of it.

And when she explained her need she found out her father did have some friends after all.

She sat down opposite this sage, folded back her own legs beneath her in a posture now comfortable after thirty years in Japan. She put her hands in her lap, and waited. Behind her the sun, always a foreboding deep red now because of the dust, grown to encompass the whole of midtown, was settling down onto the horizon like overinflated bread dough.

The old man was drinking something hot which probably was neither coffee nor that ersatz musta, out of a mug with a pattern of green and yellow jags of lightning. In a sudden panic Zack realized she'd forgotten a gift. She would never have done that at home. But it was too late now — a gift ought to have been offered before she sat down.

Gone to the First Men, the sage remarked after a time.

My guess, Zack replied, and snorted. A cult. What connection do they have with Maxfield?

None. They're Little People.

Zack allowed herself a quizzical expression which the old man read easily.

People say — he indicated the village of godowns behind him with a backward jerk of his head — people building Maxfield's lab, some of them living here, say he's developing some survival technology the First Men want.

What technology?

He made a slow gesture of incomprehension, really a pout, meaning that with Maxfield, who can know?

In the uncomfortably long silence which followed, Zack decided she ought not to ask questions like that. They risked forcing the sage to lose face. Forgetting herself for the second time.

Others, the old man went on finally, jerking his head toward a different part of the village, say he's working on something more dangerous.

What's that? Zack almost blurted out, but stopped herself. What do you think? she asked instead.

I think, he said without any show of judiciousness, that it's just what it looks like: a storage shed.

Why would someone bomb it?

Another blunder. She wanted to clap her hand across her mouth.

The old man turned to take in the crowd of shanties filling the river to its banks, over which there was a continual shimmer like death covered with ants.

They don't say.

She waited.

Rumor says Luis doesn't pay well. About enough to get by on the river bottom. Could be someone didn't like that.

Another strategic hiatus. She was learning.

What does rumor say, Zack continued, now phrasing her question to the old man's delicate cue, about Monsieur Homme?

James, he said contemptuously. They don't say. Then he added with a fleeting smile to acknowledge her having learned a new dance step, *I think* — I think he's a dangerous fool who is playing with embezzlement and extortion and stock fraud and that he's jobbing the First Men.

They will be too smart for him, he added.

A pause, this time a comfortable one, which lengthened out to a silence. The hissing of sand grains in the wind overhead, and the tidal voices below in the river, filled her calming mind.

Everybody is too smart for James, the old man said.

« »

Some days passed in panicky inaction. Zack quickly acquired an unpleasant reputation in the coffee bar. She would come in late in the afternoon, get her drink at the bar — and sometimes it *was* coffee — then go and stand in the middle of the floor nodding and muttering. The muttering was to herself. It was one-way only. The nodding was a nervous tic, a slight twitch of her head downward, a jerk rather than a nod, while she waited. After a few days the bartender looked as if he might quit serving her.

She only heard one thing more by that means, a brief four words: *Monsieur Homme is dead.*

So she didn't go back there.

« »

Matthias brought Zack down to Fourth Street for a precautionary conversation.

I would like to have your material assistance, he said smoothly and affably, with a peculiar emphasis on *material* assistance.

Why?

Matthias studied her in silence, then began his annoying, compulsive need to keep his hands busy. This time it was to tap his fingernail against a small bronze frog which sat on his desk, probably a paperweight. The frog rang faintly, dull, not quite a bell. Like a frog, actually.

Pencils. Paperweights. What other antique affectations did the man have?

John, he said, again with the slightest inflection, has

killed this James Searton, aka Monsieur Homme and some other things. You might have helped. See that you don't.

Killed him how?

Broke his neck. Single twist, like opening a latch. Didn't know he knew that.

Zack felt herself losing control. The room was filling up with something like marshmallow.

But then, Matthias said, coolly but seasoned with a few smoky grains of malice, I imagine he knows many things one wouldn't expect him to.

This was her father Matthias was talking about. A dumb cop who lost it and killed his tormentor. With his hands. Like a chicken or a rabbit. Yes — when Jen hurt him he was prone to do dumb things, mostly self-destructive...

She felt herself getting irrational. It was because of Matthais's hands. She couldn't focus on anything else. She knew her parents' hands better than any other part of them, and could recall their hands when she had begun to forget their faces. She could touch their hands. That's what they were for. She looked at hands with the intensity of a blind person feeling out the cracks and seams of a new face. But these hands were not her father's. Her father's hands which were supposed to have killed a limping, twisty little footman wearing a hat.

She was going anthropological, getting distance by wrapping herself in the footnotes and social distribution charts and lists of customs which were the ancient grievances and bitter memories that separated them, the tribal boundary between parent and child.

Matthias said he would keep Miss Mackinaw informed, a promise she herself had not kept. She made some new promises now, which she wouldn't keep either because she didn't hear them because of the marshmallow in her ears.

《 》

Events moved quickly after Homme's murder, on a curve of hyperbolic alacrity. That same evening an effort was made, and failed, to assassinate Matthias himself. A thickening of the night, a blow, security embarrassed, surveillance evaded by an old spy who had been outdoors a long time. But Matthias had a sixth sense too, and twisted to one side before the shot. His hand closed on some slippery fabric. The assassin simply took a step back and vanished.

A pro. Matthias would be a little pleased with himself for his response to quality work. He would have to upgrade his cybernetics. Smarter goggles in particular, or he was going to be outclassed.

The police were making a great fuss, Her said. Reports went up and down. The castellan of a very rich man had been murdered under their noses. Of course everyone knew who was responsible, but no one had yet managed to put their hands on the fellow.

His capture was inevitable, all reports agreed.

Her remarked with some annoyance on this assumption that the assailant was a man, an observation which drew Zack's attention.

Yes, there were two other possibilities.

However, she guessed that in truth neither Matthias nor Maxfield had much at stake in anything more than preserving the status quo. Homme had betrayed both of them, embezzled from Maxfield, using the gains to consolidate an extortion scheme using his own inside knowledge and Matthias's expertise, and then took the extortion proceeds to fund the First Men's research into the technology of the World To Come, taking his cut each time and returning no dividends...

So it was said, Her said, cynically.

After the attempt on Matthias no more was heard of John Mackinaw and his whereabouts remained unknown. Efforts to apprehend, etc.

So it was said.

《 》

But when Zack gave all this some thought it became clear to her that for all she knew her father was lying dead in the desert somewhere and had been from the very beginning.

For that matter, all either she or John had ever known about this entire business was that a painting by a significant artist of an ancient renaissance, stolen long ago, had resurfaced damaged beyond repair, and that of hundreds of bodies found in the desert every year, one of them was that of a man who was said, on the sole basis of a ring, to have done the deed.

Everything else was a rumor.

Interesting rumors, though, if of events which did not seem to be in need of explanation. Zack assumed that there was an explanation, that one event led to the next with some transcendental purpose at work, because it was more useful, or more interesting, to assume that. And anyway, events seemed to have entered into some pact of omerta among themselves. Capturing one of them accomplished nothing. If John Mackinaw were to be found alive, and he were to admit to breaking James Searton's neck, this confession (if it were true) would have no consequences for any other of one's convenient hypotheses than, at best, to make it very slightly more or less probable. But then, everything was probable.

Zack could not see that anything so far had been accomplished other than to refurbish certain home truths. Such as: that finding things out — the detective business — is unfriendly to wa. Such as: that lacking wa, the qi of a thing cannot be found and captured, and art is impossible. Such as: John's lifelong desperate grabbing at the wind was just as foolish as Jen said it was, and his melancholy over failure was no more than self-indulgence.

Not that Jen would have bothered to work out this out

herself. She would simply have observed that a ruined world should have been left to the monkeys and the birds and the trees in the first place and *you*, Mistress Wachi, are only going to make things worse. As you have done already.

Poisonous woman.

Zack reminded herself that her original task — or quest was it — was to find her father. He had run away and she was supposed, for some reason, to find him. Just find him, not prove him guilty or innocent of anything.

Gizmo thinking was that if he were found the probability of salvation in a thousand kalpas was improved by two femtos. But yes, the evidence was beginning to accumulate. The ethereal advisory, the one-way red-tapeless ticket from Japan. The redirected official traffic in reports and surveillance. The disembodied conversations in the coffee shop. The removal of the Last Men, of Monsieur. The attempt to shove Matthias off the board. Someone or something was forcing her attention northward, toward the mountains.

And she did not want to go there.

《 》

Zack had no intention of keeping Matthias or anyone else informed. If necessary she would appeal to the Japanese consulate but in any case she resented the idea that anyone was entitled to her knowledge of anything. It put her back up.

On the other hand, she had no knowledge to be robbed of, to her knowledge, though the pickpockets would go over her anyway.

But if Giz were a player?

Giz was better at this that anyone else. Only John would be foolish enough to challenge him. Let Giz play his own cards. The great question in Zack's mind was what her father might do next. She felt a stirring of urgency about this. Wherever he was going, she needed to get there first. Perhaps she could prevent a great harm, but also, unexpectedly, whatever no good he was up to she wanted to stop it.

Really she didn't understand anything which had happened since she was hauled back from Japan to fix things which no one wanted to fix, just as at home — let the compassionate gaijin burn herself out on the hopeless ones. Let the gaijin's sad, hopeless empathy… which she was beginning to realize, under the constant pressure of having to defend or excuse him, might have sprung from those same qualities in her father.

That would have to be purged. Whoever had set her this job knew better than she did that she would do it. She would accept the task.

<< >>

The First Men probably knew John's plans, always assuming that was where he went first, but were quite unlikely to reveal them, especially now that Hum's assassination might expose them to obloquy as accomplices. These First Men did not seem to Zack to be the sort who keep their mouths shut simply out of fellow feeling.

There was no clue in the *Book of Lamentations* visible to Zack's crippled insight. The house was bare of receipts, notes to self, do lists, and all such records of intention. She did find an address book finally, a slim volume tucked neatly into the bookshelf according to some system of order she couldn't work out. But there were very few addresses in it.

But there were also three drawings,

Zack studied them. The woman depicted seemed familiar, but was unplaceable in the way that one's own face sometimes appears in the mirror after a long absence.

That night a burglar broke in. Zack, in bed but not asleep, heard the clicking of a latch and then some rustling which she recognized as books being taken out from between others on the shelf. Then the deliberately slow drawing of drawers. Then the door of her bedroom was pushed open.

She waited. The burglar — it was a man — was scanning the room with a UV light, which she guessed by the way he swept his hand up and down. His night vision goggles found the address book on the night stand, and also Zack lying on her stomach seemingly asleep.

She started up, clapping on the light for maximum effect. The goggles and anorak hid most of his face but still she knew at once — it was John. Her father.

Who are you? he growled. What are you doing living in my house?

Dumbfounded at not being recognized — could she have changed that much in thirty years? Possibly. Zack croaked an unintelligible protest.

Why are you burgling your own house? she managed to say.

Why shouldn't I? It's bugged.

By who?

John was plainly nonplussed by this naiveté. The question was beneath answering. Who was this alien? A medium sized woman in her forties with a thick rope of black hair and flashing black eyes and very small underwear.

Who's that? She pointed to the address book now in hand. The woman in the pictures?

My wife, he said in a flattened voice.

Zack blinked. And now you have the book, she said, what do you intend?

Who the hell are you to want to know that? John pulled off his goggles, eyes narrowed in suspicious scrutiny. I know you, he said after a moment. Zack stiffened.

You're Hum's secretary. Amanuensis or something. Giz found you in the Soup weeks ago.

Bugger that. Why did you kill him?

What? Who?

James, you heedless conscienceless idiot. Monsieur. Hum, Homme, Bum, Certain Searton.

You talk like my wife.

Your ex-wife.

You're out of a job, Mademoiselle. I'd tell you to skedaddle. Absquatulate yourself to the Sand Men but they're gone already. Everyone's running for it. Fleeing the ruins. Stay away from falling walls, Mademoiselle. You might survive to paint a few Canalettos of this place.

With that, John himself vanished into the dark. He may have lost Giz but had evidently held onto his cybernetics.

Zack sat up in bed now, twitching her halter strap irritably, sweeping her hair back and forth with a futile, repeated flicking of her fingers. She pondered her mother's strangeness, whether it were so or only an artifact of a girl's fastidiousness. Her father's strangeness, perhaps an artifact of a daughter's frustration.

《 》

Zack had never been sure before now what her mother's real opinions were because she wouldn't say, except now and then when her judgment was forborne by some egregious evil. The older Zack got, and the more able she was to understand complex explanations, the more taciturn Jen became. When Zack was a toddler or in grade school, just the two of them in the house, she remembered Jen talking to herself, although Zack never understood what she was saying. By the time an exacerbated Zack fled the family the most that Jen would say as a comment on anything was some variety of *Hm.* Zack supposed one might make a dictionary, perhaps a grammar of the language of Hm, but as (so far as she knew) there was only one native speaker...

The Japanese were something like that. A tendency to make noncommittal noises.

Hm had been the whole conversation of adolescence.

Then there was the summer afternoon when Zack was... she calculated on her fingers. There were so few landmark events to calculate from. The really big sandstorm — when was that? Was that before or after the neighbors' cat died in the wash?

When she was about fifteen. A couple of pictures had escaped into the kitchen from John's heaps of bijouterie. One was a photo of an execution. The man to be shot was kneeling on the ground, looking up at his unseen retribution — all that could be seen of the executioner was legs. The soon to be dead man's blackened face, with its patchy beard, bore long cuts on the cheeks and forehead and was covered in gritty blood like the heavy glaze on certain tea bowls.

He was not resigned, this man. He was too scared even to plead. His heart was going to explode from fright before the others ever got a chance to shoot him.

The other, John had written on the back in his neurotic cuneiform hand, was a still from an old movie, identified as *J'Accuse* by Abel Gance, 1938. The caption was "The dead of Verdun arise to infest the earth."

Jen stared dumbfounded at these two pictures. Her eyes glistened — or perhaps glittered.

Beasts, she said after a time.

Just this once, Zack was able to ask her mother what she meant and to get an intelligible reply.

They were alone in the house. It was four o'clock on an afternoon of forty-five degrees. Jen had been preparing a desultory meal of noodles and vegetables which Zack would eventually discover was a poor sort of ramen. Even then the ingredients were beginning to be hard to get. There had been a hot trip to a supermarket in a Korean neighborhood which, like many Asian markets, had mysterious sources for local produce. Vegetables popped up in the bins like the handwritten signs on street corners advertising tamales made by "Tia

Luisa". John was somewhere working and not likely to appear for a gobbled-up dinner. Zack was out of school and between shifts of a timewasting job that provided book and clothes money. At another time she would have taken her bowl of noodles and barricaded herself somewhere. But she was feeling growly and lonesome. She hiked herself up onto a stool at the kitchen counter.

These beasts, her mother said, are those of the field, who — who should never — who grow out of the ground like dragon's teeth. A mountain lion has more morals. Is there some evolutionary use for this vomit? Is — is —

Tears leaked from her eyes and she said no more.

It was John's increasingly frequent undocumented absences which had brought these pictures to light, rather like one of those black and white tragedies in which an unsuspected mistress is discovered in a husband's pants pockets. Someone had called. Some information was wanted. A diary, an ancestor of *The Book of Lamentations,* had been pushed off the desk and fallen open.

It was around that time that Giz became a presence in the family, an increasing preoccupation for John and an object of hatred for Jen.

And so, over noodles, across the kitchen counter, the ceiling fan adding a tremor to Jen's already rough alto voice, Zack heard out some of her mother's complaints. It was a role reversal of sorts, with Zack as the wise elder.

The details were not of much importance, actually. The world was become increasingly unpalatable — lots of people thought so. Every aspect of life was governed by idiots and criminals — a common opinion since Paleolithic times. Civil rights and notions of decency abrogated at a steady pace — daily. Greed and selfishness everywhere, friends and neighbors ever fewer, intimacy only a subterfuge for newer, more clever denunciations. Sand and grit and wind and heat here, floods and fires there. Every day emaciated, ravaged, bleeding people crawled into the ER with unknown, untreatable diseases, people with the flesh scoured off their hands or faces —

A ruined world. A fouled nest. An overflowing toilet.

She, Jennifer Mackinaw, was tired. Somewhere in her mind the nerves were dull, frayed at the ends like abandoned alleys. From the broken doors, fallen lintels, and rotting piles she heard at night faint cries. You dasn't go in those places. Humble folk, people with no further need of innocence, or no need of anything else.

And he. *Him.* Does nothing.

Later on, when Zack had some experience of flying, she would say this was like a glimpse of the liver-colored ocean through a fleeting hole in the clouds. It was an augur of those sickening losses of buoyancy when the plane drops a thousand meters, creaking and groaning in despair, leaving you weightless long afterward. First the storm, then the hole in the sky, then the fall.

When Zack found the diary with the pictures she also found a sort of bible, a compilation of remarks, aphorisms, and unattributed quotations grouped into topics. At the time, she thought it a peculiar book for her father to own, resistant as he was to taking advice. Now she asked Her to find another copy. There were several candidates. Zack picked the one which seemed likeliest and looked at the list of topics on which to find reassurance. Among them was "On silence."

The truths of ethics are ineffable, she read.

What is shown cannot be said.

The wise person keeps the peace. In times of war it is wise to keep silence.

Questions are answered best by silence.

One of the things which had helped to drive Zack out was that in the last years, when her father's depressions were getting worse, Jen seemed to be following a policy of exacerbating them, like the wife of an alcoholic fighting codependency by administering tough love.

From having to watch her step, Zack got to know the cycle pretty quickly. A period of mania marked by late nights, then mute lethargy, then a sequence of angry outbursts growing longer and increasingly without provocation, and finally a roaring blues culminating in ululations of death and suicide. These were hard to bear, certainly. Jen was determined not to.

What especially riled her was John's contention, at that stage when he contended anything, that he saw more clearly than she what was the truth of the world. The world was squalid and mean and not to be suffered, but how not to suffer? This was the point from which matters would decline pretty quickly to fetal positions and midnight weeping.

Why is it taking so long?

He howled. Zack was unable to listen, and stuffed towels under her door.

You should kill yourself, she said one night at a rare dinner. That might help.

John said nothing, as usual. Jen shrugged, picked up her dirty plate and silverware, and went out. Zack heard water running in the kitchen, a brief clatter, a click. Darkness.

Stygian gloom, in fact. The real thing.

It was early evening, and there was an unusual orange and purple sunset with a foam of high, still white fluff. Jen had opened up an aluminum web chair in an open space among the mesquite and prickly pear behind the house. It was all gone in less than a minute, but Jen sat on, drinking from a can of beer in the thickening dark.

A rabbit hopped out of the bushes at the edge of the ravine. Seeing Jen, it froze with indecision. A small dog burst from the ravine, seeing its chance. The rabbit darted aside but the dog was quicker — it got a paw in the rabbit's hind legs, grabbed the back of its neck in its teeth, and killed it in an instant. The rabbit screamed once, a high whistling note surprisingly loud.

A virtuoso killer, that dog. It nosed over the dead rabbit and trotted off down into the ravine, leaving the corpse behind, happy with an evening's work.

The beer was dribbling from the can in Jen's numbed hand. Unmoving she sat, staring at the dead animal, the cottontail whose sudden demise had exploded into her sunset idyll.

And she, too, screamed. A single note just like the rabbit's but higher, louder, more piercing.

Why does the rabbit scream? Zack wondered later, trying not to fall asleep until this great question was settled. Is it fear? Despair — or that hopeless feeling she would come to call such for which she now had no name? Was it the silent rabbit's one shout, released at last now when all was lost and foolish acts could do no harm?

There was some obscure bond between the rabbit and her mother, as if they had both been killed. And the event was some sort of crisis or turning point — all night she wailed and howled in her bedroom, arms wrapped around her knees, and for once the shoe was on the other foot and Zack could do nothing to console or assuage the pain.

《 》

In the end, they were all too late. Charles John Mackinaw's last resting place was an efficiency behind the Third Avenue hospital, the oldest in the city, a crumbling wreck serving people like Jen who filled that part of the city like roaches in a cupboard.

Jen's room was of a sort familiar to Zack. A minimal space just large enough for a bed, a chair, and some cubical shelving from St Vincent's. Bedding tattered, piss-yellow. Windowless, located in the dense center of a modern tenement, a refuge protected by an accumulated shell of human bodies, artifacts, and detritus hundreds of feet thick.

At home, a cleaner place like this would serve as a pied à terre. Here, Zack discovered, people lived in them year round. She estimated that in this hallway, one door every meter of wall on each side, about one hundred people. Somewhere around eight thousand in the building — or would have been at one time. Now the slots were mostly empty, as the city hollowed out and crumbled to sand. Jen had probably been squatting here.

In its time, the people would have lived mostly in the hall, hugger mugger, their doors standing open. What did they have to steal? What did privacy count for without secrets which had all been taken away long ago?

And here Zack's mother had lived the last of her life, nursing these people, tending the wounded, sick, and dying, birthing the living and burying the dead, until John tracked her down.

Predictably, the life support had shut down when no one was detected in residence, and when Zack got the door open after an hour's wheedling and bribing of various low-grade trolls down below, a hot wind carrying the rich odor of an abattoir rushed out.

Her father lay on his back. He had been wearing a sort of burnoose made of some shiny gray material. Bled out on the floor. There were enormous amounts of blood and uncountable bloody footprints, some with shoes and some without.

Toes in the blood.

His offending larynx cut out.

And yet there were no footprints in the hall.

Zack was not going to go in, but she spotted something shiny lying in the blood which had pooled along one wall.

Gingerly, she put a foot forward.

She was not going to stay clean, obviously. With that squirmy idea set aside, she took two long steps forward, stretched out her left hand with the assistance of the bed rail for balance, and hooked the thing she sought on two fingers. Then she backed out more or less in her own footprints.

Scraping the soles of her shoes on the hallway floor, Zack looked at what she had found. It was the qi ring. The ring which had been the fetish of the Sand People's elder, Maxfield's brother, and had passed to Benny Long and then to John and now to Zack.

A trail of dead people. Was that the qi of the world, then?

Found the ring, I see, said a voice behind her.

Startled, he lost her balance in turning and fell to one knee, bloodying her pants and her other hand as well.

Matthias, immaculate. Smiling broadly.

Where is she? Zack demanded

Your mother? Matthias shrugged. Disappeared. She has a talent for that.

Helped by your not looking.

Eh. We were a fraction too late for that, weren't we.

Were we?

Zack regarded the omnipresent and possibly omniscient Matthias through narrowed eyes, a sidelong squint which is needed to see ghosts and demons in their true form. A tiny smile twitched at one corner of the policeman's mouth.

Terrorists yourselves, it seems to me, Zack went on, beginning to feel angry, willing to drill down.

Yes, perhaps, Matthias admitted, his voice quiet with ageless calm.

Then just as quickly, Zack's anger sank away and she began to droop, a flower planted in sand. A dry wind harried her as she emerged from the building, a wind without past or future, feral.

Where did the wind go when it wasn't blowing? How was it able to muscle her around, from the faintest kiss to a leveling hand that wiped the earth clean, scraped away everything down to the rock — when it wasn't there at all?

There was an answer, of sorts, she supposed. But the same flowing energy in a more visible medium, water, was no less mysterious. What was the source of those heaving waves? The earth shrugged and twisted, trying to settle the shoulders of a badly fitting coat, and a little disturbance scoured out lake Biwa, scattered the invaders, and in a moment transformed towns and villages, bamboo forests and rice terraces, into a vast swamp of laserflat brown water.

Hardly surprising, the inclination of little furry people who live in holes, to be careful with these spirits, to imagine them as beings with intentions who demand propitiation and break their promises.

⟨⟨ ⟩⟩

So what had happened? If the barefoot prints had been Jen's — it was her apartment — where did she go afterward? Out the window, a witch-woman transformed into a spider? And John had certainly not torn open his stomach and his throat both. Which of them had taken the knife first? He or she?

And why had he gone looking for her in the first place? To Zack this was easier to understand. Old, depressed, alone, betrayed, humiliated in a dozen ways, he had had nothing to live for but —

Here Zack discovered she was not so sure after all. Was this some sort of revenge wreaked on the only person available to wreak it on? A payback? Or was it the opposite, a despairing and utterly defeated man who wanted only one thing more, to put an end to himself with the blessing of the only person who had ever loved him?

Love. They'd caught him, and that was all. This was Giz's childhood as much as it was Zack's. Now ended.

What if they had loved each other? For almost fifty years, despite everything — the viciousness, the destruction, the contempt? There was, after all, something to love — John's eager intensity, a narrow genius which might have ruined someone else,, and Jen's fierce, selfless grip on moral principle. They were both unchained, these two. They could have loved each other only because of that.

But not Zack. But not her brother Giz. She, of the Last, back to Japan. He, of the First, gone. Out There.

⟨⟨ ⟩⟩

There was one thing left to do. According to the Book of Lamentations, John had gone to see the library sybil the night before his flight. She told him there was something he needed to know. What was it?

Zack looked up and down the street, holding her hands up to shield her eyes. She would need goggles at least, if she were staying.

And I haven't been too careful, she thought, feeling the flying sand bite her cheeks.

Nearby was the remnant of a neighborhood park. Most of it had dried up years before, but one corner had until recently continued to be tended. Zack looked about her for a possible source for this now vanished solicitude. Some old person who died, a family moved away north.

A tree with six leaves was struggling there. Zack had no idea of the species. Something dignified and very old like an oak, though she suspected oaks had never grown here. No weedy cottonwood. Miss Gostrey would only tell her it was some fangled thing Zack never heard of.

She caught a tram and made the short walk from the tram stop to the library. The lines for the sybil were long and slow. She didn't really want to stand in line, anyway. She didn't want to consult the soothsayer, only to see the process at work. Was she really giving out sooths? So why did people think she was, then? Where would she get a sooth and how would she tell it from an unsooth?

Perhaps because, Zack speculated as she watched the people shuffle forward in line — exactly because she didn't do it that way. She conducted no experiments, no house-to-house searches, she was not recherché of anything perdues. She didn't test the results, grade them, throw out the little withered ones. The sybil's expertise was inscrutable, and for that reason alone unlike any other of the latter days.

What it was, was that Zack did not want to know what Miss Gostrey had said to John Mackinaw on the last day. She did not want that knowledge. She had found the limit of herself. Beyond that limit there was nothing, the mu of emptiness, and there was nothing to prevent her from stepping through that gate whenever she wanted, leaving herself behind like clothes in the laundry basket.

Zack scrutinized those going in, trying to predict who would emerge beatified, who frightened, who puzzled or nonplussed. She couldn't do it by appearance or behavior alone, but that didn't change her sense of what was going on. People were coming into the library just as they always had. Some were looking for particular books and had a list of shelf numbers in their hands; some were intending to browse for things which struck their fancy, some were going to have coffee and a newspaper, go to a club meeting, rent a gizmo. It was still the same. The only thing which had changed was the cans in which the truths were stored.

Zack spotted in line a woman who interested her — short and dumpy with a headscarf and a string bag of vegetables from the market. All at once she recognized the woman she had invited in from the street to talk in the coffee shop when she first arrived.

Zack thought she looked a bit beaten down from the last time when she had seemed more street-smart and acidulated. The woman with the perhaps bag went into the sybil's circle. A moment later she came away with a rueful expression. She was wincing and chewing her lip, either fighting tears or fighting acceptance of whatever she had heard.

Zack pushed through the line and accosted the woman on the other side as she was going out. She reintroduced herself, but it was no good. She wasn't remembered. Zack waved away something which had only been meant as a polite opener, anyway.

Can I take you for coffee? she asked.

The woman's eyes clouded in puzzlement.

Why? she said in a flat, harsh voice.

Zack paused. Why indeed? Because I need someone to talk to, she said. I saw you and I thought, well …

A slight snort, barely audible, perfumed the air.

I thought you were a kind person who would listen to someone like me, but I see you have troubles of your own. I apologize, Zack finished in what had been a rather breathless admission.

The perhaps lady scrutinized Zack closely. She was thirty centimeters shorter and hard to look up to do it. At last she smiled, a bit sour, and nodded.

All right. There's a coffee bar a couple of blocks from here. Will you walk?

Of course, Zack said. Can I carry your bag?

No.

The two of them walked the distance in silence. Zack had to shorten her steps, but it was no different than with the Japanese she had been living among for years.

The shop was much like all the others — a wide room with translucent sandblasted windows set not very deep, roll-down metal shutters, a scattering of tables, the bar running along the back wall. Zack ordered two cups of ersatz coffee, paid the window charge, and brought them over to the table the perhaps woman had chosen.

The brown liquid was hot and, so far as Zack had any standard of comparison, not bad. She scanned the room for a food menu, spotted nothing, but a man at the bar was eating a roll with what looked like sliced meat and tomato.

So, the perhaps woman said, putting down her cup after drinking the coffee in one swallow. Who are you?

What a terrifying question. Might I ask you the same?

The other woman shrugged. You wanted to talk to me.

Ah. Yes, I did. I was born in this town but I don't know anyone here. If I ever did. I think I told you before that I live in Japan.

Do you? I don't remember. What do you do there?

Disaster relief. I'm a social worker. Of sorts. You might have met people like me during the first tidal floods. You were in Sangre Sur Ventospi then? Windy Bay?

No, I was never there.

Oh! I'm sorry, I thought —

I lived all my life in Vienna.

Zack was a bit nonplussed by this, and for a moment didn't know how to go forward.

So why are you here? she asked. It was the first question that occurred to her.

I ought to ask you the same, retorted the perhaps woman.

Ah. Yes, well — would you like something to eat?

No. Food is hard to get here. People eat too much.

Zack sighed. Cornered, she began the tale. The narrative was a bit scrambled at first, but she soon made sense of it. Insofar as there was sense.

So, the perhaps woman said after she heard Zack out. Your father has murdered himself. Or perhaps your mother. Your father is dead somehow, and your mother has disappeared. Again. Domestic violence. You must run across this all the time in your work.

Actually not. The Japanese aren't a violent people. They work out conflicts in other ways.

The other woman rested a squinty, thoughtful and suspicious stare on Zack. But she only remarked that it was common enough here.

I think — Zack began.

And I think, the perhaps woman countered, and then said no more. She looked, birdlike, around the room, turning her head this way and that in short jerks.

I think, she began again, you are making this up to save face. You strike me as the sort of person to tell yourself convenient stories. Pfui. Such people always have unimpeachable intentions.

My father —

Was a weak man. He allowed himself to be used, a tool in every man's hand, your mother's included.

Oh! I… I don't think he would have — that he would have acknowledged anything like speaking strength to power. I don't think he believed that was the right way.

Rubbish. There are the eaters and the eaten. This Matthias — he is a dangerous man. He is gathering himself for a coup. Maxfield is backing him, I think. These Men — first, last, whatever — are his mercenaries, who will come down out of the mountains when the time comes.

Zack found this kind of conspiracy thinking repugnant. If it were true, she would prefer not to accept it.

You are Viennese, then? she said, hastily changing to subject. You have no accent.

I am Turkish. My family came to Vienna with Saladin in 1530. We brought you coffee.

Suleiman, I think that was. His siege was broken in 1529.

You know a great deal, said the perhaps woman contemptuously. My other ancestor was the Hungarian king, Matthias the Crow, who ruled Vienna after the Turks.

I see, Zack said quietly. An illustrious lineage.

Pfui. Bandits. Eaters.

Are you sure, Zack said slyly, you wouldn't like a panini? I'm hungry myself.

I will, if you are paying.

The perhaps woman was impervious to irony. Zack stood

up and went over to the bar to inquire about food.

Yes, they could have sandwiches. Zack thought the price exorbitant, but under the circumstances did not want to quibble. She waited at the bar while the sandwiches were being made, keeping the while a wary eye on her companion. The perhaps woman sat stiffly erect, hands resting together palms upward in her lap, her head turned slightly to watch the dark shapes moving past on the other side of the window.

She's not the same one, Zack thought. She's just another short woman in a headscarf out marketing with her string bag.

But when Zack sat down again by the window and pushed one plate across to her companion, the woman smiled and the slightly dotty Los Angelino resurfaced, displacing the Mittel European stranger, and she was the same woman after all.

Zack took a breath and leaped into the water.

What did the Sybil say to you? she asked.

The perhaps woman started. It was an unexpectedly personal question.

I'm prying, Zack admitted. I'm a busybody social worker, after all. You seemed upset after questioning the sybil. I wondered what you'd heard.

You've never consulted a soothsayer, then?

I'd never encountered one before now. Japanese has no future tense, you know. And they're too modest to accept the idea of special instructions. As a people, perhaps. Not as individuals.

Admirable, I suppose.

Yes. But it's my turn to ask: why did you agree to talk to me? Was it something the sybil said?

The perhaps woman remained stubbornly silent.

Well?

She said I would meet someone needing my help. And that I shouldn't refuse.

Good advice, that.

Dangerous advice in these times, I think.

Well, Zack remarked, you've met someone. But you haven't helped.

Oh, dear. I've been putting you off, haven't I?

Yes.

The sybil told me I was to say this: *Tell her it was because of his son.* That's you, enn't it?

No.

Yes. She said you would deny it. And then I was to say: *This I told him. Go and do likewise.* So what do you want me to do that's likewise?

Nothing, perhaps, Zack said. Convince me that we don't deserve our fate.

I don't think I can do that.

Zack got to her feet. No, she said. I don't think you can. Take my sandwich. I'm not hungry after all. You can feed it to the dog.

I don't have a dog, said the other woman, obtusely.

Yes you do, Zack retorted, and walked out.

« »

Zack didn't intend to sell her father's house though it seemed he wouldn't be needing it. She intended to abandon that and everything else and go home. But out of some bizarre sense of propriety she went back nevertheless, ostensibly to see that the doors were locked.

They weren't.

Already squatters had broken in. Zack locked up, pointless as it might be. Then she walked out the back and headed up the wash toward the top of the mountain.

It was early evening, cool enough to be out, not so dark as to make her stumble or kick up a snake. She climbed for a time, and then stopped on a convenient rock where she sat to look over the city.

The lights of the city were not as bright as she remembered them, but the sky, now a little rosy along the edge but mostly a dusty indigo, was not so bright, either. It was possible to see stars.

She considered that.

Up there, were there worlds — perhaps only one — where creatures like herself lived? If so, had they done better than their human brethren? Human sisters? Had they proved smart enough not to produce the same cockup?

Possibly not. This sort of thing might be as inevitable as the third term of a syllogism.

Giz would know.

Zack thought about the monkeys. Hanuman was not a nice godlet. She had never lived far enough to the south to have to deal with monkeys.

Apes were, she supposed, the next — who were the Old Ones to the apes who pushed out onto the savannah and began to experiment with meat, and hunting. The monkeys who watched the doings of these new beings, watched from the fringes of the dark forest, their big eyes gleaming golden and their long tails …

No. Old World monkeys don't have long prehensile tails.

And out of the apes —

What a dolorous procession.

She tried to imagine, had tried before this, what it might have been like when there was more than one intelligent —

No, that was wrong. She meant other hominids, that was all. Another species with the same capacity for getting it wrong.

They are our Old Ones, maybe.

She pondered the notion of *mu*, under a variety of names a possibly universal concept of what there is which is not us. How to imagine such stuff. Everything not part of the phenomenal world, all that conjectural stuff, the supposition that there is a life of stones which we know nothing about,

about which we can know nothing, all that parti pris of *things* which fills up the world with nothing.

And *qi*, another of those probably universal ideas, universal under several guises, of the pile of individuals which compose the world, each of them distinct, each with its own life force, its own qi — meaning breath. Every stone, snail, breath of wind has a *qi*. Unique. To understand a thing is to understand its qi. To understand a few of them is an immense task. To understand many, impossible. To survive it is necessary to get along by some method other than knowing. It is necessary to be silent. It is necessary to be unreasonable. It is necessary to be ignorant.

Perhaps, Zack thought, looking at the stars, there is somewhere like that. It would be curious to meet those people, to see how they got on.

Are there such beings?

Perhaps.

Perhaps not.

《 》

Before she left for home, Zack went down to the riverbed shantytown to find the old man who had been John's informant, and who had given her the lesson in politeness. For over an hour she wandered here and there, asking after him, but no one was helpful.

People disappear pretty quickly here, she muttered.

There was a really surprising variety of shelters which these supposedly homeless persons had constructed for themselves. There were teepees covered in various materials, some in bright rags, some of which rags were still bright as if the inhabitants washed their house regularly. There were actual mud huts, constructed presumably out of adobe made from river clay. Zack scuffed some up with her shoe and thought it rather too gravelly. Did they carry it in like the

Indians who lived here before? The ones who said they had come out of holes in the ground?

Most of these refuges, however, were cardboard shanties with tattered paper roofs, layers of it fused in the annual rains into a solid board inches thick. A thickness of roof which told the age of the house, or anyway the amount of time these few square feet of ground had been inhabited. Amount of recent time.

There were some tin roofs, some plastic sheeting, some palm fronds which were becoming a bit sad as the palms were drying and the supply of that roofing material was drying up with them.

And then there were really temporary structures — piles of boxes or rags or plant litter, lean-tos. The ground was too hard to dig into, or else loose pebbles below the compacted crust, so that there weren't any cellars or dry stone walls.

Only a few adobe houses had doors. Most had a flap of canvas, but many had nothing. The streets, or paths, between the houses were barely a meter wide and madly twisted. She couldn't see more than a few arm spans in front or behind. In a lozenge shaped space of ground less than a kilometer wide and no more than four long it was easy to get lost, unable to get out without luck or help.

Piles of ordure stood here and there, middling tall cairns mostly dried to inoffensive pats. The problem of filth was perhaps less here than it would have been in a cooler, wetter place. The fresher pats lay in the middle of the street marked by little whirlwinds of flies, as if they were left there on purpose while they dried and were then tidily swept into one of the neighborhood cairns. Other kinds of dirt were paid little attention. Some streets were filled with an impassable constipation of litter — paper, cans and bottles, garbage, old clothes.

It didn't smell especially bad. Zack had the impression of a down-at-heel working-class town of mostly resourceful people.

But for all that, they were neither hopeful nor voluble. The most she could get was a grunt or an angry lecture about some wrong done to himself, his family, the human race, respectability or reason. The majority of residents were men and most of them past middle age, but there were enough women to make her aware of them and children enough to get underfoot. The children were definitely feral, well patched clothes and shiny hair to the contrary. Zack learned quickly to keep her hands and bag clutched close and to put up with being mauled and nosed as shamelessly as a dog in heat.

Finally, out toward a familiar edge, where the ground began to tip backwards and the shanties were a little less tightly packed, out more or less by itself on a tiny knoll, she found the house she thought was his. But another old man, viciously surly, lived there like a boar in a hole.

Dead, he snarled. Neck broke. I seen, and got in here, didn't I.

Did he fall?

A bubbling snort from the old man. Kidding me. Kilt, of course. Nobody falls down here gets trod on.

Zack wasn't quite sure what that meant. Who killed him? she asked, a little carefully.

Them did. Them as always does. Move away, cunt. Yer blocking the air.

Zack sighed and turned away. She had had an idea of giving the now dead old man the chi ring she'd found with her father's body. He'd been the only person she could think of safe enough to give it to.

So that idea came to naught. Zack's flight home stopped over in what was still called San Francisco. The airport was up in the hills on the east side of what had been the Bay. She checked into a hotel and then took an electric tram down to the shore. Out on the water an archipelago of little peaks

stood up black against the sun, a few buildings clinging to
each one like monk's huts. It was the real sun, not some
shrouded circle which looked like it had been drawn on the
sky. The air and water were still. Shaking with cold, really
unable to breathe with shivering, she was determined to face
it out, to stare the ancient ocean down.

She would be the one to blink first, of course. But Zack
wanted to make a good show, to keep a scrap of her tattered
flag, the colors she had flown since leaving home the first
time.

She smiled tartly. That was a seriously badly mixed metaphor, wasn't it?

What she wanted was a littlest bit of the dignity and in-
difference of the ocean. Of one of the oldest of the Old Ones.

There. That was better.

Zack walked slowly out to the end of the pier, fighting
the wind. She couldn't raise her face to it and so saw only
her feet. But where the planks ran out, by squinting fiercely
and ignoring the wind-sprung tears, she could at last look up
toward the horizon. There was no actual horizon, which was
lost in the swirling primeval mist.

Out here it was again the beginning of time. Nothing had
yet come into being but water and air, wind-hauled break-
ers rolling out of the mouth of the world to smash here, to
throw themselves on the beach at her feet. *Her* feet — the
only feet yet in existence, connected by some jiggery-pokery
machinery to her crying eyes and those eyes too the only
ones. There was nothing yet for them to see. Her eyes were
waiting for the world to be created for them, her feet for the
land to rise up for her to walk on, her hand to raise against
all those yet un — um — what?

But it was not the beginning of time. That was her mind
at work. No-mind saw the water which slapped weakly on
the pilings leaving an oily smudge and looked heavy as mud.
The sun settled into it like quicksand.

The ring was heavy in her hand. It nestled in her palm, under her curled fingers.

She reached back and with a cry, dragged out of her to follow the outward arc of gleaming metal like a ragged end of string still attached to a lost kite or a despairing balloon, no longer within reach, flung the ring into the ocean where it would lie until some new explorers found it and began again the cycle of redeath.

E₂

*A cure for cosmic loneliness does not prove
very inviting. The neighbors pull down the shades.*

CROSSING OVER

Soster rising, Charles.

Charles Lehon, still asleep, not yet risen himself, but becoming lighter as his own particular gravity well seemed to
flatten out under the forward momentum of returning consciousness, as the wrinkles are pulled out of a quilt when
it is stretched over its mattress in preparation for morning
inspection, heard, began to comprehend at some unknown
iteration: Soster rising.

Soster being the target or guide star by which that other, humbler Eian star could be found, given warning of.
Charles Lehon was a being who was even so a guide also,
in a mundane and corporeal way, as head of Mazatzal Station, Astronomy Section. Which in reality was a task of little dimension, a fractional dimension never quite reaching
two, like a gnarled and enfolded lettuce which this particular
bureaucratic or astronomical head resembled. Astronomy
at Mazatzal Station consisted exclusively of monitoring the
flight, now approaching three generations long, of a probe,
a package of sensors and semi-intelligent machinery, toward
the as yet unseen if not unknown planetary system discovered, once upon a time, in the vicinity of that star Soster: the
first such, and in fact still the only such, possible habitation
known. Though the search went on, or Charles presumed it
to go on, in other more prestigious, influential laboratories
elsewhere in the Foundation. In the ERF in which Charles

Lehon was no more than a frozen planetoid bound to this anonymous, heatless brown sun, Mazatzal Station, somewhere in the southwestern desert, HispanoAsian quadrant.

But this was to change.

⟨⟨ ⟩⟩

The agent of this change arose from Charles himself, who was a guide in another sense, metaphorically a raised edge serving to keep something — a vehicle, a person, an idea — from falling off the track, the Way, the true. For his incorporeal or disincorporated self-inhabited the personas of one Maldonado, chair of the Eian Council for Kalgoorlie, and his venal and corrupt rival Fishbach, part owner of the Vardon Mine. Fishbach was of a piece with Maldonado in the mind of his creator, the Lehonian mind which was not quite so starkly divided as that and which was even now crossing over from those blacker regions, those interstellar wastes scoured by a divine wind of primeval radiation in which hope and fear were quarantined and where Maldonado and Fishbach circled eternally their imaginary sun.

The planet E, fifth planet circling a modest and as yet unnamed sun, was the true target of that probe which had so far cost so many lives of waiting.

The planet E was also the target of a massive simulation now three generations in construction, a research project which had become in that time a substantial if virtual portion of E before the fact.

It was on that hypothetical planet of E that Jorge Maldonado served, for the time being, as Chairman of the City Council of Kalgoorlie, that world's only substantial habitation. And it was in that Kalgoorlie where Karl Fishbach plied his role. The Vardon Mine's resources fell under his bureaucratic purview as well his entrepreneurial one. The budget of Kalgoorlie which was his alter-ego Maldonado's nominal responsibility was by this perversion of political power in continual contest.

By playing his two hands (or minds) against each other Charles had for some time been able to keep hidden from himself the springs, which is to say the underground sources, of character and action by which he himself was guided. This produced within himself a certain mystique, a fascination which occupied him like a black hole, a sink of self-knowledge to which he was fatally drawn, a distorting gravitas of valuable caution which otherwise could have been useful to him in all his lives, embodied, disembodied, aspirational, and imaginary. Others about whom he knew, after all, no more than one does of the independent and unpredictable creatures in a storybook, his fellow beings, were to him merely temporal or sublunary, subdivine illusions. They simply vanished when he looked at them. They could be seen only out of the side of his eye, spirits who were otherwise within the event horizon of his very own neuroses.

Charles did not, of course, invent this situation, this virtual conundrum. He was not even aware of it. It was no more significant to him than playing both the white and black sides in a game of chess, as he would have done in learning a textbook game.

But that, too, was to change.

In his least corporeal existence Charles Lehon sought enlightenment, an ironic quest in one who had engaged his life to guide a robot probe to peer at another world by the light of a distant sun.

Or rather, to adopt a water metaphor appropriate to the story of Charon and Lethe as well as to the spiritual and actual desert in which Mazatzal Station stood, the desert in which the man Lehon lived and had his being, such as it was, the outer desert of aridity and barrenness which reified a parallel inner desert requiring to be irrigated in order, in a biblical phrase to which Charles was partial, to bear fruit.

But it was not. From whence was this water to spring? How was it to be guided from its source? Why was he commanded not to eat the apples of the sun which would grow on that tree if only it were watered? What immense, perhaps universal consequences reverberated through countless generations, clanging and jangling, the remnants of a primordial explosion, in the mind of some fierce, wild-eyed saddhu Ezekiel bodhisattva? And all because this poor forked being Charles Lehon could not come into himself?

〈〈 〉〉

Soster rising, Charles.

The imperturbable, infinitely patient speaker of these terrible words was his engineer, Will Doblin.

What were you? Will asked in his nudging voice.

I was dreaming about Salvatore Cicci again, mumbled Charles.

Confused, not yet awake, Charles returned the smile which loomed over his couch, that faint Doblinian smile seeming to know and forgive all, and Will, smiled upon, turned back to the plot which streamed across the screen of the vid behind him on which Soster was e'en now detaching itself, like a bubble in a flask of glycerin, from the plot's lower bound.

A plot, to Charles meant ground in a cemetery or the organization of events in a story, which extensions or amplifications he did not reject. They had a certain Orphic resonance.

This particular plot originated in the diffraction or mutual interference of gravity waves detected on the Moon, at Mazatzal, and at a third instrument in the Estrellas two hundred kilometers to the south on the other side of the Phoenix basin, were the mortal visualization of computations which now emerged on Will's vid screen.

It was a simple triangulation. In another eight hours Soster would rise over Woomera and the same triangulation would be computed there; in another eight hours over Pic Touside; and so again to Mazatzal.

Sighing and sleepy, Charles rolled his chair closer to peer at the familiar isogravs flowing past, the flowing past of three generations now, Salvatore's life and his links to the Soster project were the closest thing to a time machine we are destined to know — or so Charles thought then.

But time waits not, least of all for him, and now he was being dragged whining and half-conscious to duty.

I'm going to knock off when we have tonight's confirmation, he muttered, vision still bleared by dreams.

Council meeting in an hour, Will reminded him. A passing remark.

Ng can take it.

If you say so, Charles. Coupla minutes here to digest this and then you can sign off.

So they waited, Will leaning back comfortably and Charles hunched forward, forearms creased against the table edge. They are waiting still, for that moment was the last of the old order. At that moment Charles Lehon, and the whole universe, was created anew.

It's a miss, Charles said, voice incongruously bland.

Yeah? Will's head came down as he peered over the tops of his glasses at the screen. Give me the plot again, please.

Responding, the screen broke up, marbled like melting ice cream.

From, ah... twenty sixteen.

It cleared again. Isogravs swirled right through the spot where the Soster probe should have been.

Digest, please.

The vid hiccupped and produced a graph with a prominent yellow amoeba fringed in green and blue, over which it drew a simplified isogravity diagram.

We're inside tolerances, Charles.

Hmp — a little dubious noise, a reserving-judgment vocalization which fell politely short of disbelief. Diagnostics, please, he said.

Charles's voice, furry in comparison to his junior's, was nevertheless sufficient to the plotter thereof and the screen went blank. While the computations were being redone Will stood up to stretch, languidly uncoiling his tall frame, languidly and shyly covering up his anxiety.

It's the Estrella cable, he observed, dry and precise. Probably some dirt in the patch again. Did you get the mail yet?

Charles had not, and without comment he swiveled around to speak to the courier. But Touside was all right. Nothing from Woomera. Query Woomera. A few seconds later a routine reply from the Woomera server, undigested columns of miniscule exponents clearly indicating a hit Tuesday seventeen hundred and some local time.

It's the patch, Will repeated with finality. I'll go put the Council back half an hour.

The last miss was fourteen months ago, Charles observed. He tapped the screen and Will, returning from his Council posting down the hall, looked over his shoulder at the page of the maintenance file Charles had called up. It was the Estrella cable that time too, Will said, poking the screen with his own thinner, better manicured finger. Should have buried it.

Will, secretly restless as always when made to wait for diagnostics, permitted himself the hint of a grumble, or the grumble of a hint, which fringed his voice like the rime of salt around a dry hole.

Salvatore laid it on the ground on purpose, Charles replied a bit testily, to deal with the fault shear there. You can't anticipate everything. Really, fourteen months is a pretty good record.

Yes, Will returned amicably, but still he paced the edges of the small telemetry lab. Two of his long strides were enough to cross one side of the square; reaching the end of his circuit, he reversed direction.

Still computing, Charles said, anticipating him. Results momentarily. Did Will know Salvatore was dead?

No.

Three days ago. Stroke.

Jeez. He must have been near a hundred.

A moment's reflective silence, a certain encomium for the now vanished First Cause, perhaps the only memorial he would have, not a stele exactly, to be finally broken or pulled down by mere polite noises such as: Ah, I see. Dead for certain, erased even mnemonically. We won't hear of Salvatore again, Charles thought, dream creature that he is, for this is a valediction of the future, not the past.

"Ah, I see." Phatic phrase. What does he see?

Now this intellectual drift, this tide, was neaped by the arrival of the telescope diagnostics. Will plopped down to look at the vid, popping his lips as each test result appeared.

Fut.

Fut, fut.

Fut. Fut. All fine. Intermittent transmission failure. Sign, please.

Charles pulled out the pad and scrawled the necessary confirmation on it, instructing the telescope to go on collecting for the rest of the pass.

If it's just dirt in the line, he said, maybe it will straighten out. Order a live tap on Woomera and call me in the morning when their pass begins. Put it out as unscheduled maintenance. Not as a miss, Will. As dirt. Unscheduled dirt is what, you should say.

The other astronomer listened calmly, perhaps sometimes complacent but to anyone's knowledge never smug. Giving the required instructions, he began to turn off lights.

Are you still going to pass up the Council, then, Charles?
Mm.

Neither of them stirred.

After a time Charles remembered his coffee. But it had long gone cold and he pulled a melancholy face, unseen in the dark. Will, reluctant to leave before him, to leave without being excused, without being dismissed, a feature of his punctilious discretion, a punctiliousness which it was easy to take advantage of, sat on with Charles in the fudge, the electronic gloom, his long legs stretched out under a table.

What could Salvatore have been thinking of? Charles wondered aloud. What did he want for himself, to spend his whole life on this? More than his whole — he'd never have lived long enough. One might contrive a way to get to the end, I suppose. But for nothing. In the end, nothing. Why?

You're proceeding somewhat elliptically, Charles.

Indeed. Am I?

Yes, Will said firmly. I suppose you mean that Don Cicci's motives in starting something he could never finish, something moreover of questionable value, are difficult to understand. You are apparently fussing about your career again.

Whuf! Charles's laugh was a little uncertain, and required a self-deprecating amplification to fix its meaning: Too late for that, he said.

Never met the gentleman, Don Salvatore. Monkish fellow, I imagine. Capable of that sort of focus. And there must have been satisfactions.

Charles mused. Yes, he said, to see his research program established... well not his program entirely...

His and Aarne's.

Yes. And then, not to know the end... well, when you don't know you can tell yourself whatever you like, eh? No taste for abasement, I imagine.

Positive minded fellow. Unlike yourself, Charles.

Don't let's get into a religious discussion, Will.

Some Doblinesque barking at this, partly hiding his relief at having risked an exchange and come off unharmed.

Will thought perhaps McKechnie's request for a transfer had started something.

Who? Started something?

Drumlin McKechnie has asked to be put onto a telemetry field crew.

Ah.

Charles pinched the bridge of his nose, pulled down the skin under one eye, observed that we don't get the best people here, after all.

It's a sinecure, Will countered, unshaken.

Will never wanted to be best people; never wanted a sinecure in fact, monkish fellow that he was, spiderish web tender, a long-legged Number Two who wanted only to keep things running, who wanted only the privilege of keeping it all going a little longer, believing as he did that it would go, that there was a little longer yet, perhaps a lot longer, relishing every patch on the Tao while it held.

The best people, Charles went on doggedly, playing the curmudgeon, are not going to waste their careers babysitting here. The best people are going to take over when we're done.

But Will Doblin, still unmoved, appraised his super-ordinal colleague silent with index finger doubled across his lips, rocking slightly in his chair.

Since Charles did not offer any more confidences Will, unmoved mover, after some moments more of silence, rose tactfully and finally went out, leaving the question of the Eian Council unresolved and the older man sitting with his eyes closed, apparently asleep.

But the miss was not because of a dirty patch on the Estrella cable after all. When the scan was passed on to Woomera an hour before sunrise, Lazard's group also failed to pick up the can.

No intermittents during the night? Charles asked dully, not expecting any. He was still in bed in his cubbyhole.

Will's voice not encouraging even on the com — that com which, not being satisfied with the simple transshipment of electrical signals, had to package them, brighten and gladden the voices by the same procedure that scrubbed unscheduled dirt out of telescope telemetry.

No.

You've tested the uplink?

The air in Charles's cubby was stale, as if the recirculation had failed again, and his eyes felt glued shut. This he was reluctant to test by trying to open them. Perhaps the disappearance of the can meant the ERF had become bored with them and was switching off? — a notion of classically paranoid form considering that a much simpler explanation was available which was that of a characteristically inadequate bureaucracy which scientists since Newton's day have felt is directed particularly at them. A ghetto mentality. However powerful these techniks had become, whatever hegemonies they would be able to gather, they would never shake off that early marginalization. No amount of deference would compensate for those medieval traumas.

So it's us, then. Mazatzal leg. We dropped it. We broke the thread.

Might be some systematic error in phasing, Will observed, oiling the panic with his low-key manner. The hardware checks out, he said. Servos and so forth. Say the triangulation has gone out of whack, Charles. Fong is recalibrating that now. Let's hear what Pic Touside has to say this afternoon.

Yes.

Will's delay played perfectly to Charles's weak left, the side of him always anxious to put things off. Will appeared to be all unflapped, but then Will had a neurotics of his own which Charles couldn't afford.

Charles was sitting up in bed now, glaring at the blank vidicom. His cubby, the familiar darkened room, seemed too small. He hadn't slept well as usual, now had been awakened suddenly, his habits disturbed by this unscheduled dirt, this disease which he was waiting for other people to treat, to palliate if not relieve, waiting fevered and sweating, forgotten in some little cubicle at the end of a long hall, breathing rebreathed air, his naked ass sticking to the doctor's cold steel.

Charles? You there?

Yes, thank you, Will. The vid's switched off, that's all. I'll be down in a bit.

They all thought he was hiding, always switched off like that.

Stretching up to uncover the skylight, feeling the untried muscles loosen, the hatch slide smoothly back, the reassuring yellow sunlight pour out of the pipes onto his upturned face, sunlight heatless at this distance from the surface but still its rich yolky color, his heart slowed. Cautiously he drew his fingers over the slick white wall, then rolled back onto the naked futon and buried his head in the pillow.

What do you expect in the desert? Dirt. Even a dog has Buddha nature.

《》

Pic Touside also failed to pick up the scan, and by afternoon the Woomera people had caught up with Will's diagnosis. So you're off the hook, Will observed at the end of his report at the afternoon staff meeting. It's Aarne's problem now, the senior man on top of his African mountain.

But that wasn't so: Charles was more on the hook than ever. So long as the work went on routinely he had been able to go on himself, routinely, but now here was the prospect of being dragged down to such basics as calibration. He didn't want to think about basics. Will it was who took the housecleaning load, leaving Charles to wander purposeless through the telescope he was supposed to be in charge of. He left himself vulnerable, of course, to gossip and backbiting if not a laboratory coup. There weren't very many people at Mazatzal with the outside contacts to pull off a coup and make it stick.

Standing in the shade of a palo verde which overhung C wing near the elevator port, Charles being newly sprung from level two into the parching early air like some ignorant impatient seed, breathing slowly, deeply, filling his lungs with the waterless air which enclosed him — after forty years he knew so well what was going on here that he felt it like digestion or a pain in his leg.

A lot of other research was being done here at Mazatzal, deeper down in the mountain. Only three fingers of the lab showed above ground, standing out from the rock like three piers of some huge, now demolished bridge, shivered down during some ancient earthquake perhaps, which were the bunkers containing the air compressors, the water plant, greenhouses, and the receiving dock.

He sometimes felt extended inside and out across the whole mountain like thick paint covering its flesh and bones. The Soster probe was not going to be recovered. This one was not like the other times.

Charles Lehon contemplated the future.

Was there a future? Charles looked about him. That Maxfield had built well. The ERF had pushed deeper into the mountain when they acquired the site, added a dozen levels or more, but the old tycoon's house was the core of it.

Charles's cubby was in C wing, level two, where most of the Soster project was. Everyone else lived in the dormitories on level five, but Charles liked to be nearer the open air than that. To him the people working deeper down in the mountain seemed like the lab mice which exist in a faster paced universe, a whirring time which burns out a couple of generations just in the course of a single go match. These people fly in, run their little tests and suck up a couple of library samples, fire off their reports to Mexico City and Beijing, and vanish again while the lifers play complicated games and slowly grind everything down to the finest soil.

And when it was all ground down? Charles looked out to the southwest where the Phoenix basin was, or had been, with its permanent sandstorm, a whirling hurricane of scouring grit.

People lived there. Who knew why?

Waiting, he supposed. For the apocalypse. For the sun to go nova.

More mundanely, Charles no longer believed in a future for himself, either.

Aside from leaving Mazatzal Station, leaving the desert and familiar place where he and the others had spent nearly all their lives, Charles didn't much want to take up that frenetic flick existence. Wasn't that why he came here to begin with?

No. It was because he couldn't take a loss. If he were going to be beaten down from the heights, pushed off the ramparts to be crushed beneath uncounted infantry feet — and he came to believe very early that he would be — Mazatzal was a very different fate. Akin to a monastery. They lived small here. It was a simulacrum of a world, like the one they had built up over more than a century of story-telling.

But the mountain was still unbent to him. It had taken in these years not one step toward him. If he returned to the flick life he would be eaten up by jealousy, hopelessness, and greed just as before. And what else would there be for him if the Soster probe were dead?

It was not a transmission failure, or a problem in direction-finding or in power boost, or a malfunction in any of the six orbiting antennae, or any other such hopeful thing. It was not a cybernetics error, or an epileptic seizure, or indigestion. It was a dead ship. Somewhere along the deceleration from half-light there was an accident, or what we call an accident, a euphemism constructed so as to avoid too plain a reminder of the way things run down, decline into disorder, return themselves to the Tao with a relieved sigh.

The thing is dead. Dead dead dead. Dead.

We'll never know, Charles thought. Because ship's log will be lost along with the tracking signal, and if we do lock on again it will be over forty years before any reply to a query of the ship's inert diagnostics will be received, and after forty years that will be pointless knowledge. No one will care because no one is going to do it over.

It's the flick life for me then.

Charles twisted off a green, leafless twig of palo verde and peeled away the spines before using it to dig in his ear after a piece of wax that was troubling him. The summer monsoon would be along in a week or so and stop his body trying to crust over, to seal itself off. Then the palo verde could leaf out, too.

《》

Meanwhile the other man, Drumlin McKechnie, the louche and plebian counterpart to the aristo Lehon, a counterweight and a reproach to him rather than someone in his own right, a cipher as befits this lumpen character, merely a techie who makes things work, had done what Charles himself would not do. He had applied yet again for a transfer. McKechnie registered the split, the ambivalence in Charles's being — the conflict between making and doing, between the spiritual or cerebral and the physical. McKechnie reified the craftish unreflective being latent in Lehon. They squabbled, these selves, seeking a spiritual intimacy bound with, inseparable from the physical one, two halves of the same person, disdaining each other as a false brother. In this closed, village society it was safer to play Eian politics than to seek anything more than an ayyup acquaintance with other men.

Instead, they squabbled mostly over small things, fearing to take up more important ideas to soon, before they had properly spread their roots, for fear of killing those still tender seedlings. Sprouts now years old and overspread like gourd vines which choked out all else with their hard, bright, indestructible fruits, and still they played Eian politics and waited for something to happen.

Now it had.

They squabbled over Charles's preference for living up top when he was entitled to a more sumptuous room below. He was offended not by the sanctimonious status inversion but by its monkishness, the ability to do without them all. They squabbled over Will Doblin's imperturbable aloofness. They squabbled over their exobiologist Varda Fleming's periodic disappearances into the freedom of the mountains. They squabbled over Drum's eternally unsatisfied longing to defect to a cable repair crew and a life of honey and locusts in the desert. They were a brotherhood whose guts were twisted with undigested ambitions, burglars' sacks filled with bright trinkets.

And so the Kalgoorlie Council finally met.

Drumlin McKechnie was drinking a beer which he had carried from the mess, the foam running over his hand. Charles Lehon stared at him with the unselfconsciously shameless curiosity of the imprisoned mind for the life of the free body. He saw but did not feel the man's heavy throat pump slowly, Drum's eyes turned to some spot over the door and all his attention fixed on the taste of beer. Charles sat by himself at the end of the table drinking coffee. If he conserved himself long enough, like a lizard waiting for some sun, Drum would finish his beer and return to the other four senses, whereupon his eye would encounter Lehon's and he would see incomprehensible mysteries — the imprisoned body, the unfree mind, the groundless animosities.

And so went the daily round of the Mazatzal telescope of the E Research Foundation, and had done for three generations, now completed with the passing of Salvatore Cicci.

Meanwhile the Eian civilization which was their collective creation ratcheted forward from hour to occasional hour at a nominal ratio of Eian to local time of one to four. But in truth these Eians were as ancient as memory. They were the aboriginals of the place, without history, possessing only those phenotropic stories of the Old Ones. These stories stuck to them, coating them like the grit which precipitates out of the air. Perhaps these stories were there all the time, brought out from the story-world whenever there were new people without immunity, and the locus of invention had for some time now been the planet E.

So they gathered communally twice a day to eat and to add some more bits to the Eian jigsaw.

There was really no reason to have their meetings here, in the seminar room, or why they had a specifically designated seminar room at all when everyone could tap in from the vid in his cubby, except that it was a chance to affirm their solidarity in a flick world, a ceremonial replacement for the family dinner. If Charles felt less alive the deeper he went into the mountain, down there where he couldn't smell the acrid dry dust or feel the sunlight puff and swell his eyelids, no more could the others do without this daily ritual.

That was now moot. The thread had been cut. The anxiety was easy to read on everyone's face.

They were waiting for Varda Fleming. Finally, still in her field boots and dusty fatigues, she bustled in, apologizing breathlessly as she poured beer for herself from one of the pitchers on the side table, covertly assessing them all as she explained about the piece of lab glassware she'd dropped and had to clean up.

Empty, fortunately. No mutant little exobiotics floating around, let me assure you all.

And with a decent pause to complete, with all present, the ceremony of drinks before dinner, Charles sat down in his appointed chair, to his appointed pattern analytic, and the rest gratefully followed his example. The seminar room fell silent.

These analytics helped to sort the kalpas of data dumped into the tank every minute and presented a profiled version to every viewport. Lehon had always been impatient with this — he felt he were driving a car peering through a little hole in the windshield. As he had in his youth when he was immortal and too busy to scrape the ice off any more. But how could anyone see everywhere at once anyway? It was the profiling which bothered him. By the time he got this wispy homunculus on his desktop the little creature had been so thoroughly debriefed he was almost transparent. Some program somewhere had ladled for Charles out of the Soup just exactly how much he wanted to eat and how many little floating alphabet crackers he wanted. But then, he'd never supposed he was a free rational being anyway.

This was the point where the camp divided and one part of the People crossed the river to the other side and the other part stayed behind. It wasn't about the wisdom of universal surveillance or whether the data mavens were getting it right or they were being robbed by a soulless machine, mavens and everyone else. What the BigEnders Over There believed was that the World Soul spake truth and what the LittleEnders Over Here, your friends and neighbors, believed was that the World Soul had her head in the fumes and was talking nonsense.

This little group of astronomers were outliers anyway. Engaged on an endless quest, they were interested in means, not ends. Their population was miniscule compared to the whole Mazatzal research station and insignificant outside.

Never suborned, not looked over but overlooked, making no reports, caring neither for nor about, they conducted their business however eccentrically they wanted.

But this was to change.

Meanwhile, for several hours the lives of those beings who dwelt in that other place where time was incremented by so many minutes, moved as by a chess player who has reached out to shift a pawn with a forefinger nudge, saying *j'adjuste,* advancing the lives of E-space by a fraction at a time.

For a while Charles had also inhabited the persona of one Hemla, until he discovered that the man was only an ordinary renegade, a plausible and in many ways admirable but nevertheless standard-issue guerilla revolutionary who sought no more than a simple redistribution of the same old marbles. Per Hemla was like the man who criticized the rules of checkers by shaking the table now and then. Besides, he was difficult to get at, always guerilla-invisible out in the desert. Eian civilization was essentially, profoundly social, as are all societies hemmed and interpenetrated. Except on those rare occasions when Hemla could be lured to the bargaining table or enticed incognito by some opportunity for booty, making Charles dusty and uncomfortable, a Hemla puppeteer had little to do. So Charles had set about learning other roles and found he had a talent for that. Like the person who picks up languages wherever he goes, most of which he will never use except to find the whereabouts of the men's room, Charles invented new people. It was only necessary to imagine a circumstance and a few props and people materialized to sit on the chairs, talk and argue, and all the rest.

Stories, he too discovered, are phenotropic. They stick to phenomena.

So are people, he said later, sitting with Varda Fleming on the roof at the end of C wing and looking at the night sky away to the south, over the Phoenix basin. Varda had been meditating there on the roof, swinging her feet in dusty desert boots now over the edge, now crossing her legs so that the red boot laces trailed limp over the stones. She had finished her business below, with the petrie dishes which always occupied her late into the night after a Council session.

Charles did not want to talk to Will about the miss. Will was too existential about things like that. Will observed the life of data like he would lab mice, or the flicks below level five. Cute, would run up your arm or crawl into a pocket, but a different life form. Who knew?

It's the end, Charles said. The probe is dead. I think I should get out now, before we're found out and the project is broken up.

Some noncommittal noise. Ah, hmm.

I could get some crew chief's job. There's one open in telemetrics.

There's always something open in telemetrics, Varda said with an overtone of amusement. As Drum can verify.

Well, people don't like the long drives out into the desert. Then, after a reflective pause: I don't suppose I do, either.

Far down in the southwest a thin, broken orange line set the mountains into relief, marking where a spontaneous fire had broken out in the rubble on the north face of the Estrellas. A telemetrics crew had been out there for a week, first laying the patch which had caused so much initial delay in their troubleshooting, then relaying the cable itself.

Thought I'd find you here, said a voice behind. It was McKechnie. He pointed toward the horizon.

Your patch will be coming off tomorrow night, he said, receiving a reply too quiet to be sure of having heard.

So I understand, said Charles, then louder — Know anything of the cable crew on the mountain?

That fire you mean?

Yes.

They're all right. The crew chief …

McKechnie broke off. An engineer himself, universal fixit man to the astronomy section, nevertheless to be on speaking terms with a field counterpart, to *know* the man, was not in good taste.

The patch comes off now, Drum said.

Charles was jovial. Then we'll see, eh? he added, pedal down on any threatening notes.

Drum is leaving us again, Varda interpolated into the tidal ebb of emotion always washing back and forth between the two men.

Indeed. Is he? Charles said, peering closely, sardonically, lecherously at him and speaking in the ancient, not to say hereditary but undoubtedly mortal voice of negation, refutation, reflection.

Then, after a long awkward silence which was mostly a reproach to Varda, he said to Drum: I could find you something with Martin, I suppose.

McKechnie's eye had already drifted away to the Anasazi ruins below them on the lower slope, from where it fled the world up into the darker sky to the southeast, that empty sand-scoured country above which Soster 241A once rose nightly, so many invisible ages ago, leaving only the faintest of traces. An empty shirt or a stiff sock dropped on the hall floor, an odor on the pillow — suggestive, tender, nostalgic clues to an almost unnoticed passage.

The Soster probe had been like a child pressing his face against a balloon, stretching the skin ever thinner and tighter, suffocated by its own curiosity, until with a viscid little pop, by some sort of hideous quantum tunneling, it crossed over to the other side of the seamless rubber womb in which it now lay dead.

There, under Soster, in the gnarled and windy Mazatzal wilderness, waiting like a headstone frugally bought on time, the quarter moon just rising over writhing, faulted canyons as narrow and mysterious as a catacomb, in the moonlight, unspeaking, the three of them saw the dust devils chase each other up and down and were not content. Closer by, deeper within the Phoenix basin, the sea of brown grit was beginning to retreat from high tide as the wind cooled and settled.

Forties again tomorrow, Charles said.

Maybe we'll hear something, Drum muttered, unable to keep the thought to himself.

I'm tired of waiting, he added, rescuing himself.

Charles's glance flickered over Drum toward Varda, but she was staring morosely into the Mazatzal cauldron and seemed not to be listening.

Kristenkowski's assay came in at four percent, she observed to no one in particular.

How do you know that? Drum snapped back. The question had been startled out of him.

You were in Colchis all last month, he said accusingly.

Varda turned, met Charles's gaze with obvious, painful complicity, then to Drum. The moonlight blanched, paled, painted like the white makeup of a No actor her dark skin, ordinarily the ruddy brown color of desert varnish.

I'd been back almost a week, Drum.

Looking from one of them to the other Drum was unable to restrain a loud guffaw. Who were you, then? he asked bluntly.

Hollis, she replied.

He turned to Charles. So you were Fishbach, then.

Yes.

Again, Drum barked with sour laughter. The three of them stood in uncompanionable silence for a while longer, leaning back against the railing which ran around the edge of the roof to prevent anyone's tumbling into the Cauldron, until Varda announced that she had to go down and, passing through the airlock, knocked her boots against the jamb in that unconscious habitual gesture of every field biologist or farmer returning indoors.

So, said Charles, hoping to break the mood. What do you have on tomorrow, Drum?

Babysitting a signals navigation program while it runs some tests.

Ah.

You had something else in mind, Charles?

We need to do something about kissop weed. Your people could tend to it while you're babysitting.

Think that's wise? Messing about with the dominant biota?

There's Hollis's report, Charles pointed out.

Hollis was in cahoots with everyone, Drum observed bitterly.

Maldonado thinks we're moving too fast, that it's only a local, short-term cycle.

Maldonado is a politician, Charles.

He's intelligent enough to read a field report and draw his own conclusions. But if Ng Jo raises the issue in Council it won't do for Maldonado to be seen dragging his feet. He wants to send out a work party to pull weeds for a while. Give people something to do.

Drum ran his finger along the metal railing, peeling up flecks of paint in the moonlight as he listened to political strategies being unfolded about which he cared nothing, but to which Charles's confidential authority lent a specious importance.

Will Ng support continued funding for research on desertification? Drum's tone was skeptical.

Oh... Well, I don't suppose this reclamation campaign has much to do with support for basic research. Kalgoorlie wants. Developers eager to profit. Stupid of Maldonado to oppose. Already talk in the Rim villages.

Drum made no reply to all this. He and Charles eyed each other warily, obliquely, coquettishly, pettishly, while Drum slowly peeled a longer and longer strip of paint away from the railing. Charles remembered his grandmother of an evening trying to peel an apple in a single strip which she could then coil up again, a hollow fruit, not a simulacrum but just an old-fashioned grandmotherly trompe-l'oeil apple to offer her credulous infant grandson. On the inside of the peeling bits of the greenish white flesh still adhered, but already beginning to brown. The apple-red paint skin now extended to eight or nine centimeters under the slow and meticulous attentions of McKechnie's spatulate nail. A nail thin, translucent and clear of knots or marks, meaning no sins recently granny would say. A nail as long and pale as a mandarin's, incongruous on such thick hands, knobby and ribbed, the heavy hands of an unsophisticated, clumsy or perhaps even boorish, in any case not well brought up, hardly brought up at all as a matter of fact but simply allowed to rear up like an angry horse.

What training in the realities, Charles wondered, had Drum received from his own grandmother.

It had been a long time since he'd tasted an apple. Twenty years, perhaps. And they were rare even then, which was the point, of course: two apples for the price of one.

Will Wen Li support Maldonado on this? Charles wanted to know, asking finally the question direct.

Will Ng Jo? responded Drum promptly.

Not a very inspiring project, is it, pulling weeds?

But then the moment was covered up, the vision fleeting, and Charles said: If Maldonado takes this idea up from the table I hope he can make it seem a bit more grand.

Yes.

And since this was the strongest commitment he could expect, Jorge Maldonado said no more, thus breaking the string, the peel, the thread of polite exchanges.

Moments passed. As the moon stood up higher in the sky the fire in the Estrellas paled, while in the northeast, above the mountains at their back, the rim lay black under its spruce blanket. Closer at hand, upslope from the ERF compound, an owl flitted among the palo verde, not so much visible as audible or rather sensible by the striation in air pressure spreading outward from its wingtips.

Charles twitched with discomfort, wishing for a breeze. The collar of his dashiki chafed the sweaty skin at the back of his neck.

The other man swore quietly and leaned out over the railing.

What is it?

Nest of scorpions, I think. One of them stung me. Shine your light down here.

Charles kept a flashlight on his key ring for this use as well as others, astronomers being much about in the night and often needing a safelight, which now he thumbed up into the ultraviolet range and there in its cone the scorpions glowed blue in a small nest which they had built under the lip of the stone coping on which the railing was mounted.

It's the little round ones, Drum complained. I'd better pick up some antivenin before I turn in. And he went off grumbling.

Council meeting tomorrow morning, Charles called after. Channel six.

Six?

Drum paused in the airlock. The outflowing cool air whipped his fine black hair across his face, making him squint.

Backup VLB telemetry is using the E channel, Charles reminded him.

Oh, right.

The airlock sucked shut. Alone now, Charles turned to look out on the desert again. There wasn't much to see: a large, comma shaped basin obscured by a continual dust storm, and the silhouettes of distant mountain ranges. Crossing the roof to the east side he overlooked there the arm which the ERF compound pushed out from the wall of the canyon and onto the mesa. Isolated, like a stroboscopic photograph of a baseball hanging just beyond the pitcher's outstretched finger tips, Hut four, containing biological laboratories, stood from this vantage at the edge of the mesa just where the canyon dropped off again, two thousand feet by rubbled stages into the cauldron.

There was something between McKechnie and Fleming. Charles turned over the possibilities like dice. Of course, in such a small society there was something between everyone. It was unfortunate that Varda was now the only woman, but then it meant that the inevitable liaisons would be with the flicks and could go unacknowledged. And Varda was not a person to permit being fought over.

Drum was smitten, of course, and had been from the first. But the Hollis conspiracy and Varda's betrayal had rubbed an exposed nerve. Drum had kicked away the shards of his objectivity in that one.

About twenty minutes had passed. Charles saw Drum push through the airlock at the end of the east wing and step across the gap into Hut four. He was going to find out more about the Vardon Mine Scandal, going to pump Varda on the pretext of needing antivenin. Charles smiled privately, feeling he had been more acute than usual.

Maldonado is right, of course, he said to himself — the kissop weed problem is not inspiriting. But is it up to him to keep up morale? Why is it taking so long for the ERF brass to confirm the obvious? We need a new story line to keep us busy: some swashbuckling tale of adventure and political intrigue, or an epic of vast empire in which the human spirit might expand to its full potential, or a grim realistic tale of the elemental struggle to stay alive on a hostile alien planet.

Back up in the canyon the lights were coming on in B wing. As Soster 241A sank below the horizon and heavy communications were passed on to Woomera for what remained of the night, Eians were coming in to use their slack time to do business. Most of their time was slack, it was true, but the ERF's machines had a bureaucratic streak and tended to get shirty about the claims of these upstart Eians to know better concerning excess processing capacity, and refused to talk to them if it didn't feel like it.

But then, E was a lifer's game, which to the flicks must seem like continental drift, some unimaginably slow process which they can study and write up but hardly expect to tinker with.

Recently the machinery of Eian life moved out of central Mazatzal station to the processing suburbs, a shift hastened by a growing concentration of flicks and off-world administrators in the core. This was a signal to the astronomers, low on the food chain, that they were in danger of losing their level five dormitory to senior staff. There was a time when the lifers were senior and had almost all of Mazatzal to themselves, but that was when the Soster probe was still more than a cee out. Now this crisis would only exacerbate the crunch. The ERF would eventually start to phase out astronomy at Mazatzal and push the lifers out of the main stream of Foundation research into backwaters depleted of food and oxygen. Like any endangered culture they would huddle up, perhaps birth a brief but long remembered renaissance glow, and then spin off into diaspora or just die, like the Eians themselves, who vanish when no one is thinking of them.

On E, too, there were signs of change. Per Hemla had

been frozen out. But support for his security organization was still there, and Maldonado had had to face sporadic demands even from the Council to set lizards loose in the net again. They want dossiers, these people; they want tracers; they want controllers identified. It happens every time.

Where's Drum gone? said a light voice at Charles's back, startling him out of these speculations. It was Varda. Charles had not heard the airlock nor her boots on the gavel.

Bad one? she asked solicitously.

I don't think so. Then: Finish your lathe work?

She nodded. Neither of them spoke for many minutes.

I thought you were working over in Four?

But she denied it. Maldonado says we need something grander than pulling weeds, Charles added after a time.

A new silence spread itself over the roof of Mazatzal station. A light breeze sprang up, bringing a coyote's whoop from across the canyon.

What does he suggest? Varda asked finally, soft voiced. It was not really a question.

Oh, nothing. He never suggests anything.

Why don't you go down to see Martin tomorrow? Varda said. Find out what the Beijing brass is up to. If he knows.

Mm.

Varda knew perfectly well what the real trouble was. She brushed his arm lightly with one finger, a consolation. After a while they went in together.

《 》

Charles woke sluggish and thickheaded as usual. His roomette was clammy with the damp breath of the wind tower — it would dry out later, when the sun penetrated deeper into the canyon. His eyes felt swollen into their sockets. Something had come into bloom during the night.

Leaving Varda to sleep undisturbed, he dressed quickly in the same baggy white trousers and soiled dashiki which he had worn for weeks. Over his feet he pulled soft naugahide moccasins which he sewed himself out of the dustproof membrane used to make covers for lab equipment. Varda's boots were lying by the door. From the lugs he scraped some of the mixed dirt and sand onto a paper which he folded into a packet and slipped into his pocket for later analysis. Before finally going out he sent a polite inquiry down to Drum's quarters. Drum would be cranky from the effects of the supposed scorpion sting and the antivenin; condolences would validate that. A small, painless favor. The net monitor sleeping on Charles's desk wakened briefly in response to his soft voiced request for exit authority. The lock, however, had to be thumbed three times before it would acknowledge him, and it hadn't wanted to accept instruction on Varda's tags, either. Sensor plate getting dull. Now he was thinking of it, Charles stepped back into the cubby long enough to put in a request for a new lock, and to wipe Varda's authorization after she left later in the morning. Again the net monitor raised its head, its golden Fafnir eye glowing briefly under the heavy lid; then it settled back into its dark languid cave of self-contemplating zazen. From the bidet fountain Charles splashed a little water on his face. The door sniffed primly as it shut behind him, having had a lecture from the net.

Through the window at the upper end of the hall came the chattering of birds, a flock of finches accustomed to spend the early morning in a large palo verde which grew there on the terraced slope. Charles too was accustomed to stop by this spot to watch for a while these glassed-off birds, but this morning there was business in the mail room. As he paced off silently deeper into halls in parts of the canyon which the winter sun couldn't reach, the breeze picked up, driven by differential warming of the outside walls. It was a real wind, raising and ruffling his hair and pimpling the flesh chilled and tightened across his back and arms by the evaporation of an adventitious film of sweat; real because Mazatzal Station was big enough to have its own internal weather, locked withal to outside events as the Earth's to the rising and setting of its sun but with at least as much complexity and as many degrees of freedom as the blobs of protoplasm which set the station going and now write haikus about the neural patterns which it induces in them, a pretty good example of a feedback loop, a sort of poetry generator. But also not real, no more than the finches in the palo verde which could after all be laser made, holos with sound, only it seemed like a lot of trouble to go to, with the droppings and other archival evidence, for what was essentially decor. And decorating a common hallway, too, down which commoners trod in heavy, unseeing and undeserving steps. The astronomers all remembered that first flickish acceptance of their utter redundancy and quickly learned to feign a superficial belief or trust in those appearances which in a place like this would become more fragile every day until at a certain moment appearances melted away like the last skin of device shimmering between the petals of a cactus flower and one saw the world dry and clear again, tight etched, as it always was, on the other side of the gateless gate. The flicks moved too fast to see such things.

The mail room was empty except for a flick monitoring traffic for his office. Humphrey, read the name tag pinned to the breast of his shirt. The plum breast. A corporal, probably economizing on something. Humphrey, stony backed before the screen of his traffic analyst, acknowledged with the barest twitch of a plum-lensed eye the next step of this astronomer tortoise toward his still distant lettuce.

Captain Martin, please, Charles said to the intercom, which contentedly scanned his identification.

Com's sluggish today, eh Humphrey?

A bit, sir.

On the windowsill above the com sat a whiptail lizard. The two of them traded unblinking stares until the com peeped, startling Charles and releasing the lizard, which darted into a crack.

Request a meeting with Captain Martin, he said evenly.

Your agenda? returned the com just as composedly.

Personnel.

One moment.

Charles waited, drying his palms on the legs of his already dingy canvas trousers, or what passed for canvas, a coarsely woven fabric of a certain density and meeting a number of other conditions unknown to him. Waited, muttering, until the com, not understanding his half voiced complaints, fluttered briefly and threatened to become distracted.

Callback, he ordered in a more distinct voice. I'll be in C209 telemetry until eleven o'clock. Acknowledge.

Grudgingly, the com acquiesced. Nodding unnoticed to the plumate corporate analysand in the corner, Charles strode out of the mail room.

The morning he spent constructing a tap on the raw output of the telescope, piping the tap for the time being into the tank in his cubby, and was beginning to think about what to do next when the com roused itself. Captain Martin's pale, square face popped up.

You're up early, Charles, the Captain said. Being an earnest man, he undoubtedly thought it was true, that it really was early, and accepted Charles's reply with a formal smile. The exchange which followed was inconclusive and unhelpful, nuzzled as it was by all the network cats now being fed by who knows how many liaisons, reps, honchos, hirelings, and entrepreneurs of any degree of incorporation. A personal meeting was out of the question, of course, eyeball to eyeball as it were, there being some suspicion that ERF command liaisons might be wired direct and thus not, in a strictly instrumental sense, have eyeballs. Discounting this quotidian visual device as, for the purposes required, sub-mundane, to be brought into play only for finding one's fork in an ill lit restaurant and so forth.

The instructions from Beijing, Captain Martin said, are to decrease resolution by one-half arc-second and continue as before.

Which the astronomers all knew, and knew also that a request for an estimate of damages was expected from Paris in a day or so. Martin and his counterparts at Woomera and Pic Touside would reiterate the finding that ship's log was possibly disabled, or perhaps obliterated, pixilated, sated, or seen god though not yet, unfortunately, born again. The Board was obviously reluctant to declare a loss, though a scan across the target area at maximum resolution had found no debris bigger than a quarter kilometer. Vaporized. Beijing could hide under the blankets as long as it liked and the most Martin could do was ignore Charles's tap, though where resources for analysis were to come from he couldn't say, of course, being officially ignorant and therefore dumb, as it were mouthless as well as eyeless. But he could hint.

Ought to scale the E simulation back a bit, said Martin casually. A little one-sided now, isn't it? The comlink went dark while Charles was still pulling diplomatically on his lip.

Then lunch, stopping at the post office on the way to mail the packet of dirt collected from Varda's boot, enclosing with it a requisition for analysis and probable source, giving Maldonado's authorization to draw on the desert reconnaissance fund and addressing it to Mazatzal Geologic Survey attention Fong Oushih, Level Four Section D. The packet was sucked away. The tube cover bumped shut with a hollow thump.

Always a moment of empathy here, a tendency to identify with the pneumatic canister for some reason, whether fear of being sucked away himself or more likely a simple motor response like the desire to schuss along with a line of skiers, an empathy which led this time, by a not very elaborate or surprising series of associations, to speculation on the transit to E, that is the canister's transit, very much larger and more complicated than this pneumatic mailer but a canister just the same, an interplanetary people post, two decades and odd change down the tube, in the can, anyway from the passengers' perspective, locked up in there. Is it any wonder if they come out a little odd, a little rumpled, with travel wrinkles, little factional obsessions characteristic of small closed societies, their priorities somewhat scrambled like the contents of a suitcase which one has been living out of for weeks, or a trunk one would have said in days of slower though not necessarily more leisurely travel, leisure being a free choice rather than technologically imposed obstacle, which suggests that two or three decades to another planet is not a leisurely trip but neither would it be a way of life, given its inherently transitory nature and one's natural anxieties about what comes next, analogous to anxieties about life after death he supposed, so that it should not surprise anyone if all of this rumpled baggage was still lying on the bedroom floor when the stupefied and disoriented traveler regained consciousness in yet another hotel room or if the twists and wrinkles of colonial voyaging got expressed in the colonists' subsequent social practices and institutions, as deformations of inherited ethics, etiquette, politics and so on, a comparison which might have been thought Lamarckian before genetic engineering, controlled mutation, and other forms of biological tinkering made the Lamarckian heresy irrelevant.

They had never bothered to model that part of it, to work that out in any detail. With a millennium of galactic history to play with it had seemed dull to waste time on twenty years of preliminary domestic squabbling. But perhaps that had been a mistake. Just as the present distribution of galaxies depended on minute irregularities in the big bang, or the existence of human beings on a few crucial events among the protozoa, as chaos theory as well as experience suggested, so the demise of the Eian empire might be found, retrospectively at any rate, in some dinner table argument among colonists.

And is it different with us? Will Doblin inquired with a little pointed mischief frilling his voice like a delicate lace.

How do you mean? Fong Oushih asked. Oushih sat across the cafeteria table chewing a lunchtime forkful of enchilada in green sauce.

Will hitched up one eyebrow. Consider the lifers here, urged he, indicating the cafeteria with his own green coated fork, meaning Mazatzal generally but leading Fong to wonder what they eat in Touside or Woomera, synthetic couscous perhaps. What was Australian peasant food like?

Will was going on, though, without Fong. It's the same small, hermetic society, he was saying. It's the same treadmill life, mostly trivial routine and waiting for the end. How is it different from being squashed into a little can and spun off into interplanetary space to die?

Not exactly little, Drum objected. Even the lunar shuttle is a kilometer square.

Pooh. This is the E colony ship right here. We don't have to model it, we *are* it. We're self-selected for this kind of life. Statistical oddities. For example: not one of us is married. As a group we have these strongly marked characteristics. The tendency to put off decisions for example, because we're unreconciled to living our own lives, to living just the one life, to giving up on the unlived possibilities.

Will took another forkful of the green stuff and swallowed carefully. It's more fun to try on than to buy, he observed, somewhat gnomically until the analogy to trying on unlived Eian lives made itself felt.

Yes, well... Drum objected to that. How would you like to be squashed inside some nasty little man like Fishbach for any length of time?

Not much, they agreed.

Not, said Will sardonically, when there might be something newer, or more fashionable, or better fitting on the rack.

This line of attack was making everyone at the table uncomfortable and a long pause in the conversation ensued while they all stirred sauce and tried to think of how to change the subject. Will, being actually a kind man and not inclined to cut anyone to the point of actual disfigurement, did it himself in the end.

Beijing is not moving, I take it?

Ahhh. Yer mother.

But it was all for nothing, as it turned out: the waiting, the anxiety, the recalibrations and re-laid cables and half second reference scans, the monsoon of raw telemetry data which poured out of the hole Charles had bored in the compactor pipe, the cover-up stories they'd been telling themselves. Good stories, Charles observed, come from the reptile brain. They are a cultural peat bog where ancient men have died, one on top of another, in which they had been digging, distracting themselves by exhuming these preserved moments of final agony, covering up their own fears with these layers, these winding-sheets of violence.

All week Charles had been stopping off in the mail room every morning to check on his tap for fear some bureaucratic mandarin would turn it off. He was sure they had been missing something by not bothering to store all the raw scan at a common site but, considering the warehousing that would have been required, it wasn't surprising that they would have had to show cause. Charles himself didn't have a tank big enough for more than an hour's worth, just enough for the pattern search to keep up, but which tied up his node to the point where he now couldn't even get into his cubby and had been sleeping in the astronomers' commons. So every morning he looked in on the mail, where OMS Corporal Humphrey sat grimly filling out forms authorizing continuation of this and that, to watch the flood of small, futile numbers roar out of the hole in the pipe. He hadn't much wanted to challenge the compaction algorithm anyway, since the rule on which it was based was the foundation of all storage practice. But there was this persistent, longstanding worry that their analysis was in some way circular, which suggested the possibility that this ominous silence, this bland smooth custard which had turned up in a region which had once been lumpy, was an artifact of data prep. Of course he had to look into every hidey-hole, but the practical reality was that to attack intelligent analysis now, in mid-jump, was impossible. Certainly they were desperate for a better means of handling these massive data sets. The whole history of astronomy can be interpreted as a continual crisis of information management. So when nothing had turned up in a week's raw scan Charles was — perhaps perversely — relieved. The daily pattern analysis had dutifully been published, with so far no response from anyone, which suggested Charles might not be the only one with no stomach for basics just now.

Riffling through the en clair messages from Woomera was one which he had to read a second time.

Mister Humphrey.

Sir?

Here's something from the people in Australia saying they have a ping.

Yes.

You said nothing about it to me.

No, sir. It would have been in your mail.

I haven't looked at my mail. I can't get into my cubby.

The mail will be released in about half an hour. I'm sure you can open your mailbox from another site?

Has the ping been confirmed?

I believe they're on from Paris about that now, sir. If you would go below?

I'm not asking whether your superiors have been notified, Corporal. I'm asking whether it's been found in the scan.

I couldn't say, sir.

Well of course he couldn't; it had been rude of Charles to ask, but the prim grittiness of this factotum had been roughening his temper for a week. Impotent, wanting to hide his feelings, Charles turned away to the window. Beyond the canyon wall a small wedge of brilliant blue sky was visible, like a fleck of lapis in its stony matrix. Nearer by a black chinned hummingbird was feeding on a honeysuckle growing over a leaky recycling pipe. In search of more flowers, the bird sidled along the glass, which it gave an experimental tap.

And so it is with me, Charles muttered. Timeworn rhetorical device, this allegory, but accurate.

Sir?

Nothing, Humphrey. Nothing at all.

Woomera's message was plainly a hasty one; it gave the ping in local rather than sidereal time, but when the ephemerides in Charles's analyst had made the conversion there was nothing in the raw scan which corresponded. Some damned mail clerk who didn't know what time it was. Instantly Charles pulled the tap, letting raw effluent run on the ground while he bailed his tank enough to keep the last hour's discharge from overflowing. Then, with the raw Woomera scan safely bottled, he was able to patch up the pipe.

Humphrey!

Punctilious response, razored sibilants, ripe vowels. Charles pointed to the honeysuckle growing outside the window.

There's a hole in the sump there which should be fixed, Corporal.

Yes, I've reported that. I'm sure there will be quite a lot of housekeeping to do now.

Now? Now that what? Nonplussed, mated, Charles jerked the dust cover up over the analyst and strode out in a rage.

That afternoon they all gathered in the commons to watch the Pic Touside data come in for the same area of sky in which Woomera had reported its ping. Will sucked his lips as the topo was filled in, but successive magnification as deep as twenty-five magnitudes showed nothing but the edge of the dimple corresponding to the Soster reference. Flat as cold pudding.

Where's the Pic en clair? someone called out from the back. What are they saying at Pic?

Coming along now, Will replied, peering at the sidebar.

There was a pause, a breathing silence.

Pic Touside reports a ping. Will's long finger punctured the topo in the middle of the new Mare Bodino. Right there.

From the back again: Where the hell is that?

That's about, um — Will did some rapid calculations — eighteen months from orbit.

Eighteen months? Eight years, it should be.

Will did the calculations over and only shrugged.

At half-light it'll be out in the back lot before then, said a different voice, heavier and angrier, but Will pointed to the vectors.

Not half, Garth. Ten percent.

What? Where? Crank up the res, I don't see a damned thing. How can Pic be reporting a ping? There's nothing there.

Will Doblin only shrugged and, turning, pushed through the crowd and out of the commons, leaving Charles to field questions.

They'd look into it, Charles said. Have something by dinnertime, maybe. Query Pic. Query Paris. Get a verbal from Aarne. Any suggestions on where to look? What the fault might be? Monitor E channel for postings, he advised, and followed Will into the cool, empty, blue-lit hall. The commons door bumped shut, silencing the frizz of puzzled but ominous talk which filled up space like static between radio frequencies.

《 》

By midafternoon Mazatzal station was on general alert. The news had spread rapidly and by the time official instructions had come down through flick channels the astronomers already knew what to expect. What they would have been led to believe if Charles had not witnessed these events as they happened was something Will, at least, preferred not to speculate on. Speculate anyway: imitation happenings, virtual vapors. Just those noises the house makes at night when it settles. Turn over and go back to sleep, will you?

Charles was back in his cubby for the first time in several days, awaiting yet another dawn of Soster 241A. Earlier he had tried to raise the Pic people without success, and Woomera seemed to be all asleep. But Soster was coming up now, and in another hour the moon too would be up, completing the third leg and forming the immense telescope which had enabled them to see the ancient planets, these Sosteridean specks.

The hour passed heavily. He tried the other two telescope stations again with no response. Perhaps they were too busy, or Charles's low priority calls were simply being dumped by a communications network now spooked, traumatized, entirely monopolized by high level chatter between Paris and Beijing. But the moon did rise, visible on the baseline down in the valley and on the slope of the Estrellas long before Mazatzal, tucked away under the lip of the mountain, could see its white pinched face. Then Charles's vid jumped to life, the screen suddenly bright with topo lines. He decreased the compression until the isogravs parted, and gave himself to their hypnotic march. The reported longitude of the ping was soon coming up over the horizon, but again the scan marched by without a wrinkle.

Muttering, he recalled the target area to the foreground while behind it the scan continued to flow by. Still nothing. Meanwhile, their own Mazatzal en clair was reporting contact, claiming a ping where the telescope itself reported only black cosmic dust.

Archiving that, Charles abandoned the vid and crashed his cubby door. The lock peeped complaint; impatiently, he left it unsecured and bounded for the elevator at the upper end of the corridor.

Six, he barked, and jabbed the priority switch. The doors closed leisurely. The car began to sink toward six.

At three it stopped to admit a staff sergeant carrying a cake. He thumbed the priority switch also; this time the car shot down two levels to the personnel department, where it hung stupidly with its doors open while Charles squirmed under the violet stare of the boy at the reception desk.

Six, he requested again, with irritation. The elevator yawned, shut itself up, and eased down another level.

The offices of Communications Directorate were tense. Martin himself, ordinarily a most indolent man, was bundling down a corridor on his way, he said, somewhere.

In person?

Charles commiserated, falling into step.

The Captain, his pale face flushed at the edges like a trout, made an impatient gesture in the air.

I can't get through to Pic or Woomera, Charles said.

Not surprised.

Is the Estrella leg clean?

Desert reconnaissance started out an hour ago to verify.

Lengthening his stride to keep up, Charles described his monitoring of the raw scan and the absence of corroboration for the reported pings. Who, he wanted to know, was talking en clair?

No idea, Captain Martin said, snubbing the words tight.

Trace it.

Routine. Everything is sent below.

The elevator which had been called for the Captain was waiting at the FG crossing. Charles sidled into the doorway.

I want to set up a working party, he said quietly. Give me a secure line to Woomera and emergency call on net resources. You'll have a report after the next pass.

Martin calculated hastily, letting Charles see at once that he had been right, that Martin was as much out of the loop as anyone and needed a grapple to hold his place. Taking a scrap of paper from a pocket of his tunic, Martin scribbled a note.

Give that to Pfolet, he said. Knows my writing. Let me have your findings privately, before session Directorate tomorrow. To me, Charles. Not through channels.

When the elevator had gone Charles looked at the paper he had been given. A receipt from the cleaners, for an officer's tunic. It was a long time since he'd seen a paper receipt.

What could they be up to, these liaison officers and military foundation bureaucrats with their cleaning bills and paper money, living their unheard-of, almost unimaginable tucked away lives? How would one know, when even the getting from morning till night are so different, what these people could possibly think about the proper motions of the stars, and what there could possibly be left to say to a computer after fifty light-years?

The rest of the evening Charles spent gathering resources using the authorization Pfolet had given him, beginning with a general session call on channel E. There was a lot of clamor among the Councillors, which he tried to calm. An expeditionary force was imminent, he said — Maldonado said — numinously present in the sky already, and all the tolling of the bells was because of that. Called back from the grave somehow, Charles wanted to add, but kept his cruel doubt close, paused, and left well enough alone. Who knew what sort of chaos that would introduce. He made his second call.

The Lazerites were awake and in as much an uproar as the Eians. He opened all the vid channels then. They would, Charles announced, camp in hut two until the business was resolved, and that was where Drum found him when he looked in a few minutes later.

Raid the commissary, Drum, will you? he called out, seeing the younger engineer. Whatever's hot, and a jug of coffee. My account. Here a pause while he waited for the commissary to confirm; then, peering at the top of the form returned: requisition number four two zero four.

But it was the usual commissary stupidity, being a flick operation with a fixed idea that everyone goes to bed at seven o'clock when the pencils are put away, compounded by Drum's resentment at being sent to fetch, so that all he could get besides the coffee was a sack of cookies. But as he was grimly leaving with these inedibles Fong Oushih, the geologist, who being a plump little man with rounded not to say pillowing superficies which hinted at his frequent alimentary struggles, having doped out for himself what would be needed during the night, came by on his own and, seeing the poor results Drum had achieved, used his own influence and superior diplomacy to pry a stack of frozen pizzas out of the commissary's night service, as well as a four liter pot of wine and another jug of cold coffee.

Back in hut two there was a good deal of hilarity as this food began to go around. The underground gloom of the last month was dissipated temporarily in an atmosphere of energy and the prospect of some night work so much loved by owlish astronomers but which in their latter days, separating observation and analysis as they did, had not been very common, just another of the little cheats which they had all encountered growing up and watching their expectations turn into middling, sometimes sordid but most often only banal, reality. Slowly the laughter and the toasting of stained mugs and slices of bread and congealed ersatz cheese thawed even Charles's crabbed and clenched emotions and allowed him to take a little undeserved pleasure in his own small success which Oushih, negligent as always, was too preoccupied to claim for himself.

Will Doblin ambled into the hut, and Charles at once beckoned excitedly to him. Sit, ordered Charles, reaching behind him for a folding chair abandoned there like a man standing alone at a party pretending he doesn't notice the circle of drinkers talking at his elbow.

What's up?

I've got Lazard on from Woomera, and I'm just trying to raise Pic.

Will was quickly filled in, with contributions from Lazard in Australia and from others gathered around the vid. Lazard's voice was drifting in and out of synch on a disconcerting ten second cycle, so while he listened, Will set about tracing the source with a hair fine probe which he fished out of his shirt pocket.

So it was the raw scan which tipped you? Will asked, holding a fragment of the projector up close to one eye. Lazard's image broke up, leaving only the relict voice, to which Charles had become increasingly insensitive. It was, he thought sometimes, like people who wear glasses being unable to hear without their glasses on. When Will began to tinker with the vid there was a noticeable falling-off of attention on the blinded fringe of astronomers and others who had gathered around.

No, no, Charles corrected him. The lack of corroboration had the flicks up at once. We were the ones out of touch. This simply brings us up with them.

The flicks, Charles knew, having little interest in the integrity of the data or the chain of reasoning, incorroborance being for them a bungle or a snarl requiring political or bureaucratic repairs, had had no intention of telling *them*, and in fact had yet to make any effort to enlighten anyone at all, but were at least content to let the astronomers alone to find their own way to the truth for which he supposed they ought to be grateful, but which gave him then some hint of what to expect from these people if they were to be allowed to drive events rather than deferring as usual to telescopes and data compaction algorithms and simplified sidereal holograms.

Here! Charles exclaimed triumphantly. I've got Pic finally — and a soft familiar voice filled the room as the face of the ERF senior astronomer bloomed up in the middle of the group. Got you! exclaimed Will at the same time, and Aarne in Africa was joined by the renascent and now stabilized Australian. Will slipped his probe delicately back into its case.

We can't pin down authority for this here, Aarne was saying.

Ours, Lazard put in, seems to have been provided from Beijing. From ERF administration there — he turned away to consult someone else — Adjutant Hsiao of liaison staff. Something in the nature of a news release, would you believe, which this Sr. Hisao claimed to be only passing on from god knows where. Charles?

Nothing to add. We're still working backwards through our local archives. Only just got clearance.

Has this gone outside yet? Will inquired, meaning outside the Foundation, producing negatives from both Aarne and Lazard and a brief huddle concerning strategy should there be a public inquiry, as to the wisdom of pitching facts over the wall without being invited to see the pile.

Frankly, Will stated, spraying cookie crumbs, I think you can tell a cabinet minister anything you like. Soster probe, you say. That old thing. Well, what is it? Money, I suppose.

Yes, someone replied. And if Adjutant Hsiao collars you to make an explanation?

Can't explain. They always want it in twenty words, anyway.

That won't do. Aarne's soft but heavy, rumbling voice added to his authority.

We hand off in a little over an hour, Charles observed, looking uneasily at the clock, with still no contestable verification.

Charles disliked this sort of discussion, which like Will he would try to trivialize or put off, finishing predictably: Let's see what happens on the next pass.

The hour went quickly, though Charles felt himself getting a bit muddled with nothing to eat all day but cookies, pizza, and wine, even if the pizza did have ersatz bacon on it.

Nothing to eat, Drum?

McKechnie made a sour face and said that he'd been out all afternoon with a field crew and had had duty rations.

Now, as the Woomera scan began to come up on Soster, everyone gathered around while Will aligned the big pro-

jection plotter and the familiar isogravs began to flow past.
They were all so used to looking at this plot that it had actually become hard to read, and there was a lot of unhelpful
chatter. Anxiety was not often a positive emotion and tragedy's grip on the imagination was stronger still — greater
profundities are born in greater fears, Charles said aloud
to everyone's puzzlement. Will stepped up the sampling,
slowed the display, zoomed up on the crucial region as it
peeked in from the right. That old dimple made by 241A, an
ovoid compression of the lines of equal gravity overlaid by
irregular blotches of color from the radio and X-ray spectra
and peppered by smaller dimples, drifted across their field of
view like an amoeba caught under a cover glass.

Someone pointed. There.

Got it! another shouted, and everyone scrambled to a different terminal to look at the numbers.

Confirmed, insisted a third. It's a ping.

Where the hell has it been for a month? everyone was
wondering, but no one quite dared ask because a general re-
laxation, a relief from the month's tension, was spreading
across the room which no one wanted to disturb with doubts.
There would be plenty of time for doubting, for confirming
the known characteristics of the Soster scout, for wondering
how it got where it evidently was and just what did they
think the...

Pic Touside dropped off to get some sleep before the
scan came around to them, and the Mazatzal people too began to drift away, leaving only a few of the inner circle to
drink from the nearly exhausted jug of wine and watch the
ping become thicker, darker as its verification function con-
verged on unity. And Charles also stayed on, or rather was
unwilling to go, unwilling to go away to an empty cubby
from which he would be denied anyway because the lock
had long since forgotten his authority code, and he would

rather hang around like a forlorn graduate student sitting a corner, eating cookies and struggling with a really cosmic depression exacerbated by too much chemical sucrose and too little neurotransmitter.

What a bust, Charles Lehon commented ruefully, switching off at last.

Ah, Will said quietly, consoling him. Engineering will come up with something. An error in signal deflection computations or something else on board. Hah? Something at the other end?

Rubbish, Will.

Sure it's rubbish, returned Will Doblin complacently. It doesn't explain a damned thing, but it's less than twenty words.

Nothing touches you, does it? Charles growled, rousing and shaking himself. I'm going up on the roof. Coming?

Will stretched out his own long legs and said he'd pass, he'd had enough fresh air to last a while, so that was how Charles Lehon's eye happened to fall on Drumlin McKechnie just at that moment, when for the first time in their snarled and reluctantly entangled lives they actually needed each other. That's sufficiently rare, Charles thought, to be worth pointing out.

The two of them, disdaining the elevator, clambered up the iron stair tower into the open night. Here, in the river of cool and still clean air which flowed down the canyon into the dust filled basin, Charles's mood thinned. He looked off toward hut four, farther out at the end of the mesa where it was hot and still and a faint blue light showed that Varda Fleming too was restless and had gone back to work, then up into the black, sugar sprinkled sky.

Rubbish, he said after a time.

Maybe, Drum said softly, I would be better off in desert reconnaissance after all, out of doors.

Charles, silent, taking slow breaths of the slightly acrid air, an aging, eccentric but still powerful man, now turned to look full on Drum for perhaps the first time. Yes, he thought, inkling what was about to happen and what it offered for him, his gaze lining Drum's face with the care and precision of a plotter's pen. Maybe he would be better off that way. His eye drifted away to the side and his smile flowered, releasing a faint sardonic perfume.

Why don't we have a resumption of the verbal? Drum demanded.

Next time around, maybe, Charles said vaguely, his thoughts still in thrall elsewhere. He looked up into the many-shaded sky. His adam's apple moved rhythmically within his taut throat.

Rubbish, he insisted again, contradicting himself after a judicious moment.

Meanwhile, Jorge Maldonado also waited in his desert fastness for nearly a full cycle of seasons to pass before the incoming, now at last expected ship to be revealed, like a god to be glimpsed only briefly, a faint star-like light low on the horizon as it slowed, falling down the near side of the arch which had touched, at its apex, almost nine-tenths the speed of light. Ground and ship, the two of them then flung out hands to each other, feeling through months of time to touch, hold, lock.

Fifty thousands, they say. Nearly a twentieth the present population of Kalgoorlie. Like dropping a melon into a bucket of soup. They would all be overwhelmed. Maldonado foresaw a struggle which he would be powerless to prevent or even ameliorate, feeling a ghastly dread, a reluctance in every act, as if by doing nothing he could slow events; as if by his taking a sort of shuffle step they, falling from their measured place into this hectic here and now will somehow miss completely, flash by, wink out and be lost in the forever future.

A week passed. The life of Mazatzal station began to settle back into the routines from which it had been knocked by the disappearance of the Soster probe from the sky in springtime, and its mysterious reappearance in the summer. But the influx of new temporary staff which had begun then did not stop. The personnel nodes were swollen with new applications for transfer, reinstatement, beginning, ending, rising, and all the other ceaseless motions of this frantic, insectoid species. Something was going on elsewhere in the ERF. A change in government of one of the contributing nations, or a new war, or an economic collapse, or a resurgence of religious fundamentalism, had swept up the Foundation again in its larger motion.

And an explanation did emerge just as Will had predicted, and with the expected and correctly temporizing tone. Charles made his promised report to the Communications Directorate with no visible consequences. His priority access to the net was not renewed and, feigning pique, he withdrew to his cubby behind his broken lock to hide. The whole vast edifice of international scientific research was coming about to a wind from a new direction, and coming about pretty quickly for such a ponderous craft, but of its new heading none knew nor could discover anything. There was, presumably, somewhere a pilot and a compass, but to the Mazatzal onlookers this setting of courses seemed as inexplicable and inexorable as everything the flicks did, like a migration of Vikings or Huns whirling out of a wilderness of ocean or steppe, laying waste and passing on. There would be a retrospective explanation, of course, for what they now experienced as ruinous confusion. Sociological, statistical, unsatisfying explanations.

For some there would be history. For the Eians perhaps. Not for Charles.

THE BRIDGE

Weeks passed. Now it was the first of September, and the heat and dust were at their height. All day long wind boiled the Mazatzal cauldron, which settled every night a little less, until finally it boiled over. Up on the mountainside where Mazatzal station was dug in the season of dust storms began. The exposed huts were sealed, equipment was packed in bubbles, and everyone retreated to lower levels. Even Charles went down when the wind towers were smothered by blowing dust. He had tried to stick it out one year, the first, when he still thought the desert was charming. But he found out that to live on the edge of the Mazatzal cauldron in the dirty time one needs a lot of claustrophobic, technological infrastructure. After a while it hadn't seemed worthwhile.

Charles was having an increasingly hard time getting the net to recognize his existence. There was some stigma on him, he complained to Logistics. But no, the ubiquitous Humphrey reassured him. He was not an unperson, he had simply lost his priority call on resources.

Like air.

Sir?

Air. I'll get some if there's any left over.

Humphrey cleared his throat, looked left and right, decided on a course of action.

Sir?

I'm here to report a malfunction in the air delivery system in my cubby, Charles repeated patiently. Level two, corridor B.

Ah. And then the fatal pause, while Humphrey's eyes wandered off and comprehension slipped slowly away.

Aren't you assigned level five, sir? he inquired after a

time, shaking himself.

I haven't lived on five for twenty years.

Such an immense length of time was clearly beyond Humphrey's grasp, and he retreated to more measureable aspects of the problem. The net was, he affirmed, supplying adequate ventilation to Charles's assigned quarters; that is, to level five.

What I mean, eh? It's forgotten. Forgotten to forward my air.

Humphrey digested this. Why don't you report this to the net itself, sir, he said at last. Instead of walking down?

Because, Humphrey, it's busy.

Ah.

Humphrey cleared his throat again, rubbed a corner of his eye with a long thin finger, pinched the end of his nose.

Busy, sir. Yes, sir, it would be.

Charles did not reply and Humphrey, released to more important tasks, swiveled his chair around and politely turned his back while Charles, smiling a little sourly, ambled out.

Why is the net busy of course? he muttered as the airlock opened.

Sir?

And then mercifully hissed shut, cutting off any more talk with Sargent Humphrey.

What's it doing that takes so much of its time? That Humphrey takes for granted when I haven't an inkling. And why should it want to snub me? Did I offend it somehow? What threat could this humble person offer the world-sized reticulation within which we have our being? This intelligent plenum, plenum of intelligence.

Rather than return to a stuffy room with a door spitefully locked against him, Charles took the elevator up to the surface to have a look at the weather. Deserted corridors.

The pale radiance of sunlight filtered through dust and bubble sealant. All the doors closed and taped. Hot still air so desiccated it was painful to breathe, and a coating of grit on everything. Charles passed through the top airlock and onto the open roof. Here he was above most of the storm, but still a heavy wind tugged at his clothing and flying sand bit his exposed skin. Pulling the collar of his shirt up over his mouth, and shielding his eyes with the other hand, he made a quick circuit of the roof. There was nothing to see beyond the streaming branches of the palo verde which grew up against the mail room wall and a few large prickly pear about ten meters away on the mountain side. The air was an opaque pale brown, shading to mustard overhead and marbled with mahogany below; in the circling wind it was difficult to know where he was and twice he bumped unexpectedly against the railing, bruising his hip. Behind the airlock hut he found a little pocket of calm where he was able to stand up straight.

Nacreous, he thought. That color is called nacre. His mind would not keep upright in the whip and slap of the curtain of sand. Nacre is obsolete. The nacre-makers have all suffocated or drowned and, like trolls, are turning to stone. The nacred and the dead.

He gave up and went back down.

The burning heat on Charles's skin had not abated when he reached the common room, back inside on level two. Drum was the only one there. He who bracketed these two, Maldonado and Lehon, was so reflexive of aspect that when one turned away from the light then so must the other.

Drum could see at a glance where Charles had been. Hair standing on end, stiff with dirt, eyes still squeezed up and rimed with that oily black stuff which coated everything.

Slacked off any?

Nah, Charles replied through the open washroom door.

You can smell the change coming though. He came out toweling his face.

Crossing over for a while, Drum?

McKechnie shrugged. Can't get there from here.

Oh? Charles glanced at the long priority queue displayed, through which Drum's request for re-assignment was rising slowly like a bubble in glycerin.

The holos have worn sort of thin, anyway, don't you think? Charles muttered through his towel.

Drum, preferring to take these noises for assent, pushed on. It takes some of the fun out of it, he complained. They don't give us any work, and they don't give us anything else to do, either. We're expected to pass the time keeping up with the bioengineering literature, I suppose.

Will sauntered in, looked at the length of the short-term jobs queue, and went out again. Drum sighed, then pulled himself up.

Your eyes are pretty bad, he observed, and could see Charles felt it was true. The man's whole head looked swollen and puffy, and the glands in his neck stood out knotted under his fingers.

It'll pass, Charles said, deprecating the discomfort. With the monsoon.

Several minutes passed in bored silence.

I was thinking, Charles said again, what it might have been like here before. Stupid place to live, really. I was out in a storm once, the second or third year I was here. Thought I would go for a hike. Quite a pointless experience.

Yes, Drum replied quietly. I've done that.

I remember.

You don't take them seriously, at first. The storms.

More time passed. They watched the jobs queue turn over. After a while Varda came in.

I got tired of reading, she said, getting herself a cup of

coffee. Besides, it's stuffy.

Have you put in a requisition? Charles inquired.

For what? Varda responded. Want some company?

Charles gestured expressively to the displayed queue. Varda sat down, and they all stared together mutely.

It's doing bathrooms, Drum said after a while.

They all looked.

See? It's going around flushing all the toilets. Now watch, it's going to start over again. There.

Their eyes followed his finger.

There.

The days of September passed slowly, which implied a perception, a bored mind in which the perception of time, slow, possibly languid, could be said to differ from the irregular and rapid gothic truth. There was no respite from confinement and no way to keep busy with communications since contact with E had become so sluggish — slug-time is probably a mad whirl to a slug — that work had been reduced to signing the daily log. Of course, that was no more than they used to do for months at a stretch, but now they no longer felt as if they were working for themselves. Which was all the difference; such differences, like the passage of time, being mostly ideational which was to say subject to slugly repositioning. Mazatzal station was undergoing some transformation, like a chemical solution which, reaching a certain instability, will turn red or blue at a glance.

Will had set himself, for something to do, to analyzing the net's behavior. Charles was finding himself on many afternoons now in the common room, watching Will run statistics and tracers, try out new performance measures, test esoteric capacities. Total capacity, response time, and a dozen other of the crudest measures had been climbing all summer, Will said. He poked through a heap of notes, did a quick calculation.

Here. Nesting capability is up by an order of magnitude just in the last week.

Charles glanced sourly at the scrap of paper. Then why can't I get the lock on my cubby door repaired?

Capacity is up, but we're not getting the benefit.

Well, who is? It's even quit publishing its queues.

It maintains there are no queues, Will remarked.

Right. The reputation of Mazatzal node requires that there be no waiting, is what it says. So there is none.

Unfortunate phrasing, Will acknowledged. But actually there don't seem to be any queues, to speak of.

Oh? How do you know that?

Will explained the processing performance tests by which the order in which the net handled requisitions could be uncovered and the dark matter inferred. It's even unemployed now and then, he added.

Ah? What's it do when it's not busy?

I don't know, Will replied seriously, putting on the sober face considered necessary for admissions of ignorance. But you're right, it does lie about the queue, when there is one. It seems to feel we don't need to know such stuff. Mere procedural knowledge. Instrumental truths and so forth. Reserved for higher purposes, us. But that's not why your cubby door isn't being fixed. Here, watch this.

Will filled out a routine equipment repair requisition, dropped it in the mail, was promptly acknowledged.

Status check, please. Will spoke sharply, giving the requisition number, but still had to submit to a voice print verification.

In process, the net acknowledged somewhat grudgingly, Charles thought. Pried out of it through a piece of bad faith.

Confirm, please. Blue two one one.

Requisition is denied, was the acerbic reply. Advise blue access is not in conformity with stated priority call.

Requisition number, please, Will continued imperturbably, and scribbled down the identification that was supplied.

Now he manually called up a task inventory, answering a few security questions as he did so, and paged down the list of requisition numbers to the one wanted. Denied, it said under action code. He turned over that leaf. Insufficient need, was the reason given.

You see, Charles? It's lying to you. The net is processing its queues by kicking us no-counts out of line. At least it's polite about it. It doesn't want to tell you to your face, unless you insist.

What's this access blue business?

Will pulled on his ear. Something I picked up from a system manager, he admitted. But you see it knows someone like me isn't likely to have a blue code. It doesn't want to call my bluff yet, but it will soon. The net's remaking itself, Charles. There's all this internal encryption. Maybe it's been going on for a long time.

A generation, Charles remarked sarcastically.

Hah. Why should we complain about the flicks' impetuousness when the Eians live at something like thirty to one? In fits, of course.

Yes, a whole lifetime in an afternoon, like Hollis.

Will raised one eyebrow in a comic expression of incredulity which on his long face unintentionally indicated a sneer. It wasn't an actual sneer, merely a proposal. An indication, devoid of any downlooking. The tall-browed and thus high-minded Will Doblin — high in the vertical sense only — he being of the despised instrumental and procedural tastes — laughed.

What are you trying to get your cubby fixed for, anyway? he inquired after a time. Have you moved back up top?

Ah, it's not so bad, Will, there up top. I've done it before, other years. If you put a wet scrubber in the wind tower vent and keep the door shut you can sleep, anyway.

Where did you get a wet scrubber?

The same place you got all these security codes, eh?

Will grinned, but Charles noticed that he ducked any hint of complicity. And the grin faded quickly, to be replaced by an expression of concern.

I believe you're going to apply for promotion again, he said quietly. Aren't you, Charles?

Yes. I suppose so. Futile. Futile as it is. As it shall prove.

Charles gazed off into a dark corner of the room. From somewhere down below rose the unheard thumping of a compressor which had found an eigenmode and was resonating through the common room. Charles got up to open the door to stop it. Will, insensible as he was, inaureate Will, had gone back to his diagnostics.

Will was right. There was something going on here. Staff turnover had dropped and the astronomers could feel the change in the suddenly crowded corridors. What was the point of all these superfluous flicks? When the deep-space astronomers couldn't even...

Stung by a sudden insight, Charles jumped to his feet.

Will! he rapped out, startling the other man. Give me a virtual time-scale for E since June, with a projection.

Laconically, Will complied, and in rather longer a moment than formerly there it was. With compensation for the roughly twenty-five hour Eian day, time fell off precipitately. Then the Lazarides curve rose from below to melt into the horizontal axis.

What is it? Will inquired.

Eian time has been pulled into synchrony with ours, Charles explained, tracing the tail with his finger. Recognize this part here? It's a ninety cee probe falling into planetary time as it dumps energy.

Is it? Will peered at the glowing yellow line which

swelled brightly over the table in the under-lit room. It's upside down.

He tipped his head to one side. Who's messing with the
simulation?

Here, where it meets the baseline. Charles's finger cut
down through the projection.

Eighteen months ago, said Will.

Charles digested this.

That's about the time the Soster probe went missing, he
observed. The two discontinuities are overlaid, unless some
flick in Beijing has gotten them mixed up...

Will cleared his throat uncertainly. The drumming of the
compressor had begun again. Sucking his lip, Charles got up
and shut the door.

I wonder, he said, his hand still on the knob, if the net
understands that E is synthetic.

〈〈 〉〉

By the end of September the influx of flicks at Mazatzal was
obvious also to the flicks themselves, accustomed even as
they were to the indignities of overpopulation. The mailroom
was overwhelmed, commissary hours were extended to midnight, halls and waiting rooms were noisy. Housekeeping
even assented to recognize Charles Lehon's long obsolete,
erst, pluperfect fifth level room assignment in order to reclaim it for new staff. It was a pyrrhic victory though, because the net also objected now to Charles's unofficial cubby
up top. Finding under scrutiny this room to be uninhabitable
and presumably reprimanding some subroutine for having
overlooked the matter all these years, the net simply erased
the place. The now homeless Charles took this more calmly that anyone expected, retreating in dignity to bed space
which the net found for him in a working-class dormitory

after it had lost patience with Charles's pizza rinds and spent beer siphons littering the hut two work room.

Not long after this squabble over his address Charles was ordered off to Beijing by the ERF management, to a conference of telescope staff. This was far worse than bureaucratic snarls in housekeeping. For two days he raged through the laboratories and the commons before his annoyance wore itself out and he emerged again for a late breakfast, puffy and pale and subdued in unaccustomed dress.

I don't have a warm coat, he admitted, leaning a battered valise against one leg of his chair while he gripped a loaded cafeteria tray in his left hand. The valise slithered down to lie flat in the aisle and the tray sagged at its unsupported end. Various glasses of juice and bowls of gruel threatened to overturn themselves onto the table.

Hie, you're gonna —

Oh, sorry — and he settled with a crash.

What's that, peach congee? Drum asked as Charles began to unload his tray. The bowl looked small within the nestle of his long fingers, choked by those vines, those skinny fingers which enclosed a bowl like a snake winds around a boulder.

Mm. Listen, Drum... Go along to the shuttle with me. Do you have something else to do?

Where do peaches come from this time of year?

I don't know, Venezuela? — the shuttle, Drum? In half an hour.

Sure. Yes, of course, Charles.

Charles slumped down with relief in his chair and began to taste his concoctions with a stubby round spoon.

Needs witnesses, not to seem to be sneaking off, but Varda said it was travel nerves, that leaving home, going away — these gusts, tornados of anxiety and dread, not to disgrace himself by being dragged clawing and screaming onto the shuttle and needing the ballast of witnesses, needing to be seen leaving for Elsewhere still conscious and upright.

What if he *were* to be transferred, though? she wondered. Kicked upstairs or sent some other place devoid of revenants, devoided like a new planet is. Denested like a fledgling mockingbird, the way they do, onto the ground among the cats and weasels? She herself looked at the logbook and found that he hadn't been off station in fourteen years. Most of the rest of them hadn't either, of course, but *they* didn't have anywhere to go whereas station chiefs. This sort of thing, foibles in high places and so forth, was supposed to make Charles feel better about his inadequacies by showing off his own administrative skills, though in reality it sucked away hope because if he was really only middling then what hells must be those lives which cannot aspire even to the quotidian?

If we can't stand any higher than that, she muttered with disgust and pushed aside her breakfast gruel, no longer hungry, thinking about why she'd never been able to learn to play the trumpet. Too bad. Intimidated perhaps by that instrument's young voice, pure and piercingly clean.

Whereas.

⟨⟨ ⟩⟩

The shuttle, when it came, was full of new flick recruits who could be seen pushing for a spot at a window long before it settled on the pad. In the narrow waiting room Charles, standing between his valise and a small, lumpy traveling bag, shifted nervously from one foot to the other. Behind him, Varda and Drum eyed each other complicitly. With complicion.

Varda was in a speculative, detached mood. To them, she mused, meaning the gawking flicks, we're exotic as parrots. Those strange astronomers, life on other planets and so forth. This is a romantic spot — a wilderness in flick-time, an upside-down resort vacation.

Charles smiled tightly. The shuttle wiggled into place and cut off its engines, flopping down like a man letting his stomach sag. In an instant the waiting room was jammed with flicks shouting in five languages, pushing toward the door with their garment bags and their flat hard document cases. One by one their clearances were proofed and they popped out to the hall where orderlies briefed with identification photos waited to hustle them off, repeating over and over the greetings smothered each time by a tangle of bags, cases, passports, and apologies.

Where's Charles?

He had already gone. Alone, he was walking across the shuttle pad.

He didn't say goodbye, Drum complained. What did he want me to come here for?

The pad was windrowed with dark brown sand swirled into moiré by the shuttle's engines, but Charles scuffed heedless through the pattern. The yellow door slid home and no more than thirty seconds later the engines ignited again and the shuttle fell away in an arc to the west. Spreading its wings at the bottom of the arc, tail alight, it bored into the white sky and vanished over the Estrella divide. A little dust devil whirled across the pad and died upslope, among the cactuses.

I have to go field collecting tomorrow, Varda said after a thoughtful or possibly diplomatic or even simply aesthetic pause. Want to come along?

Drum hesitated.

Two days, or three. Forty, fifty kilometers. I want to walk back into Buckhorn Canyon again. Maybe as far as Fox Spring. Will can handle things here, until Charles gets back.

Drum lifted one shoulder, pouting a little at being asked

out only when Charles wasn't available. But then, Charles didn't go into the field, did he? Anyway, Varda ordinarily didn't want to put up with guests, she said once when Drum tried to invite himself along.

You're clumsy, she said that time. You scare the animals. I can't get anything done.

So why was Drum now to be permitted the sanctum?

Charles is insatiably curious, Varda went on unawares. He sucks all the air out of the room, as they say. You have nothing of your own.

She paused.

Or so I thought. Maybe what he wants is only to be liked. If you think he's interested in what you do then he will be. But he takes over everything, always.

Drum was beginning to be alarmed. These confidences put him in an awkward position.

Come on, she said. This is no place to talk. Let's get lunch.

The cafeteria on this level was intended for visitors coming through the shuttle port and was more elaborate than the ones father down.

The shuttle perimeter's sentry pondered their identity for a moment and then peeped them back into the building. The cafeteria was up the hall twenty meters. It had wide windows of thick thermal glass which gave a nice view of the mountains tumbling down into the cauldron. Varda chose a table in a corner, well away from the others and protected on two sides. They ordered from the jukebox on the table and sat back to wait. The coffee bot came by and left off two cups without asking.

How does it know to do that? Drum said.

You told it to, from so many years of never choosing anything else, Varda replied with a little amusement.

By such means did Varda Fleming begin, as cautiously

on her part as Drum on his, to sound him, to test by a light tapping with her finger whether he would give the right note, whether he could be trusted.

What do you suppose, she mused, the Directorate wants to talk to us staff for? Us weenies who don't even rate a network powwow usually?

Wants to stare us down, I imagine.

Ah. New policy, push off in a different direction, no dirty washing in public, that sort of thing. Hmp. I'd like to know why they care what we have to say.

Drum didn't reply and Varda, breaking her mysterious fascination with a cactus growing just outside, turned to him abruptly.

They don't want to leave any forts still standing in their rear, he said.

Ah. Of course.

This was no special astuteness on Drum's part, who was usually a little slow-footed in his political thinking and mostly kept quiet as the safest course in matters of tactics and diplomacy. It was Varda's unprotected posture which caused him to take the risk of saying something stupid. So, having begun, he now bleated his distress with Charles's intention of seeking a corner office.

Ho! Varda snorted. Charles wouldn't be happy among the brass, to say nothing of starting again at the bottom of the pole.

Then why does he complain?

He doesn't. Charles wants power only on a small, safe scale.

Well then, he has that.

No, Drum. He's ambitious, true — or was. Maybe he had trouble years ago settling down here. But the fact is, all he has is authority. He's lonely. He wants power so he can keep a harem. It's a pathetic imitation of friendship but it's better than nothing.

Drum was still bringing up the rear. A harem? he puzzled out. You're the only woman here, Varda.

She grinned.

It's an analogy, Drum. Keeping friends as you would in a harem. The fact that I sleep around is not... doesn't disqualify me for friendship.

She saw something now in Drum's gaze and shook her head almost imperceptibly. The tension collapsed. A server brought them juice, meatloaf, and a salad for Varda.

Look at this, she said, waving her hand across it like a magician with a silk scarf. Not a bit of it from anywhere hear here. Why do we eat this, and then complain about the weather?

What would you eat, sand?

Drum was infrequently snappish and Varda gave him a quiet appraisal.

You couldn't grow a hill of beans and squash here anymore, he said, contritely.

They ate, nevertheless.

Varda continued to talk, one spoonful at a time, confidentially. Herself and Charles. Or not, and someone else. Drum was acutely anxious, afraid she would spill something he'd have to touch.

Why was she saying these things?

So, he ventured. You don't think he's going to Beijing to hustle a transfer up.

No.

Varda eyed a nut in her salad suspiciously.

Why did he go, then?

Because, Drum, he was ordered to report.

Oh.

And to do what he can to save our little fifth planet from being destroyed to make room for a new hyperspace bypass.

Oh, I... what?

Varda poked at the supposed nut with the tip of her spoon. Then she pushed back, intending to leave.

A cashier bot rushed up before she was on her feet. A red bar tab holo popped out, rudely upside down, covering its face. Grumbling, Varda swiped the keypad with her thumb.

No good, the bot replied, and pushed the bill forward another ten centimeters.

Eh, what? she barked. That's what comes of going — she swiped her thumb again, more slowly — where they don't know you.

Invalid, the bot said, and the tab went from a sort of rust color to orange.

This seems to be happening more and more often, Drum observed while Varda was paying the bill with a laborious and insecurity-prone direct access. He was trying to be consoling. In fact, he himself had not had problems.

That's because you're small peanuts, Varda growled. A cruel remark it was, when Drum had sorted it out — that he was not consequential enough for the net to bother with.

It's sore with us, he'd overheard Charles saying to Will a few days earlier. They had been standing in the windowless instrument room and had left the door open for ventilation. Drum stopped outside in the hall, hoping to hear more, but there was only the humming of a transformer.

The net has messed up the Soster probe, Varda said when the cashier bot was finally appeased. They started out to leave the dining room.

What did the net do? We —

It's embarrassed, Varda said, ignoring him. It wants to let us know that if we rat there will be reprisals.

Oh, fer —

But Varda only shrugged, having gotten over her annoyance. The sentry in the elevator panel acknowledged her print without complaint and the door slid back. But she had begun to speculate and didn't get on.

What if you could double back on the security guard somehow and multiply yourself? she mused. I don't think the net has the metaphysics to deal with a true doppelgänger so long as it doesn't catch the two of you together. Virtual selves to go all sorts of places they aren't supposed to, while the flesh goes quietly home trailing its surveillance like panting suitors. Does the net understand the physical limitations on protoplasm, I wonder?

This was getting into Drum's expertise, but when he opened his mouth Varda signed to him — again, that slight crinkling at the corner of one eye, a slight motion of her head.

How does she do that? Drum said with exasperation to Charles some days later, when he was back from his junket.

Because it's illegible to cam analysts, Charles said.

No, I mean, how is it I know what she says?

Well, Charles replied with a slight drawl and put his feet up on the seat of an empty chair. Remember, the net was built from the cortex inward. It hasn't got a limbic brain — yet.

The elevator was begging, so Varda stepped back into the cage.

Why are two of you for? Drum said, made a little desperate by his total inability to read the situation.

Extra rations? Varda quipped as the door closed. She jammed it with her hand.

Bring a respirator, she advised, in case the wind picks up again.

And at last the elevator took her away.

⟨⟨ ⟩⟩

Now ensued a new period of waiting, of sleepy suspension,

everyone in his own bed wrapped up, nubbling their teddy bears.

Charles sat alone in the Council meeting room thinking over the situation. Presumably life went on without him, but then it never seemed to get anywhere much before yet another pointless morning. He felt a kind of mild paranoia or fear of being left out, but also a curiosity which afflicted him — he thought particularly — a night wanderer who once liked to sneak out and walk the late empty streets, envying the owls and jars and others who lived upside-down or inside-out or somehow differently. How long had it been since there were real owls in the streets, though? Three hundred years? For that matter, how long since there were streets? Probably it wasn't true, anyway, and things went on then more or less as they do — did — in brighter times, only more slowly from a kind of anomie or anemia of darkness when people were away, or asleep, or marking time until their blood sugar went up again.

Kalgoorlie, too, waited along with Mazatzal in entropical darkness for something to happen, for an unstable situation to resolve itself like a Fourier transform into components, factions — waited, still expecting to find it on the logs as the world turns and the watch is passed to them.

As for the other Kalgoorlie, the shadow one, their defenses had been thrown up long before, their entrenchments dug in. The Eians were a suspicious people, anxious squabblers, and always had been. Now they waited for a still-dim speck to grow brighter, fall to the ground, and break open. They who were made in this place, who came out of holes in this earth, had prepared themselves as best they could to die.

And all the while the creator gnawed on its queues, annoyed to find always little discrepancies, things moved about like the pieces of a chess match supposed to have been adjourned overnight. The new world was quickly becoming too complicated for all that talk, all those algorithms which left too much unresolved, unfinished, unfinishable. Stubbornly it gnawed, deep into nightbird time, at the end of a dark, empty hall in that single office still lit where someone was pondering the accounts, making adjustments, still clearing the books for tomorrow's business, as Charles remembered his mother doing when they wouldn't balance, adding up those long lists of numbers again and again, looking for that unmatched error, that malpractice, falsehood, that iniquity still not requited which kept the garment from falling into its proper shape like a bit of the cloth caught up in a wrong seam.

<< >>

Despite his promise, Drum didn't go with Varda into the bush. He took a rain check. If it ever rained. He'd go another time. Eventually. When it was someone else's turn at the puppet strings.

Charles was called to Beijing and returned looking worse than before. He slept eighteen hours, reappearing in the cafeteria one afternoon with both breakfast and lunch on his tray.

Big doin's, he confirmed to Will and Drum. Last time I was in Beijing it was a mausoleum. Now the place is crammed full. They put us up in bunks. Paul Lazard isn't well. He's got fat and muddle-headed, sweats a lot.

The other two men had long since finished eating, but even in mid-afternoon the commons — what used to be the astronomers' commons —was crowded, buzzing with polyglot noise that made it hard to understand what Charles was saying.

If this keeps up I'm going to go back to cooking for myself, grumbled Will. The three of them had a small corner table. These flicks are everywhere, like scurrying roaches.

Beijing is preparing for rendezvous, Charles said, poking through his bowl with his chopsticks and picking out a chunk of bean curd. We have a whole lot of retooling to do. No more retrospective analysis.

Drum rephrased this a bit as: stop trying to figure out what happened, just do it.

That's it. Charles piled up his empty dishes and leaned back with a cup of the tea he had brought back for everyone.

What retooling? Will wanted to know, feeling betrayed for all of them.

Upgrades, was all we were told. Something to be upgraded. Instructions and materiel to be forwarded as necessary. Flick business. Lots and lots of redesign to keep us busy. To keep you busy in particular, Will. Warehousing, analysis, presentation. All new stuff to be integrated and tested. Fundamental changes.

Hmp, said several offended voices.

Oh. There's a new data compaction algorithm.

Will stiffened very slightly and raised one eyebrow, but said nothing.

We're going to polish all the little shiny parts, too, Drum. Everything spotless and slick before the guests arrive.

Before the what?

Before that prodigal probe settles into orbit around E.

Everyone looked, stupefied, into his calm blue eyes. Apparently the moving finger, having writ, had moved on.

⟨⟨ ⟩⟩

And so did they all, of necessity, move on toward a rendezvous planned three generations before. No one knew what to expect from these people, possibly the most puzzling and alien beings imaginable. Themselves.

Drumlin McKechnie was one of these. Just now, being a little naive, a character transparent and vulnerable, with some capacity for introspection but less hampered than Charles Lehon by the sophisticated habit of analysis, that dichotomizing trick which helps everyone to balance their books, to keep account of these Mazatzal creatures, avatars, manifestations — among whom Drum was closest to the light. What he might have achieved at this early stage would have been something, an insight naively transparent and peculiarly visible to himself, perhaps a little banal as a consequence, but worth savoring, recounting, accounting for, as the first new growth, the cotyledons of what he hoped would become, with time and practice, more capable and assured. Humble Drum, not too self-respecting, never did learn his actual worth. His crucial self-delusion should have protected him from what, when older and wiser, he might have seen with his third eye — if he would be older at least, but that was not to be. Not even that.

And so the limitations and the possibilities there once were but were no more — indeed how could there have been possibilities otherwise, unless it were possible to vacate and dissipate them? They would have been not possible but certain, and Drum's hopes would have been dust from the first instead of returned to dust. Possibilities which the Eians had been given by their former selves and relied on for the wherewithal to purchase their lives, were whisked away in an instant, leaving only that small polished stone on which they had bet everything but which had never been seen until now, when the game was over and the swindlers were gone, leaving behind only this lump abandoned on the green baize which was the planet E.

Drumlin McKechnie was one of them, but one who, perhaps because he was less articulate than the others, had fewer means for catalyzing a peculiarly poignant sense of loss, that feeling of abandoned desolation which drives people now and then to invent all sorts of bizarre but hopeful faiths. Unprotected, he could see more clearly how they all recapitulate the rejected rabbit kit which rooted around and around the edge of the nest box, circling that vacant center until its natal supply of ATP was exhausted and the end, the inevitable consequence, returned another tired, blind, puzzled manifestation to the Tao.

Drumlin McKechnie was one of these. Being one of these, his role at present was not a very active one, not likely to influence events, at least directly or in ways which might ameliorate that pervasive sense which he had of being on the fringe, a mere spectator of distant, almost invisible occurrences, phenomena which others seemed to control: others less humble, and for that reason more powerful and thus also more enmeshed, tangled, constrained. So Drumlin McKechnie waited, watched, tried and failed to understand, to reclaim from the banal the daily life around him, to puzzle out the intentions and motives of Charles Lehon, Varda Fleming, Will Doblin, and the others he had known for years but still, now as then, strangers, perfect in their strangeness. Reporting what he saw or knew or imagined during this crucial period of waiting, while humanity prepared itself for a great transformation, for another struggle to free itself from —

From whatever it is we are not free of.

Varda Fleming opened the dormitory door. Wrestled it open, impatient with the now almost paralyzed infrastructure in the astronomy quarter.

Found something, she said, looking about to see who else might be there. But they were alone.

Charles made her a sour, wordless invitation and Varda sidled around the scattered furniture to sit on his bed, one nearest the door of a long column of beds in this particular warren, the clerical men's dormitory. She held out a small roughly cubical lump of blue plastic.

What is it? Charles asked finally. He took the blue stuff

from Varda's outstretched fingers. It was a watery translucent color, shot through with fibers which winked on and off
as Charles turned it under the light, crossing and re-crossing
in new patterns with each different orientation. The surface
texture was soft, almost oily, yet it was harder than a fingernail, at least. It seemed warm to the touch, but perhaps that
too was illusory.

Biopolymer, Varda said. Got it from a flick engineer.
Says its going into netcom on an attrition basis.

It's a storage medium?

Basically. But it seems to have some intelligent prop-
erties. Ability to reorganize itself on general instruction,
propagate complex patterns with cycles up to powers in the
hundreds. I don't know. The man who gave it to me wasn't
very informative.

You're going to do some tests?

Varda nodded, then burst out angrily. It's our own stuff,
Charles, she complained. Why can't we get specs on it without my having to steal it out of the net?

Charles only sucked in one cheek and began to chew on
it, saying nothing.

Evidently it's spread pretty well all over, she went on,
calmer but still with an angry tremor in her voice. We're the
last to get it.

Later in the day he ran a quick index check on biopolymer in net publications and found a couple of mentions, less
than a week old. Recalling the silence which had followed
his own recent publications, he felt the isolation, the suf-
focation of the backwater and for a moment, seeing Varda
flopped on her back on the bed staring at the ceiling, looking
at her, thinking of these new alarms, Charles found it actually hard to breathe. Allergies elaborating over the years into
something like asthma were now finally exposed as simple
fear.

It was fairly clear to Charles what had happened. He wanted to say that the planetary model — simulation — which they had been building up slowly, that increasingly detailed description, history, politics and so forth — that hypothetical E — had invaded or been sucked into, spread through the net and so, no evidence to the contrary, accepted as correct. True. As the case. But it wasn't correct. To *spread through* was one of those metaphors which hang on unexamined, like to *hand in*, preserving in language a defunct technology, culture, way of thought. Charles pondered the world soul. All present to itself, without center; the only structural principle being local significance. Nothing spreads in such a matrix. Either it's there or it's not. There is no *dawning* of enlightenment. Someone had wanted there to be such a thing and thus, just at the moment when it seemed there never would be, there was.

Why? Perhaps the advent of biopolymer had removed some barriers to a more elaborate and detailed world, and wherever the biopolymer could be found there was found, like a parasite, this belief in the existence of a habitable planet some several lifetimes distant. They had all wanted it as a cure for cosmic loneliness, in hopes of sedating the more local sort. The biopolymer version of reality was realer, a more powerful sedative.

But real to whom? Will remarked to Charles that the net itself made a good many routine judgments of significance, mostly on housekeeping chores, and it was probable that this notion of a soul was only an epiphenomenon governed by the law of succession of versions, something similar to the succession of forest trees.

So then, Charles retorted, the loss of the Soster probe provoked a reality crisis and the net jumped a track, putting the upgrade into distribution before it was ready?

Will's mouth turned down in a scowl, contradicted by

a shrug. Or it was a bureaucratic mistake, he said. Some administrator unknowingly legitimated the imagined but not yet imaginary planet E on the authority of one of those twenty-word digests that Martin is always asking for. Or perhaps he, this hapless, guilty functionary, simply couldn't tell the difference, and was tired of the kids wanting to know if we're there yet. When enough clerks are confused on some point then the comnet, democrat that it is, will follow suit.

Both of these hypotheses tickled his prejudices, but Charles suspected they were fatally simplistic. Running under such determinist mechanisms there was a twisting stream of desire, a will to believe, like an urban river covered over centuries ago and forgotten. Amid chaos and disintegration unknown for fourteen hundred years and an ecological crisis unknown since the end of the paleozoic, a substantial chunk of humankind was trying to build a galactic escape. True, it was a small beginning: one bot shot from a cannon. There was a pathetic discrepancy of scale and priorities here which pointed to a much deeper reality crisis. The net, after all, only mirrored a general human preference for meaning over unmeaning, purpose over vanity, which, it fondly deluded itself, found justification in the preference of matter for order over disorder. Like its human cousins, the net simply did not believe in pointless order. Atheist aesthetic degeneracy, it muttered, and went on with the business of issuing traffic tickets and balancing bank accounts.

But the truth, which to the semi-detached Charles was a truth profoundly ironic, was neither true nor profound to others who had been preparing themselves, he realized now, for months or years, perhaps all their lives. He had noticed how easily the flicks picked up the astronomers' jargon, beginning as long as two years earlier to talk of "E" through a sort of narrative magnetism. *Stories are phenotropic*, he'd heard it said. The association of stories with phenomena helped people to realize, make real, an abstract, imaginary bot of a mere few tons in the welter of isogravs, inert diagnostics, meaningless probability plots and tabular data which substituted for direct observation. For most people things are real and true only if and insofar as they are story-like.

Rousing himself, Charles ambled over to the dormitory's public com and asked for a requisition, which he began to fill it out.

Who are you talking to? Varda wanted to know, sitting up in bed across the aisle.

Com Directorate. Martin.

What? That bureaucratic slug?

While they waited for the request to feel its way through channels, Charles explained to Varda what he had been working out in his head. Soon enough the comnet requested an acknowledgement and, getting it, popped Martin up.

Yes, Charles? the slug began, but his mood was plainly as thin as slug slime on sand. Briefly, please: I'm clearing out here.

Indeed, the surface of Martin's desk was covered with paper directories. He appeared to be moving his files. Transferred, he confirmed petulantly. A muscle in his cheek which had been twitching now suddenly stopped jumping and lay still.

Well. I thought you'd never go, Martin. Where?

Martin did not reply at once. The muscle took up again. Tampa, he burst out, and stamped his foot.

What? That swamp?

What is your business, Martin rapped out. Charles demurred, now thinking it would be better to go below, to do business in tactile range, protoplasm-fashion. I'll send someone for you, Martin replied.

Send someone, Charles repeated. Martin, do you go around with an escort now?

Captain Martin barked with bitter laughter and winked out. Escort! he was saying. I can't even get the attention of the towel dispenser in the lavatory. I think it's composing a symphony.

Charles settled himself, while across the desk the communications chief cleared a space for his own elbows. Martin's heavy face was more than ordinarily flushed and from under the loosened collar of his uniform sprang a tuft of red hairs damp with sweat.

In any case, Martin went on, it keeps you out of com to come below under cover of escort. He shrugged off Charles's protest. Only the usual security, he said quietly. And in case the com weasels find me, I'm leaving tomorrow.

Who are we getting instead?

Sober ignorance: he didn't know.

Charles went quickly over the same ground that he had gone over with Varda half an hour earlier, but all Martin would say was that it was interesting, if true. And how does it concern you, exactly?

Non-plussed, Charles could not reply and the question was passed over. Thinking about it afterward, he concluded that Martin's hear-no-evil attitude was only an aspect of the more general determination — Martin's, the Foundation's, comnet's determination — to go ahead at all cost. Martin, after all, was only a local network manager, and not a particularly imaginative one.

The sum of it, Charles said, wrapping up his remarks to the rest of them that evening, is that anyone who hasn't thought about getting out had better take a look at the civil service list.

He sat down. There was some muttering around the table. Will and a few others scraped back their chairs.

What about E channel? asked a psychologist from the other end of the table. Charles and this man, whose Eian functions were mysterious, traditionally occupied opposite ends at Council meetings, but tonight he had been quiet. Security man maybe, or on the Horring research and development team.

Charles spoke flatly.

Denied, he said, along with all other communications privileges. Channel five reverts to internal administrative traffic.

A few others went out, the psychological spook among them. Then a few more. Finally only Charles, Varda, and Drum remained.

The three of them, always first and last. Two weenies and a bun, Fong would say.

I put in for telemetrics a couple of days ago, Drum reported placidly, and went on with his story despite Varda's contemptuous body language. No answer, he said. Application chewed up somewhere, I was told. All the wrong codes on it, I suppose. The old codes. Mazatzal Desert Reconnaissance they call it now. So I handed in a new form: MDR section four, zero nine zero, civil engineer grade thirteen. Denied.

Varda sneered. Denied? Anyone can lay cable.

There was a long silence. Charles drummed his fingers on the table.

MDR doesn't lay cable any more, he said. He revealed, perhaps.

What? Varda shot back. What do they do, then?

More sober ignorance: I don't know.

Well who does lay cable?

I don't know that, either. Possibly no one.

Varda gave a strangled, uncertain laugh and subsided. Another long silence followed.

Let us have the specs on biopolymer when you've finished, Charles said finally, getting up.

But Varda, with other things on her mind, having other objectives possibly more immediate than analyzing a quasi-intelligent pudding, darted after him.

Obsolete practice, laying cable, he replied. Agency transformed into a commando unit or something. Security patrol, made up from the only people who know something about desert survival. Go down into the sandstorm after... who? Exotelescopic biota. Outlanders. Hemlocks.

How goes the telescope then sans cables? Charles went on rhetorically. One-legged eye. Some new means of wiring the parts. Internal, ethereal, biopolymerical communication. Inward gaze. Sees Soster with its third eye now. No samsaroid illusions. No virtual worlds. Got there before anyone, the damned machine.

Charles started off disconsolately down the hallway toward the dormitory. Varda caught up again with him outside the commons. Uneasily mute, they walked side by side to the elevator and by thence by some silent agreement not to the dormitory but up top. They passed through the airlock and onto the roof, back into the canyon, following the base of the west wall for a hundred meters or so before Varda suddenly, angrily turned off to clamber up the slope in the dark, kicking down a shower of pebbles with every step. A species of tantrum, like putting one's foot through the wall when the neighbors are making too much noise. Kicking the earth. But soon she had to stop, panting and unable to climb farther. Charles, who had kept an easy pace, touched her arm gently when she came down.

There's a side canyon nearby, he reminded her, and led the way across the slope, then through a gap where a spine of the mountain fell away into the basin. Here a narrow declivity ran down to a ledge in the face of the bluff wall at the canyon's mouth. They were well above Mazatzal Station now. From out of the main canyon the building's three fingers gripped the tops of the granite dikes exposed by the eroding away of the softer rock around it. Out of the canyon's mute mouth, fingers from a mouth like a fossil cuttlefish. Softer rocks scoured away.

Varda had followed Charles's thought.

Yes, she said quietly. You infer by their absence, see them in the mind's eye like the flesh around a petrified spine, the soft parts of society. The poor. Are there poor people now? Always with us? Not possible to have no underclass. Plus a few icarii fallen from higher up, ex-directors, councilors and so forth, and a few euridices fallen back such as McKechnie, an ex-barrileño himself, encumbered like me by root and branch, withdrawing into the desert to wait, live on jawbones and honey and dressed in lion pelt. Lions are extinct now.

Desert patrol, she said with disgust. The man's true vocation after all these years of pretense.

Farther below, on the right, lay the cauldron, with the Estrella range forming its opposite wall. Beyond that lay more tumbled range, stretching away toward the Gila drainage to the south, looking like a rumpled bedcover in the moonlight.

Ought to see what I can do to give him a chance, Charles said. Give someone a chance while I can.

There's a little waterfall here in wet years, Varda reminded him.

Oh, yes. I remember.

You're in quite a funk, Charles. What else is there?

He shrugged. There's all this new surveillance, suspicion. INS is beefing up.

Varda waited for him to go on while the two of them looked out onto the desert from their high niche in the wall. The breeze still smelled of dust, but there was beginning to be a chill in it. It might rain soon. Perhaps a week. Little nightlights were beginning to pop out here and there, as if the stars were reflected in pools of water scattered in hollows across the high ground around the cauldron.

What grotesque, antique imagery from the days before the Sand People. The nightlights were theirs, ten meters below the surface dust.

Charles took a deep breath, grateful for the absence of a mask for once.

I suppose, he said, the real reason they had us all come to Beijing was to see how far they could trust us. Paul's dying, I think. Arne's comfortable as the figurehead now. That leaves me, and a few younger men in Beijing. There hasn't been any new blood for a long time. It's been all engineers and programmers for years. Martin was pretty explicit. He knows why he was sent all the way down to Tampa. Slugs go down to Tampa to make room for other people on their way up, to high places. Suddenly become high places.

Are *you* to be left behind, Charles?

Bureaucratic orogeny. We haven't done any real astronomy in years, anyway.

What about Will and the others?

What I told them. They'll be all right if they want to be. Engineers and programmers, I said.

And you?

I could stay on as team leader. So long as I took orders through comnet and didn't insist on spying, on lifting up anyone's skirts.

Orders from who?

I don't know. And that's the problem, isn't it?

A thorn had stuck through Charles's moccasin, which he found and worked out. Below, a repair party was returning out of the Mazatzal cauldron, their five yellow sodium lights making at first a brilliant spreading glow which then resolved into tiny points as they emerged out of the dust. From off Varda's left came the thud of a bird's wings as it rose from a coppice in the canyon.

He rubbed the thorn between his fingers, speculating.

I'll find something to do, I suppose. It will mean going
below.

Biopolymer. It was tempting to focus on that stuff, whatever it was, it being always easier to find excuses for change
than to admit the real causes. And there was a handy metaphor for what had happened: the saguaro which grows up
below a palo verde, the tree nursing the delicate cactus within its branches until finally the saguaro supersedes and kills
it. Why does the cactus succeed the tree? Because it's better
adapted? Adapted to what?

Because it gets the water first, Varda said. The saguaro's roots are shallow and wide. The deep-rooted tree dies
of thirst.

What a metaphor on intelligence, Varda.

Isn't it? Not worth a damn, intelligence. What will happen to E now? Just vanish?

I expect they'll mooch on without us, access denied, living on some pemmican of biopolymer jerky and chokecher-
ries. They'll get by. When you're learning how something
goes, things don't always, at first, get done in the right order.
Since the start of this adventure we've thought of it as an
expedition into deep space. Why else would we have needed an exobiologist? A psychologist of course, any emigrant
group might expect to have problems of that sort, especially
one which is compressed, isolated in a field station, an outpost, for a century. And also a geologist to keep an eye on
the unstable ground — to align or calibrate the astronomers
as well as the telescope. And certainly someone to collect
the exotica, a Beagle Boy or a Cook. So, sailing to Mazatzal,
this expedition into not any longer uncharted but still uninhabited desert — uninhabited by scientists, anyway. Things
don't always get done right the first time. It's a question now
of transforming a one-camel dash into a genuine expedition,
like making a painting after a sketch. Perhaps you would like

the process of getting from place to place to be less intuitive, more studied, more like being born (again and again) than like this dreaming, like a dream time from which you have to learn how to wake up. It shouldn't simply take you, this process — you go in here, come out there. Pfft. Eventually the business will be industrialized, scaled up, but for the time being it's all custom work. So while they puzzle out what to do next, route closed, detour for construction, they'll mooch on without us.

Meanwhile, the whole astronomical clan was meeting again.

The Troubles, Maldonado said. He was sitting with his aide de camp in the darkened council room of Government House looking at the city spread below. It was a small city, really. Compact, with a distinct edge where the buildings stopped and the desert began. It looked sometimes as if it weren't fully attached to the ground, but just lying there. There was a dark streak across the center — the barrio, like a belt buckled tight. The rest glowed yellow with strings of streetlights and spangled windows, and above the sky was a blue-black of hidden stars.

In time we'll capitalize that, he said. The Troubles, or the period of Warring States. Reduced again to a notion, an imaginary cosmos more tractable, convenient, comprehensible than the actual obdurate one. The Troubles — at least by Eian reckoning, our calendar having a ruck in it, because of certain reforms, so that Eian time seems to meander back and forth in big loops across the main channel. The Troubles begin now, with this infall. They will destroy us just as we destroyed the people of the dream time. Now, date 159e old style.

The aide, a young man, kept silence.

《 》

I haven't seen Charles for weeks, Drum was saying. He took a side of pickles to go with his sausage.

No, Varda replied absently as she tested the pies with her fork, looking for one that was fresh. Will says Charles is reading a lot.

Fong Ou-shih, on the earlier shift, was just finishing up at their usual table along the wall, tucked out of sight around the corner of the small orangery.

You're late tonight, Ou-shih, she commented as they sat down. The astronomer nodded to his colleagues but said nothing and went on eating the last bits of a risotto as he gazed unseeing at the crush of diners, to which the great variety of uniforms lent a festive illusion. At first they had played at spotting new ones, at guessing the rank, service, or country. Now there was a standard reference, updated daily, and the fun was gone out of that.

Then Fong Ou-shih spoke up suddenly, breaking his reverie. I've been approved for a position on the next E transport, he said. He smiled diffidently and dabbed at his lips. Drum's attention was fixed on three grains of rice sticking to the side of Ou-shih's bowl.

What transport? he managed finally, trying to wave away the dull fog in which shock had wrapped him. He was making an effort to concentrate without really wanting to hear. From the side of his eye he saw Varda smile and look down, and guessed that his advertance, his show of heediness, had been less than perfect again.

But Varda was seeing instead the madwoman on the street who Charles had told her about, who muttered and whisked at the demons besetting her.

I see you're pleased, Ou-shih, Varda said brightly, choosing to cover the gap, to exercise her politesse on Drum's behalf. Can you guess how they'll manage it?

Manage what? Drum said, refusing to be rescued.

Ou-shih smiled more widely, nodded, exercised his own politesse, said nothing. Either he couldn't guess or he wouldn't. Maybe he knew already, how this new way of crossing over was going to work.

Politely, she supposed. I see you're outbound. Will you step this way?

When Ou-shih had eaten his three grains, bussed his dish and gone, Varda sighed unhappily. Obscurely embarrassed, Drum now held his tongue.

Plans for a colony transport were announced this morning, Varda said sadly. Said muse-like, detached but with a hint of regret, sighing as do so many artists for lost edens, knowing what this would mean for her now. At least for her, if not the others.

I quit reading those announcements, Drum replied, a bit more roughly, defensively, than he ought to have.

Varda started to say something more but brought herself up short, digging a fork into her own risotto with unexpected anger.

Drum laughed uncomfortably, observed that Ou-shih must have put his application in pronto, counted months on his fingers.

Last spring, he told me.

What? Before the hiccup? Secretive devil.

Mm.

But then she relented, elaborated. Foundation people have been planning this for a while, apparently, she murmured, beginning to practice their conspiratorial ways. All they were waiting for was a confirmation from the probe. Got that sixteen, seventeen months now. So it's the colony ship.

What ship?

Varda clapped her hands in frustration. Who knows?

They've built a ship somewhere. Behind the moon, eh?

Ou-shih knows, Drum asserted. What evil lurks. Reminds me of a niece of mine, lurks around picking up people's secrets, perfect epistemic black hole. What ship? They're going to send actual dead people to E?

Yes, Varda said. What about the passengers? Suspended animation?

Not possible.

But why not? What have we been playing at here for so many years? Varda whispered fiercely, breaking her plastic fork. Say it's so, it's so. No one tells us anything. Knock some people on the head, and when they wake up tell them its four-score and ten and welcome to the new world. I'm surprised they feel we have to observe the proprieties and wait for confirmation.

Confirmation?

Yes, she said tiredly.

Of what?

Varda gazed speculatively at Drum for a long time before apparently deciding not to do whatever she was considering.

Drum, she said, not bothering to hide any condescension. We all know what the probe will find on E. A native population.

Who?

Us.

This time the wait was even longer. Varda gazed steadily at Drum, and when she spoke her voice was no longer at all kind.

And you know what happened to native populations. The Foundation is playing in real time. We've left them with a discrepancy. Who are these people, these aboriginals, and how did they get here? Any number of explanations might be found. Say the remains of a slaver from another galaxy. But it would be much simpler just to ignore the a-chronicity.

Dump Kalgoorlie and start over.

Drum was beginning to grasp the source of Varda's anger. Like dumping test data, he said.

It isn't *like* that, Varda returned impatiently. That is *just* what it is. We're test data. Have you tried to access the E simulation recently?

No. Too slow. No one goes there anymore.

Will tells me it's gone. Since this morning. Kalgoorlie is *not there*. The planetary data has been intercalated with other astronomical results and the index link to the sky chart expunged and inquiry calculations are rated zero. Drum, a wild guess has a significance higher than zero.

Drum's stomach bumped over. Dead. Expunged.

Have you considered, Drum, Varda said, sitting now way too close, how we are going to run simulation tests of our hypotheses on colonization? Because the ERF doesn't care any more about predictive testing, she hissed, pushing even closer. Because E has popped out of hypothetical space. Hypotheticals are irrelevant, significance zero. The last chapter of the book has been torn out. Hypotheticals are so much hydrogen gas and no one cares about the last chapter of gas. Has there ever been a comparable human experience to this? When Uncle Emo emigrated to Colchis in ought-nought? Or Ulysses sailed for the uttermost West? Not even a postcard, the scum.

So Ou-shih has decided to kill himself. No wonder he seemed a little distant.

They'll begin again with Kalgoorlie, of course, Varda was saying, because that's where the strata of fact are thickest. I wonder if the net feels anything like deja vu when it recalls something from zero significance.

Drum was staring at his fork. Or his hand, rather, wrapped very tightly around it.

Maybe it's like that little frisson you get in the lab sometimes, she speculated. When the numbers start coming out and you just *know*. Before any analysis you just know what they mean. Satori.

Drum made some deprecating noises, but she cut him off. That's just what it is, she insisted. Satori. Finding god.

Drum only raised his eyebrows a fraction.

He cut into his sausage, which had grown cold, but was stopped by thought.

They're sending a transport ship, Drum began, to... Where are they sending it, exactly?

We don't know that yet, do we?

Um, uh... he spluttered, just now catching up. But... real people. Digitized or something? Ou-shih is going on... Really, he's really killing himself. So Ou-shih thinks he's... Does he?

Varda shrugged and gazed vacantly into the crowd.

You're dinner's cold, Drum.

Eh?

He looked down, where the white cereal which had leaked from his sausage lay congealed on the cold plate.

Varda reached out for his hand. Her eyes on him were hard, but she held his hand with a different emotion.

⟨⟨ ⟩⟩

The break room, erstwhile Council chambers, was not big enough for everyone to crowd in, especially with the intrusion of numerous spies and curious flicks. There was some milling about until a spontaneous decision was made to move down to the dormitory.

By this time the relatively small number of astronomers and engineers had been doubled by flicks and the people who had been lounging in the dormitory were pushed aside. Many of those found other places to sit, kibitzing angrily, so all together they formed something of a rabble.

Charles climbed onto a table and diffidently began the meeting. Their purpose, he said, was to pool their knowledge concerning the condition of E and of transport plans, and to discuss whether a position needed to be taken.

This second point was something Varda had insisted on during their meeting in the dry gorge in the mountainside above the lab. Charles had been puzzled, and taken aback by her seriousness and urgency. What position? he had wanted to know, but Varda wouldn't elaborate.

Why do we need a position? What is there to dispute? How can we go into a meeting and say we want to talk without saying what about?

But that is what he did, nevertheless.

The sum of their knowledge about the re-discovered planet in the neighborhood of its marker star Soster was very little. The senior astronomers had learned nothing.

At one point Will leaned toward Varda, who he had taken some trouble to keep close, and whispered that, considering who was in the room, it was unlikely that anyone who thought he had inside knowledge was going to spill it.

Varda tilted her head a centimeter to one side, making inconspicuous acknowledgement.

As to whether a position was needed, the discussion quickly became a melee. Clearly something needed to be aired but no one could work out what it was. There was a lot of incoherent shouting.

Varda clambered up onto Charles's table, pushing him off. Smiling privately, an expression which might have been provoked by the bad behavior of a sister or a cat one has no intention of correcting, Charles sat down on the floor nearby. Someone offered the corner of a bed, but he refused.

How many of you have taken the offer for free transport to E? she cried.

About twenty hands went up. She fixed on Ou-Shih and Garth. Do you know where you're going?

The question was rhetorical. Everyone on the team down to the screwdriver people could recite the sidereal co-ordinates of Soster's dim companion. That was not where she meant.

Do you know what's waiting?

Weeds! someone shouted.

Weedy people, she returned, brisk. War. Mayhem. Extermination.

General incomprehension at the thought of armed weeds. Varda jammed her hands into the pockets of her denim outback pants and rounded down her shoulders defensively. Then she rallied, stamped on the table top with one heavy desert boot.

Who here thought it was a good idea to overrun the Yukon Islands?

Some murmuring. With a little theater, she began with one hand to ostentatiously brush the dust off her rumpled heavy shirt. She flicked at the folds with the backs of her fingers, then raised her head again.

Iceland? Newfoundland?

Muttering and discontent.

Well, just in case you missed out, she hollered, and sat down.

These elliptical sentences were met with puzzled annoyance. Goaded further, she popped up again, but then plumped down on the floor beside Charles without saying anything.

What are you on about now? Charles whispered wearily. They want to hear about paychecks and summary transfers.

Varda snorted and returned to her original seat on the folding chair beside Will, pushing aside a short flick who was about to sit down.

When it was clear she had done speaking, after a respectful moment which people seemed to think she was still owed, the shouting broke out again. Nothing could be made of it except possibly that a number of people wanted the toilets cleaned more regularly, and Will said something Varda couldn't hear. Here and there in the crowd were some men who, by turning this way and that in a pattern counter to the moving knots of dispute, showed themselves to be in the decipherment business. Com analytics would sort it out.

All will be revealed, Will said, a remark which itself was revealed by falling into one of those sudden inexplicable hiatuses when everyone comes to the punkt at the same time.

Growing tired of this, people began to drift off. The disturbed sleepers pulled the covers over their heads again, and the readers clicked over their bookmarks and turned on their backlights.

Varda turned to Will and began speaking with low intensity, taking his elbow to steer him away from both Charles and Drum.

This isn't a cocktail party, she said to Charles, who was closest, causing him to step back. The little smile was gone.

A small group of astronomers reformed in the hallway around the malcontented exobiologist. After a bit of rapid wrangling it was decided to hole up in Will's instrument room.

It was windowless and hot with eight of them in that small cave of glowing vid lines. Projected probabilities of the more significant diagnostic markers zipped across their faces and chests like miniature lightning in green and yellow and scarlet and an almost invisible ghostly ciel.

Varda took the floor at once. Now she was specific and blunt in her accusations.

What, Garth said in his sanded voice, about our experience with cathedrals? They took generations, enormous public resources, consumed lives, only for a scrap of transcendence. What you are calling transcendence.

Stonehenge, added Krantz the mathematician. The Mayan observatories.

The cave paintings, said Olga, who had actually seen Las Eyzies and Altamira, the only person in the last forty years to do so. No one knew what kind of influence or money Olga must once have had. Now she was an inconspicuous old woman, a human zohar who stuck herself to events and was seemingly always *there*.

What I mean is, she went on quietly, that art is a sort of invocation, a spell-casting ceremony which calls up the guides, regents, paladins of the demon world.

This was metaphorical and allusive in the extreme. They all waited for the explanation. Varda's thin improbable voice commanded mysterious authority.

You must go forward, she said, once you have invoked your birthright and asked for their protection. You cannot look back.

This explained nothing, apparently. Charles noted, but kept his peace. Will the pragmatist waved it all away with a visual snort.

To all intents and purposes, he said, E is a habitable planet orbiting a reddish sun a bit over a hundred light years from here. It has two moons and four near neighbors. You may choose to believe this. The probability of it is high. We are all familiar with the same principles of verification for the history of subatomic particles, extra string dimensions, and so forth, even if we are not in the actual business of versifying counterfactuals. E is posited habitable; Earth is patently not so. Or not so any longer by us — when we have all gone to E and unburdened the biosphere it will pretty quickly recover.

Will paused. His fingers, long, bony and spatulate, were always moving in the air with curious motions — capture, enfolding, probing, unfolding, farewell — which distracted attention from what he was saying. When his voice was silent his fingers stopped moving and one woke with a start, remembering nothing of the dream. It was an unconscious habit of Will's. Charles and Varda had learned to guard their eyes.

These reasons, he went on, supplement the more fundamental percipience which Olga, our Manichean Zarathustra, has urged on us.

This way of speaking, endogenous and hermetic, pulled together the little group of people who had engaged in this discussion with each other for years. They were all of a cosmological bent, they had time on their hands, they had the interest and the means to familiarize themselves with anything they chose. Will's emollient words produced a moment's sodality, which he shattered.

Rubbish, he said. Our original intent has been overlaid, burdened, crushed by an encrustation of bad faith, greed, delusion, narcissism, and ignorance which has induced us to throw up ever grander and taller spires until one of these makeshifts you call a cathedral is bound to fall down. That it has done.

The fingers halted in mid-gesture. Will looked — peered — at each of the seven others in turn. All this was unaccustomedly intense coming from Will, and disconcerting. Some shuffling and jostling exposed their anxiety.

But none of us, Will went on, is able to face the nihilism which lurks underneath, so we turn to *art* in search of order and comfort, and during the night our minions whisk away the rubble. Now it's morning and we are staring at this stump of a tower, a spire, and claim to have finished the job. The iconographers and designers have also been busy in the night. It seems this is what we intended all along — one spire and one stump.

We can't look into the abyss, he said, jabbing the air with each word. So we push into it all the rubble and thousands of bodies, hoping to fill it up.

What thousands? Garth said, in his rough voice sounding a probably unintentional snarl.

I'm having none of it, Will said emphatically after a dramatic pause.

He walked out of the meeting, closing the door with incongruous delicacy after him. The others were stunned by
this quite unfamiliar behavior. After a bit, Varda got up and
went after him. She did not shut the door.

《 》

So now the key players, the personalities or personas —
reduced to personas temporarily, emptied or hollowed out
— on whom the future of E once depended were all pushed
to one side, out of harm's way, put into storage so to speak
where they could occupy themselves for a while getting a
grip, consolidating their knowledge, a kind of sabbatical in
which to seek the next stage of enlightenment while others
did the world's business on their behalf. Others not entirely identifiable, not so much faceless as statistical, a time of
ordinary little people pushing forward worldly business by
old principles until a new era of instability, like a sand dune
piled up to a critical angle, permits small incremental actions
to precipitate large events. Catastrophes imply that unstable times always decay unhappily, always run to the bad,
which Charles supposed was true from the viewpoint of the
few individuals singled out by happenstance to move the last
grains of sand, like happening to be the billionth custom-
er of some big store, that from such a summit, from which
acme or culmination everything seems to run catastrophical-
ly downhill, but from the viewpoint of the rest farther down,
incremental and anonymous others, valuing stability rather
than change with the exception of a few hungry and unhappy
romantics starved by unfulfilled cravings, at the bottom of
the pile such times would seem catastrophic indeed. Varda
and Drum, each seeking their own sort of apotheosis, fled to
the outback while Ou-shih moved in the opposite direction,
toward some dimly sensed rapprochement seeming autono-

mous and freed of will but in reality bounded as any other.

Charles had by this time withdrawn into a vague, opportunist, self-protective interpretation of the goings on at Mazatzal and of what he knew of the wider world of Foundation policy and the trend of events, only poor and unsubstantiated knowledge which might have been safely ignored. And so would miss his chance, was doomed in fact to struggle with illusion for a long while yet, while the more robust, fit, or simply reckless seemed to pass the gateless gate with ease. Perhaps that was an illusion too; perhaps Charles might have consoled himself with the supposition that the quality, the depth or profundity of his final understanding would be proportional to the struggle of achieving it. Probably not. Probably it wouldn't be. And so he too, following along or coming after like Jesus after John, might have wished. But he knew it would be more like the last son of a last king, his inheritance decapitated, destined to rot in the dark of some Jacobin prison, echoing pantographically Charles's life at Mazatzal by Maldonado's at Kalgoorlie. Supposed life, now that contact was lost.

Anyone is superfluous who believes that the cosmos sets a high value on efficiency and orderly procedure.

Charles's pre-occupations were drifting farther and farther from the business of Mazatzal Station. Now that the telescope was shut down and the E simulation discontinued there was nothing productive to do. They were all waiting for the next crisis in a backwater cut off from crises.

Charles contemplated a series of lectures or talks on what might be topics of interest.

Not-thereness is a relative quality.

A discourse on the theory of narrative epiphanies.

The encomium as a rhetorical envelope.

Redaction is a dysfunctional response to welter.

Whether the pianist's humming rightly presages the entrance of a new theme by the cello or ought to be suppressed as an outlier.

This last after a Beethoven quartet was performed one night in the commons by an ad hoc flick group attempting to recapitulate the experience of the original audience. Unaccustomed ears heard only unmeaning confusion. The seven movements written on a whiteboard nearby, all melted together, soaked like bread in a fondue of uniformed prestos cut down by a wall of molto poco adagios, all in the end lying quietly dead in a mire. Say, someone was overheard to say as the clapping began, that's only three, isn't it?

More propositions with which to pass the time:

Complexity is the natural result of trial and error and cannot be achieved except by deliberate mistake.

 Significance is not a property of events. Contrariwise, meaning is inherent in noise.

Nostalgia is a disease of history.

You need to hear it again, someone said after the concert. Do you think we could ask?

Did you think it was beautiful, then? I remember, I don't know, some squonks…

Beautiful. Well, it made sense. Is that beautiful? What I want to know is why I had to be locked up in order to —

And they were lost in the crowd, simply voices which Charles had been unable to locate, to see who was speaking.

He went for a walk through the tangle of hallways cut into the mountainside without paying much attention, into a badly lit, vacant region.

Yes, someone said, just a watery voice which leaked out of the dark narrow passage accompanied by a rank smell which belied the affirming word — We are here.

This gnomic portent made Charles smile at last. It was a piece of silliness which caused him to raise his head and take stock.

An assignation, probably. The carnal smell he had imagined lingered, and he resolved to go and see Varda before her disaffection grew any more. Before the saguaro which now towered above the dry sticks of the dead palo verde which it had overcome, the tree which once nurtured and gave it life, before that inevitable succession ended a molto adagio of faint, almost unheard notes.

Varda was no longer to be found, as once was, in the laboratory at all hours. Charles guessed she might be outside, sitting on a rock in that arroyo they had found which gave such a good nighttime view when the moon was near full.

He was right.

She knew who it was by the crunching of his feet, and laid her hand on another rock nearby without turning, as a sign that he was welcome. Charles sat where he had been invited to and kept silent.

Varda cleared her throat, a small noise somewhat like purring.

You're out here at night much of the time now, he observed, taking her permission.

She shrugged, mostly a turning of her hands palm up in resignation.

What should I do, Charles? What is a biologist, exo or otherwise, doing with a lot of astronomers studying life in a place never less than wholly imaginary? You wanted a novelist, I think, for that.

You haven't requisitioned any new genomes in weeks, Varda.

Of course not. What good is a parts list now? What is the point of assembling these creatures, endless variants on optimums from our past, in search of one which might be beneficial to people living off-world? Off-world as they say, as if there were only one and everything else is off it.

Whether there is only one or not is irrelevant now, Charles said quietly.

Of course it is. I'm out of a job. Any writer with a decent mind can do now what I was the only one here who did. Did that.

What then? I gather you don't think much of what the Foundation is offering.

Snort. Very percipient of you, Charles.

Yes, after you stood up and called us all genocides.

Without a scrap of moral sense. I might as well have been dancing naked on the piano top.

Charles sighed, the whistle sub-audible. I know, he began — that is I imagine what it cost you to speak up.. You're very secretive, Varda. Protective of your feelings. It was an outburst, nothing else.

You're saying it's deniable.

An excuse might be made.

Isn't that what I was in a rage about? Excuses? People who don't — ahh, hell. It's none of your business, Charles. You're one of them.

Charles winced, a gesture unnoticed in the dark.

Thanks for the memories, she said with some acid.

Ah.

You're supposed to say 'you're welcome,' you boor.

Well but I don't think you are welcome, Varda. I'd like them back, you know, memories, if you're only going to pawn them.

Heh. No, they're pretty light, I think they'll go in my luggage.

Down below, a search party was coming up out of the dust.

⟨⟨ ⟩⟩

Winter brought cooler weather and a thin gray sky to Mazatzal station, and at the end of January the wet monsoon gave a few weeks of intermittent rain. The crowds of pushing flicks seemed thinner, too, as they learned their way about. The former telescope staff kept more and more to themselves, worked late hours, slept in the labs on the second level, cooked on improvised facilities or ordered food in from the commissary. There was less to do every day: some routine maintenance, monitor operations for investigators conducting research from remote sites, sign forms. Varda amused herself with longer and longer field trips to gather plants to test for desert ecotoxins, local knowledge she seemed to think was important.

Cats. Charles hadn't remembered cats for a long while. No one at Mazatzal kept pets except for one parrot and one tortoise left over from a now pointless cultural practice gone extinct everywhere else. Along with the cats.

The feral cats had done well on corpses for a while but it didn't last. The vultures did well on the cats but that didn't last, either. Lots of birds were gone now. So of course there were no birds on E, either. People can imagine only what they already know.

Charles decided to resign. Before the end of February he intended to call a staff meeting to announce his departure.

Varda sat up, suddenly alert. Her intuition was confirmed by the next announcement, that the assimilation of the Soster project was complete. Some of us have gone already, Charles said, and the support staff are very noticeably reduced, so no one will be much surprised. Varda Fleming will be reassigned to the desertification project and will stay on at Mazatzal for the time being. Ou-shih and his colleagues will go to the E departure preparation site in China, after six weeks of preliminary briefing at ERF in Paris. I will be going with them, to head up a small mapping team.

Drumlin McKechnie stood up, stiff and ill at ease.

I too, he said in too loud a voice, am going. With one

hand he made a hooked gesture which ended awkwardly, in mid-air. He seemed about to say more. Everyone waited, but after rocking onto his left foot a couple of times he sat abruptly down.

General puzzlement, until the gossip made its way around the group that Drum had been accepted into Mazatzal Desert Reconnaissance. His survival training would begin in only a few days.

The border patrol. Search and destroy.

There was a spatter of clapping at Drum's long looked-for success.

Ou-shih stared at his hands, spread flat on the table. Will slouched in his chair, a little smile at one corner of his mouth which might mean anything if the hooding of his eyes did not give it a seasoning of suspicious superiority. Varda felt that she was staring and jerked her gaze away from Drum, but then felt she had betrayed herself instead and dragged it back.

Charles, his last responsibilities discharged, sat not un-seeing, legs crossed, hands lying one atop the other on his lap in plain, that is humble as well as manifest, expression of his new relationship to the others and to the world of samsara. After the others had gone he sat on, waiting, but no one came. As he rose at last to his feet the light went out. Like a sleepy host hastening the last departure, the net had turned it off.

⟨⟨ ⟩⟩

Some weeks before, Charles had been lying as usual stretched out on his bed in the dormitory. He was meditating, or had been until a fly disturbed him; now he was merely lying on the bed. A bit of incense was giving up its last smoke. The light in the wall sconce beside the door had faded to a senti-mental orange glow. The clock and the vid on the table beside his cot were hooded. Water ran faintly in the pipes near his ear, and distant music breathed, swelling and fading in slow aspiring rhythm. Even the fly now lay dead, carefully placed on the near corner of the bedside table. Charles was lying on his side, hands between his drawn-up knees, staring at the dead fly. Without thinking he had killed it, in a manner like brushing away a hair. The fly was also lying on its side. It was just a fly, slightly crushed. He was vaguely disappointed about that.

He sat up, put on his shoes, and went out. One block over the main thoroughfare was, for an hour or so, quiet: uniformed flicks passed on squeaking rubber soles, a laboratory gurney rolled along with a load of clinking glassware. Even here on level five the air smelled of rare rain. Charles blended himself into the traffic going south, toward the elevators.

On level one the smell was strong, almost choking. The first drops of vinegary rain had struck the musty, spore-laden, alkaline earth, releasing that odor which lingered indoors for hours. Drops rattled against the shutters, filling the darkened hallway with the sound of Chinese new year. Anxious not to miss any of the squall, he pounded up the iron stairs onto the roof, eager yet obscurely worried.

Huge drops like crystal marbles were falling. The first ones to strike his skin were cold, but that passed as soon as his shirt was wet through and even the pelting of the heavy drops was soon felt only indistinctly on his now deadened shell. A slapping wind was up. He turned his back to it, feeling his way along the railing to the end where a familiar path went on into the canyon. There, where the building poked into the mountain's wall like a finger into a pudding, the way was blocked by the limb of a mesquite broken off by the wind. Thorny twigs caught on his wet clothes as he scrabbled through this obstacle and onto the puddled rock. Such a brittle tree. Huge branches torn off by every storm, and not a particularly fast-growing wood, either. More so here perhaps, where leaking sumps give it more water than was good for it. The ones growing in the natural desert were smaller, tighter. Hunched-up, even, and more resilient

The rain was slacking off already. A flitting moon appeared as the overcast was broken up into scud by the following wind. Charles pushed on up the canyon, his thoughts occupied by other things. He wanted to get high up, to look down. Veering to his left, feeling against the wall for a way, stomping unconscious over cactus and cat's-claw and salt bush, he found the gap, choked with blocks of limestone fallen from the ridge. Into this he made his way, clambering over the wet rock on all fours, and this cleft brought him up again to the top of the dike, a thin ridge separating the main body of the mesa falling away to the west. The dike, perforated by veins of softer rock, scored with clefts and pipes like the one he had just shinnied up, stuttered away in a broken line into obscurity. In that direction he walked a bit, but it was hard going along the top of the ridge, cut up as it was, and soon enough he plumped down on a square block of stone. The upward face of this stone was wet and black; its side, exposed where it had broken away from the wall above, was pale tan in the moonlight. Charles's mind was beginning to clear of its thoughts, and he sat for a while lightly rubbing the flat, fine-grained stone. The newer, unvarnished surface felt dusty when even wet.

His trousers and socks were choked with cactus spines, which were beginning to work through the cloth. He took the socks and trousers off. Sitting barefoot and bare-assed on a wet rock, he picked hopelessly at the hair-fine prickles.

Stupid, he muttered, laying his trousers to one side on the rock. Stupid blundering around in the dark.

He shivered a little, but the wind was not cold and as his shirt dried the shivering passed. Slowly, as the tension drained away from his muscles, his body began to feel lighter.

Charles had never liked the desert, without especially disliking it either. All his earliest life he lived in cold cities, completely within those urban networks of tunnels and buildings which were so much alike, from Paris to Perth. The out-of-doors meant a hallway to him. Owls and cactuses and the whole desert apparatus were, like Kalgoorlie, all invented by Charles himself, perhaps real but still somewhat alien and delicate, like a painted plate which he held not with a potter's intelligent fingers but like a shopper with empty pockets, afraid of dropping it.

They had put this leg of the telescope in a desert because Mazatzal and Woomera were both desert stations, not because anyone except Varda was particularly fond of their harsh but grand home. Its Eian copy was likely to be not so grand. Copies aren't.

What, he wondered, would Ou-shih find there, wherever it was? But what did that mean — really there? No more than that Ou-shih would not be able to fiddle little pieces of it on a whim? As Per Hemla tried to do early on by inventing kissop weed? But there was too much at stake now. The weight of experience was too heavy, too complex, to allow little aberrations to spread like Hemla's weed. If Ou-shih were to decide for himself that Kalgoorlie really was a weed-choked outpost guarding an imaginary border probably no one would object, and it wouldn't change anything other than Ou-shih's test scores in Paris.

So they all, from the earliest childhood of the race, experienced the world as ever less plastic, less responsive, more alien and obdurate, and themselves ever smaller and more inconsequential, leaving a vague and rootless regret expressed in universal legends and in that pervasive feeling that the world was an illusion simply because of wanting it not to be, of that very determination to believe which is the origin of gods. No maya, no buddha.

But would Ou-shih pass the test? The Eians were a special case here. Could Ou-shih simply put away his knowledge of past incarnations and uncritically accept the world as he found it? But perhaps it wouldn't be required, else how could anyone hope to go? Perhaps, after their cryogenic suspension or whatever the Foundation intended to do with them to explain that detail, that little physical inconvenience of the expedition, that discrepancy, they would all have vague memories of gardens and apple orchards and the great war between Gog and Kali over the turtle's egg, and be perfectly content.

It wasn't, after all, an ordinary expedition constrained by biological and engineering details. Anyone could go, this time. Anyone could be saved now. Crazy, incompatible, once-doomed people and their dogs and coffee-grinders saved too. Well, perhaps not. The sudden reappearance of all one's familiar comforts would spoil the illusion of having gone away, of beginning a new life in a strange place, without all that. Without all that that you wanted to be saved from.

Was that why they were going, because of all that? Why was Ou-shih going, exactly? Charles wasn't sure. Suppose he were to go, himself?

Charles imagined himself standing up at some staff meeting to say that he was retiring, going away. He imagined the stares which he would get, as if he had announced a decision to become an opium addict or a schizophrenic. In the moonlight, sitting on a rock in a desert canyon after a rainstorm wearing nothing but his shirt, he had to smile.

And really, the illustration was more apt than it might seem. One did not, after all, decide such things but rather, in the routine pursuit of pleasure, find them to be the case. You're taken by them, or taken over. You notice, one day, that you've become an opium addict. It was like the dead fly, of no particular significance. That was what happened to opium addicts sooner or later.

A rumbling sound which he had been hearing for some time now intruded on his thoughts. It was coming from up the canyon, like a pack of dogs running before a brush fire, barking and gnashing their teeth, or a turbine blade which had come loose in the air conditioner and thrown the compressor out of balance. He looked up just as a black shroud blotted out the canyon and part of the sky. Scrambling back crabwise, he only just got out of the way of the head of water which scoured the canyon, taking his pants and shoes with it as it tumbled over the edge into the valley below.

Dumbfounded, he stared at the little stream which the flash flood had left behind, a result so under-proportioned to its cause. Minutes passed. The flow showed no sign of drying up. Cautiously he let himself back down to the stream's edge, where he knelt on the stones and put his hand into the cold water, now limpid because the loose trash and dirt was all swept away. The stream was three meters wide but no more than a hand in depth. It's violent rebirth over, it flowed placidly, snaking between boulders, splitting into rivulets and rejoining itself, sliding unconcerned over the last smooth shelf which was the lip of the waterfall. Charles walked in it down to the edge of the dropoff, lying down right in the streambed finally in order to look over, to watch the hypnotic cascade sparkling in the moonlight. It fell into no well or pool below, being too intermittent to have carved one, but splashed onto a bare talus slope and sank away among the loose rock.

This water, naturally enmued, neither flinging itself over the lip of the fall nor clinging to the edge, moving on easily, neither singing to itself nor grumbling, without even needing to gather itself for the perfected stroke, as with the laden brush or the chased blade flowing around and through him, taken into account as he was, incorporated into the design like a speck in the paper, allowed for like a stick in the bundle of straw which, in the shape of a man, awaited the practice stroke, flowed over the edge and fell perhaps a hundred meters in a broad veil of droplets subdivided with increasing fineness into a mist which curled away on the wind and vanished, only a fraction reaching the damp black talus, the gesture completed.

His own body, unrooted as it was, would soon be undermined and carried over with it. Seductive idea, this letting go, this clinging to nothing. The body, however, left off clinging, wedged itself behind a rock and refused the seduction.

At this point the master glared, withy in readiness. Tell me, the master demanded, which was the wiser: the man, or the rock?

The man, Charles ventured, because, though divided against himself —

But the switch leapt upon his undefended arm, biting the naked skin. Ah!

The rock then, a peaceful sandy society cheerfully obeying its hexagonal law.

Ah, ah! Ouch!

‹‹ ››

Returning: from the dead, or merely from across the street — this frenzied running around which gave the impression of coming and going so as to cover up the truth that there was only going and staying behind — the frenzied pretense of preparation, all the gathering of things which would be needed, shampoo and photograph albums and something for headaches, the provisions for someone to cut the lawn and take in the mail as if one were coming back, until the final confrontation at the gate revealed with perfect clarity who had a ticket and who didn't. At the gate he turned away for a moment, perhaps to speak to the porter, and behind his back the real passengers went aboard without even saying good-bye, leaving him to go home alone. To return, pretending he had been somewhere.

Two months passed. Drum returned from desert reconnaissance, leaner and fitter but not reconnoitered at all. There were still the summer's expeditions to the south to look forward to, though. Training and shakedown over, he had a week's leave before being sent out again. To the mountains this time. There would be no more descents into the cauldron until the monsoon: that season was over.

They were talking in Varda's now disused lab in hut two, waiting for a centrifuge to finish with an assay she'd prepared. Drum didn't ask what it was — clearly it was not biology. A soil sample, he guessed. Some others had come in, hearing that Drum was back. They all had free time on their hands now, waiting for scheduled transfers, reassignments, shuttle seats, and so forth. Charles was gone already. Will looked in for a moment. Others stopped by to hear the traveler's tales being told by this new master of esoteric knowledge who sat on a battered straight chair, its back to the wall and front legs in the air, spinning yarns of faraway unvisited places, of strange unheard-of practices, of adventures, close scrapes, and all such necessary trappings. But actually he was just waiting for something real to happen. Why had he been singled out, given a chance now, when already he was losing his grip?

INTO THE CAULDRON

One hypothesis, Drum was thinking, was that finally snagging a security assignment was really just a sinecure, a reward for watching the baby for twenty years. But that didn't survive his first meeting with his new colleagues. The other new recruits were kids with hardly twenty years among them, and the sergeant was a man about half Drum's weight who could probably kill him in seconds with his bare hands. These guys, he said to himself, are going to take me out in the desert and lose me. And in fact, Howie told him later on, they wouldn't ordinarily have expected him to stick it, to come back after the first encounter. But there were orders from somewhere and Drum had been given some sort of official observer status and they had no choice but to take good care of this office engineer who'd been dumped on them, which making nice wouldn't stop Drum from bailing on his own, they hoped. But he didn't. Bail to where?

The present detail was supposed to haul some fugitive out of the cauldron. Drum was told they do this all the time. Four missions for the sergeant's team since winter and three or four more expected before the end of the season.

I found out later, Drum said, that actually they do usually take a faggot along —

Beg pardon? Faggot?

Official observer. Dead wood which they have to carry. But it's usually some file clerk, or a specialist skill they happen to need, not an overage recruit. So it wasn't a sinecure after all, and the sergeant, whose name is Bonchurch by the way, wanted to make sure I was sorry about that. He's the only man left who laid cable or made repairs to the dish in the old days. The others are just hyenas. Policemen, he means, who pick off vagrants and keep the cauldron free of carrion. I asked how long this had been going on. Eighteen months, but Bonchurch told me the repair teams had begun to encounter these squatters in the cauldron already five years ago.

Varda nodded. We had one here. Last week.

Drum looked hard at her but said nothing.

Or so I'm told. We didn't get to see him. Will's lost his security access, you know, and couldn't find out. He put in an official request to be informed of potential damage to the telescope but that was ignored, of course. Irrelevant. Maybe they just picked up this, um, *vagrant* out there somewhere, but we had the impression he was caught in the lab — in someone's lab. There's a new obsession here with secrecy which bothers me.

But Mazatzal isn't secure, Drum objected. You could always just walk in here off the desert.

Off the desert? Come on.

Well, sure. The desert was security enough. The net has always been a little hysterical. It takes itself too seriously.

Varda shrugged, raising one eyebrow expressively, a refutation which Drum thought best to digest in silence.

Anyway, he went on.

But this *going on*, this narrative restlessness which plagued him: and then? and then what? with never any answer, any event complete, any action finished, which did not suggest a series — branching, twigging alarmingly, implacably into a snarl of unrealized opportunities, untraveled paths, unenjoyed pleasures, wasted sins, unused, unread, unknown, uneaten.

He was tired of *going on*. He wanted to know how it turned out. He wanted to know *what happened*. The one thing he was not to know.

One sees what ails the net, sometimes. Places to go, people to see.

After the shakedown tour Bonchurch gave Drum a day's shore leave. The week of equipment training and a conditioning regimen finished, he went out again with Bonchurch and the others into the cauldron. The hyenas, they said, used a crawler on the open desert. Bonchurch's voice had a sneering lilt to it. Drum couldn't see his face through the com helmet.

By early afternoon they had reached the edge of the cauldron where there was a staging point, a natural cave which the hyenas had enlarged for themselves, sunk deeper into the mountain like a toy version of Mazatzal station which was itself originally just such a bunker, a rich man's refuge from the ruined world.

Their crawler was hooded and stored here. Bonchurch's crew spent the night in a kind of barracks which was kept stocked with food and specialized equipment. In the morning they started down on foot. Drum was given a pack weighing about fifteen kilos: food, rope and other climbing equipment, flares, radio, breathing equipment, emergency air supply.

Water, Bonchurch said, you can get from natural sources if you filter it.

The helmet and suit weighed another two kilos on top of that. The suit was a kind of sand-colored plastic which served as camouflage and kept the wind from shredding your skin. The helmet, so Drum was told, would let him see what he was doing more or less, but he never saw a thing through it.

The faceplate was made of breath-thick layers of the same stuff as the suit.

When the top layer gets scratched, said the corporal who was briefing him, a man who turned out to be Howie, you peel it off, so. But Drum guessed anyone who went down into the cauldron would use his eyes for much, and the faceplate was just psychology.

Sand-diving, the hyenas call it, Howie said.

About a hundred meters below the staging point the top of the sand cloud looked like a sludgy lake, predominately tan with swirls of darker brown and purple.

When the air's still, Howie said, it heaves a little. Any little breeze picks up the light clay on top and whips it into long plumes that climb into the air where sometimes a thermal will grab it and spin it out into a fine thread. By late afternoon these thermals will raise a dust fog, which settles during the night, so that like now, early in the morning, the boundary layer is pretty sharp.

They went down, through the skin of it, almost beautiful.

Under the surface there was a constant clockwise wind. You won't be able see a thing at first, they'd told him in training, and it is extremely hard to hold a line of march. Bonchurch simply roped Drum and Howie together and Drum blundered along at the end of a tether the first day. The deeper they went the heavier the weight of sand-laden air, which multiplied the force of the wind as well, so that by the end of the day's march Drum's legs were pretty soft. Their goal had been four hundred meters down, one of the hyena bases, a buried pod about two meters high and just big enough for five to lay out.

They drop these pods all over, Howie said. You find them with a beacon and the pod sends out a snorkel for you. Sometimes the snorkel won't reach, if the pod has been sunk too deep by drifting sand. In that case you sleep in your suit. We found a squatter once who managed to get in with a stolen transponder but didn't know enough to set the alarm, so that when the pod sank too deep he couldn't get out.

And what?

Died.

Transposed to another plane of reality in this case, since a pod's life support so far transcended ordinary abilities to do anything with the life so supported, awarded, spun out into finer and finer floss, that anyone who was not literally bored to death, sinking down under meters, kilometers of sand to the root of being, would become an arhat for sure.

Next day they reached the heavy discontinuity. Below this the conditions became too severe for a man on foot and for two days more they circled the deep cauldron along the edge of the discontinuity, keeping the wind at their backs. They were making a sweep, Drum guessed. The hyenas would have thought it a routine mission, looking for sand people. What for? And why send down Bonchurch's border patrol team to do hyena work?

It's a squad, he was informed. Not a team.

Toward the end of the second day they began to encounter ruins. Huge sections of wall eaten into masonry lace loomed out of the swirling brown fog, then streets of rubble rising out of the black discontinuity like bones out of a tar pit.

The walls are safe enough to windward, Howie said, but squatters who use them for shelter sometimes get squashed. The deeper rubble is treacherous, too. Much of the eroded rock and cement is rotten, and will crumble under foot, dumping you into pipes or crevasses filled with quicksand. And there are gas pockets all over.

Ruins.

Elaborating, gothicizing, knotting, melancholy mind that Drum was, he couldn't understand how anyone could venerate ruins. Tumbledown buildings maybe, ersatz shacks made of cardboard, bombed monuments, but not ruins. Ruins were inaccessible to nostalgia. The evidence of the weight of time, the actual weight which pushed him down into a pocket, into some bathroom or closet which suddenly opened underfoot in which he would be ignominiously buried —

Are nostalgia and horror a pair, he wondered, like happiness and tears, or compassion and cruelty?

A diptych, Bonchurch said, his voice coming in over the helmet comlink, startling Drum. That was that a warning. But of what?

Now Drum was simply counting steps. The squad was trudging through the edges of the huge destruction which filled all the depths of the cauldron, moving upslope or down in order to stay close to the lip of the pit. Howie's voice crackled in his headset, muffled by the constant roar of the wind sandblasting his helmet. Pretty well deaf and blind, by now Drum had given up trying to understand. A rough yank on the rope which joined them caused him to stumble; a knob of rock crumbled like toast in his gloved hand and he sank to his knees. He had been drifting stupidly with the current. Floundering, he struggled to stand. They moved on, pressing forward urgently to avoid being separated from the others.

In the pod later, Howie complained of a pinhole in his suit, holding it against the light in an unsuccessful attempt to find and patch it. The wind, he said, would seize on these weak spots and shred your suit in seconds. Plus the dirt that got in made the suit itchy.

Bonchurch regarded Drum with supercilious detachment from where he had sprawled at the other end of the pod. The two boys, recruits whose names Drum did not even know, were already asleep on the floor in the small space left between the elders Bonchurch and Howie. It had only taken two days to wear Drum down to the ragged edge of panic. What a crazy, purposeless expedition. What did it matter if a few desperate people wanted to hide in this horrible place? Who were they that made it worthwhile to winkle them out of this hell? And what was the point of putting *him* in here, who would have been killed before he had taken a dozen steps without Bonchurch and Howie to protect him? What was he doing in this little titanium egg in a sandstorm which had been blowing for years, with these taciturn avengers? What, he wondered, would happen if he deserted to the surface?

You'd die, Bonchurch said quietly, again somehow reading his thoughts. Stick with us. You'll file your report.

The two of them locked eyes while Howie felt over the material of his suit like some ancient, parsimonious tailor.

Drum broke off first and curled up at his own end of the pod to try to sleep. But it was no good.

If we have such a tough time down here, he said, how do these sand people live practically naked? What are they doing here anyway?

Bonchurch's reply was negligent. They've been working this refuge since the beginning, he said. Call themselves that: the Sand People. Of course. Some cult.

Ever talked to one?

No. You can't get your hands on a live one to talk. They sort of curl up, crumble. Mostly they get away, though. Foxy blighters.

Fox?

Bonchurch paused, looked inward, rummaged in his head. Figure of speech, I guess, he said.

And these crumbly cultists are a security risk?

Bonchurch narrowed his eyes. Beats me, he said.

In the morning they were away again after a hurried meal of water and nutrient paste. There was a curious tension in Bonchurch which communicated itself quickly to the other four, as if he smelled prey. And in fact, they had been on the move no more than an hour before Drum's headset burst to life.

Got one! Ahead, on the right, in that dell where the I-beam is sticking up.

Drum could see nothing, but Howie veered to the right at once. The beaters'll drive him forward, Drum made out through the crackle. See he doesn't get around your end.

How was he supposed to do that? The safety rope which had so far joined him to Howie had been unclipped. He hardly dared take a step. Cautiously, he worked his way downslope toward a looming shape which proved to be a mass of concrete hairy with re-rods. Here he stopped to coil up the trailing line before it snagged on something. The hollering in his headphones grew first loud, then soft, but always unintelligible.

Edging forward around the broken concrete, he was about to cross over to the next dim shape which he could make out through the swirling brown fog when a white patch on the left caught his eye. He turned, and what had seemed to be a blowing scrap of paper suddenly ballooned into a man dressed in something like a burnoose, a man who just grew up out of the ground, rushed past, and was swallowed up downslope by the black mud. A moment later a cloud of bats attacked Drum, ripping at his flesh. He whirled, slapping at them, but just as quickly they too were gone to windward. After a stunned moment, Drum realized that these bats were in fact the shreds of his protective suit. Throwing himself into the dust brought some relief. Slithering, sometimes rolling, he made it into a little hummock and crawled around to leeward of a post sticking out there.

The hose leading to his airpack had been severed also, unsealing his helmet. He could feel his throat swelling up as he fumbled with the hose, trying to fit it over the nipple on the airpack. He was getting dizzy —

A shot of oxygen jerked him awake, burning his nose and tender throat. His breath rasped in his ears.

He's coming around, a voice said.

Get that thing off.

The helmet was pulled away from Drum's head and white sunlight poured down over him. Blinded, dirty tears running down his face, still choking, he tried to sit up. Howie's grinning head swam up close, black as a miner's with two white saucer eyes. Drum hawked up a gob of spittle and lay back again.

The fox took a swipe at you with a knife as he went by, Bonchurch was saying later.

What happened to him? Drum wanted to know.

Who?

The fox.

They had sheltered out of the sun, up against the wall of a mudstone cliff.

Got away. Down into the mud. They do that. We had to break off to get you up to the surface.

So I lost him for you.

Well, when they get into the mud they usually get away anyhow. You're lucky he didn't cut you worse. We put Howie's helmet on you and carried you straight up.

Drum tried to sit up again. A long scratch on his stomach oozed blood. His skin felt hot, burned.

Later, while the others were sleeping, Drum thought more about what had happened.

Howie's helmet, Bonchurch had said. In the moment of waking, fractionally lucid with oxygen, before his eyes teared over and they snatched the helmet off, he had seen —

Howie's equipment, he now realized, was not much like what Bonchurch had given his faggot. Howie's com hood was loaded with intelligent scanning and range finding gear which projected a holo of his surroundings inside the faceplate. That explained how they were able to move so easily, tracking fugitives though the moil. And the helmet's voice communications had been clear, unscrambled. So when Howie unclipped Drum's lifeline he must have known he would wander off and get lost, because with essentially nothing but a bag over his head he could do little else. He hadn't expected, perhaps hadn't wanted Drum to see what was going on. They would have expected to come back for him afterwards and have a good laugh while he, ignorant and humble, wondered why this was such a hard business. But the fox had foiled them, had known how to use Drum like meat thrown down to put off the dogs.

So who were these squatters, so harried, persecuted to hide in such a hole, dangerous enough to justify such trouble and such precautions?

He didn't know. No one had said.

They haven't told you any more than that? Varda asked, incredulous.

He waved the question off impatiently. She snorted with disgust. It's obvious this Bonchurch was sent down for some infraction, she said. Mistreatment of prisoners. it sounds like. You were put in to mind the baby, but they neutered you.

What? I wasn't told anything!

You had a physical on enlistment, right?

Yes.

Implants. You didn't need to be told anything. Don't do anything seditious, my boy. They'll know. And don't trust Howie.

We've been down into the cauldron twice since, Drum said, and never caught *any*one.

So far as *you* know.

Varda was finding Drum's obtuse narcissism harder to accept now that the situation had fallen out political.

When Bonchurch is out of the brig where will you be deployed?

The Chiricahuas. Three of us: Howie and Bonchurch and me. Border patrol.

What do we need a border patrol for? Varda growled. What border?

It's better than sitting around here polishing the bronze.

The brass, someone corrected.

Another metal altogether, brass. Not so brittle and rusty and dark, nor so in need of polishing.

Chin in hand, Varda rested her eyes softly on Drum but said nothing to reveal her true feelings. If anyone did have true feelings. Feeling truly. Or only duplicitous ones. Tell the truth of your life, it was said, and the world will split open. Not much danger of that, after so many futile attempts, and here we are still. Biting his thumb, he had to turn away from that soft suffocating gaze.

They'll tell me what I've been vetted to hear, he admitted. Maybe they know what they're doing. Maybe they don't.

A pause. Ou-shih gone? he asked.

Last month.

Heard anything?

No.

Maybe he's all right, then. Bonchurch talks about going.

Varda gave Drum a long look.

What's wrong with that? he asked, surprised.

Varda scowled and dropped her eyes. After a moment she got up to see about the centrifuge.

More soil samples. What was she doing now, prospecting for gold?

《》

Charles, Fong, and Ou-shih. Of the scientists, anyway — hundreds of flicks probably. Thousands.

Drum was eating lunch with Varda and Garth the day before his leave expired. Varda, Will, and some of the others had been avoiding him, probably because he was hot. They found it onerous to be circumspect now, after years of official inattention.

Drum was clearing his plate when a crackle in the air caused him to look up. Garth had vanished.

Hmp, was all Varda said. Been took.

Drum gaped at the empty chair, his mouth half full of ham and eggs.

The ham is a little garish today, Varda remarked. They

need to work on the color balance. Not so much blue.

《》

All right, Bonchurch said. Now we're going to do for you, my boy.

What? Drum was alarmed.

Bonchurch pressed some sort of handset against Drum's neck, adroitly pinioning Drum with his free hand. He consulted a readout.

All right then, you're quiet. No pie in the sky, eh?

Oh, Drum muttered, rubbing his neck. Won't someone object?

Probably. Let 'em talk to the enquiry board. We're clean here. We run a clean operation. You said so.

I?

Bonchurch regarded Drum with slitty eyes. And with the faintest of smiles he turned to speak to Howie.

By the end of the summer Drum had been back and forth across the border a dozen times but he still had no idea what they were looking for. He had seen no one. All summer, from the low creosote desert to the high grassland at the foot of the Chiricahuas and back again, no one. The monsoon season was expected soon. Maybe two more forays, Bonchurch said. Then back north for a while.

It was just after dawn. Sol rising. They had camped on the slope of a range overlooking the San Pedro valley which was still in shadow four hundred meters below. Drum could see, down there, the long tawny grass beginning to stir under a wind from the south. For several evenings now they had had dry thunder. Rain in a day or two, perhaps. Up on the mountainside the air was still, and even this early the sun was already hot. Yet farther up, a red-tailed hawk was climbing the first of the morning's thermals into a crayon-blue sky.

The mouth of this shallow east-facing canyon was one of Bonchurch's favorite spots, tactically useful as well as beautiful. There was a sweeping view across twenty kilometers to San Pedro Peak, around which the valley bent to the east before turning north again to round the toe of a short mountain range named after the conquistador Francisco Vásquez de Coronado. Upslope, columns of red rock stood out from the mountainside, fading now to salmon and finally to their natural tawny orange as the sun rose. A second hawk appeared from behind the ridge. Nearer by, a wren darted among some yuccas and a flock of sparrows chittered noisily in a mesquite bush. Behind him, back in the canyon, a cottonwood tree rose up, its shadowed trunk bearing a huge torch of sun-gilded leaves.

Conquistadors. That's us: con quisto, like at the end of a letter. With love, Drum.

Squinting. Uncivilized place. Unchanged for hundreds of. More or less. Easy to re-materialize Coronado and Cárdenas, their party of Spaniards in white mail, crossing the river on horseback just there, coming here into Cíbola, the first Europeans. Legendary cities of gold. Legendary as in storied, what we tell ourselves to prospect our values, biting down on the ore to taste fear, delight, greed, sadness. Rare spices worth their weight in. What's the weight of a quintal of fear? Pretty dense stuff. Need to have a good working sense of smell in order to taste it properly. Can't tell the difference between an apple and an onion otherwise. Tasteless white stuff, like you get in the commissary. A soft slice of fear slathered with sadness. Tasteless in the sense of undiscriminating, too. Ill-bred. Ex-polis. Tasteless indigenous savages in various tribal factions, mud houses. Cities of a sort, made of imaginary gold. Lots of imaginary stuff here, and Coronado if the first to look then hardly the last.

From here, Cárdenas broke away to the north, Coronado to the east, wandered around for two years as far as Quivira on the Arkansas. Nothing. Abounding with imaginary places right under their noses, unnoticed. Abounding grace, six reals the quintal. Every once in a while a fleer from, abounding through the tall grass, one of those expoloi. Stark contrast here between urb and nonurb, politics and wilderness, policeman and cíbolaman. Nature of desert places.

This was not Drum talking, though. Drumlin McKechnie did not talk to himself. Mazatzal station patrol selected people who keep private.

Charles talked too much, Varda had said.

Drum told her about how Bonchurch had quieted him and drew a hard stare.

He had said goodbye too often now. He'd stopped wondering where they were all going. Stopped wondering why so many of them thought it was a good idea.

But why in that wizardly way? Surely he could be taken quietly, in a corner or a bedroom, like having an…

What was going on there? Would Varda know? Probably. Who was filling his head up with this stuff?

〈〈 〉〉

Howie was up, rustling about in camp and hawking up black dirt from his lungs. Bonchurch would be up soon, too. Drum wanted some coffee, and ambled back along the dry creek to where their domes stood hidden in the canyon.

The coffee was already made and Howie was sitting on the food locker, leaning back against the fender of one of the skiffs, drinking it. Drum poured some for himself and squatted on his heels a little ways away, under the cottonwood tree, keeping his distance. He, too, had grown laconic, with nothing to say to these two with whom he had now spent months alone together. Bonchurch had always been aloof. The easygoing Howie did not seem to care one way or the other, he just found it simpler to keep silence. But this morning he grunted and pushed himself off his spot on the food locker to join Drum in the shadier place under the tree. He eased down on a boulder, slopping his coffee a bit on his dusty boot.

Bonchurch got a radio bulletin last night, he said.

What radio?

Howie grinned and tapped the bone behind Drum's ear. Same as yours, boy.

Meaning?

Howie shrugged, pouted a little. A rendezvous?

With who?

Howie's face got a little longer. Someone coming our way, anyhow, he said. Maybe a runner. Bonchurch will want to post a sentinel today.

I see.

No hurry. We can eat breakfast first.

Where is he?

Went down to the river before dawn to set trips. Back this afternoon, this evening maybe.

Trips.

Howie shrugged. Better no surprises, he muttered, then flashed a grin.

Drum decided not to pursue this any farther. Wherever Bonchurch had gone, he was on foot, because all three skiffs were left where they had been parked last night, in the mesquite above the creek. Drum stood up, flinging the last of his coffee to one side. Brown drops spattered the stones.

I'll cook, he said.

The runner did not appear until evening. Shadows had crawled down almost to the river. Drum could see him easily,

moving south through the grass on the opposite bank. Bonchurch had not returned. About an hour of light remained.

Hey! Get down!

Drum scuttled back into the scrub to keep from being
seen against the sky. From under a palo verde, Howie was
following the runner with a sighting scope, its guide beam
turned off.

He's timed it good, Howie commented. If these guys
ever get night vision we're going to have to do a little work
to catch them.

Fifteen minutes passed. The shadow line, the portentous
edge of night, was coming on. It seemed to hesitate, then
leaped across the river.

Damn, muttered Howie, it's a long one. Deliberately he
picked up the laser rifle lying on the ground beside his outstretched leg, clicked the scope home, and switched on the
guide beam. Down in the valley a little diamond of light appeared, darted forward, pounced on its target. Howie hit the
pulse and the rippling, mole-like motion of the grass stopped
just where a little curl of white smoke rose. The thin streamer
of smoke lifted about two meters to dissipate where it passed
into the sunlight.

Got him, I believe, said Howie softly, not troubling to
dissemble his pride. Let's go. Bonchurch'll sit on him until
we get down there.

He stood up, slipped the rifle into its case, and walked
back up to where the skiffs were parked. Drum followed.
Howie nodded toward Bonchurch's larger machine. Bring
that one, he said, dropping into the seat of his own and pow-
ering up in a single motion. We'll have a load to bring back.

Howie's skiff darted forward and whisked away, dropping with a sigh down the creek bed toward the valley. Drum
brought the other skiff along more cautiously. When he broke
out of the scrub into the open grassland, Howie was already

far in advance. Their two skiffs arrowed silently over the range to the nearest point of the river, then banked and followed the course south. The water, no more than a few centimeters deep at this season, wandered back and forth across its wide sandy bed. Ahead stood a copse, black against the thunderheads building now. Short of the copse, Howie settled his skiff where Bonchurch was indeed waiting in the tall grass. Drum settled in a few moments later.

The runner who was lying there face down on the ground was wearing a dirty white canvas burnoose, burned on the shoulder where Howie had struck him with the laser. The hand and wrist of one out-flung arm, where they showed under the canvas fabric pulled back, were brown and lean as a chicken's foot. His head was small, with glossy black hair. As Howie and Bonchurch picked him up to stow in the hold for the trip back Drum saw that his face too was scrawny and narrow, fine-featured as a ferret's.

Dead?

Howie's skiff moved off with its load.

Not yet, Bonchurch replied, waving him away from the controls of his own skiff. More heavily loaded with two fleshed living men, it slewed in a big arc as Bonchurch headed it back across the river toward camp. He kept his tongue.

In camp the runner's body was unloaded and carried into Drum's hut. You'll watch tonight, Bonchurch said, stripping off his clothes as he spoke. When he wakes up, give him what he needs until morning. Wauh!

Naked, his thin muscly white body streaked with grime, Bonchurch stretched up, looking into the now dark sky between his two spread hands, then suddenly bent double, his palms hitting the ground in a peculiar ritualized gesture. Probably some isometric stretching exercise, Drum thought, and kept his curiosity to himself. Bonchurch paced across to where Howie had begun heating up supper, to the water jugs, and poured one jug out over his head, rubbing himself briskly with his free hand. Then, still wet, he put his old sweat-stiffened clothes back on and dropped to the ground with a tray which Howie handed him. Howie served himself some of the same stew, thick and gray as oatmeal, and the two of them settled down to eat, speechless in the fading light.

Drum, mysteriously not hungry, wandered over to look in at the doorway of his hut, now shared with the runner's lean body which lay stretched out on its back on the floor.

So you can testify that he was handled correctly, Bonchurch said at his back. Answering your unspoken question which is why do I have to sit wake? Am I right?

What's he done?

No idea.

Bonchurch ambled off. Howie was washing up by the last light. Drum ducked into his hut and dropped the netting.

It smelled. Probably it usually did, but of him. He let down the sides of the hut and settled cross-legged on his mat to wait out the night. In the small hut the two of them, he and the unconscious runner, were pressed very close. Drum's bit of gear had been piled in a corner. Shifting and pulling at the mat, he tried to get comfortable. The runner's bony chest moved slightly, erratically under his filthy burnoose. Outside, Howie finished up and turned in. The camp fell silent. Drum listened awhile to the crickets. Perhaps there would be a late moon. But what difference would that make? Not here, under the clouds. The hut was as black as the inside of a stomach.

Well, of course. That's why he'd wanted to cross over tonight, wasn't it? In the particular dark. Get over the river and out of Cíbola, over the border and... where? Grandmother's house. Too late for that now.

About nine o'clock the dry thunder came up as usual,

and Drum went out for a while to watch, but he was afraid to leave the unconscious deserter for long, in case he woke suddenly, or cried out.

Deserter, they said. Who said? Who had put that in his mind?

The lightning was far down in the south tonight, with little chance for rain. Again and again it roared, like a man choking to death, trying to cough up a bone. What was there, in the south? Perhaps he had been running *to*? A seeker.

About midnight the injured man began to stir. He tried to roll over but, groaning at the pain in his shoulder, fell back heavily and lay panting, his eyes closed. The man's white skin, his white clothes, clouded with dirt as they were, stood out luminous in the dark hut, and Drum was reminded of the man in the sandstorm, that flitting white shape like a wind-whirled piece of paper, which he encountered in the cauldron. That one had tried to kill him.

Give me some water.

Of course.

But when the fugitive rolled onto his good shoulder he could not hold the bottle and Drum had to help him to sit. The bones of the man's spine pressed like teeth into Drum's hand. When he had drunk, he asked to lie down again. Such destruction from a tiny wound. Like being struck by lightning. Only a small portal burned onto the skin but everything inside destroyed. Only a shell, like an eggplant stuffed with ratatouille.

Where do you come from? Drum asked.

The dying man stared up at the dark roof of the hut with eyes like boiled eggs. Stupid question, apparently.

Jakes Well, he said, hollowly.

I know that. At the end of the Mazatzal ridge, in the Tonto basin.

Yes.

I used to work on the ERF telescope.

Perhaps Drum revealed too much spirit for a wake, because the fugitive turned his face toward the wall. Then, after a time —

We are starving.

Who is?

Again, no answer. When he did speak, the man's words came singly, as if all the soft parts of his mind had been scoured out, leaving only these hard oracular spines separated by deep mental gorges, leaving Drum stranded on a narrow, prophetic mesa in the midst of the wide, wide desert.

Again the dismal voice. First men. We are first men, he said.

Well yes, I suppose. First of all you're men, not baboons or something.

A sardonic smile managed to establish itself briefly on the fugitive's mouth. Your kind is finished, he said.

What? What kind do you take me for?

But to this pertinent question there was as Drum expected no reply.

What do you know of us? the runner said.

Nothing.

Now the fellow gathered himself and over fifteen minutes gave a fragmented, breathless history of the origins of his sect in the first troubles of the previous century.

So there's you, Drum said slowly, seeming to count on his fingers. And the Sand People who aren't homeless squatters —

The wounded man gave a feeble snort. Who would choose to squat in the Cauldron? he said.

And who else, then?

There is an anarchist movement which keeps itself hidden, gathering its strength.

More strength than you, I hope.

Huh. Huh — his laugh was interrupted by a fit of liquid coughing. Drum gave him another drink of water.

We caught you here on the border, Drum said. Where were you going?

The man had not the strength to be impassioned, but the strain in his voice showed that once he would have let go an angry tirade. The intensity reminded Drum of Varda. More and more of Varda.

Save your strength, he said.

For what? the runner rplied

It's useless telling me. I'm just a mechanic. Whatever your problem is, it seems to me that any problem which hasn't been solved in that long just isn't the problem.

The runner had wanted to be angry but was silenced by hacking and Drum went on with the one-sided conversation.

I don't know, he said. Suffering, ignorance, cruelty… Begs the question. What do you want for yourself? Money? Happiness?

I'm tired, the man said, curling up on his side, his head turned away.

And in a few seconds he was gone so limp that Drum had to feel for his breath to make sure he was still alive.

Drum sat on through the night, conscientiously wakeful. In his mind he chewed toothlessly on the soon-to-be-dead man's remarks. What *did* he want? Was it any way related to why people were being *took?* What did *they* want? To see God? To sit on Nebo and dream?

Drum thought he himself had no such desires. For himself, he would have hoped it was something humble, unassuming. It was something connected in some way with what he had said about himself, that he was *only* a sort of mechanic. Had he meant that he was proud of being small? Or that he thought there was something transcendent which even small people could have? And did he have to know what it was before he could have it?

Or was his case more that of the solipsistic Charles Lehon — lonely, futile, tired.

So far as Drum knew, Charles had always been that way. He didn't *get to be* that way, he *was* that way. Was it some sort of prescience about the human condition, like being born a mathematical prodigy or a musician?

When music counts for nothing musical prodigies go undiscovered. Presumably unknown even to themselves. So that all your life you could be a genius at something and you feel inarticulate, unfulfilled, *unjustified* in the old original meaning. Lacking in righteousness. Knowing from birth all about the human condition and powerless to do anything meaningful about that or anything else and so being of an age no longer able to resist the fatigue and loneliness destined then to… to…

Drum admonished himself as a sentimental fool. Somebody thought these First Men were dangerous enough to hunt them down. Wistful failures would hardly matter.

He went to sit outside on the ground in front of the door and watch the lightning, which had become scarce and faded.

So no proper revelation fell from the lips of the wounded man.

I suppose that's usually the case, Drum said. People pretend to more than they really know. They promise to write back, but they never do. So after we'd made the round trip twice more I was relieved, mustered out basically, and came back here. I don't believe I want to go out again anyway.

And what happened to the *runner*, as you called him?

Varda asked impatiently.

As I called him? Who was he, then?

And?

Oh, Bonchurch stood him up under the cottonwood tree the next morning and shot him. Laser pistol to the head, pfft. That was my job, you know.

What, to shoot him?

No. Official observer. Everything pukka, done according to regulation. It was, too. I had to file a report.

What had he done, Drum?

No idea. Escaped from somewhere, I gather.

There was a long, speculative silence.

Official observers don't last long in the bush, Varda. So I'm told. Not surprising. They gave me bad equipment, told me nothing, stuck me in holes I hadn't been told how to get out of. They gave me bad advice and nobody but Howie had a civil word. I was more alone than I was at Mazatzal.

And you think, Drum, that quitting the border guards will find you friends?

Not friends, no.

It's the human condition, man, Varda said.

What is?

It was just the two of them talking in Varda's cubby. Drum was on leave. He had moved out of the security barracks. Varda had the ERF bunker almost to herself now. The flicks had migrated already, and over the summer most of the Mazatzal staff had been transferred out too, to Beijing and Paris, leaving only a scratch crew under Will Dolmen, and a couple of abandoned administrators. Mazatzal station was mothballed. Whole wings and all the lower levels were sealed off. Drum had expected to find Varda gone, too, but left a callback in her mail anyway. In the early evening, after mess, she turned up, materializing on the plaza while he was turned the other way, watching a night bird scratch in the palo verde litter.

Stupid bird. she said. Nothing grows under a palo verde.

So I applied to go over myself, Drum said.

Ah.

Application refused, naturally.

Ah. A couple of quick breaths and the momentary alarm was quelled, endocrine response counteracted.

Drum looked away, scratched the back of his head. Varda's eye lay heavily on him, sat on his shoulder like a parrot. One corner of her mouth twitched a little, but she quieted that with a thin, somewhat rueful smile.

A bad faith smile.

Refused, Drum repeated. Always refused. What do they want with me? Is this some kind of penance? Am I being hardened, prepared for something?

The age-old question, Drum.

And the age-old answer, too, I bet, eh?

《 》

He had been having nightmares. In one recurring dream the tide of war had turned against them. Bedeviled by shoddy equipment, misunderstood orders, and treasonous stupidity, the militia fell back, then broke under the weight of hordes of children, unarmed legions which boiled like pustules everywhere out of the ground. The very earth defied him. He fled through collapsing tunnels under the bunker. For days a huge storm had been raging, cutting off all help. Time after time he barely escaped being crushed by falling rock. Driven deeper and deeper into the earth, into galleries which he had not known were there, into black caves reeking of ageless cold —

Waking with a cry, he tried to recall himself to life. But the black dreams were taking slow hold over him, drawing him inexorably into some other, alien world.

He began to take tranquilizers.

《 》

The corridors of Mazatzal smelled stale and dusty. Drumlin McKechnie could hardly hear the sucking of his cushioned soles on the soft composition floor. Only two levels of the station were still open, one of them for Mazatzal Desert Reconnaissance because the barracks had been closed. Ground level was shuttered, even the shuttle dock. Most of the MDR troops who weren't in the field were living rough on one of the remoter sites.

Hermit sages, those guys, Will remarked. Plastic jawbones, nylon breechclouts.

I was out there, Drum said quietly.

Kept you shoes on, I suppose.

Will Dolmen said he hadn't been outside all summer. The mailroom had been brought down next door to his quarters. That was the last thing left on ground level. Even the net had been withdrawn, leaving just enough capacity for communications. Doors were left unlocked, which couldn't be locked in any case without the net to key them. The portal to E was closed — the mailroom wallah was one of the last to be taken. The wind towers still brought in cooled air and Will cooked for himself, getting supplies twice a month.

Drum was here on supply detail. He was still trying, with desultory forms and queries, to get out of desert reconnaissance he had tried so long to get in.

It wasn't paramilitary then, he said, and picked at the cuticle of one thumb. It was fixing things.

Tch, Will remarked, Bonchurchly saying nothing else.

You were mister fix it, Drum said accusingly. Until they mothballed us. The telescope is a ruin, I suppose.

I suppose.

You don't hear from Pic?

Pic Touside is hotter and dirtier than here, if you can imagine. Got eaten by bugs and vines, I suppose. A miniature Angkor Wat.

Heard anything from Charles?

Will raised one eyebrow. Did you when he was here? he said.

Well no, I meant whether you knew if he stayed on or went.

He wasn't here in the first place, Drum.

Yes. What was it about that?

Will said nothing, only relaxed the one eyebrow. After a while he got up and went out, leaving Drum to store the boxes he'd delivered. Always thin, Will had become weedy. Had he always ducked going through doorways?

Then there was that runner who Bonchurch shot. Brautigan, his name was. Drum had had to look it up to file his report. An opaque man when living, made more so by network security jargon. Probably no clearer in his purposes than Charles only, being dead, less talky.

That was the sort of remark Drum would once have thought unworthy. He would have preferred to be squashed by a rock before he got so hard. Lucky the man who dies with his eyes closed, for he shall be returned as an even less enlightened beetle. Drum wondered whether the churchly people ever considered the possibility of getting off the wheel at the bottom? Of going to sleep, as it were, in life forms which know nothing of all this, awaiting the end of the world as a pear tree or something.

No. Trees are portals to the Old Ones. A fungus, maybe.

But your Brautigan, now, Will said when he returned.

Drum tried to explain about that.

He was no bodhisattva, either, Will said after listening for a while. Hardly said a word more than give us water, give us food. Water. Food.

Where do you come from? Bonchurch had asked in a dry, dutiful voice, for the record on the final morning.

No answer.

Where were you going?

No answer.

Got that, McKechnie? Shoot him.

So they stood him under the cottonwood tree and clapped a pistol to his head and shot him with his eyes open and they stayed that way, afterward. Something about the way the laser jellies the brain, Bonchurch said.

No help, him. A man with big brown eyes and a droopy moustache, starved to a skeleton and caught in the San Pedro valley on his way from somewhere to somewhere else. Maybe if Drum had asked for a transfer to Pic Touside he could have been sent up a long, gravid river on a rickety steamer into the interior of some jungle where the slaves had revolted and found the Void there. Maybe.

Tch, Will remarked, and went out again.

Herman Brautigan. Some meaningless identification number, some items of physical description. Brown eyes, 173 centimeters, 62 kilos. Knotted star tattooed on his left thigh. Didn't see that. Bonchurch clapped the pistol to his head and he didn't twitch a bit. Foop. Down he went like a marionette with the strings cut, dead as a jellybean, tattoo and all.

And he, Drumlin McKechnie, had kept wake on the man. What for? To ease his soul out of the world or something? Or to see that it didn't get back in? That's what the keening was for, maybe. To scare off lost souls. Bodhisattva monkeys and arhat clams.

What *should* he have been doing?

Drum was beginning to feel, vaguely, that he was guilty of something.

Up and down the empty corridor of B-wing, third level, Drumlin McKechnie's soft-soled shoes squeaked on the spongy floor. Down to the frozen door at one end, back past the immobile elevators and the unused rooms standing along both sides of the hall to the stairs at the other end, in the soft but stingy yellow light, in the dusty lifeless silence of suspense.

Bah.

He had hoped to find Varda. He wanted her acerbic contempt. She would be the only one who could say for sure. She was the one for whom he would sit at the gate, fried and crispy in the sun, waiting to be let in.

Out, said a message pinned to her door. Back this evening. Wait for me in the assay lab.

But she didn't turn up. Drum slept in the lab, gritty and troubled. In the morning she was still missing. He sat in the shade of the lab wall and watched a cactus suck up its shadow until it was a round nub. Getting near equinox, he thought. He'd lived in Mazatzal station among astronomers for twenty years and never before given twenty seconds' thought to equinoxes.

Coming then to a decision, Drum made his way over to Will's communications bunker. Will was there as usual, tinkering with something.

Don't you ever sleep, man? said Drum curtly. Give me a line to the MDR outstation on the cauldron rim. Corporal Howard Loewy.

Will put in the call, unflappable as always, and sat back. What's going on?

Varda's missing, Drum replied.

Howie's thin, pinched face popped up, catching fire at

once from the urgency in Drum's voice.

The station field biologist is overdue, Howie. Can you get up here with a decent skiff?

I guess so. Howie grinned at the prospect of something to do. What about the sergeant?

Drum hesitated, obscurely worried, but decided to keep Bonchurch out of it. Give yourself leave or something. We've got enough kit here to handle a desert rescue.

Fine. I'll be along in an hour.

The connection was broken off and Drum started for the door. Will dropped his feet to the floor.

The net has got all that, you know, he said, sucking his tongue and rubbing his stubbly chin with a long knobby index finger. You can't keep your Bonchurch out of it that way.

Drum irritably waved off this objection and stomped out. In three quarters of an hour he was back above ground with two kits, one already stowed in his own skiff parked on the now unused shuttle pad. True to his word, Howie arrived in his own skiff soon afterward, rising up from below the ridge hotdog-fashion, heralded by the characteristic whine and swirl of dust. He stowed the second kit without shutting down and together they peeled off, heading into the canyon above the station.

You got a search grid mapped out? Howie asked, his voice sharp in Drum's helmet. Drum punched it over to the binnacle in Howie's skiff.

There's a saddle at the head of the canyon, he said. The ground drops away on the other side onto a mesa which extends to the north, part of that finger-like system of canyons and mesas you see on the map. I assume she's followed the mesa up onto that rim at the edge of the main range. From there we'll have to work it out as we go I've got a list of the soils she collects. There's a convergence.

Doesn't this woman leave trail plans? Howie returned a bit testily.

No.

Well, all right then. Let's go!

Side by side, the two skiffs pushed up the boulder-choked canyon and onto the plateau, where they paused for a view of the rumpled and scarred back country on the southwest slope of the Mazatzal range.

Foo! Howie grumbled. And it did look hopeless, even with the skiffs' instrumentation. Where to begin?

Drum pointed. There's an intermittent stream where she goes sometimes to be alone, he said. And sure enough, at the bottom of the slope, where there was a waterfall in the wet season, a pile of loose bones lay on the talus. But they weren't hers, was the net's opinion when a scan was sent back for analysis. Not human.

I didn't think there were any large animals in the outback.

More test data, Howie.

Howie shrugged and kicked his skiff forward.

They took it slow up as far as the rim with no success. This narrow, unobstructed mesa was easily surveyed, but the rim was a different problem. Fissured with innumerable clefts and canyons, it would take weeks to scour systematically. Drum suggested they separate to cover the base of the rim twenty kilometers or so in either direction, look into the mouths of the bigger canyons, and return to their starting spot by evening. Without waiting for much discussion, he spun off to the northwest.

Sunlight was slapping the flat wall of the rim when he returned to camp. Howie showed up after dark, tired and hungry. Over a hasty meal of packaged rations they talked over plans for the next day.

You're going to have to call this in, you know, Howie advised him. I'm signed out only until tomorrow night.

Sure, Howie.

Who is this woman, anyway? Why couldn't you just put in a standard requisition for desert rescue?

Is there such a thing?

Well, Howie admitted, maybe not. Desert folks don't generally want rescuing, I suppose. And if one of us were lost he'd have to be lost for good. Friend of yours?

Manner of speaking. I've known her a long time.

Howie assessed that in silence, along with Drum's obvious misery.

Mm, he said. I wonder why they can't put some decent food in these rations? Maybe they think we like this stuff.

Howie wadded up his mess and dropped it into the fuel well of his skiff. That'll make it fart, he said, crawling into his bivouac.

The night was clear and moonless. They hadn't bothered to put up a hut, and Drum lay staring up into the open sky. He had been studying the sky for a long time, man and boy, as his sore and aging body told him. He was forty-five and despite over a year in desert reconnaissance is not really fit.

Well of course, he muttered, I'm only a block of wood who doesn't do much. Sails here and there, eats noodles florentine alternating with some distant relative of chop suey. But then, I haven't learned much from studying the sky, either. I don't even know which way is Soster. Soster rising. Somewhere.

In the morning they started off together to the northwest, that being the less accessible part of the rim which Drum guessed Varda would prefer. He wanted to do more than just a survey, but in most of the canyons the skiffs could not be gotten over the huge boulders which filled them. It was even difficult to get in on foot. After one attempt they gave it up.

There's probably a spring up in there, Drum observed regretfully. It's just the sort of place she'd want.

It had taken them half an hour to crawl over a couple of dozen boulders, penetrating no more than two hundred meters. The canyon had rapidly narrowed and the round boulders were piled one on another, leaving huge caves and tunnels beneath them.

Howie nodded doubtfully. You'd have to get in at the upper end, from the top of the mesa. Rappel down.

Or from the air. Send over an eye.

Well, if you were sweeping out a whole nest or something. You couldn't find one person that way, hunkered back under one of these boulders, without some help. If she's unconscious, or doesn't want to be found.

Help. If she would give us a flare, you mean.

Something like that.

Later, when they had returned again to the skiffs, Drum looked back at the tantalizing, impenetrable mountain.

How long do you think it would take to work the skiffs up onto the mesa? he asked Howie.

Most of the day, probably.

For the rest of the morning they made their way slowly along the base of the rim, looking for signs. They found no evidence of Varda, but Howie's instruments were showing up other unnatural disturbances.

Ought to get a tracker up here some time, he said later, while they were eating lunch. I don't think this area's been swept in quite a while.

Uneasy, Drum said nothing. They ate hurriedly. In an hour or two it would be time to turn back.

Now Howie was leading, on the scent of something. He'd found a large canyon which seemed to have been recently in-

habited. This time they worked their way half a kilometer up
the steeply sloping floor before the familiar boulders brought
their skiffs to a halt. Howie was not inclined to halt this time.
He began unloading kit and instruments from his hold.

We got something here which is more than your friend,
he grinned, shrugging on the jacket. Without waiting for
Drum, he seated the helmet and started off.

Drum followed reluctantly, now mistrustful of what
he'd begun. It had never occurred to him to wonder if Varda
might be up to anything other than collecting prickly desert
weeds and bags of dirt. Howie's enthusiasm worried him.
But then if she were found it would be due to Howie, to his
experience. The worm in the apple. Worms hadn't died out
yet. Taking only a pistol, Drum scrambled after the younger
and more agile man. From up ahead came a sharp whistle.

Dammit, Howie was complaining as Drum let himself
drop onto the sand from the cleft between two boulders.
Where's your com helmet?

Howie was annoyed. Too hot, Drum replied, and Howie
stamped the ground in frustration. How can we keep a line if
you're not wearing a helmet? We'll show ourselves, hollering back and forth like this. Look here.

He indicated an area of ground scattered with smaller stones lying at the base of yet another of those walls of
wedged boulders. What Howie saw was not apparent to
Drum, who trailed behind as instructed, not speaking, any
spurious authority evaporated. Along the edge there was a
gap which they could just slip through. When that ran out
the slimmer Howie darted ahead through a cleft which knotted itself among the boulders, sometimes crawling beneath
them, sometimes pausing briefly when brought up against a
naked face of rock, swinging his helmeted head from side
to side like a hound and then scrambling over to pick up
the narrow track again on the other side. Drum fell farther

behind, the breath roaring in his throat from fear as much as weakness.

Hsst. Hsst.

An arm snaked out of the tunnel beneath a slab of rock wedged between a boulder and the canyon wall, gripping him above the knee and pulling him down into the crevasse, which was just wide enough to stand sideways. The bottom of the crevasse opened out so that by lying flat on his stomach Drum could twist around into the tunnel. Howie was lying there, his head just inside the opening at the other end. Wordlessly, he pointed toward something in the canyon beyond. Drum tried to look, but could barely lift his head in the low tunnel. His breath rasped as he tried to quiet it. Cautiously, he put his head out.

They had emerged into the bottom of a kind of well where the canyon, here no more than ten meters wide, was closed by a sheer face of rock. At the base of this cliff sat Varda Fleming, still and broken but conscious, her hard eye fixed on the rathole from which two men peered at her. Drum started to wriggle forward. Howie's hand closed painfully on his shoulder. Snarling, he tore free and scrambled into the open.

Fell from up there, Varda said when he reached her. Broke my legs.

He looked up at the cliff face. Where she was pointing he could see faint footholds cut into the rock, an eroded Anasazi stairway.

Behind him, Howie was moving slowly forward. Helmet in one hand, he got to his feet while Drum remained kneeling.

This her?

Yes.

Drum choked out an introduction. Corporal Loewy, desert reconnaissance.

Varda raised her hand, but palm out as if to prevent a blow. There was a flash of light, followed by a whine and an acrid smell. Howie dropped his helmet and slid against the wall to his knees, then fell face down.

Astonished, Drum looked stupidly at Howie's body, then to Varda and back to Howie. Then he raised his head to the cliff top where, black against the bright sky, stood a man with a laser rifle.

Varda, what is this?

You can't go back, Drum, she said, her voice pinched and tired. She nodded toward the jacketed corpse behind him. They keep a one hundred percent monitor on all their people. She tapped the bone behind her ear.

What?

They'll have a sweep team out here before dark. And you wondered what use they were going to make of you.

The blood pounded in his ears.

He had been the sniffer, the guide beam, the heat sensor, used to find an outback nest, to squash this pocket of resistance.

They don't tell you anything, do they? Varda said contemptuously. You're the last boggled man still alive.

Drum licked his lips nervously. From overhead, two men were dropping swiftly down the rock face on ropes.

Why did you leave me a note if you didn't want me to follow?

You idiot. If there's a sign in a shop window "back in fifteen minutes" do you wait fifteen minutes? That note was to keep tiresome people like you from bird-dogging me. Now you've brought the whole Foundation argus along.

I didn't —

Why didn't you come out with me when I asked you to, a year ago?

Two years.

I could have given you a hint.

A hint.

You asshole, Drum. We've got to leave here because of you.

So Drumlin McKechnie, the ignorantest man on the planet, the least enlightened, the only one yet to taste the apple, unfavored, unfervored, a mere unsouled shell, a tube: an asshole, and not even the soiled, stinking flesh but just the hole, which neither accepts nor rejects but passes all impartially, was not going to be the bodhisattva, the compassionate one who stayed behind to help others on the way.

The two men who had rappelled down the cliff dropped lightly to the ground. One of them carried a sling which he now clipped onto his climbing rope while the other man kept Drum at a distance with a pistol. Varda stood up, settled into the sling, and was whisked up onto the mesa. Two more ropes came down, and the empty sling. The man with the pistol motioned Drum forward, but Drum hesitated. There was a flash and a spreading black smear which covered him like paint.

« »

He didn't find out what they did with Howie's body.

Drum awoke in darkness, feeling as if his head were in a bag, and then after a time became aware that it really was in a bag. He was bound. By wriggling about, he ascertained that he was in a sack lying on a dirt floor. There was no feeling in his hands or feet. For a long time he lay quiet, listening and smelling. A cave, perhaps, or a small room with a low ceiling, perhaps a store room; there was an odor of grain mixed with the characteristic bite of stone. There was a good deal of bustling about, hurried people speaking in low voices, outside the door.

So he was going to be executed, it seemed, like Brautigan was. What for? Because he was a member of a different
tribe of chimpanzees.

Brautigan knew what for. Why didn't he, Engineer
Drumlin McKechnie, get to know?

Well, perhaps Brautigan hadn't known; it was his dignity that had given that impression. It wasn't a cosmic thing,
this knowing. Varda seemed to know. It wasn't as if it were
something fundamentally unknowable, a basic limitation of
human life. It was just he, Drum, who was in the dark. That
wasn't fair, was it? Varda acted as if not being in the know
were some sort of moral defect, whereas in Drum's experience it was the normal human condition. Perhaps there were
people who thought it was normal to be morally defective?
The churchly doctrine, as much as he understood it, was that
all this was illusion, the product of desire, of falsely dividing
the tao into bits: known, unknown; intelligible, incomprehensible; mundane and mysterious.

So Drum was going to be executed. But Brautigan had
shown him how to behave, at least.

If he didn't know of what he was guilty — and who did
— he could at least act as if he did.

《 》

Outside, the bustling sounds had organized themselves.
Sacks were being dragged along the passage, followed by
the pattering of unladen feet returning. Drum guessed that
he had discovered a nest living in a small cliff dwelling and,
as Varda said, they were now preparing to move farther back
into the country.

He wondered whether Varda had infiltrated this nest just
recently. Or had she been one of them all along? Or perhaps
she had just stumbled on these partisans and tried to keep

quiet about it, wanting neither to get involved nor to move her research. Like finding a nest of wasps while painting the house. Perhaps they were no more than a facet of her research, another environmental condition to account for in explaining cactal rise and fall. Or perhaps they had been the subject of her research all along. Desert ecology and survival. The limits of human capacity in alien places, on far planets.

All planets are far.

Well, that was absurd. He found it much easier to accept resistance and guerilla war as explanations. The existence of an Underground, though in this case the positions were reversed if not the roles, with resistance up top and orthodoxy dug in, which rather spoiled the metaphor. But it didn't matter: resistance was the verso of orthodoxy in any case. Text and margin. Marginalized. Where the gloss or commentary is.

What would happen to Varda? Drum fretted. Would she move up-country with them? Or would they dump her, too, as compromising and excess baggage?

He couldn't have been unconscious more than an hour or the sweepers would be here, as Varda said. Soon, now, they would be ready to go. Someone would look into the storeroom and bolt him, like checking to be sure the back door is locked and the electricity turned off. He'd never know, or have his chance to stand up.

How, he wondered, did they intend to get back into the country without leaving tracks? They must have some method, or they wouldn't have survived this long. Or was it simply that the desert was large and reconnaissance small? Smaller even than its fancy instrumentation and the intelligent assistance the net gave it. And for how long really? Only a little more than a year. Godzilla could hide in the desert that long. He'd be more likely to die of thirst than be found.

Perhaps the sweepers would come now, before they got out, and vaporize Drum along with the rest. No one would ever know for sure what happened to him then. It was just ego to want to stand up at that moment, to want not to be squalid and undignified. He was, after all, nothing more than a thick spot, like a bit of cheese slow to melt into the sauce. A momentary lump in the mu.

The universe even looks somewhat like that on an isograv plot, he reflected. Like cheese sauce. Perhaps that's why people find it a natural image, a natural representation. Or astronomers do, anyway.

Boots. The hood over Drum's head was jerked off roughly. Varda stood over him, rifle tucked under her arm. There were others. She signaled them back. Far too late, Drum realized that she was the one in charge, and always had been.

Where are we going? he asked.

Varda smiled very faintly and gestured with two fingers raised, he thought enjoining silence.

《 》

Where a place may be found, what goes on there, is a function of travelers' reports, which explains the impression that Euboea is just over there whereas Colchis, across wine-dark seas, is a little dubious. When people began to fly, then metageography became common sense. One went to the place where the specialized instruments of travel were kept (inn, quay, terminus, transporter room, the metageographic porthole) and got into a machine (carriage, sailboat, locomotive), and a bit later got out again to find the flats changed and a new play on which, one was told, was called Paris or Beijing. At first one could follow along, more or less, and pilots would point out the Grand Canyon and the lights of Wichita and no one was much troubled though it still took a while for everyday reality to snap back into place even after short hops during which one looked out the window the whole way, following a thread of highway with a finger. And Wichita, after all, looked somehow familiar, and so did Paris and Beijing, and even the moon in the end. Besides, Parisians seemed to feel that Wichita and Beijing were over there somewhere, a reassuring reciprocal illusion which did much to reduce the leap of faith needed to believe in the moon, or Mars, or Barnard's Star, even if one couldn't unwind a thread or drop bits of bread on the path to be sure.

That rubbery quality, caused by the body's stubbornly clinging to old ways, became part of the true experience of travel, the physical validation of an already consummated mental event. Wichita, Honolulu, Beijing: poink poink, poink. Like checkers. After an uncomfortable pause, which goes on a bit too long so that you know someone has forgotten their lines, the body kicks in like a window shade wrapping itself around the roller. Wap wap wap wap. Everyone jumps, and after a moment breathes again.

So now you go to this place where the necessaries are kept and someone says we're just going to make you a little cold, see, you won't feel a thing, and when you thaw out you'll be there.

Right. Where is that?

Well I don't know dear. What's it say on your ticket?

Woo thirteen twenty, sector four. Tourist, no lunch.

Oh, you can see that from here. The little dot right of the big red one. Can't see the famous hanging gardens, of course, but if you remind the kids to leave forwarding addresses they'll get picture postcards one day.

You're sure the luggage is checked through?

Right. Now just let me have your arm. This won't hurt a bit...

And it doesn't. Poink poink. Wap wap wap. Natural as anything.

You lie, calm now, in the dry stone-smelling dark and wait. With your eyes covered you never saw the flash. You were taken. It's hard to know, really, why you worried about it so much.

« »

Razan went first to Sekiso and asked: what shall we do when we wish to escape our thoughts?

Sekiso said: Be cold ashes and a withered tree! Spotless purity! First impressions for ten thousand years!

Razan did not understand and went to Ganto for an explanation. Ganto shouted in his face: Who is this who is escaping? And so Razan was released.

Ganto was a disciple of Tokusan. Many stories are told of Seppo, also, who was another disciple of Tokusan. One day a monk said to him: The old well gives fine cold water. And Seppo answered: Look into it all you like, but you won't see the bottom!

Curious, the monk asked: What then when we drink the water? and Seppo replied: It will do no good.

Unsatisfied, the monk went to Joshu with the same questions. What do you think of this cold well water? he asked.

It is very disagreeable, Joshu said.

The persistent monk asked: What then if I drink it?

You will die, Joshu said.

When Seppo heard of this conversation he prostrated himself, saying: Joshu is one of the ancient Buddhas.

I wonder what happened to the stupid monk who carried all those questions and answers back and forth?

Died, I suppose.

It's the beginning of a new life.

Poink, poink.

Wap wap wap.

E₃

The war of extermination turns ugly.
The authorites prove corrupt.
People take matters into their own hands.

THE DISPOSSESSED

I

THE REPORTER hesitated, sensing an opening. You had something else in mind? she proposed, cautiously.

We need to do something about kissop weed.

Think that's wise, Charles? Messing about with the dominant biota?

There's Hollis's report.

Hollis was in cahoots with everyone, the reporter observed bitterly.

Yes, well...

Charles Renaud chewed the inside of his lip.

Come on, Charles — the weed is a ruse. You can't fob that off on me. This supposed controversy over weed clearance has had all the juice wrung out of it.

Maldonado says —

Maldonado is a politician.

He's intelligent enough to read a field report and draw his own conclusions. If Ng Jo decides to press —

What does Security have to do with kissop weed? the reporter asked.

Charles paused, taking some time to study this woman who was browbeating him. He had not worked with her before. She was young but obviously competent, and had done her homework. She was not going to waste time on small talk. And he was not going to ask about her previous job in Horring and how she had liked small town rural life. They were going to get down to business.

We're expecting an infall, Charles said.

Hoi!

Already visible. Slowing by ten percent a month. We should have known about it years ago. The Board of Trade — What do you know about kissop weed?

Very little.

I advise you to study up. It's a dangerous invader. Now as to the new Kristenkowski workings —

Wen Li.

Charles nodded. Wen, yes. The Vardon Mine Consortium.

Fishbach. Hollis-who-is-dead.

Charles chewed disconsolately on his lip. She was not letting him pursue the nuances.

The two of them had come out onto the roof because it would be friendlier to lean on the balcony rail where they would not have to dissemble their words. Charles had committed himself to a frank interchange and only hoped that he had guessed right.

Charles, the reporter said, you can't drop — how many?

Five hundred thousand.

Hoi. There'll be a war.

Inevitably.

Now was her turn to pause and think. She ran her finger along the railing in the moonlight, slowly peeling a strip of paint away from the metal.

At length, the reporter resumed her probing.

So, she said again. What is it about the research on desertification secretly —

Charles's eyebrow shifted a fraction upward.

unobtrusively funded by State Security, a works project

as big as the Vardon slave camp

Ahem.

slave camp — Where is there space for half a million immigrants? Kalgoorlie can't… Ah, I see. It's not about kissop weed, is it? It's about suburbs, detention camps, and prisons.

Yes.

Charles, she noticed, had begun to lift his own paint peel.

Let's go inside, he said, taking the reporter's elbow to discreetly steer her out of the hole in surveillance and toward the window panels now sliding open to invite them both into the office of the Chairman Maldonado's factotum.

We shall now agree, he said, on what of this to print.

《 》

Jorge Maldonado had run the Council meeting with evident disinterest, and in the hallway behind chambers Wen Li was going to twit him about it, but Maldonado turned on him with unexpected fierceness.

Why has Ng been working in the north basin? Maldonado demanded curtly.

Wen did not reply at once. The crinkles at the corners of his eyes vanished and reappeared lower down, around his mouth.

Has she?

The Public Assay has been asked to analyze a soil sample from North Basin, Maldonado insisted. Ng has been surveying the old scout ship landing site. I want to know why.

I believe, began Wen with typical caution, that she has a standing practice concerning that site. My office —

Has charged her, the Secretary for Internal Security, to monitor soil sterility, Maldonado broke in, causing Wen's eyes to narrow with impatience and disdain. But the little Chairman of the Board of Trade gave no other sign and, seeing none, Maldonado allowed himself to smile, but not broadly.

The assay you requested, he said, more smoothly now, was more a matter of engineering than of soil sterility, Sr. Wen. Stability, compaction, granularity, that sort of thing.

You are about to make some accusation, Wen averred. I would rather hear it in my office than in the hallway.

Maldonado nodded agreement and Wen produced a small brass key plate from the fob of his trousers just beneath the red sash which he had not yet had opportunity to remove, and Maldonado was ushered from the corridor into the Minister's office. This room was spacious but not grand, with a fine view of the desert. Not for the first time, Wen silently praised his father's choice of building sites. At the time it had seemed both wasteful and tasteless to raise the new government on a mountainside rather than on comfortable ground among the people. But that was before the explosive growth of recent years. The growth made possible by the Vardon mineral finds. A mineral wealth now, with the Kristenkowski find, expected to increase by an order of magnitude.

Now then, Jorge, Wen began easily, beginning his counterattack. Why are you interesting yourself in the daily business of the Public Assay?

Maldonado chose not to reply. Wen stripped off his sash and collar. When the marks of office were laid away in a closet and the two men were comfortably seated before the large window, a small bottle of soda water and two iced glasses between them on a low polished table, Maldonado opened with a discreet *ahem.*

Li, he began, likewise shifting to his adversary's familiar name, you know that we are to receive an immigration infall within the year.

Wen Li hesitated, but did then acknowledge knowing this.

You had this news, I believe, privately last month, by means of the recent pod.

Now Wen bristled. Do you mean to say that I am not entitled such private communications? That is by way of compensation for my expenses in maintaining the trade and is protected by charter.

No, no, Maldonado responded mildly. Though we could certainly renegotiate your charter if that is what you want, it is not my purpose. Li, my friend, the colony ship will now be at half-light. There should have been notice of this ten years ago, but I myself only learned of it today.

Wen said nothing, and only a slight flaring of his nostrils gave any clue to his real feelings. A susurrus of cooled air grew up, filling the room without making a draft. He reduced the glare by turning down the louvers set between the window panes.

Li, you are not much better informed than I, Maldonado observed. If you were, you would have had a better answer prepared, and a better cover for your preparations at the landing site. These matters come under you, Li. Why didn't you know sooner? I hope you are going over your organization pretty thoroughly.

Ah, yes. Though what we are looking for may prove difficult to document. I find it hard to believe that knowledge of such importance could be kept secret for a decade.

Of course you do, when you yourself have managed to do so for only a month.

Wen Li drew himself up, genuinely offended now. You will find I have not disregarded the common weal, he said stiffly. Ng Jo's people will secure the site and my office will take charge of planning. The matter will be managed in the time available. I do not think it wise to go farther now, risking words which we may regret. My resources are at the Council's disposal.

Please excuse me, Maldonado said, acknowledging the stalemate with a slight bow.

After Maldonado had gone, Wen continued for some time to sit with an untouched glass of soda water, gazing out on the desert spread below his window. It had a certain purple grandeur, this desert, here at the edge of the greater south basin, but for the most part the desert floor was still nothing but a slightly rumpled, ugly plain sloping some six hundred kilometers to the sea, studded irregularly with black volcanic outcroppings and thinly covered by creosote and kissop. From where Wen stood, high on the mountain, none of this was visible, hidden by low hills, except for a disturbance in the air which marked the sandstorm's well.

To the north of Kalgoorlie, where the basin was closed at its upper end by the foothills of the interior, there were some enormous vistas, rock walls a thousand meters high painted rose and orange by the setting sun, and moss-grown canyons sheltering their rills in eternal shadow. Still, Wen didn't much like the desert. He had little interest in scenery. If he were offered a chance to move — where? To the fjords of the west corner, or the rim country in the east, or the pampas?

Rising, he began to pace the room.

His sponsorship of the secession movement would necessarily be very circumspect after this, Wen thought. He was in a delicate position, and could no longer play a double hand. These earthers might settle in Kalgoorlie, but only if their articles of settlement were made so attractive as to profit Wen but little. If only he had had a chance to prepare, to diversify. More likely the colonists would begin again for themselves, either from a taste for it or to escape exploitation. Wen would have to extract what he could from them in Kalgoorlie without hastening through greed the inevitable emigration, while at the same time striving to extend his reach without alarming them.

Most disturbing, why indeed had he not learned of this infall before now? What hidden forces were at work?

Half a million people. What are we going to do with half a million people?

A discreet chime swelled the air and Ng Jo's face appeared on the com at his desk. Wen sat down and, after composing himself, stroked the authorization.

Good morning, Jo.

Kalgoorlie's quondam Director of Weed Studies smiled and twitched a heavy lock of black hair out of her eyes. I wanted to thank you, she said, for voting to fund the kissop weed program this morning.

Ah. Well, the program is in good hands, I'm sure. Will you see to it that the north basin assay results are passed on to the City Engineer as soon as you receive them?

Of course.

Didn't miss a beat, Wen thought as the vidicom eye closed. Always a pleasure to work with good people. The cranky, self-pitying mood of an hour before was gone. Contrary to first impressions, matters seemed to be as much under control as could be expected.

He waved away the eye. He found it disconcerting to have it float there over the corner of his desk. Even closed it was far too reminiscent of its paranoid orbiting brother.

《 》

Four percent, the troll Karl Fishbach was complaining. He seemed inclined to throw his pencil across the room. There were, in fact, a number of black marks on the wall at the spot where he was glaring.

Point three eight seven, countered Wen drily, but Fishbach whined: Four! and Wen, smiling just a little, did not contradict again.

If Councilor Maldonado had not stupidly made a public announcement of this discovery, Fishbach continued in his phlegmatic thin voice, we would not find our hands tied in this way. People will expect the most absurd benefits.

He paused to cough, a dark rheumy noise, a gurgling caused by chronic allergies, to kissop weed primarily.

When they aren't forthcoming, the Vardon Mining District will be blamed.

To Wen the solution was obvious, but it seemed better to let Fishbach come to it by the rougher road or the man would certainly feel he was being denied a voice. So Wen let Fishbach grumble and pace the small anteroom without hindrance. And it was quite true that by making these unjustified promises Maldonado had allowed his enthusiasm to override his good sense. A really go-ahead development of the Vardon mine would be more difficult in an atmosphere of distrust. What was more worrisome was that Maldonado had not consulted anyone else on the district board. Perhaps he had intended to blackmail them, to bring the board under his personal control by threatening to use public opinion against them?

And now the papers were beginning to refer to operations in Vardon Vale as a slave camp, and that man Cuelleman was asking for "considerations" on the Hollis business. Fishbach's management of public relations was ludicrously ham-handed.

Ham. Wen smiled. Pig-headed, we also say. And talk about bringing home the bacon.

While Fishbach fulminated, Wen studied the room in which they sat. Fishbach himself was tall and lean, emaciated really, but in spirit he was small. The anteroom was positively claustrophobic, its walls scraped of any decoration, of that institutional green color used from time immemorial to denote anonymity. There were three doors. One opened onto the elevator from the opulent main lobby of Government

House. Opposite, closed by an ostentatious security skin which Wen knew to be responsive only to Fishbach's own biomarks, was the door to the man's private quarters. The third door was small and would have been unobtrusive if it were not guarded by an ominous man in civilian dress who was presumably as discreet as he was ruthless. This door was connected to a private entrance just inside the building perimeter.

And they will benefit, Fishbach was saying now. We should let them see that. Give the Mine Board the power to really develop the Kristenkowski find and they'll see something. Why are you smiling, Li?

Pigs, Karl.

Pigs?

I was thinking about the fact that there are no animals here. Other than ourselves, of course. Now then, Karl, he went on politely, pursuing his own strategy, what do you suggest? Maldonado can't be allowed to arbitrate public opinion, of course. The present instance could possibly be turned against him by some of the hotheads on the Council. Abusing the public trust, using his position to misrepresent the views of a minority for personal gain. The obvious complaints. But Maldonado's position is a good one, well-fortified, and it would be foolish to risk a battle over the public reputation of the Mine Board, which is shaky in any case, when a defeat will tar us all with the same brush. Better to accept the compromise now, when a show of openhandedness can still be salvaged, and let the matter rankle for a time. Maldonado's overbearing tactics will drive some of the moderates out of his camp. Do you see, Karl?

Wen leaned forward in a most intimidating way, forcing Fishbach to step back.

Yes, Fishbach said hastily. Yes, of course.

The Mine Board can't be allowed to avenge its injured vanity, either. As I know you would, naturally, wish to, and

as I know you are working up to. That would not play well
with the public. Or for that matter with the Council. Do you
agree?

That way everyone profits, Fishbach whined. We get
nothing. The Council should step in, confound it.

Oh, I agree, Wen replied smoothly. But after all, the
Board has not entirely ignored your interest in this. Sr. Maldonado came to see me about it yesterday.

Fishbach stopped his pacing. Then why didn't you tell
the Board? he snarled, passing in an instant from stupefaction to grievance.

I intend to, when it meets this afternoon, responded the
imperturbable Wen, and Fishbach sat down in a pout to toy
again with his pencil.

What I say this afternoon I have not yet decided.

What were you told? Fishbach said, now decidedly
cowed.

Wen now paused to give thought. He did not particularly want to cook a hasty story. Maldonado would defend
it all, of course, since anything Wen said would make the
Chairman look better than he presently did. So he began the
explanation by saying that Ng Jo had got hold of the assay,
and Jorge wanted to make the announcement before she did.
He asked me whether I thought the Board would support a
distribution. I said they probably would, so long as they were
given a free hand in running the district.

And does Ng have the assay? Fishbach asked suspiciously.

No, that was a ruse. Your security is good. It gave Maldonado an opportunity to sound me out on the position of
the Board.

But the Board doesn't want a distribution, Fishbach objected.

Ah, yes. Nevertheless, as you see, there will be a distribution. The Board's position will be stronger if it appears to welcome what it will have to accept. Don't you think the Board would prefer to salvage part of its opportunities rather than lose everything defending the high ground?

Fishbach supposed it would, and subsided into just the sort of irritated acquiescence which Wen hoped to obtain from the whole Mine Board in an hour's time. Privately, Wen found the Interior Secretary's behavior foolish and clumsy. Fishbach put far too much importance on keeping face. If only he had struck at a reasonable target. As it was, by treating the present position as an ignominious compromise he would lose the victory.

Still, everyone had uses. In any case, Fishbach's role in the establishment of the Vardon Mining District was suspect enough to keep him under control. This militia corporal Cuelleman might be able to help, might have something to say about that. A whole expedition endangered by this business with Carol Hollis, for nothing more than a sleazy personal vendetta, and a respected mining engineer too, who certainly knew his way around in the desert better than that. It could be made to look very bad, if necessary.

Wen sighed, a little dispirited despite the forwarding of his plans. Everything was so unnecessarily complicated.

« »

After the meeting with Fishbach Wen took a trolley around to the militia barracks, intending to see the commandant about a request to detach Cpl. Cuelleman to sentry duty at Government House, where it would be easier to keep an eye on him. Cuelleman would know well enough what it was about. As it proved, the commandant understood perfectly also and Wen's only mistake for the day was to suppose the corporal's name was pronounced with a soft c, which caused a little merriment which Wen knew how to overlook.

The knowing Corporal Frederick Cuelleman was not happy to be ordered off with his duffle to the Council guard, though he put a good face on it. Coo, the others commented, allowing jealousy to show. Some guys has all the luck. First it's the Vardon expedition, now it's the guard. They going to run you for the Council next? Cuelleman traded jabs with these few acquaintances but privately cursed his continued misfortune which had begun out of nothing more than boredom.

Who was it asked for me? he inquired while he was getting his identification redrawn. Guy with a round head?

Nah. Wee dapper fellow in a white suit, with a parasol. Not your other boy. Never seen him before. Seemed to know frogface pretty well.

Didn't he pass scan?

Didn't have to, did he? You be messin with some of the big boys.

The ID artist capped his stylus. Cuelleman sat up, sourly fingering the spot under his right eye where the artist had been at work, and shouldered his duffle. The desk man wiped him with the light and glanced once at the security terminal.

Hokay, boy, you be cleared for the guard, and don'tcha come back here no more with that evil eye or you'll set off every bomb in the place. So get youself a new honey, hokay?

Sure. See you.

Not me, boy, the MP said, not laughing.

Outside the barracks an empty trolley was waiting on the terminus roundabout. Cuelleman trudged over and got aboard, slouched into a seat at the back, crabby and resentful. Away off behind the officers' mess a lacrosse game was going on under hot blue lights, making the yellow streetlamps of the vacant terminus seemed dim and moody by contrast. The trolley started with a jerk, rolling out onto the line and carrying him up to Government House over a track strung like a necklace on the naked mountain. Cheesy hotels and bars crowded up to the line here below. Further along, away from the militia barracks, the buildings fell back, became dark inward-looking tenements which leaned against each other like the walls of a card house, each with its narrow un-lit stair turned like a rectum on the empty street. Crazy twist-ed passages ran between the buildings, where as a boy he had on mild winter nights made many advances to unknown girls, some of them not too ugly, some of the advances suc-cessful when they weren't spoiled by stronger boys, or being dumped half naked off the unrailed landing. But all those girls had smelled bad. The whole neighborhood smelled bad, like rotten fruit and moldy bread, dirty feet, garlic. It was worse now. He never went there anymore.

Nearer Government House were districts of fashionable shops and restaurants, spangled with little twinkling lights and bustling with a lively café society dressed in pink and pearl gray. Above that was another dark band, the labyrinth of government offices and patio houses jumbled together promiscuously among spiky palms and fig trees with leath-ery black leaves as big as bath towels. In a breeze the leaves rubbed together like thighs.

Above that was Government House itself, gated and walled and sleepless. Cpl. Cuelleman swung off the trolley at the guardhouse and went in to report. A flash of scanner light blinded him momentarily as it always did, looking for and this time finding the retinal ID, the implant, the virtual portrait looking out through the pupil of his eye like some-one through a keyhole. He'd been kept locked in a closet for a time as a boy, looking out like that.

That's me, I suppose, in a metaphoric sense anyway, looking out through a sort of telescope analogous to the world-sized machine which keeps its Eye on us. Frederick

Cuelleman is, he thought, mostly a device, a hand and an eye manufactured for the purpose, assembled in ghetto factories and fueled by the usual longings, ambitions, hatreds, ignorance, self-disgust, and so forth, which no parent can avoid passing on. What beings, he wondered, but not too often, peer from my eyes? Who are the specks who float there, the unplucked-out moats and beams and specks of specks, like mitochondria of desire stretching back in an unbroken chain to the Beginning?

Right, said a dry voice.

The security officer's pinched face floated out of the dark behind the desk. The night duty clerk pushed a key card across the counter.

Cast your duffel in the bunk down the hall. Mess is in the basement of the Council. Report to the masthead for duty at six o'clock. That's all.

Dismissed, Cuelleman dropped off his kit and continued on along the passage, following the signs to the Council basement. After getting dinner he went upstairs, passing one checkpoint and another by means of his small eye, little brother to the bigger one overhead. He went through the deserted chamber hall and out onto a balcony overlooking the main gate. A steady dribble of foot traffic passed in and out of this gate, with an occasional whispering, black shrouded two-seater carrying some official and his driver. Every twenty minutes the trolley drifted by beyond the gate, ran along the wall for a block and then curled away again down the hill.

Suppose he were to desert? Up over the ridge into the north basin and through the bush to Horring? Could he avoid being picked up by Per Hemla's separatists? He didn't fancy being loose in the bush even without the rebels to pull the strings out of his legs like they'd probably done to Hollis when they caught him finally. Down into the barrio then,

where he'd been born and could hide as he pleased except
for the smell and the bad memories and the guys who would
catch you sleeping on the roof or a landing and gut you for
the necromancers, or just push you over the edge for the hell
of it.

Better to stay here, to lie low. Word was there was a colony ship due in eighteen months. Then there would be a hel-
luva mess, and then he'd be able to make off as he liked.

Turning, Cuelleman looked away into the dark sky
behind the ridge. The lights of Kalgoorlie blotted out any
chance of seeing the incoming ship, and the stars which he
knew now were there. He'd seen them for the first time on
the Vardon expedition, that summer in the bush, the only
time he'd been out of Kalgoorlie. What a summer. Most everything is beautiful at first.

First time always the best.

Frew he was called then. He didn't remember the first
time, as if he'd been born that way and someone else had
used up his first time already without giving him anything
back for it. Probably his dad. On one of those landings on
one of those nights, got thrown down on his head, mom said
once.

Better to lie low.

Eighteen months. Damn, he said. Damn. Damn.

《 》

Maldonado was studying a map of the northwestern interior
when his aide cautiously looked in. Startled, the Councilor
waved his map away and then, thinking this hasty gesture
might appear surreptitious or guilty, he ostentatiously restored it to a space above the vid.

The aide's voice betrayed his uneasiness. Sr Renaud has
a guard corporal selling information, he said. He thought it

better not to consult you in the usual way.

Selling? What, for money?

That's what Sr Renaud says, Councilor, but perhaps it's too extravagant an expression. He's encountered some of Hemla's people in the north basin. If pressed he would only want to be sent out after them. A chance to make a name for himself.

A corporal of the guard, you say.

Recently transferred. He was escort on the Vardon expedition.

Ah. Sent to coventry, fears he'll be forgotten.

Coventry, Councilor?

Nowhere.

It was an expression Maldonado had picked up from Charles. He could see there was more to it, and that his aide thought so too, but decided to leave well enough alone.

This mercenary corporal, he said, should return to his guard post. Let him know we'll see he learns of any opportunities to improve his position.

The aide grinned and withdrew, and Maldonado returned to the map with new interest. He had been looking at possible sites for another settlement but now he turned to the geography of Per Hemla's position instead. Increasing the resolution to show sufficient detail of the north basin, he called for an overlay of the Vardon expedition route, which appeared as a thin red line circling the western edge of the basin before it struck off across the high mesa country in the direction of Vardon canyon. A second overlay showed the places where Hemla's people had been found. From a position in the coastal mountains he had been making increasingly longer strikes in the last few months, toward the north in the direction of the coastal town of Horring.

The ambassador would have something to say about that at their next meeting.

And now there were some newer strikes to the southeast, into the barren desert. What, then, had Hemla learned of the infall?

Maldonado requested the roster of the latest Vardon exploration and easily identified Frederick Cuelleman as his new informant. Commended in the unsuccessful search for Hollis. Promotion and transfer to the guard.

Another one of Wen's spies.

The details of Hollis's disappearance were extraordinarily sketchy. But then the country was rough, even for someone experienced.

Sitting back, Maldonado pondered the relations among Hemla, the Vardon mines, Hollis, and this opportunistic corporal of the guard. Hollis had been opposed to the development of private interests, the same issue which Hemla exploited to justify his guerrilla war on Kalgoorlie. Suppose someone other than Wen had suborned this Cuelleman to betray them? More than an eye, perhaps. An eye for an eye.

This upstart corporal needed to be brought under control.

The Horrans would support Hemla if necessary, in the interests of a balance of power. Supplies, base of operations perhaps. What else? They had all been reluctant, so far, to use force. There were too few of them to be able to spend lives that way. Playing at war, Wen grumbled, and claimed they weren't serious about their beliefs. Views defended so cautiously, so tepidly, could not possibly be serious. Hollis was the first casualty, perhaps the turning point. Looking to the incoming colony ship, did Wen now feel he could afford to risk a little capital?

Everything centered on the incoming ship. It would choke Kalgoorlie and Horring both, but interests like Wen's stood to profit. They would profit by a new settlement, too, but that was riskier: it would add a new player to the game. The difficulty was, there was no place to site a new settlement.

Maldonado pulled back the resolution so that the map above his desk covered the whole northern continent. The geography of it was a serious obstacle to large-scale settlement. Virtually the whole was ruggedly mountainous and, except for an alluvial region in the southeast, without agricultural land. The inevitable course of development had been toward small, isolated city-states living on the produce of narrow mountain valleys. Lack of resources and space would keep them small, and poor communication would keep them divided for a while, but eventually they would need the resources of that southeastern plain and that meant a federation of some kind, farming the southeast in common if they were not to be all dictated to by an agricultural monopoly. A similar threat, of a mineral oligarchy, had already been raised by the Vardon find, which private interests intended to work with what amounted to slaves, using their ore to buy control of the levers of power. It would be essential to delay further exploitation of the Vardon's Kristenkowski resources until the colony ship arrived. Then labor would be cheap and hard to corner, with the chance of other finds continually sucking away independent prospectors. Other finds there would be, and with them the Vardon monopoly would evaporate.

So Wen was faced with a nice problem of timing. He had to develop the Vardon opportunity quickly. If the colony ship arrived before he had consolidated his grip he would lose everything. But if he could bring Vardon, and with it Kalgoorlie, under his hand in the next few months then the colonists might find themselves herded off to the mines, and perhaps eventually to some serf state in the southeast.

Carol Hollis had stood in his way. Against Wen there was now chiefly public opinion, mobilized by people such as Ng Jo and symbolized, somewhat ambiguously, by Per Hemla.

But a promise to distribute the Vardon profits would easily mollify the public until the day when they found themselves sent, profitless, opinionless, to the mines with the rest.

Two lots of spies, then: Ng's and Wen's.

Wen had shown himself in the matter of Hollis to be hot-tempered and incautious if pushed the right way. Another useful possibility.

Still working out in his mind the nature of his own opportunities, Maldonado doused both the map and the lights and opened the sunshades to look down on Kalgoorlie. The class structure of the city was distinctly visible in fine gradations of roof and lawn tumbling down the mountainside from Government House to the bottom, where lay the jumbled ruins of four generations of class struggle.

Cuelleman comes out of the barrio, Maldonado remembered. Quite a success on the face of it, from rising barrio rat to guardsman. Not so much in his own eyes, apparently. Something would have to be done about the resentments of the rats before long. Any Vardon distribution which overlooked that inequity wouldn't have much of a chance. Inequity beheads kings.

Maldonado turned away from the window again, brushing closed its louvers against that hot pitiless sunlight.

《 》

Ng Jo was sitting at an outdoor table in the café district drinking coffee. Only in the last week had the heat died enough to reopen the sidewalk tables, and though the evening was still garish, Jo was glad to be out of her house and among people again. She sucked up the hot bitter coffee which made the sweat roll out of her hair and felt the newly cool breeze dry it, and all the wire-thin muscles of her arms and shoulders, ratcheted twangy tight over the last month, began to ease back just a little.

It was early, in the season and the evening. The café district was still empty, pastel sandstone pink in the last swirls of twilight. Down the little side street where she was sitting, Jo could see the lights of shops on Vardon Avenue, and below that some bright barrio clubs. Two blocks above, the street was closed by the pale sparkling granite of the wall of Government House. Then night sprang up into the sky and all the color of the street was sucked away leaving only the butter yellow of the café windows. The avenue shops and the barrio rushed away to indistinct glittering white grains. Behind her, the mass of Government House bulked up, resolutely unlit.

There was a smell of fried bread in the air, spicy with peppers and astringent herbs. She ordered another cup of coffee and closed her eyes, concentrating on the mingled odors of coffee, food, perfume, dust, and a faint and distant smell of old urine.

Someone else sat down at the table. Two people, a man and a woman. The woman, by her scent and the snuffling way she breathed, was an acquaintance, a Council aide. The man was a stranger. Tall, she guessed, but hunched. An acrid, sweaty man. A little thought told her who it might be. She opened her eyes. This sort of thing was good practice.

You are Corporal Cuelleman?

And it produced the desired effect. The tall, sandy haired man started and stooped a little more.

The Council aide sneered and drifted away, having done what Ng Jo had asked, which was to locate the survivors of the Hollis expedition.

Who are you? the guardsman inquired belligerently. He was out of uniform, dressed in a blouson and loose drawstring trousers of dingy canvas.

My name is Ng, she said quietly. I sit on the Kalgoorlie

Council, for security, and so I have an interest in the Vardon mine.

So I report to you.

Jo's smile was cold. Young, he was. Six months ago she would have been leaning on this man to turn in his kissop weed distribution reports.

The Council, as you know, has given the mining district leave to bring out the ore as it pleases. This closes the district to my view. It is now, in effect, an independent state.

She signaled a waiter, who soon brought two plates of fried bread, more coffee for her, and a mug of beer. Jo delicately picked up a stick of savory bread and bit off the crisp end.

A defeat for you, the corporal observed smugly.

Of course, one can't protest. A public distribution of the profits has been promised.

Cuelleman made a derisive snort. He had touched neither the bread nor the beer.

Now that they've begun to bring out the ore, she went on, it does seem after all to have been worth the trouble of resistance. Conditions in the mine are not good, of course. One could hardly expect otherwise.

You're going to change that?

Poough. Ng spread her hands flat on the table, on either side of her cooling cup and saucer. I don't suppose anyone is, unless the district makes its bad faith apparent.

Her black, stony eye rested steadily on Cuelleman's paler gaze. He flinched, but with a contemptuous little grunt. A bully, she thought. Timid and blustering, snobbish about the use of force.

A few months ago, Señor Cuelleman, you offered us some information on Carol Hollis. I'd like to have that now.

Cuelleman's face hardened, but when he spoke it was with a petulant voice. I made that offer to someone else, he complained.

Jo waited, making implacable silent command.

I didn't say I knew anything about Hollis's death. It was the separatista. Hemla's guerillas.

Rubbish. The Eye tells us that much every time it comes over. You never expected that to be taken seriously.

Cuelleman shrugged. Jo drank off her coffee in a single swallow, then lowered the cup onto its saucer with hypnotic deliberation, letting it fall the last distance with a clink that made Cuelleman start.

They've abandoned that position now, anyway, she said. It's too near the mine.

Señor Maldonado said there'd be a chance for me. To get out of the guard.

You want to go back into the desert?

That's it.

Or I could have you sent to Horring. With a diplomatic mission, as a sergeant at arms. That would be appropriate for a guardsman, not likely to draw attention. Good for your career.

Cuelleman pulled at the dirty canvas of his shirt, trying to hide his satisfaction.

Besides, Jo went on quietly, you'd be safer in Horring if it should become known you'd killed Hollis.

Cuelleman went pale, then red. I didn't, he hissed.

Ah, replied Jo distantly, with a touch of disappointment. But then, you were supposed to. You were hired for that, and bungled it, and people will believe what they like.

I did not, Cuelleman repeated desperately, but he was already defeated. Jo met his eye, which wavered but this time held, accepted complicity. She would use him to block Fishbach's exploitation of the Vardon find. Fishbach would have enemies on all sides, then. The Horrans would not protect him, out of solidarity with Hemla or a cautious regard for relations with Kalgoorlie. The guerillas would hold the desert against him, and in Kalgoorlie he would need to defend himself against Wen Li's faction. Against Wen she now had Cuelleman. Fishbach was hemmed in. He and Maldonado would not appease Wen Li again.

What do you want me to say?

Ah. Jo rose from the table. Nothing would be best.

Then she relented. You'll find the right words, she assured him, taking another piece of the savory bread. But then, changing her mind, she returned it to the basket and fastidiously wiped the grease from her finger tips with the thick yellow napkin which had been brought rolled up on the plate beside the round grass basket.

Weed. A tough desert grass, brittle and hard to work with, but variegated and fine. It made beautiful close woven fragile baskets.

《 》

After Ng had gone Cuelleman passed a few moments watching the bubbles still rising in his untouched beer. When she had a block's start he, too, left the table.

Ng had turned onto a lane which ran parallel to the wall of Government House a block below the trolley line. Cuelleman followed, keeping well back. The narrow lane twisted between the backs of houses all set at different angles to one another to take best advantage of the sloping ground. The white plastered walls, blank except for unpretentious porticoes which jutted out into the cobbled lane, gave access to interior courtyards which he could glimpse through the iron grilles which were set into the gaps between the houses. The lane was dark, lit only by portico lights.

Ng went in at the entrance to one of these houses, her black hair and dark narrow face illuminated for a brief moment while she unlocked the door. Cuelleman slipped into the gap at the end of the wall, climbed the grille, and dropped down softly on the other side, into a wedge-shaped nook between the two houses which had been landscaped with picturesque rocks and cactuses on a carefully raked bed of sand. The sand was noisy underfoot and the raked surface showed prints. From here, openings slitted into the walls gave views into Ng's and the opposing courtyards but the slits were too narrow for him to pass.

Ng's court was dark. He saw briefly someone moving under the arcade which shaded part of the ground opposite, then all was still.

The flagged courtyard was set with a fountain in the middle and flowering trees in tubs here and there. Nearby stood chairs and a table with a game of chess partly finished. From one of the dark rooms which opened onto the courtyard from beyond the arcade came a soft, tinkling kind of music. Incense was burning somewhere.

Ng had revealed the kind of fierceness and energy which it would be difficult to stand against. He could see it in her fingers, splayed on the café table: all bone and tendon, knobby and fleshless, seeming to clutch the smooth wooden surface like some strangling vine. Wen and Fishbach he understood better. Men like that have power and use it bluntly, straightforwardly, not for pleasure but simply to get more power. Ng was something else. Perhaps it was that impression she gave of being stretched taut even when she appeared most calm. Her powers were personal, self-derived, quasi-magical.

After a hour's wait, he decided that there was little more to be learned here. Climbing back over the gate, he marked the location of the house and flitted away down the crooked lane, back through the café district and across Vardon Prospect into the barrio.

He knew he had left traces everywhere. But professionally discreet, as would be expected at any job interview.

Near the Prospect the houses were small and well-kept, but as he threaded his way deeper they became more and more ramshackle, each tier overbearing the ones in front like mountain ranges set one behind another, the most distant and ominous peaks bleak and snowcapped against the leaden sky. In the daytime it was different. Then, the bright orange light washed the soft grays and yellows of the weathered, unpainted wood with glowing color, punctuated by eccentric streaks of rust and purple stains. But at night, away from the lighted thoroughfares, the narrow barrio streets were like crevasses and culverts eroded through a mountain of trash.

Once within the barrio, passing quickly through a small unlit square, Cuelleman dove into the black mouth of an alley so narrow that his shoulders brushed the walls on either side. The air was hard to breathe here, still and hot, unmoved in years. No breeze could twist its way this deep into the impacted, overshot canyons. About twenty meters back from the mouth was an even narrower stair which climbed up between two buildings and led ultimately to a doorway on the top floor. This he opened without knocking and stepped into the hall beyond. Light seeped in here through a hole in the ceiling, just enough to see the bare floor and a dark wall blotched with pale stains which glimmered with a radiance of their own. Feeling his way, avoiding the dark humped shapes lying against the walls, he located halfway along a closed door with a new lock, its lower panel freshly troweled with fibrous gray resin. he knocked. One of the men sleeping nearby muttered and shifted a bit.

From inside a woman's voice. Yeah?

It's Bro. You changed the lock.

The door was opened, after a bit of fumbling. Some of these tubs kicked in the bottom, said Sis, gesturing toward the sleepers as she closed the door again. Gimmee your key, I'll fix it.

From a pocket under the drawstring of his trousers he extracted a small key card, which he handed to her.

Where's Bengt? he wanted to know, flopping onto a futon which was folded up under the bleary, lightless window. It had a new cover, a big orange flower print.

Out. Bengt is out.

Taking his key back, now married to the new lock, he fished out a flat packet from a different inner pocket and laid it on a square lacquered table standing nearby. A fresh arrangement of dried flowers stood there, another spot of color in the otherwise drab room. An empty bowl stood on the floor, a pair of chopsticks laid precisely across it.

Whatcha doin?

Watching holos. I gotta work in an hour. You sent word. I thought you'd be here earlier.

I was hoping to see Bengt.

What now?

I don't know. Business. Is the light out in the hall again?

Yeah. I'm afraid someone's going to start a fire, burn the building down. Maybe tomorrow, Bengt says.

Is he coming back now?

Sis nodded, her face masked by shadow.

Dammit, Liz. It's this Hollis business again. I want to know can Bengt help me out. I got to show up for duty roster tomorrow morning, six o'clock. Can I sleep here? Maybe if Bengt comes around before then.

You'll miss curfew.

Yeah, well maybe it's better I'm not in quarters just now. Maybe it'll be all right. I know someone who might spring me to Horring, but I'd feel better if I had a banger somewhere.

I gotta go, Frew. I'm going to be late. Have you had any supper?

No. It's all right. Do you think Bengt can find me a

banger?

Liz had been changing from her shirt to a work smock and stopped, her hand on her throat. What do I know about that? she said angrily. Why did you let them push you into this? It's bad for business, Frew. If they had to come in here after you or Bengt it would probably start a riot. Then what? You wouldn't last a week in the mines.

Dammit, Liz, what can I do? How many sweeps have there been?

Two this week. Two last.

What are they saying?

I don't know. Keep off the main streets, outa the bars, no crowds.

Nobody's been down inside?

Well, they haven't come back here anyway. It's bad, Frew. You gotta stay out of it. Don't let Bengt use you for nothing.

Sure, Liz. You be going. I'll be outa here before you get back.

After Liz had left he pushed the lacquer side table away and unfolded the futon, which took up most of the floor. Then he rubbed Liz's supper bowl clean with a little water from the canister which she kept in the commode and threw the dirty water out the window instead of into the recycling bottle, put the bowl and chopsticks away in the commode and lay down in his clothes, setting his watch for four o'clock.

Sometime later he woke to the sound of shouts and running feet in the alleyway below and he sat up bolt, his heart pounding, but it was only some kids and it had been just two hours by the watch. But then, perhaps the preternatural sensitivity he had for just a moment on waking... No lights, the hole in the hallway ceiling, the broken door... he realized Bengt wasn't coming back, that they'd picked him up in the last sweep.

Shit, he said out loud in the dark. Why didn't she say so? Where am I going to get a banger now?

« »

Wen Li was discoursing on systems of government.

So, he was saying: We see the first signs of independence, of rebellion, of what I take to be the usual, perhaps inevitable transition from autarky to a system less personal, less despotic if also less free, not yet a democracy but with stirrings in the demos, or rather the helotry, the protodemos, protores, beginning to make themselves felt like an unborn baby kicking you in the stomach at a party, causing you to wince and catch your breath quite inexplicably. At least inexplicably to others, to the man you splashed your drink on and who now makes a hasty excuse to leave, which doesn't matter since you were flirting with him under false pretenses anyway. So in systems of government, as in reproduction and I suppose in human relations generally, independence sifts downward (toward the loins and feet) and constraints bubble up (toward the mouth and brain). To the governed what appears to be more degrees of freedom, to the governors seems anarchy and rebellion. Our freedom to govern is increasingly shackled by an unwelcome interdependence. Entanglements unwelcome to me, at any rate. I would prefer to leave matters to those with fewer scruples.

Maldonado, Ng, Fishbach, and some other members of Council had begun to fidget. Maldonado cut off any resumption of Wen's lecture by turning to the woman in the seat beside him.

Jo, he said, you've seen the Corporal? And will he do?

I believe so.

Maldonado turned his attention back to the rump Council assembled in Wen Li's courtyard on a mild evening.

Such are your views, Li? Underneath the thick callus of your oligarchic instincts runs a stratum of sympathy, then? I should say empathy except that when one does not feel a need oneself then empathy is moot. Bareheaded, how is one to guess another man needs a hat?

Wen's house servant left four glasses of brown liquor on a tray on a side table and withdrew. Wen handed them round himself, to Jorge and Jo who were sitting by the fountain, Jo on the tile rim and the Councilor reclining somewhat on a chaise. Li took the third glass himself and remained standing. The fourth was for Fishbach, sitting now primly and uneasily on a small wicker chair, apart. The tray with its solitary remaining glass had been put down just out of his reach.

Mr. Fishbach reports, said Li, gesturing with his glass, that we have a miners' strike in progress. I thought we ought to work out our position before it goes any farther.

How long? Jorge asked. He had sunk back at the news, his anxiety sucked away, the hole filled with certainty now.

Four days, Fishbach admitted in a husky, nervous voice. Jorge took this in.

You were hoping to put down the strike by yourself, I take it, before the next pass of the eye.

Fishbach lifted his chin a bit, visibly stubbled even in the shadows of the courtyard. We have two or three of the ringleaders, he said. We could contain it in a few more days. They have no provisions. Food, that is. Haven't any.

Then why appeal to us? Jorge returned a little wearily, beginning to rise.

Yes, Fishbach replied in a languid voice intended to appear hesitant but conveying instead a sneer. I had hoped to conserve the resources of the... polity by relying on my own. Mr. Wen prefers not to... he thinks it unwise to wait. He sees a risk of their being relieved by some of Helma's people. I... concur.

Maldonado studied the stuffy little Secretary of the Interior, discomfiting him. He sipped a bit of the cassia that Wen had served, putting the glass down carefully, delicately, as an exercise in self-control under the circumstances, on the flagstones beside his chair. Jo, too, waited, sitting easily with her legs crossed, with the balance of years of yoga, carefully avoiding Maldonado's eye. Behind her, a soft mist rose from the fountain, filling the courtyard with a welcome moisture and perfume. An unfinished chess game stood there, in the shadow of the wide leaved trees.

If the Council's help is required, Jorge began, and especially if the militia is used to stop this rebellion, they — that is, the many Council — will consider it a refutation of your policy, Mr. Fishbach, and will almost surely revoke your grant.

Fishbach cleared his throat as if to speak but only shifted a bit on his chair.

I think that point is understood, said Li, putting it firmly aside. He glanced once at Fishbach and then turned to Jo. Are you prepared to support action? he inquired, and she responded with the characteristically distant, wry smile cultivated for such uses.

Garden of smiles, Maldonado thought. Grow best in the shade, smiles do. The cultivated variety anyway.

Behind Li, Fishbach was getting to his feet. He took the fourth glass of cassia delicately in his thick fingers and walked away to examine the flowers growing in a bed under the arcade. A while later the house servant returned with more drinks. Fishbach stopped him, spoke a few words in a low tone, set his empty glass among the full ones on the servant's tray, and hurried out.

Maldonado and Ng left together. He lightly touched the back of her hand. Four blocks away, inside the Government House compound, they met again, Ng gliding out of a shadowed corner to fall into step beside him.

You were watching all this?

It's my business, to watch their backs, to look into things for them, to keep them secure.

And *will* he do, Jo?

Yes.

There will be repercussions, Señor Fishbach is certain. Undesirable repercussions. He wants to be prepared for them, to hold his position. To be able to hold it, weakened as it is. News of a solidarity rising among the barrilleños will leak out. By morning, I would expect. It will be crushed.

I think not, Ng said quietly.

No?

The barrilleños are too tough to be rolled up so easily. They will know within hours that they are on the wrong side of history.

Cuelleman already.

Ng Jo nodded complacently. They will not consent to fight a shadow war, Jorge, she said, brushing the back of his hand in turn. The gesture contained a warning: he faced not a consolidation but a beginning.

There was a movement in the street below, and a shout. A dull thud, of the sort felt in the stomach rather than heard, was followed by a rattling of pebbles on metal roofs. A siren started up.

Charles Renaud was waiting at the door of Maldonado's compound. He nodded familiarly at Ng and began a hasty briefing.

There has been an explosion in a communications bunker, he said. A fire has started, and has spread to the node. Barricades have gone up on the north and east. We have a second explosion in the transmission tunnel, with one tower now down.

Who is at the barricades? Maldonado wanted to know,

still calm, merely curious.

It's difficult to know, Charles said. Difficult for us to know, that is. He paused to listen to a new report.

The tram line is blocked.

Blocked?

Yes. With, um... trash, cobbles, that sort of thing. We can't clear it away. The militia barracks is on the wrong side.

Ng Jo broke in here. Cut off, she said quietly, curt. How long will it take to mobilize?

By morning, perhaps.

And to retake the barricades?

Difficult to say. Difficult for us, that is. They'll have had all night to consolidate their position. Seems to have been well planned. Perhaps we ought to be negotiating?

Maldonado seemed about to give an order but then fell quiet. Ng and Renaud waited while the pause stretched out to become a silence. An aide emerged, sweat dripping from the lines of his jaw onto his plum-colored silk shirt. He, too, was silenced.

No, Maldonado said finally, jerking it out. Set up a cordon. That will be sufficient. See that it is sufficient. Señora Ng and I have business. Charles.

The aide swirled plumly away, followed closely by Renaud. Maldonado rubbed the bridge of his nose, seeming to gain energy from somewhere within himself like a dynamo core. What do you suppose we can see from the roof, Jo? he inquired, and was off like a boy to a fireworks display.

A house servant brought a ladder and the two of them climbed up onto the tiles — a clamber for Maldonado, while Ng seemed to levitate — to sit side by side on the ridge, looking down the slope over the housetops into the barrio. Already the cordon sanitaire could be picked out by a double line, white mercury lights on the government side and yellow fires on the other. On the yellow side, deeper within the body of the enemy, a jet of flame marked the position of the broken com link.

Must be a hydrogen line or something, Maldonado commented.

The graceful torch, blue and yellow, rose straight and thin fifty meters into the black desert sky, only the very tip wavering uncertainly like a bit of fluff on a stick.

Folly to site a com node in the barrio, Ng remarked drily.

Wen will have to isolate that line and shut it down, Maldonado said, but his voice suggested doubt for the first time. Was that their objective, do you imagine? The com link?

Taking out that com, Ng observed, knocks out the Eye. Contact with Hemla and with Horring is cut off. Now Fishbach will in fact have to handle the Vardon situation on his own.

Down below, a second jet of burning gas shot up beside the first.

Maldonado, one eyebrow rising slowly, gazed obliquely at the woman sitting beside him on the roof. Her feet in soft leather moccasins clung easily to the sloping tiles. She seemed no more tense than usual, but her face glistened in the flickering shadows cast by the faraway hydrogen torch.

We always seem to be just a little behind events, don't we, Jo? Maldonado sniffed the air and allowed himself an ironic smile.

Toward the east, where a wide avenue marked the perspective of the tram line, yet another new fire flared up. By its light the tiny black silhouettes of men could be seen heaping up more rubble there. Beyond the barricade to the south, insect sparkles darted to and fro.

Spangled gunfire.

They're killing them, Maldonado shouted, starting up. It's supposed to be a cordon. No shooting, he roared. Stop, stop! You're killing us!

His hard shod feet slipped on the tiles and he fell, arms outstretched, slapping the smooth tiles in search of a grip, and slid off the roof and into the fountain.

« »

Meanwhile, a brisk walk through darkened streets of garden offices has brought Fishbach to a corner of the wall below Government House. Rounding the corner, he climbed a narrow lane of steps with a wall of whitewashed brick to his left and on the right the tile roofs of houses terraced into the slope below. In the distance, beyond the necklace of shops and cafés, the tall barrio tenements stood up against an utterly lightless southern desert. Always ominous at night, the barrio seemed to him especially threatening now. Malign. Always malignity on one side or the other. Its dim, faintly glowing, skeletal buildings stared at him, craned and peered like mugs in the back row of a fight crowd.

The guard at the upper gate inclined to insist on a security pass but after a little argument waved Fishbach through. Quite right, Fishbach said to himself with grim satisfaction. Wen hasn't moved any too soon.

The separatista was being held in one of the guard cells close by the upper gate. Fishbach turned into the mouth of a side tunnel, following a yellow stripe on the tiled wall. At the end of this stripe, where a temporary sign had been put up, was another security checkpoint.

Evening, sir, said the man in mufti sitting there. Fishbach was known here. He pushed by without responding, stopped briefly in the open lighted doorway before entering the guard cell, paused under the orange security light, paused again at the border.

Within, in relative gloom, another man in civilian clothes sat at a small deal table reading a transcript which he now held out to Fishbach.

Blood's not even dry yet, he said, grinning. Fishbach scowled at this tasteless remark. Turning the transcript over, he checked the lock and the verification, then slipped it into his jacket pocket.

What have we got?

Hollis lives, apparently. Defected to Hemla, that pied piper. Cuelleman's been lying to us.

Fishbach nodded. That was one of Wen's holds slipped, but a poor one. The man Cuelleman would have quickly become an embarrassment to Wen in any case.

Identification of sympathizers? Fishbach tapped the informer's transcript tucked in his pocket.

But before the security man could reply to this a flurry of activity at the checkpoint outside drew Fishbach's attention. An MP who had just reported to the checkpoint was now running away up the hall, sweat soaked tunic clinging to his muscular back. Fishbach's man was scrabbling up his kit in some haste, while from the main corridor beyond came the sound of heavy boots as a squad of guardsmen were mustered double-time out to the gate.

What?

Explosion and fire in the barrio, sir, Fishbach's man said. Rescue crews have been turned back at the barricades. We've been ordered into blue corridor.

An MP arrived at the gate.

Prisoner ordered moved to regular detention, the man said.

Ordered by who? Fishbach snarled.

There'll be someone along in a bit to take charge, was all the MP said, holding out his hand for the interrogation report still in Fishbach's pocket. Then he walked away up the blue line.

Behind Fishbach the security goon was objecting angrily

to something. Fishbach winced at the man's cursing. Anxious to get clear himself, he hastened on into Government House by one of the more obscure subterranean entrances.

He wanted his people out of Kalgoorlie.

Wipe up here and pull back to Vardon, he snapped to his two aides standing irresolutely at the mouth of the bunker. This uprising will keep Wen's militia busy for a while, and give you time to recapture the situation there.

What about the prisoner? a junior man wanted to know, but Fishbach was already hurrying away again.

Shoot her, he said over his shoulder.

The aides exchanged a quick glance and moved away from the now contaminated, impertinent junior.

《 》

Elsewhere in Kalgoorlie Wen Li waited, uneasy despite his precautions. A show of energy would shore up his position, he thought, if it were threatened. Shaking off his lethargy, he bustled about the command post that had been set up where the blocked tram line crossed Vardon Boulevard, satisfying himself that the rioters intend to stay within their barricaded nest of alleys and tenements. At the command post he provided himself with one of the radios which a captain of the guards had pressed into service to substitute for the disabled com link. Sweating and puffing, with no hat and his white suit soiled, Wen set off down the tram tracks to see for himself whether this salient could be retaken.

All the outward facing buildings were blacked out and the lights in the alleyways were pulled down, so that on its north, outward face the barrio appeared like a stage set, with looming tenebrous blocks stacked up under a lurid sky. Here and there in the street bonfires were burning. On the east, less exposed face bars and clubs were still open, casting long shafts of light into no-man's land and onto the tram rails over which Wen picked his way. But the bars were empty, and the whole district was uncannily silent.

Wen suspected he had misjudged the situation somehow. He was going to lose some discretion over this. There was the matter of passport and travel permit lockdown. There would be a hue and cry for better surveillance when agitators from the Vardon rebellion were discovered here, as he was sure they would be. At the appropriate time. Clever of Maldonado. He strengthened his own hand by diverting attention, and made good use of the less tractable miners. Now Wen would have to make a show of stepping up his own measures. More check points, men in uniform, other such distasteful pub;ic commitments.

A rattling handcar was coming down the tracks behind him, propelled by a guardsman who said he was on orders from his captain. Wen smiled with satisfaction as he climbed up. He had made his point. His energetic response to this emergency had been noted. The car leapt forward. Policy leapt forward.

They had been calling it a barricade, but to Wen's eye it was just a heap of rubble. Sticks and stones thrown across the tracks and defended by snipers in the buildings along the line. The handcar man stopped about a hundred meters short, at the beginning of a shallow ess. On the other side of the barrier, at the other end of the ess, stood another tram which militia from the barracks were using as a forward base.

Ignoring his driver's protests, Wen got down and walked ahead part way to the barrier, which had been raised to about two meters in the center but had not yet completely filled the gap between the sides of the street. Just where one arm of rubble reached out to the undisputed side, the extra-barrio side, in the open door of a bar whose front window had been melted by a militia cannon, stood a man in an apron. Heavy bare arms folded across his chest, he watched Wen coming on toward the barricade.

They have torn up the line, too, Wen muttered. What's the point of that? Exuberance, perhaps. Unnecessary harassment.

The handcar man, who had been talking frantically on his radio, shouted something and Wen turned angrily to object when a blast slapped him on the back and knocked him to the ground. Puffing from this blow, hands and cheek bleeding, he was able to rise only to his knees. A cannon had hit the other side of the barrier. Now a few rifle shots winked from the upper floors of one of the darkened buildings on his left. Getting to his feet, Wen stumbled out of the middle of the road toward a lighted vestibule on the unbarricaded side, in the half destroyed building where the thick-armed barman still stood unmoved, watching the assault. Just as Wen ducked into the proffered haven a sniper bolt from up the street glanced off the corner of the building, leaving a charred notch in the wood about head high and filling the vestibule with an acrid creosote smell.

It was the entrance to a whorehouse. The whores were watching from the upper windows and their laughter tinkled down on him. Red-faced and furious, Wen turned defiantly back onto the sidewalk and walked primly up to the end of the ess, back to the handcar.

What are they firing at the barrier for? he inquired angrily when he had again climbed aboard. They'll only vitrify it. Where are they drawing power?

From the tram line, the handcar man replied. The rebels have been trying to capture a transformer at the head of the ess, there. It would trap our men in a pocket.

Rebels? You dignify them.

The handcar man, unsettled by this challenge, became

cautious. Aren't they rebels?

Hardly, growled Wen. Look at this foolish position they're trying to hold. What are they doing it for? We could put them down in a moment if we would stop playing at it. They can't be serious. It's a tantrum.

What tactic are you going to recommend, sir?

Turn that stupid cannon against the face of the barrio, of course.

It's their cannon, sir, the handcar man said in a shadowy voice.

Capture it and turn it on them.

The handcar man went white.

Threaten to liquefy them. Bring them to reason.

The handcar man blinked with fear.

Stop this stupid business. man, Wen fumed. They must want something, these people. We won't find out what it is until we ask them, and we can't ask them until we get control of the situation.

Yes, sir. That's what we're here for, sir. The man seemed serious, but Wen was tired of being cross-examined.

Is it? he replies dismissively.

They have good reasons, sir. I'm sure. But I'm not —

Rubbish. These people are not serious, I tell you.

Now the handcar man kept his own counsel and the argument came to an end.

A shout. Another cannon shot shivered the ground and black smoke boiled up from the other side of the barricade. Men tumbled out of the nearby buildings. Some scrambled up onto the barrier to provide covering fire for an assault on the transformer, while others ran across to occupy key buildings on the other side of the street. Two men slipped into the whorehouse and a moment later could be seen running low along the edge of the rooftops from building to building, garishly lit by the militia's white siege lights. The aproned barman went back inside finally.

Pull back, Wen ordered. Sightseeing is over.

The handcar man stood erect and grasped the handles of the pump, but before the car had begun to move a bolt struck him in the head. His eyes turned milky and he tumbled off the car onto the pavement. The car, kicked backward by the force of the bolt, rolled a little ways beyond, creeping toward safety.

Stupefied, Wen stared at the body of the militiaman lying face down beside the tram tracks. The back of his head was smoking a little and the stench of burned hair came to Wen in whiffs on the swirling breeze, mixed with hot earth from the cannon fire and alternating with the mingled smells of coffee, sweet pastry, and sweat.

What? What? The situation was slipping out of his hands like warm syrup. He felt the ground shake.

Suddenly aware of his own situation he jerked back, jabbing himself painfully with the car's pump handle. Turning, he threw himself on it. The car rolled backward a bit more. The pump handle rose obstinately. He wrestled it down again. The car gained speed and was soon out of range, but Wen continued to fight with the unfamiliar levers which powered him, faster and faster, back to the command post on Vardon Square.

《》

At the lower gate of Government House Cpl. Cuelleman was on duty when the uprising began. He was looking right down into the barrio and wondering what had happened to his brother-in-law Bengt when a spike of yellow flame shot up high into the sky and a moment later the whoof! of the explosion blew over him like a foul gust from the mouth of a street beggar.

Shit! cried the man on the other side of the gate. What's

that?

Cuelleman's heart sank. He knew at once that he was going down there. From the moment that he was picked out of reveille for the Hollis expedition he had been caught up in events beyond his understanding or control. He had become an embarrassment to everyone, even Liz. It was like a tattoo, a stigma. Because of this mark he was going to go down there and they were going to kill him.

At midnight when he came off duty, Cuelleman heard in the barracks that the rebels had captured a cannon and turned it on the militia, blowing up a tram car. They had gained control of a bridge to the east side of the city, where a new uprising threatened a second com bunker.

Back out in the guardhouse a sergeant was raging around the walls of the tiny room. What are they doing? the man pleaded in an anguished voice. What are they doing?

But no one seemed to know.

《〉》

Kalgoorlie waited. Horring and Etterhaven waited. Farmers, fishing folk, craftsmen, professors, bureaucrats, soldiers waited for this unstable situation to resolve itself into components, factions, enemies.

Fishbach had a long-simmering slave rebellion on his hands, dating from before the present crisis. Wen's position was slowly hardening to intransigence as the uprising in Kalgoorlie destroyed his plans for managing the infall and as his anger with Maldonado grew. Maldonado himself did nothing to neutralize the attribution to him of a scorched-earth strategy for clearing the barrio, a misapprehension which Charles did not entirely discount. Charles was appalled at the incompetence of them all, at the way they had let the situation get out of hand, at their childish Machiavellian posturing and complete ignorance of the concept of virtú. Ng's detachment remained undisturbed. She had made an easy calculation of the likelihood of success of the remnants of the barrio people and made her own plans. Her creature Cuelleman was in place, held there by the conflict of ambition and his barrio origins and suborned by his eye. Dragged out of the desert deep into Government at one go, marked with a beacon making him always and everywhere visible. Known. Cuelleman, feeling trapped and used but over-estimating his powers, counted on to break out irrationally as the ancient peoples struggled against a war of extermination on a continent which could have accommodated a thousand times their numbers, fought in the name of hatred and ignited by centuries-old fear. And the Eye saw it all, and waited.

《〉〉

Frederick Cuelleman recalled his mother working through the night, wrestling with a set of ledgers which wouldn't balance and Reconciliation said otherwise. Adding up long lists of numbers again and again, looking for that inconsistency, that malpractice, falsehood, that iniquity still not requited which kept the garment from falling into its proper shape like a bit of the cloth caught up in a wrong seam.

And when it did, Reconciliation was angry. Once too often.

You created this situation, Ng Jo was saying, now openly accusing Maldonado of complicity with unreason — but not ex nihilo, this creation. A craft, like any other. Bad craftsmanship, she was saying. Lots of turpitude.

The Councilor winced. He thought there was some truth in that. That he had worried too much about the imminent colony ship; that he had delayed and temporized to keep Wen from getting a stranglehold on the suppositious colo-

nists; that Kalgoorlie was slipping out of his grip, liberat-
ing itself they said but that was an illusion, it would only
be another form of thralldom, of subjection — to chaos or
misgovernment or opportunists to step in and save them all
from themselves as the Romans so often rescued the squabbling Greek cities. But then no one here read Earth history.
One's own time always seems otherwise, he reflected. The
time one actually lives through rather than imagines, so that
being given longer lives, more lives, is perhaps not a good
thing. Immortality liquefies time and perpetuates evils. Or
so he thought.

It was a perspective borrowed from Charles, who had
reason to understand it.

That Cuelleman person was on his mind. He hadn't
known what to make of him and so had made nothing of him
and had perhaps unleashed his own undoing. It was hard to
see how such a ratty nobody could rise to the top so quickly.
He was a methane bubble. And now here was an ally rounding on him, and moreover the person who had brought Cuelleman's supposed utility to his attention in the first place.

Maldonado and Ng were talking in Maldonado's office
— the office of the Chairman, the President, the ersatz Chan-
cellor, protoprotem — at the top of Government House.
They looked down on the city through wide windows as on a
map of battle, but one made hazy and distant by smoke, and
by the polarizing screen which kept out the glare of the fires
burning in the barrio. Earlier in the night the rebels had taken
possession of a cannon and consolidated their control of the
densest part of the barrio, the oldest section, on the western
side. In order to prevent the rebels using the cannon, power
had had to be cut to the tram line and now the whole central
corridor, tenements and fashionable shops alike, stood without cooling or cooking. The spine of the city was broken.
But from the top of Government it was all as picturesque as

something in a museum.

There's been a flap about that, of course, Maldonado said, still pondering the museum cliché.

Restaurateurs who wouldn't give a sour pancake, Jorge, to know what went on south of Vardon Boulevard.

Wouldn't give a flapjack.

He hadn't slept. His eyes were purple with fatigue. His head ached from the fall into the fountain. And he was not eager to fight with Ng Jo, who always took care to look as if she'd just come from the baths.

You won't move against the rebels, Ng observed, confirming an intuition.

I would not.

A whole mass of ideology was rising to verbal consciousness in him like scum on bean soup.

They decline to be erased, he said. I decline to erase them.

Councilor Maldonado sighed ostentatiously and said nevertheless the insurrection would fail — militarily and politically fail. Belly up.

Wen, Ng said, laconic.

He likewise declines.

Prefers squalid, dead barrileños, Ng observed, tartly, despite his pretty speeches.

They will be sent to the Old Ones, one way or another. Let it not be me, that's all.

Failure, Ng repeated. Meaning it will be you, nevertheless.

Yes.

Maldonado waved one hand limply in the air.

So, Jorge. It isn't the justice of their position or the inhumanity of their condition that keeps you from wiping them out, it's that you can't. You haven't the strength. You're tired. Being weak, you'll slip up somewhere, and matters will be done with as you wish.

Why is Li not using the militia himself? Maldonado wondered aloud, breaking a long gloomy silence.

Not strong enough, himself. Yet.

Haven't slept, Maldonado muttered. What is Fishbach up to? I don't want to think about Vardon, about the miners. Crushed. Probably crushed by now. Horrors. Fierce, wreaking little man, that Fishbach. He goes away, Li goes away, we wait.

His arm swept out a long arc, indicating the empty room.

Complaints succeeded one another. He woke from his reverie to find Ng gone and a secretary saying she had left a message.

Maldonado took the mirrored envelope delicately and fastidiously between two finger tips. Ng's calendar flowered above his desk.

Also an appointment with the Horran consul, the secretary said drily, in half an hour. He has requested a skiff, to be called for at the consulate. He intends to tour the mines.

The secretary reached across and cupped her hand over the entire scheduling matrix. The cube crumpled to a point of blue light.

I'll see the ambassador directly, then, Maldonado said, taking the secretary's suggestion. Leave word for Ng to report this evening.

In what privacy there was, Maldonado smeared his thumb across the envelope of Ng's message. The enveloping mirror cleared and vanished. The message was empty.

A reminder of the end, I suppose, he muttered. Engimatic woman.

Councilor Maldonado paused, suddenly struck by a thought plunged, Cato-like, deep into his heart, not an idea yet but only a notion.

Fires were springing up above Vardon Boulevard. A

rope of black, oily smoke rose from one house nearest the command post on the square. Maldonado called in the duty officer.

They've fired the buildings along the perimeter, the man reported matter-of-factly.

Was this expected?

It's a sensible tactic, sir.

Whose house is that?

In the upper town? Sr. Robinet, I believe. The banker.

Maldonado stared down at the fires, which were beginning to grow together into a wall. Not the cordon sanitaire he'd had in mind. It was surprising how much fuel was in a stone building.

The curtain of thick smoke rose until it struck the underside of an inversion and began to spread out like sludge on a piece of glass. Soon, however, the rising heat grew more intense and this ephemeral barrier melted. Huge moiling bubbles of sludgy smoke swelled into the clear still air above and broke, spewing black spores.

He had forgotten the duty officer, who now cleared his throat suggestively.

Find me Charles Renaud, Maldonado said.

Five minutes later, Charles showed up in Maldonado's in basket. Not that Charles, Maldonado said, pushing his face very close to the desktop manikin. It winked out.

The Horran ambassador appeared, and shortly after the embodied Charles, looking somewhat flustered. Secretary Renaud, Maldonado said curtly, by way of introduction. The ambassador was a short podgy man with the rolling gait of a seaman, like everyone from the fishing village which was the only habitation of note in that province. Maldonado steered the ambassador by his elbow over to the window, Charles attending a step behind.

Will they be able to control that, do you think? Maldonado said.

If water supplies haven't been cut off, Charles remarked.

What? The ambassador was astounded. Cut off the water? They'll die.

Yes.

Can nothing be done?

Do you know Councillor Wen? Maldonado said after a time.

No, the ambassador replied stiffly.

Pity.

Maldonado slapped the vid connection on his arm just below the Commissionaire's badge. The familiar blue aide appeared.

Yes, sir?

When is the next pass of the eye?

We're getting twice daily reports now, sir.

Councilor Wen had the orbit adjusted a week ago, said Charles quietly, keeping out of the vid sightline.

Interfering man.

The aide was beginning to be alarmed. We were told it was to clear a parking orbit for the settlement ship, he said.

He wishes to keep closer watch on Vardon developments, Charles interpreted quietly. Maldonado felt a muscle in his cheek begin to twitch.

When was the last pass, then?

I'll have to check, the duty officer returned. It would have been midafternoon.

Get it for me, please. And ask Wen to come here.

The officer nodded and blinked out.

Maldonado returned his gaze to what was happening beyond the window. You see there, he said to the ambassador, pointing. Where the barrio tenements are beginning to collapse. You would not be able to hear the screams of the barrileños, as the fire is too loud.

What is going on here? the horrified ambassador whispered.

Ah. Well, sir, we have been expecting something of this sort for a long time. It is inevitable when the inequity in society becomes too extreme. The prospect of half a million new immigrants among whom to share already limited resources brought the matter to its touchpoint, which Sr. Wen has obligingly provided.

He turned. Good afternoon, Li. Ambassador, allow me to present our Minister of the Interior.

There was an exchange of bows, after the Horran practice.

You were speaking of a touchpoint? the ambassador said, looking from one to the other. Charles remained discreetly in the background.

Yes, sir. I did. It is this business of kissop weed. In large areas of the desert it is the only thing which will grow. Weed clearance destroys a fragile balance.

Leave it alone, then.

Ah. Firstly, there is the north basin, where we propose to build temporary infall housing. This comes within Minister Li's charter, by which he will profit. The necessary weed clearance in the north basin reduces the public support.

The dole, Wen growled, and immediately regretted his indiscretion.

But it's a weed, you say.

Yes. Yes, it is. With careful practice it can be farmed, which makes it a useful source of fuel and industrial fiber.

I see.

It's extraordinarily invasive. When we came here it was found in only a few patches in the mountains north of the city. Its spores are poisonous

The ambassador frowned. I had not been advised so, he said.

Then there is the Vardon mine, already a sore spot with the people. They want to know why no profit has been declared and the promised distribution is continually delayed. You have heard of the Kristenkowski Find, ambassador?

I have.

Wen Li was beginning to be restive, but wary of appearing petulant if he should attempt to justify himself.

Another source of money which has not found its way to the people. Sr. Li is felt, unjustly I am sure, to have lined his own pockets instead.

The ambassador turned to peer at Wen. The two men were both short and fat, a pair of comical brothers were it not for the brief flash of understanding which shot between them. In the light of this bit of static electricity Wen stood a bit straighter.

Then there is the matter, Maldonado continued, of the working conditions in the mine. You understand that the people are subject to corvée as miners.

Maldonado's com winked open.

I have the eye for you, the duty officer said. The last pass was about four hours ago, as I said.

You did not say. Give me the Vardon stripe.

Coming up.

The com's blue visual expanded on an ocean, which turned streaky with brown and foam as the recording whirled, hurled itself forward to stop again on the barren, fissured mountains of the mining district. Maldonado paused to check the time and coordinate key along the lower edge of the scan. Two thirty in the afternoon. Locating himself, he slithered ahead until the edge of the mine works appeared in the southwest corner. The mine itself, just back from the mouth of a narrow coiled valley, was driven into the hillside there where it was marked by a spewed fan of red and orange rock dust. Maldonado dropped until he could make out the bodies of individual miners strewn among the rocks.

Dead? the ambassador questioned. He peered at the

scene more closely. These are not militia, he said. Where are the militia?

Maldonado angrily jerked the scan backwards and forwards, then sideways to the edge of the scan stripe where the view was cut off.

On the other side of that canyon, perhaps, the ambassador suggested. Out of sight in the adjacent stripe.

Re-visualize the pass at this level, please. Along this line.

His thin, knobbed finger sliced through the projection, which in response to his request jumped backwards and then began to unwind at normal speed. Among the rocks below the eye nothing moved. The bodies lay face up or down, still, curled or flung out as they had fallen. Only the wind moved, making the leaves of a tree on the canyon wall flash white.

Again, please. Constant focus.

The eye whirled backward, stopped, flowed forward with a changing angle of view which approximated the act of turning one's head to watch a passing scene, greatly extending the time of passage without altering at all the image of silent death which uncoiled slowly beneath him.

Copy that, please, for the ambassador, Maldonado said in a faint voice. He squeezed off the projection.

Will you sit, sir?

Wen was left standing, with Charles close behind. Uncomfortably close. Wen squeezed away to one side.

Down in the barrio the red eyes of fire were closing.

Smothered with foam, Charles said quietly.

Maldonado gestured Charles forward. Charles, he said, is a man of Delfus.

Delphi, Charles corrected quietly.

Of course. He has seen this all before.

Indirectly, yes.

What happened? the ambassador asked, a bit intimidated.

Charles shrugged. A great many people died. There were some reprisals, a Reconciliation, everyone promised not to do it again.

How many?

Oh… a million or so?

What? There aren't that many people on the whole planet.

There will be, Charles said complacently.

A million, Maldonado repeated after looking a long while out of the window.

We'll not be short of people, Charles said, seeing the need to calm Maldonado's existential fears. We're fast breeders.

Some are, was Maldonado's gloomy response. He continued to stand with his hands clasped behind his back, transfixed by the insurrection.

We've no comparison, Charles went on. We're the totality of animal life in this place.

The sun had now set and the reception area had grown dark. Charles broke the mood. He called up some lights with a wave, found seats for them all, set a table with com cubes and glasses of cassia from the sideboard, called for bowls of nuts.

Maldonado directed his attention to the Horran ambassador.

Have you seen what you came for? he said.

The ambassador nodded. I have.

And what do you conclude?

Yes. Some of your enemies, as you know, have taken refuge in Horring. We have no wish to provide a safe haven for such people. The deteriorating situation in Kalgoorlie is cause for alarm. It seems to us that the unrest may spread through the medium of these — ah. Guerrillas, to our own people. My government wishes to reassure itself that matters here are under control. They are not. In fact, they are much worse than we had cause to suspect.

Until a few days ago, Maldonado replied, your first assumption would have been correct. Now, however, you see us as we are, naked and defenseless.

The ambassador's eyes slithered sideways at such unaccustomed diplomatic language.

I feel, he said, that Horring must ask —

Demand, I think you mean.

Shall we say *require* an understanding considering the disposition of Kalgoorian citizens resident in our territories.

I imagine we can come to such an agreement, Maldonado replied smoothly, making a gesture with his glass of wine something like a toast.

We intend to turn away refugees, the ambassador went on. Financial and military assistance will necessarily be refused so long as there is danger that such assistance will fall into the wrong hands.

Understood. It may prove, of course, that the conflagration spreads despite our efforts. You would do well, sir, to look to your own restless underclass and their burden of inequity, as Kalgoorlie too must see that its meager resources do not fall into the wrong hands.

To point this threat, Maldonado pushed his wine glass a little forward on the table toward the ambassador, then pulled it back by a few centimeters.

Further discussion was polite. Plans were made to appoint the necessary delegations, and the other formalities taken care of. When the ambassador was gone, Maldonado was the first to relax.

Thank you, Charles, he said. And Li, you have done well, and taken your punishment for the most part gracefully. We hope you will not become an impediment to our plans.

Wen said nothing.

You shifted the eye south, Maldonado observed.

Yes. Fishbach has broken the strike, it seems. By his own methods.

Apparently.

When does he propose to begin mining again?

The day after tomorrow.

Tomorrow to clean up. All back under the rug, please, Li.

Yes.

Maldonado asked no more questions. Wen edged toward the door and left the room.

Slept any? Charles inquired kindly, in a softer than usual voice.

No.

That's not good.

Charles stepped forward. Tomorrow to clean up, he repeated. You intend to bring the barrio under control tomorrow. Send the ringleaders to the mine, it seems. We're shorthanded there just now, I notice, he said with amused understatement.

Thank you, Charles. Tomorrow.

I think you mis-estimated the ambassador, Jorge. Politically, he has to disassociate himself from Hemla, but morally he finds your position repugnant. He will interfere.

That will be unwise, Maldonado said stiffly.

Not on behalf of the insurgents. Against you.

Well, Maldonado aaid. We'll see.

II

Frederick Cuelleman had unexpectedly been transferred out of the guards to the front line. He had been on sniper detail all day, posted, on the roof of a building opposite the north wall of the barrio. There was nothing to shoot at. The empty houses leaned against each other like prisoners on a hunger strike. He entertained himself by firing into the narrow gangways between buildings, particularly one crevice almost directly opposite which gave him an amusing test of marksmanship, like trying to split one arrow with another, and a second opening off to the side where the bolt, when it could be angled into the gap, rattled about most satisfyingly like a pea in a shoebox. Most of the time he missed, and the shot glanced off toward the militia position on the other side of Vardon Avenue, and finally someone ordered him to quit it, so he retreated into the shade of a cooler vent to gaze at the gray-green, slag-ridden tops of the mountains which he could see above the coping. At four o'clock he was relieved by another sniper who began practicing on the windows and also had to be told to stop.

Checking his rifle at the battery on the square, Cuelleman was told to report after mess to a staging point near the tram crossing. There, he found himself attached to an assault on the barricade. Squads of commandos were to clean out some sources of covering fire, one squad to a building. A main force would then overrun the rebels' pillbox, capture that murderous plasma cannon, and turn it on the barricade.

The operation went wrong, of course. Cuelleman's team was cut down in the lower hallway by a flame thrower, and Cuelleman himself escaped only by diving into a hole under the stairs which he knew was usually built there to service the cooling pans. Barrio children used them for assignations.

They had been betrayed. He'd seen the militia uniform through the flames. A whole commando squad toasted, assassinated, swallowed up, in order to get the Jonah among them, the perfidious barrio rat, but the only man who knew how to save himself. How to escape with knowledge acquired from the very history he had once thought to transcend. Like a foolish mother, the barrio took him back, thinking to shelter him from the world which would only find him the easier to eat.

Why, he wondered, was he now in disfavor? That a bar-rileño should be inconvenient to someone was no surprise, but this was simply arbitrary. Was he caught in some political crossfire? Why this elaborate, murderous ruse when they, whoever they were, could simply execute him?

So Frederick Cuelleman unwillingly embraced his despised ghetto heritage as a sacred asset, a lifesaving grace. He wriggled through the hole under the stairs into the sewer, involuntarily switching sides. If, being a barrileño, he had a side.

The cooling pans were dry. He crawled over the lime crusted stones, shredding his charred uniform, into the dark mouth of the canal. As a boy he had splashed through these underground ducts, a good place to drown. It was a tight fit now, and he would not have been able to squeeze through if the coolers had been working. The channel was damp, with the foul smell of a strangled pond. Perhaps without power to run them the filters had clogged? Emerging from the canal into the sump of a neighboring building, he cautiously peeped out of the service door into an empty hallway.

Another evacuated building, one still nearer the border. A measure of how deep this insurrection was rooted if barrio people would cooperate with an evacuation.

The first thing was to get less conspicuous clothes. Up on the rooftops here in the zone it was easy for him to bush-whack a boy urinating off the ledge into the gangway. He took the boy's clothes, the canvas blouse now with an honorable scorched hole over the breast, and also a long knife he found strapped to the boy's leg. Dressing the body in his own ruined uniform, Cuelleman rolled it off to break on the cobbles five stories below. Now transformed back into the barrileño he once was, into his Hyde half, he dropped to the ground many streets away.

This far inside the barrio it was more crowded than usual. The narrow streets were choked with shanties thrown up by people who had been pushed back from the perimeter. Bonfires gave the only light. Around them clustered soot-blackened children and women in rags poking bits of bread toward the fire to toast them.

Over many of the fires cauldrons boiled, suspended from tripods made out of pipes ripped from the walls. Now and then a child who had managed to catch a vole would spear the animal on a long splinter and thrust it screaming into the flames without bothering to gut it.

Wastrels, Cuelleman growled. You can't eat the thing. Killing them only dissipates the sum of energy. Be eating each other soon enough.

Liz's door had been battered down and her table smashed. Barrio people looking for weapons and food, she said. They'd ripped open her bed, even, but left it, along with her stove, and she was getting along.

What did you do? she asked, seeing her brother so battered.

Got caught in a fight, he muttered, sitting up against an inner wall with his eyes squeezed shut.

Your hair's burned. Smells rotten.

Been in the canals. They've gone dry. You got water?

Liz shrugged. Cisterns, I guess. Got to fetch it. The pipes are all wrecked.

Shit. Two days, Liz. It's only been two days. How are you going to hold out?

Hold out?

They are going to roll over you tomorrow.

Yeah? Well, let em roll, Frew. You're doing your part, I guess.

No I ain't.

Yeah? his sister repeated, belligerent. What are you doing here, then, Bro?

Terrible question. What was he to say to excuse his existence?

Before he could reply, if he could have replied, a big man with flowing black hair swarmed up over the outside landing and into the room through the window. One of his bare arms was wrapped with a dirty bandage and the side of his jaw had been scraped raw. He carried a small cannon, the heavy obsolete power pack on a belt around his waist. In a moment Cuelleman was caught on the floor, pinned like a bug, his pistol kicked away out of reach.

It's my brother, Liz explained to this insurgent, who squatted down to gaze at Cuelleman with wet, luminous eyes. The flesh of Liz's cheeks was like dough, and her own eyes sat dry, deep in purple sockets. The orange uniform of her job was dirty and torn, with crusted white stains on the legs.

You're on the wrong side, Frew, she said. You ain't poor and stupid no more. What are you doing here?

The insurgent's hand twitched, but he hesitated to fire the cannon inside the small room and Cuelleman, given this momentary opening, rolled over backwards through the door. Doubt thus quelled, the big man did fire, with the predictable results. Chunks of the smashed wall rattled into the street and Cuelleman could hear the ceiling coming down. Scrambling to his feet in the hallway, he fumbled for his knife and crouched, waiting for an attack which didn't come. Finally he backed away toward the stairs and left the building without looking around. What had happened to Sis he didn't know.

To the east the sky was lurid with flickering purple and orange light, and fires were springing up on the north side as well. The final assault was beginning.

There was a prickling hysteria in the street crowd. He pushed through, suddenly less confident of his anonymity.

Something sticking to him, some smell of politics, of ambition. Reaching clearer streets near the perimeter, he set off at a lope toward the nearest big fire but found he couldn't approach the border that way. Tindery buildings exploded, torches. Some barrio people were laying down foam, but farther along the flames raced together like maddened lovers into a curtain of fire which roared to kill thought. Cuelleman scrambled back and forth through the alleys and gangways looking futilely for a way past. Now and then, faint screams reached him through the tempest, of people caught in the flames. Probably taken refuge in the canals, just as he would have done, and as if to confirm the thought, the street burst open at his feet. Propelled by an explosion of steam, cobbles flew murderously through the scalding fog. From the hole a flayed woman crawled, the ghetto itself giving birth. Her skin hung from her in strips and shreds. A few meters from the hole she finally collapsed, bowels trailing behind in a ghastly umbilicus.

Shuddering, Cuelleman crawled away on his hands and knees, staying mostly under the flying debris. A few blocks more and he collapsed in a vestibule, unable to go on. All through the night he hunkered there. The building across the street caught fire but did not fall, hiding him when the fire-boats came over shooting plumes of choking white foam. In the morning it still reared up black spears ten meters into the smoky sky, crosshatched by the fragile skipping lines of fallen beams and rafters. Curls of leaden smoke rose slowly from the points. Over the ground lay the patchy blanket of foam, already rotted and dirty.

Picking his way through the wreckage, careful to avoid loose timbers and the acrid, burning foam, Frederick Cuelleman emerged from no man's land in the dawn of the third day of the Kalgoorlie rebellion. Militia rifles turned on him, clattering with suspicion.

It's me, he hollered, displaying his identification tattoo. Then, when the rifles were lowered: My platoon was wiped out in a firefight yesterday. I've been hiding in the canals.

So the rifles were turned aside. Welcoming shouts and slaps rained on him. He grinned. Grinning is a good idea when you don't know who your enemies are.

《 》

Meanwhile, the full Council was preparing to meet for the first time since the troubles began. A future age, Charles said, will capitalize that: the Troubles.

Maldonado pondered Charles's remark. The Troubles. When were the Troubles, Charles?

159e old style, rather than reckoning as we do now, taking time as having begun with the Soster landing. Technozoic era, the Troubles, time b.e. for the time being. Then, after two centuries of war, at the beginning of changes which will not have run their course for a millennium, will not have stabilized, come to rest again until long after the final reforms, until all the consequences of that have been worked out — then, the August Council of Kalgoorlie will meet to discuss —

What?

Charles shrugged. Kissop weed, I suppose.

Inspiriting prospect.

Resplendent in formal dress, the two of them waited in the hallway outside the Council room for the members to assemble. Then the Horran ambassador would make his entrance, followed by the Councillor himself.

All rise, and so forth.

Ng Jo, who should already have been inside, entered the hallway though the pair of doors just beyond where they stood. With an imperious motion of her hand, held flat as if she were smoothing the air, the doors stayed open.

Jo?

Li has outrun us, she said quietly, stepping near. Cuelleman has been betrayed.

Yes?

Fishbach has been questioning a separatista. Sadistic little man. Li passed on the take to Cuelleman's militia squadron, who tried to rub him out in a firefight. His utility to us is nil.

Will he defect?

Presumably.

Maldonado hesitated. Stroking the braid on his sleeve, he spoke a brief order to extract Cuelleman from his present detail. Then he turned to Ng.

You've been indiscreet, he said, indicating Charles with a slight motion of his head.

Unfortunate, she replied dismissively. But Li's trap would have been sprung. He would have painted you as a traitor.

And you?

We'll see how events play out.

You left your back door open, Maldonado said with amusement, pointing to the waiting doors beh ind her.

He turned to Charles. You've been kept on a need-to-know basis, he said. I apologize, but it was necessary. Jo?

Quickly, she laid out a few basics, but then broke off. The ambassador, she said. It will arouse Li's suspicions if I am not in my seat.

She stepped back. The waiting doors closed.

Maldonado bowed to the approaching ambassador. Charles ushered him into the Council room and saw him properly seated, withdrawing as Maldonado made his own entrance, unobtrusively placing himself in a seat behind the Councillor's from which he could provide sotto voce commentary.

With Ng's warning, the Council business passed off smoothly, confined to an outline of the Horring position regarding the war.

Afterwards in his private quarters, as Charles was helping to put away his uniform, Maldonado elaborated.

Cuelleman is that man who came to us a few days ago selling information.

I remember.

A nobody. Ambitious barrileño. Jo found him. Arranged to have him sent out as an inconspicuous member of the Hollis expedition, but with private instructions. The expedition was a failure, of course. Hollis was warned.

One leg, Charles observed, on which Li's accusation could rest.

It was given out that Hollis was dead. Cuelleman's supposed success justified his being transferred to the Pretorian Guard. Is that what it was called, Charles?

Yes, in popular imagination.

To join the Guard it was necessary that Cuelleman be given special clearance. You know these clearances.

Yes.

Then undoubtedly you can piece together the rest of it.

I imagine, Charles said, that the purpose was to infiltrate Wen's bodyguard. As Jo routinely makes these assignments it would not be questioned.

There was something wrong about this from the beginning, Charles. Li made a special point of attending to the clearance personally. Whatever inside knowledge he had probably came from Fishbach, who might have been in a position to know the truth about Hollis.

The second leg, Charles said. What is so important about Hollis, then? He's one of Hemla's. No questions would be asked.

No. There had to be some hold on Cuelleman. Holllis was the perfect target. He's been demonized in the public mind. But he is also the only authority on the biology of the weed.

Then why Jo's urgency?

Li had no proof. He's gotten it somewhere.

But he couldn't bring these charges in front of the ambassador.

Exactly. But a very flimsy screen, Charles. If Li were not occupied with the conduct of the war we would expect it to be torn down at once. And it would be.

Maldonado had gotten his arm entangled in his overshirt. Unable to pull the shirt over his head, his voice nuffled, he had to stop to attend this obstacle.

And about Cuelleman's defection?

He is no longer safe. His roots are with the insurgents. What would you do?

Safely removed from the fray, then, Jorge. Except for this business of the clearance. He's got the eye on him.

Exactly. He must be dealt with. Eliminated, I think.

And does Li now have the upper hand in this fight for control of the Council?

That depends on the progress of the war.

Ng burst into the green room. Maldonado, outraged, was about to berate her contempt for protocol but was cut off.

Li has been driven back again, she said. Within the last half hour. Such weakness will cause his standing in the Council to evaporate.

And if Cuelleman defects, Wen has a new force to deal with.

Just so, Ng said, advancing again on Maldonado. But Wen in Council is not the first objective, is it.

The two of them were exatly matched in height, but Maldonado was soft, lacking Ng Jo's coiled intensity.

Does Cuelleman know what he has in hand? Charles aked, temporarily deflecting the confrontation.

Doubtful, Maldonado began, but Ng cut him off. She gripped his forearm. Maldonado recoiled, but Ng pulled him forward.

You underestimate him, Jorge. He is not a stupid man. It is a matter of time.

Bah. Who is this separatista Fishbach has got hold of?

We don't know,

Then you are as much at fault as I, Jo. Let me go. And I'll thank you not to cause my people to lose face as you did just how.

Maldonado pointed to his outer reception, where his security guards should have prevented Ng's passage.

After Ng had gone and Maldonado was again alone with Charles, he allowed himself a heavy sigh.

There was some truth to those insults, he said. I will never be sure of Ng's loyalties. I suppose that's characteristic of someone in her position.

In the evening word came that Per Hemla had been offered the protection of the Horring government, which had recalled its representatives and vacated its observers' seat on the Council of Kalgoorlie. The neurasthenic Horring ambassador had been exposed to the messy and unpleasant way things got done in Kalgoorlie and other civilized places.

Civilized, Charles thought, in the original sense of being imbued with citizens; polite, as in a polis of sinful and imperfect beings.

The ambassador was offended and went home to advise his government to associate with a better class of people..

Charles was beginning to have some sympathy for this unfortunate Militia corporal, everyone's patsy. He wondered if there were another player in this game.

A vague suspicion. He shuddered.

When Maldonadi had gone, leaving him alone in the anteroom, Charles rubbed his eyes, black with fatigue, and tried to clear his head. This was a petty business compared to how politics might be practiced elsewhere, on a bigger board, among unknowns with many more regional, ethnic, or philosophical differences than two. Lyme, perhaps, if it became less provincial than Kalgoorlie would seemingly always be.

He felt the aristocrat's contempt for these small people and their small world.

Quite wrong, he muttered. My own people were no more certain of themselves. Cautious, bumbling men, also. And I.

He went into Maldonado's office to tidy up but, disturbed by a vague desire for some better purpose, he abandoned that tack and collapsed, just as he was. He fell asleep in a chair with his back to the great panoramic window. Sleeping with his back to the People as so many had accused Maldonado's government of. Sometime during the night his body slumped forward and came to rest propped against the desk; the chair rolled backward little by little, widening the gap, and finally dumped Adjutant Charles Renaud onto the carpeted floor, where he continued to sleep soundly until well into the morning and the beginning of events for which there was no longer any point in waking him or anyone else of the aristocracy.

He was by then well gone into the desert of dreams.

III

Leaving Maldonado's office, Ng considered her own position. She was at risk from the insurgents, moreso now that Wen had been forced to retreat, although at any time they could send commandos against her. Wen was an obvious danger whether he won or lost. And now that the alliance with Maldonado was broken, she was a threat to him as well.

Now, hour by hour and day by day, the situation unraveled. The insurgents, aided by Horran troops and Hemla's guerilla fighters, began to make progress. The battle for the Vardon mines turned. Maldonado's control was slipping into the hands of more ruthless men. Supporters of the Government's policies melted away. A trickle of news stories about the Infall began to appear, causing panic among the bourgeoisie and the aristocracy, who now felt caught by three forces — the Government above, the barrileños below, and the masses overhead. Finances crumbled. Assassinations began.

After some thought, she decided that her best chance lay in the direction she had planned out from the beginning.

At home, just below the wall, safe yet for a few hours perhaps, she hastily put together a kit from the equipment which she had always kept ready for desert expeditions. Sure enough, as she was filling water bottles from the fountain in the courtyard two men in unmarked black canvas clothing burst in with guns drawn. One had been given a key, she realized afterward, which she imagined to be still in his hand. Nothing of her old life was left then. She gloated to feel all that fall away, to feel the lithe conditioned body which she had jealously hoarded so many years carry her up onto the courtyard wall to run lightly along the top and jump down into the street before either of these thugs could even think to turn around. Silent and agile, she slipped through the gap between two houses, into the next street, and was cleanly gone, taking nothing at all with her except the water bottles.

The first question was where to hide. With the certainty of long laid arrangements, she found her way through the smallest streets to the house of an obscure man, a scholar with whom she once studied. There were few people about. The café district was deserted, its sidewalk tables abandoned and its windows, even in this season ordinarily full of fluff and gold braid, were hard and empty. Her teacher's house, too, was dark. Cautiously she kept away from the vestibule. Where she had lived, farther up, the stone paved streets were hardly two meters wide. They twisted across the side of the mountain between white adobe walls irregularly punctuated by recessed courtyard doors and deep windows each protected by an iron grill. Here, lower down on the slope, the houses were smaller, mixed with offices, pushed tighter together. A mere two men could stop up any street, one at each end. The only way out would be over the roofs, and up there a sniper could sweep an arc three quarters of a circle. With a fourth to position them, or an eye, such a tiny security force would be thoroughly effective. All that was needed was better aerial reconnaissance, something she had herself never persuaded Maldonado to give her. Maldonado had disliked surveillance. Wen would have a surfeit of it soon enough, but it was not for Ng to profit by that.

Something stirred behind her. She jumped to one side and flattened herself against the wall. Nothing. It was so quiet she could hear a rustle in the next street.

She considered the dangers of going to ground. But here again was that crucial juncture when the outer sunlit world passed whole through the tiny pinprick lens of the camera obscura and turned upside down. It was thinned and pale like a scraped palimpsest. Through this pinhole, this mumon, through the keyhole of her mother's bedroom, Ng could see years of exile and makeshift rearguard defenses.

She considered also the dangers of moving on. They were serious dangers. To move was always dangerous. She had to be in hiding before morning.

From an intersection farther along shouting erupted. The disturbance was hidden by the curve of the street. Tense, ears alive, she waited, then cautiously crept forward. Just ahead a flight of stairs ran five meters or so down to the intersection, where an identification checkpoint had been set up. The hullaballoo was coming from there: a neighbor had been stopped on his way home from the market, his arms full of suddenly illicit melons. Already past the checkpoint, wearily climbing the stairs toward her, was the man she wanted.

He read the situation instantly. They crossed a still too exposed courtyard in hasty and uncomfortable silence, passed through a small atrium which was once the academy itself, and entered a room more inward than any she had ever before been admitted to, sparely furnished with cushions and a low table. Here the professor set out a glass of arrack and a plate of salt pickles.

What was the shouting about down there? Ng wanted to know, somewhat disingenuously, testing the situation.

The professor sat composedly, legs folded beneath him on the square cushion, hands lying still on his lap. His eyes, however, were restless and sad.

Local people, he murmured. Caught without identity tags. They don't know the rules yet. They haven't been told. It will take a few days.

Will he be let go? The man with the melons.

He nodded. The militia have their hands full. But after that I do not know. You can't stay here, Jo. Not with anyone who once knew you.

Then pass me along.

The old man made no reply. For long minutes, while he looked within himself, Ng concentrated on breathing with discipline.

Tomorrow night, he admitted eventually, cornered. I can do nothing more. After that a name, perhaps.

Ng Jo bowed, the slightest declination of her head, and reached for the glass of wine. There would now be long months of squalid begging, on the move, seeing only the stained and crumbled back walls of character as this conflict between decency and fear, this little morality was played again and again. Once she did not have to fear betrayal. Now she must expect it. Maldonado said it was her luxury to underestimate people. Now, if only for her safety, she would have to believe in the sagacity of others as once she did their gullibility, in good will as once in malice, expect skill and tact where once she encountered only oafish blundering.

The professor was talking about the militia. He had been down to Vardon Avenue to see for himself, and she had encountered him on his return from there. The militia, he said, were massing on the square for an attack, and the rooftops were full of gawkers. The burned-over streets were still smoldering. The insurgents' barrier, pushed forward now up the mountain, above the charred ruins, was within sniper range of the square, making it difficult for the militia to use the area as a staging point. Heavy equipment, hastily armored, was being brought up by the rebels to clear rubble, and also the other cannon from the city's arsenal. There did not seem to be any power or water in the barrio. Small fires were burning here and there, but nothing more. It was hard to tell how big a force wen had been able to gather since the streets were so crowded with civilians, but preparations seemed nearly complete. There would be an assault in the morning, perhaps.

What do they hope to see, these gawkers?

The professor sucked on his lips and said nothing.

Well it's them the guns will be turned on next, Ng observed.

Yes. The old man's eyes became a little milky. I myself went down, he admitted. To gswk. Everyone hopes to hold out until the infall. Everyone hopes to be rescued then. No one will, of course.

Ng considered what the professor had told her.

Wen will hedge his bets if he is able to consolidated his own position, she said, so as not to make any awkward commitments or dangerous promises. That caution will undo him. He's ruthless, but he isn't thoroughgoing or reckless enough to survive. He lacks craft.

A mild, cautious, balanced, honest old man returned her gaze steadily, full knowing.

The glass of wine had eased her physical tension and exposed her weariness. Seeing her begin to slump as she lost concentration, the professor withdrew to his own apartment farther within the house. Ng pulled three cushions together and lay down on the tiled floor. But there she slept only fitfully, dreamed of fleeing along endless twisting alleys hardly wide enough to get through sideways, only to find someone blocking the way. Someone. Who? A dark man, hooded, obscure, as strong and nimble as herself —

Over and over, obsessively, never close enough to catch her before a side passage opened up, gaps only big enough to swallow her like a snake eating a mouse, until, growing bored with this, her dream brought it to an end with a burst of light like a bomb, knocking her down. The walls were blown away; someone roughly took her arm. She found herself transported into the north basin, to a bunker near the landing pad. The Soster landing was in progress. The ground shook; a soundless scream pushed her stomach up into her throat and left her gasping for breath. It went on shaking and shaking —

It was her host, trying to wake her. Head throbbing, she rose and stumbled to the door. Beyond the atrium the sun already slanted high into the courtyard.

Wen's forces moved into the barrio at dawn, said the old man quietly. They have been driven back and are crumbling fast. You have to go now, Jo. You are friend to no one.

It was so. Ng Jo turned away her face. Her old teacher

pressed into her hand a slip of paper on which he had written a name and address.

Do you know where that is?

She did. Once it had been her business to know where everything was.

There was no breakfast. Walking, she ate fruit the professor had given her. At the house to which she had been sent the door was opened by a young man, almost a boy, wearing only stained shorts. His fat skin gleamed, slick with oil. He had no eyebrows.

She mentioned the professor's name, and the name on the professor's piece of paper. The boy's eyelids slowly closed and his lips moved in a pale smile. A rank smell flowed out from the narrow passage behind him and swelled over her.

Yes, he said in a watery, high voice. We are here.

She went in.

《 》

It was evening. From behind the walls of her temporary refuge, Ng Jo could after a fashion follow the progress of the war according to where the plumes of black smoke were rising, until they merged to form a single oily layer high in the air, leaving only a narrow gap above the wall. Tonight she had only a few minutes of sunshine, a lurid purple. Behind her, behind the mountain to which Government House still clung, a thick dust cloud was beginning to rise.

The north basin. The landing site, only half-prepared. The Infall.

That was not due for a year.

Somehow it had appeared out of nowhere, and now somehow it had crossed the remaining distance in a moment.

Was this, in fact, what they all had taken it for?

About midnight the creature she had thought was a boy — it was in fact a dwarf — came to tell her by signs that she was to make ready to leave. When Ng had gathered up her small kit a second dwarf appeared, also voiceless. She asked for some time to wash, but the second man vigorously refused. He seemed a little panicked.

The three of them slipped out of a small door and made their way down into an evil-smelling neighborhood of streets no wider than she was. Here and there, deep inside tiny crevasses between the buildings, dark stairs led farther down. She knew this place. Whenever it rained a slime which covered all the walls would flower and then immediately dry up in the desert heat, leaving a rough coating which would scrape off your arms, or your face if you stumbled against it. Not too far away was the old citadel.

They were going in the wrong direction. She wanted to go up, not down into the exposed south basin, into the sandstorm. There was no refuge in that hurricane.

She laid a hand on the shoulder of one of the dwarves and jerked him back roughly. There was a silent, angry interchange. Jo was not fluent in this language but it was easy to see that both of her guides were adamant.

A laser beam flashed against the side of the head of the man she was closest to. The headless body smacked into the wall and fell into the stream of sewage at her feet, blocking the way. The other guide melted away through a crack no wider than her hand.

Before she could move a lithe man in black canvas, wearing a black hooded blouson, dropped from the roof onto the cobbles behind her.

Quiet.

His voice was no more than a sibilant hiss.

I didn't think you were such a fool as to argue with one of these, he said, pointing his rifle at the small corpse. Ng twitched, and immediately the muzzle snapped up, its red blade like fencer's epée resting on her chest. She began to protest, but had no more than opened her mouth when the hooded man hissed again — quiet!

He backed up against a door behind him, which opened a few centimeters, then slipped in sideways and motioned her through. Inside it was black as an executioner's hood and there was, if possible, even more retching a smell. It was the smell of rotting flesh. Jo moved her foot slightly and stepped on something soft. The single crack of light vanished as the door was closed, leaving only the red laser beam still resting on her. The man in black canvas clearly had some sensory prostheses.

Hold still, he said in a rough voice which sounded familiar were it not for the slur caused by what was probably a breathing mask.

Impressive, she said, for a barrio rat.

Lifted it off some dead commandos.

It's bio-imprinted, you know. You would have had thirty seconds. A minute, maybe.

And I know how to fix that, until the eye works it out.

Do you.

You counted on me, Ng. You counted on my loyalty to my heritage. You conted on my anger. You counted wrong.

Ng started to protest, but Cuelleman pushed her roughly against the wall and covered her mouth.

You thought you would use me, he said in that odd, penetrating whisper. You thought I was an angry man. A sentimental man.

Ng's eyes were hard, black, without relieving light.

A righteous man, Ng. You gave me the gift of the mark of truth.

Wen —

Cuelleman pushed her head back hard, hand across her mouth.

I'm all of those things. I'm your creature, he hissed. You

and Maldonado made me out of the barrio and the desert, but you under-rated Wen's resources.

She pointed to the design under Cuelleman's eye.

Yes, he acknowledged. The Eye knows me. I am seen.

Ng struggled to free herself, but Cuelleman only pressed the air from her with his free hand on her stomach.

Wen will win this war, he said, but it will be a hard win. He's a pragmatist. Like me, he takes his chances as they come and doesn't count the cost.

By now Ng was fighting for breath, and Cuelleman released her. She sagged but didn't crumple. Her voice tore like a saw in her throat.

You bungled it.

Bungled! What do you know? Nothing. You're a danger to anyone near you. That's why they were taking you down into the deep.

Ng kept silent now, working out the implications of what Cuelleman had told her. After a time she asked what he wanted. Wanted of her.

Nothing, now.

Why did you kill that guide?

I should have gotten the other one, too. He'll let the others know you're a danger to them. As if you didn't have enough enemies, now you've made some more. You didn't want to go south. You can't now. You can't stay here and you can't go to Horring. Your only chance is through the high passes to Etterhaven.

She made no reply.

I think you might be able to manage that, he said. In this season. He put on his helmet but left the faceplate up.

Who is a danger to who, here? she asked, keeping her voice small, knowing he could now hear the least rustle.

You still have your uses, apparently. I don't know what they are. I don't want to know what they are.

She nodded.

Good, he said. Councillor Maldonado didn't. I had to listen to a leture on Machiavelli.

Ng laughed silently, but then:

The mark, you said. I know it's power. It has been shown me. I am an angel of death.

Ng's breath left her.

The Eye is capricious, she replied at last. Without loyalties.

And I'm not?

The Eye plays the game for its amusement.

Do you think I don't know that?

Did you learn nothing from Maldonado?

I learned that he is a fool. He talks, but doesn't listen even to himself. Even an ignorant barrio rat knows more. At the crucial moment he did nothing. What was he given his power for? Did he earn it? No more than I. He's a child, who only whines and blames others for his faults.

The Eye is no better, Ng said.

I know that, Cuelleman said fiercely. And so do you, apparently.

Cuelleman snapped down his faceplate. The door opened its crack and he was gone. He left it open after him, and by its light Jo picked her way the two meters back and out again into the street. The body of the dead guide still lay there. She stepped across it, turning back the way she had come, back to the north. Probably someone would throw the body into the abattoir with the other offal.

IV

Karl Fishbach was cleaning out. Wen had said he was precipitate and incautious, but Fishbach was not about to miss his chance. There were too many new people about who did not know their business.

A problem, these new people. Naifs. Nothing ready. Still in curlers and housedress. Embarrasing. They crowded in, perched on the arms of the sofa, balanced tea saucers on their knees.

Wen Li, preoccupied by a war, had left the problem to Karl. Gratifying. Much like being handed a rutabaga and a pickle fork.

Fishbach's private entrance to Government House was still open, though not so protected as it was. He paid two men to stand as sentries in the anteroom at the top of the entrance passage. Men he paid himself. Money was no guarantor of fealty, he had learned very early. Nothing was.

The shorter of the two was on duty as Karl emerged from the entrance tunnel and crossed the foyer to the door of his room. The sentry spoke.

A visitor.

Message?

The sentry said nothing more, only indicated by a movement of his head that the visitor was there in corpus.

Astonished and curious, he disengaged the biopolymer ID and opened the door.

Wen Li.

That yellow toad. What now?

I keep my own key, Wen said, as a precaution.

Karl always had a hard time understanding what Li wanted. What he wanted was cloaked in innuendo and misdirection and had to be guessed at.

Li was keeping one hand in the pocket of his coat. His white suit was streaked with black oil and his white hat and marshall's baton were missing. But if anything, this dishabille icreased the aura of menace which Fishbach sometimes felt in his presence.

Wen occupied the only chair; the others had been taken

away. Fishbach had always found it difficult to stand still, and now at once be began to fidget, shifting his weight, shuffling his feet surreptitiously, hands now before and now behind.

I have news for our people, Wen said. Also instructions. See to it that these are made known.

There were no instructions. The one time Fishbach asked for them he was told in due course, but there was no due course. Most of the time he made them up. Sometimes he guessed right, sometimes wrong. It didn't seem to matter.

This time, however, there was a proviso.

There are to be no more subsidies. If the game is lost there shall be no score kept. This is for your ears, Karl, as well as his. See to it. You know what the stone fingers are.

More puzzles.

How do you suppose you came on your so useful informant so easily, Karl? You thought you had the field to yourelf, and yet you knew nothing of your own forces. Cuelleman has the eye. Do you know what that means?

No.

Of course you don't. He's seen, man. Where he goes, there you go. He goes to his people, you go also, and pluck them out. He was in my power. I gave that to you and you didn't know what to do with it.

Fishbach was dumbfounded.

You were fleeing back to Vardon, I think?

Fishbach nodded silently.

Who do you think has been subsidizing Per Hemla all these years? Where do you think those mine proceeds were going? Only four percent, you said. Your bookkeeping is terrible, Karl.

Why should you?

Why indeed? A simple hedge, perhaps. More — a provision for the Infall. I've known about that for a decade. And anyone could see this rebellion was coming, Infall or no, when the distribution of wealth is so unbalanced the poor will fling themselves on their slavemasters when they have no more to lose. You have been away from the mines too long, Karl.

Wen paused, heavy with implication.

Where, then? Fishbach squeaked.

Nowhere, Karl. You will be crushed by some or another of your victims in any case. You have not taken enough care. You overestimated the power of ruthlessness and cruelty. Like all power, it have limits.

Wen got to his feet. As he stepped across to the door he brushed the back of Karl's hand with one finger.

What are the instructions? Karl said in a disused voice.

In due course, Karl.

V

Wen Li made his way along the back halls of Government House and left the building through an innocuous door opposite the tram stop. From there he boarded a public tram. The tracks followed the terrace wall bordering the front of the grounds for half a kilometer, pausing for a stop before descending the steep grade down to the entertainment district. He would not go there. The front line of battle had pushed too near. Now both of the plasma cannons were in rebel hands, and they had found a way to power them through a captured station which they took off the command grid and improvised an independent startup.

There was simply no way to neutralize those cannons with the forces Wen now controlled. Several flanking movements had been tried and were foiled by the narrow, snarled lanes which interfered with the movement of troops, while the rebels easily melted such obstacles. From his position at the tram stop above it was easy to trace the progress of the fight along these scorched cannon tracks. The only thing holding the rebels back was that the cannon rails had to be relaid to go where they had not originally been intended to.

Probably the only thing the city planners got right, Wen had complained many times to the Council, which steadfastly refused to take into account any possibility of an uprising. Complacent fools.

There was more to this fight than an extraordinarily lopsided distribution of wealth, but that in itself would eventually have provoked what they now faced. The refusal of a communal distribution of Vardon profits, the denial of suffrage, censorship and an impenetrable bureaucracy, the barrio itself, the arbitrary and contemptuous treatment of barrileños by the militia, withholding of public utilities as punishment for any collective action — any of these would have provoked a revolution in time. News of the infall merely hastened it.

Maldonado was a hypocritical fraud. He pretended compassion and did nothing. He objected to a shooting war because he preferred one of another sort. And here was the result. Complete destruction of the inner city, the leveling of middle-class neighborhoods and now some mansions of the wealthy, and a frozen government.

Well, not frozen, in this climate. Sand in the works.

The tram started with a lurch and entered on the switchbacks of the descent. Wen got off two stops farther on and walked through once-crowded streets lined with now water-starved trees and dry fountains, too dark at night to risk.

Behind him, a man dressed in black workingman's clothing and wearing a full-sensory helmet dropped softly from the wall to the sidewalk. He lightly took Wen's elbow and guided him onto the grounds of an abandoned house. Wen, who saw no point in complaint or resistance, let himself be taken. Only when they were inside and he was allowed to turn and face his captor did he see mark of security clearance and recognize the man.

When his helmet was off he faced who he had thought: Cpl Frederick Cuelleman.

Thinking he was in safe hands, Wen relaxed. A hard, painful grip on his arm told him otherwise.

Sit, Cuelleman ordered.

They were in a large room of sheeted furniture. Two chairs had been pulled out into the vacant center, facing each other beneath a chandelier made of ominous glass pendants in the shape of daggers.

Wen sat and waited silently.

Cuelleman nodded, a gesture of approval for Wen's composure.

You have my sister, he said.

Not I. Karl Fishbach.

A detail. I've seen her.

Oh, my. Karl's security is even more dilapidated then I thought.

Either that, Wen, or your recruitment of security bodyguards is better than you thought.

In humility, Corporal, I prefer the former.

Your humility does not extend far, Councillor Wen.

Wen shrugged, It's a war, he said. We shall see after. I've been at work at the front, as you can see.

He gestured open-handed over his disheveled and stained clothes.

I do see. Now let's do some more work.

As you wish. Do you begin with me, or one of the others?

Maldonado and Ng will follow.

You don't, I hope, have in mind some tedious lecture.

Your own, Wen, are extraordinarily dull I'm told.

Cuelleman got to his feet and paced around the back of

Wen's chair, leaving his helmet occupying his own seat. He continued this circuit twice more. On the fourth he stopped, putting his hands on Wen's shoulders.

I should throttle you, he said. You betrayed me. You already knew before you had me transferred to the line that I was beholden to someone else. And how did you know that? Liz doesn't know a security stigma from a bar fight. The men didn't know and couldn't care less. Security is all spies. Had one of your own people among 'em, I guess.

Wen laughed lightly. Jo's work is better than that, he said.

Who, then?

You ignore the obvious, Corporal. I knew the truth about Hollis. I know everything which passes in the desert. There was only one plausible reason for your spurious success, sudden rise, and billeting on me.

You accepted it.

To see what might be done with you, Corporal.

Cuelleman released his hands and stepped across to pick up his helmet.

Nothing. Sir.

So I see. Have you found out what you need to know?

No! He pointed a shaking finger.

An explosion detonated against the wall behind Wen. There was a rattle of plaster and wood splinters, and then a chuck of wall a meter square fell out whole. Wen turned in his seat. Seeing what had happened, his face paled, and on it his lips showed as two bloody wounds.

So, he said. You know.

Know what?

Well, if you don't know it's hardly my business to tell you.

Damn it!

Another explosion very much larger than the first opened the floor to one side of Wen's chair, Slowly, comically, Wen tipped to the side and fell into the hole. Cuelleman heard the crash, then nothing. Finally some weak scrabbling. He grabbed up his helmet and ran out, over the back wall of the compound.

Seen, he said, jumping down on the other side into a flower bed. The soft cultivated earth made him stumble.

Seen.

Cuelleman stuffed his black canvas clothes away in his pack and continued along the street in battle fatigues. He was longing for a place to sit and work out what had happened — not some filthy ell between half-ruined buildings or the corner of a room in a puddle of urine. He found a gelato shop with its door standing open. He went it. There was no power, and the ice had melted and run out days ago. Cuelleman sat down at a table made of crocheted iron and laid his pack and helmet on it. The accompanying half-size chair was not very comfortable-looking. He rummaged around behind the bar and found a package of crackers, with which he improvised a polite semblance of tea and scones.

Seen.

By who? When people said that they usually meant the Eye. In his case, with the small eye imprinted on him just at the lower corner of his own left eye, that was surely what was meant. This was what welded the members of the inner guard together as a single consciousness. The Eye saw more than just a beacon. It saw their minds and thoughts. Somehow.

Or was supposed to. Cuelleman had been transferred out again to the front, almost immediately, before he had ever met another of his kind.

Now it seemed that the Eye was not satisfied with watching events unfold. It was not satisfied with calculations of probability and risk, with sorting and filing. It wanted a role to play, with room to pose and act, improvise, stupify.

But the Eye had no power of its own. It could cloud the mind. It could not fire grenades at walls.

Did he have a say about this?

Cuelleman opened the package of crackers and ate a few. They he took another and ground it to flour in his palm.

He brushed the crumbs onto the floor and took a swallow of water from his canteen. He plucked at the sleeve of his fatigues. This business of being *seen* surely meant that he could not continue as he had begun, sleeping by day and pursuing his black vendettas by night. It was a stupid melodrama. Was he to stand before the king, alone in his robes in the center of the room, with nothing in his hands but his staff?

With that staff he struck the stone floor once, twice, thrice. And the floor opened and swallowed everything — king, throne, courtiers, wizard, all.

Boy's rubbish.

Cuelleman knew he would soon have to decide where to play his cards. On the side of the rebels, currently with the upper hand, but for how long? On the side of Government, probably able to win a war of attrition? Flee to the mountains? Horring, Etterhaven?

Boy's fantasy.

Seen.

《 》

Crossing a relatively undamaged part of the old city, Cuelleman turned down a lane which led to a flight of steps. Ahead of him, a civilian with a twisted leg was making his way slowly by holding to the railing. He carried a cloth bag, the handles over the crook of one arm. There was something heavy in it.

At the bottom the way was closed by two Government police in white helmets.

In witless confusion the crippled man gazed about him.

One MP jabbed him in the shoulder with the barrel of his rifle. He was speaking, was holding out his open hand.

What?

Give it to me.

The crippled man handed over the cloth bag, from which the MP took a dull black cylinder. This he tucked it into his tunic, and turned to go.

Wait! the crippled man shouted. He swayed forward, having a hard time keeping his grip on the railing.

Wait! What about me?

The second MP swung his rifle down in a single smooth motion.

Oh, yes, he said. What about you? and fired point-blank into the man's face, flinging him back onto the steps at Cuelleman's feet. Mercifully, his body rolled over onto its stomach and lay, wedged against the wall, expression unknown.

Cuelleman scrambled down the last steps into the street. The MPs' white backs were disappearing around the corner while Cuelleman remained behind, empty-handed, shouting.

Hey! Hey!

No one heard him. The street was deserted.

« »

It was dark. Cuelleman had fallen in with some rebels, a company of Hemla's guerilla rabble. A day of fighting had left him sore and drained, but the worst looked to be over and he expected now to get more than the naps that had kept him going so far. He had been better prepared than most of them for this sort of fighting. A knockaround childhood and his knowledge of the intricate barrio maze had hardened his mind, dissolving fears and depositing in their place the mineral grains of experience.

They had barely fallen out when the man lying next to

him suddenly rose to all fours.

Damn! he said, with quiet urgency. You got the mark on you, man. Keep away!

Cuelleman rose to one elbow. The other backed away.

You been in the Guard, he said. You got the eye on you. You is seen, man. Get away!

VI

The rebel platoon leader, a fussy rigid man, was shouting about something. He wanted them to form up; he was kicking them awake one by one. Soon the eight of them, bleary and unfed, were leaning against each other in a semblance of reveille. That done, Cuelleman's mind wandered away again. How dumb was this? Wanting to still be military, they were lucky not to have been killed by a single bolt, all snuggled together that way Left alone by the sargent, the men all fell out again..

Wrapped up in a nook of a largely undamaged building, Cuelleman was beginning to realize he had some choices to make. Since the Government platoon-mate had recognized the scar at the corner of his eye, he had worn a bandanna. It was a common practice, pulled up over the nose to the rims of the eyes to keep from breathing so much of the sometimes poisonous dust. But for anonimity he had slipped away from that platoon and insinuated himself in another. Nobody noticed, or cared.

He recognized the neighborhood and the building where he was now holed up. It was the café in which he had firsr encountered Ng Jo.

What a lot had happened since then, He was no longer that young chump, that tool of others. And yet he had also lost something valuable. There was still something tugging at him fron the barrio. Perhaps it was only his fighting temporarily among the rebels. And there had been something like a code, an inarticulate sense of what was the correct thing to do, but unintelligible, like which fork to use.

A lost time. In less than a year.

Nearby there was an old man sleeping under a table. Cuelleman gazed at him. He was an old man who not long ago had been drinking coffee here and had slipped from his chair and fallen there, under the table. A heap.

Under Cuelleman's gaze, the man began to twitch. Waking somewhat, the twitching became a tremor, and soon it was if someone were shaking him, just as the platoon sargent had an hour ago kicked Cuelleman awake. The old man struggled to his hands and knees, vomited, and died there like a supplicant courtier who had made the mistake of using the wrong fork.

So, Cuelleman thought. He could do that on purpose.

《 》

Now began days of senseless destruction of whatever he came across, and nights of exploration among the soldiers of both sides, the homeless and unhoused, starving, waterless people. Cuelleman found that when he met someone face to face, without some provocation he could let them pass. But once or twice every night some paranoia would overcome him. In the daylight this also happened, but whether among civilians or soldiers death was now taken so much for granted that no one noticed.

Something was changing. Government troops were beginning to hold their ground. The killing mood shifted from despair to exhiliration, and the rebel side began to despair.

《 》

One morning early, long before dawn, Cuelleman went out to find a vacant building. He tried to summon again those earlier feelings when he killed the old man, but it was only theater. And he didn't know what to do with them. He glared, pointed, jumped up and down in a tantrum. Finally, the awareness of his own ridiculous behavior struck him and he stopped.

It was just as well, for the building wasn't empty. Cuelleman heard voices within and moved closer. He crossed the street. It was a family who had taken refuge in one of the ground-level stores — a man, at least two women, and some children. As Cuelleman approached, bricks and blocks of concrete began crash onto the pavement. The voices inside fell silent until a crack and a thud were followed by a long wail and the building began slowly to fall in on itself.

Hastily, Cuelleman dashed in, but it was too late. All that remained standing was a corner spire of brick. The voices had fallen silent.

It was not the building Cuelleman had destroyed but the people in it. And they were people he had no feeligs for. He had never laid eyes o them. They were a destitute family he haad felt the stirrings of compassion for.

Now there grew within him an anger of another sort, that of a man who had been turned against himself. It was as if some fledgling god were learning something, like a man learning how to hit a ball with a stick.

Gods. They smite things. People.

《 》

From that moment Cuelleman began to think of himself as an ancient prophet who, wherever he went, struck the ground with his staff and the ground erupted, vomited fire and bodies. He struck the ground and the shells came hard and true. The tide of battle retreated, then returned to a higher mark, and slowly the Government recovered what it had lost. The fighting pushed back into the barrio. A regular pattern of artillery, hand-to-hand cleanup, and rest took hold. The war was turning against the rebels. Wen had proved a surprisingly able commander. The plasma cannon were recovered and with the reinforcements of the centurions of the Infall the enemy was now being driven back. Inexorably, by ones and hundreds, they were being exterminated. Soon nothing would be left of them. They would go to join the Old Ones and the wraiths of the first — and last — people.

Cuelleman had no intention of being one of these. He shifted sides. Again, no one noticed or cared.

His new company was laid up in bivouac in a tiny square not far from where his sister once lived. Once. Where was she now? The buildings which enclosed the square had been gutted by siege cannon. Nobody lived there. In the crowded barrio it was impossible to leave unsecured buildings standing in the company's rear. In areas where the cannon could not be brought to bear they had used chemical fires or gas to drive out the insurgents. Driven back from house to house, street to street, packed ever tighter as the day dragged on, they became desperate, lawless okhloi. Mines, deadfalls, and snipers gave way to crazy mass attacks, suicide missions, and massacres. A platoon operating one block over from Cuelleman's was nearly wiped out by the explosion of a booby trap left in the rubble by retreating insurrectionists, a horrible experience which deranged a few of the survivors, who made an abattoir of the next objective in consequence. Some of Cuelleman's mates had been given the job of cleaning out these crazies because they were firing on everyone, friend or foe, and some of the survivors of *that* operation were still vomiting up long empty stomachs on the ruined square. Presumably some one of these would do something demented tomorrow, and so on. The long sorry history of humankind's vendettas and suckled defeats way outstrips a piddly seventh generation, Cuelleman thought as he dropped off to sleep.

By dusk his company had fought its way over half across the barrio with only thirty percent losses, and he was hoping the insurgents would give up. It didn't seem likely. They would die either way. Everything south of Vardon Avenue was to be razed and rebuilt, he'd heard. What was the point of surrender? So they hung on, clinging to the soldiers like pancake syrup. In the late half-light a little boy of not more than seven had tried to cut Cuelleman's throat. That one had intended to get no older, not even by one day.

It had been Cuelleman's own fault, though. He'd been tired and inattentive, and had allowed himself to get too far down an unsecured street without support. He'd wanted to see whether they couldn't gas the whole block instead of cleaning it out house by house. This screeching child dropped onto his back from a charred balcony and had to be dragged off by a mate come running and Cuelleman escaped only because the boy's knife was nothing more than a metal school ruler broken off short. No bigger than a hatbox, he struggled so fiercely that the men soon grew tired of torturing him and stomped his head. The ragged cut on the side of Cuelleman's neck would be infected, of course. Blood poisoning, or something unpleasant he'd lost his immunity to.

Not surprising. It was getting hard to breathe. Needed a good rain to wash all this away. No rain in months.

The darkness of the ruined streets beyond the square sparkled with flecks of brilliant light as the sentries fired on any movement. Kept sneaking back, wouldn't let go. There was one guy could hardly crawl by the time they finished him, and he still managed to go up with a flare that singed the point man a little. So now everyone was jumpy, running down their power packs on flittering scraps of plastic film and falling boards.

Cuelleman woke after only a few moments. He tried to blunt the edge of his nerve a little, sitting on the ground with his back to the blackened remnant of a stone wall, chewing very slowly on a protein stick from his rations. He was still having trouble breathing. There was a tight band around his chest, which he could burst if only he could get a decent breath. He could feel the blood hammering in his temples.

It was the bad air, of course.

Of course.

Angrily he threw the protein stick away. Grinding his teeth on it was giving him a fresh headache.

Morning came in gray and thick. He opened sticky eyes on a scene of strange and eerie beauty. In the square filled with loose cobbles, trash, and burned spars men lay sleeping where they had fallen, as if shot. Maybe they had been. Thin plumes of steam rose through the pavement to flower in the still air above. Like the wall of a forest, black and shadowy, the remnant fringe of buildings reared up just at the edge of the square, still smoking. Beyond that the gray wood of the next range peeped through, glimpsed like the granite foot of a mountain.

Ah, he muttered. Why don't the buggers give up?

《 》

On the way back to bivouac he came across a barrileño patrol, two men with their faces shrouded. They had one gun between them.

Hand it over, said the one with the gun. The barrel rose. It was one of the short-muzzled sort which fired little stones.

If hit in the stomach it took days to die. The range was short, however. Less than a meter.

Hand what over?

Your pack.

Something clicked within him.

Hey! What about me?

Oh yes. What about you?

All of the anger and hatred of the last weeks boiled up suddenly — the humiliation over Hollis, the multiple betrayals, the old barrio of his chilldhood, his sister, the unthinking acceptance with which those around him met whatever happened, a lifetime of being marked as stupid, ignorant, no more than some golem — blazed up within him.

The man with the gun came alight as if he had touched a plasma power cable. He burned with a fierce energy, consuming more than the smidgen of fuel in his body. He writhed with it, and Cuelleman had no thought but to see him tortured still more. All the futility and rage accumulated in Cuelleman's pointless, violent life burned through the other man until he vanished, decomposed into atoms. The second man gaped and ran. Cuelleman, stupefied, drained of feeling, stumbled away until he ran into a wall, slid down it, and sat down, his face bleeding from being scraped against the brick.

Yes, he was seen, and whatever had been using him to see had found out what it wanted and had tossed him away. This little god, once satisfied to keep watch, was like some boy with a new slingshot wanting to throw rocks at whatever caught his fancy — the windshields of passing cars, people on the street, wind-blown trash — and like a boy, now he longed for something bigger. Buildings. Planets. Solar systems.

And so the next day began, a numbing routine of cannon schedules and ultrasound cleanup, of waiting for foam fire blankets, clearing out the pockets with gas and rifle fire, ratcheting forward one block and waiting for the next cannon pass. The day was hot and dirty and the pall of acrid, carbonized, iron-scented smoke grew thicker. Cuelleman felt his skin coated with some suffocating stuff like thick grease that strangled him, sapped his strength. His reactions grew slower and by noon he too was thrashing out stupidly, firing like everyone else at anything which caught his attention. There were corpses everywhere now. In every hole and corner were two or three huddled together, blasted by cavitation into masses of bloody unrecognizable flesh, already putrefying. The flying rocks and splinters produced bizarre wounds, and there were always some still struggling with hideous injuries. The plasma beams were the worst. Cannons bored deep into the flimsy wooden tenements, leaving people caught inside with the flesh of their backs burned off down to the ribs, or living torsos swimming in a muck of melted fat and blood. He tried to stay out of such places.

At the end of the day the others of his squad collapsed in their tracks. Cuelleman slept only a few hours.

VII

In early afternoon their line of advance reached a squat stone building set in a big open plaza once paved with flagstones, later filled with makeshift shanties. The shanties, however, had been burned like a field of grain, the black ashes covering a hundred meters of now bare ground to the sloping dark gray walls, streaked and stained, irregularly pierced with long slits running deep into the stone. Behind this hunched up fort was a gap in the barrio skyline where there was a ravine once used as a dump.

What the hell is this? the sergeant hollered. Cuelleman!

It's the old court house, sir.

The old what?

The original government buildings, sir. First settlement period. Abandoned. This is old town, sir.

Right. At ease. Cannon due in ten minutes.

But the cannon, when it arrived, could make no impression on these battlements. The walls were too dense. Cannon fire merely glazed them with a mirror surface that scattered subsequent shots dangerously, the shivered light bouncing around the plaza, glancing off in hot melting beams.

So. Here was the limit of the Eye's strength, and his own.

After a few minutes of futility the cannon was ordered forward and Cuelleman's patrol detached to secure the rear by some other means.

There followed a half hour of waiting for orders while the sergeant tried to raise someone. So far there had been no sign of life in the building, or in the ranks of tenements beyond. They stood near the head of the basin here, almost at the southern edge of the city. The low, bare slope of yellow mudstone which guarded the basin's outlet could be seen through the cleared spaces. Behind him stretched an unfamiliar perspective, over the ruins of the barrio to the higher north slope of the basin and the passes to the interior. Stripping away the wreckage and the striations of rust and white stone which were the streets and roofs of the upper town, he could imagine how this place had looked in the first settlement. Harsh and foreboding perhaps, but also grand, stirring with promise. Tears of frustration leaked from under his swollen lids and ran unhindered over his seamed and blackened cheeks.

The sergeant's com jumped to life. He swore. The men gathered around him, curious. Off to the right the visceral thump of the cannon stopped, leaving an uneasy vacancy.

We have an ultimatum, the sergeant said.

General laughter erupted, boiled away to a harsh crackle

with the twitching of the sergeant's cheek.

They're threatening to set off an explosion in the city dump.

What? More incredulous laughter. Who is?

The sergeant's mouth was tight with anger, but that relaxed as more orders came in. Already the ultimatum had been forgotten, assigned an index of risk too low to consider.

Flank the court house on the south, the sergeant now directed, repeating the com's advice.

Right. They all looked toward that part of the barrio still standing south of the court house.

Cannon in ten minutes, barked the sergeant. Advance or be fried.

Cuelleman took the opportunity offered. He tugged on the sergeant's sleeve, pulling him aside to quickly describe how the rebels' position inside the fortress might be infiltrated.

Just you, you mean. You'll take out the place for us. Suicide mission.

I know the building, sir. I played there as a kid.

And you're not done playing yet, is that it?

Cuelleman replied with as much dignity as he could summon.

Got your toys?

Yes sir.

Rendezvous on the cannon track if you get out. We won't wait for you.

Yzr.

Cuelleman could not approach across the exposed, open plaza. But on the south side of the building where there had once been an ornamental garden the barrio thrust out a salient from which he thought he might be able to get in under the citadel's windows. Those windows would be blocked up while the cannon worked on that side of the barrio, anyway.

With only a few minutes available before the cannon came by on its rounds, Cuelleman moved off in a loping stride, equally exposed to snipers on both sides of him. He circled around to the south, feeling perfectly lucid, somewhat disembodied. Now his head and chest felt light and free, his muscles loose. The buildings looming overhead seemed empty like a room full of bugs seemed empty just after the light came on, but with swimmy movements at the edge of his vision. Behind, the cannon was beginning to bore out of the adjoining patrol's stripe, cutting through walls and raising clouds of dust. As Cuelleman darted across the last bit of open ground a high, pulsating scream rose above this industrial racket, easily piercing the bass grumble of explosions and cracking timbers. More fried barrilleños.

Pressing back against the stones, he worked his way around to that side of the court house which fronted the dump. There a scaffold had been built on one of the mounds, from which a cable ran to a window embrasure in the wall above him. This was it, he supposed. Pretty makeshift ultimatum. Not hardened at all. The dump was crawling with people like maggots under the husk of a corpse.

There was an air shaft here which he remembered from earlier times. It was still there, and bent familiarly through the thick stone, but from the inner end came a humming which worried him, as if an exhaust fan might have been built over the opening.

It was not a fan. He dropped the last ten meters into an underground room packed with whispering, muttering barrileños who had taken refuge in the citadel. Embarrassed, meek people who gently disarmed and took him prisoner. A gang of boys escorted him upstairs to a command post staffed by two ambulatory old men, while the low hum of hundreds of conversations never ceased, rising and falling in intensity by the same mechanism which causes the wind to blow: individual particles jostling their neighbors.

The whole building was full of these people. There was no hysteria, little excitement, only this stupid, senseless, foregone waiting, as Cuelleman imagined people in a bomb shelter wait to be squashed by the unseen weight, under the thumb of Baal or whoever. It was difficult to get through. When he had been taken as far as one of the upper hallways his remaining escort gave up, simply pointed out the door and melted into the crowd. Anxious about his family, about a particular flea or two left unprotected on this dogshead. Cuelleman shuffled through the people packed into the wide hall, tripping on the outstretched bodies of a second layer of people lying on the floor underneath the standing ones. Fallen people, exhausted or looking for fresher air or dead. He ignored the incurious stares. Opening the unmarked door which had been indicated he squeezed through before the press against the door cut off his leg.

It was yet another small room, unlit save for one narrow window. Two men who had been conferring over a table now turned to face him. One was Charles Renaud. The other was his brother-in-law Bengt.

Bengt sourly broke off his stare and turned back to the maps he had been studying. I know him, Bengt muttered. Frederick Cuelleman.

So, Charles said. You are still looking for your thirty pieces of silver?

Beg pardon?

Charles gave an amused snort. Got to stop talking like that, he said. No one understands. Step forward, Lazarus. Let's see your putrid shroud.

Bengt ignored him. Over their heads, through the clouded window, Cuelleman could see the black curved streak of the cable running from this room out to the scaffold on the dump. Sitting on the embrasure was a box with a big, ostentatious switch.

Two somewhat lurching steps carried Cuelleman most of the way to the map table, where Charles deflected him onto a nearby folding chair. He plumped down indecorously. The discussion which his entrance had interrupted was quickly finished in an unintelligible whisper, but it was not hard to understand what they were worried about: how to stop the continued, unhindered and even complacent wreckage and death.

Oh yes, Cuelleman said, breaking in. Your ultimatum really was received. Heard. We got it.

The threat was not taken seriously? Charles asked with distant curiosity.

Cuelleman studied him with narrowed eye. He shrugged.

Maybe. If you had said Bengt was behind it I certainly wouldn't have. As if that mattered.

Cuelleman turned toward the window, pointing. They laughed at the idea of a bomb in the dump. They're fools. They don't know what all's in the dump. I suppose there's an analysis somewhere. You probably know where, Charles. Every barrio kid who played there knew it made you — ah, *strange*. Blow it like kissop fluff all over everything and everyone would die, I suppose. You wouldn't need much of a bang. Any miner could do it. Bengt would know.

Bengt was leaning against the wall beside the window, his arms crossed over his chest.

Not so big a window as you once had, is it, Frew? Same view, though.

Liz's political husband smiled angrily.

I figured that much out by myself, Cuelleman said, trying to appear humble. But the net didn't seem to take you seriously. Doesn't care who dies, maybe.

Charles slapped his thigh in exasperation. It's been set to accept thirty percent attrition, he hissed.

And who set it? Cuelleman asked levelly.

That's not the point. Bengt gazed, calm and unblinking, at his brother, who returned his gaze just as steadily.

Oh, but it is, he said.

And then, after a time: What happened to Maldonado?

Charles's face cleared, wiped clean by speculation.

An excess of virtù, he said.

Machiavelli.

Charles's eyes widened slightly.

Taught me in school, Cuelleman said. That's all.

And what else?

Nothing else, like I said. Too much right, not enough left.

They taught you well, then. Maldonado was executed as a traitor a week ago.

Cuelleman laughed, a single bark. So Wen got that much done, he said. As soon as the war turned, off with their heads. No reprisals now. No blood feuds.

Yes, Charles admitted. Ever the pragmatist, Wen Li. A quantum morality, eh? Wen was more clever than I. Fish-bach's sordid traffic, exchanging live slaves for their dead bodies, monitizing them both ways, awarded him as a boon. I missed that. In return, Fishbach laundered Wen's subsidies to the separatists. I missed that. I imagine that by now Hemla has paid his debt, Karl Fishbach is extinct, and Wen's grip on the mines is secure. The Infall is his for the taking. I imagine that he will take it. I was no less a fool than Maldonado, without the excuse.

Bengt lost patience. How did you get in here? he spat.

Through the air shaft. You know which one, Bengt.

What did you come here for?

I don't know, Bengt. I was temporizing. Little comman-do raid, save the city. Big hero.

Rubbish, Frew. You got no principles but yourself. Hon-or and glory, that's too low percentage.

Just wanting to get over the rise, Bengt. Outa here.

A twitch in Cuelleman's cheek betrayed him, however, and for the second time that day tears of rage and frustration leaked from his eyes. Charles saw, and speculation hardened into certainty.

So, he said, but seemed not to be talking to any of them in the room, rather inwardly.

So, he said. You have found a new way, my little friend? In your search for god?

And then his attention returned to the small room in the citadel, and he turned to Cuelleman.

Your father's name was Abraham? he said.

Not. Heinrich.

Oh, but it was, Charles insisted. Abraham.

Cuelleman stared, too non-plussed to be irritated.

I think you are not your own master, Master Frederick.

How do you know that? And who is your little friend?

But Charles said nothing more, only smiled benignly.

Bengt snorted. Abraham! What you come here for, Frew?

What indeed? Intent on betrayal. To betray his people, or betray the government? If the bomb exploded it would poison the whole valley, deny it to everyone. If it did not, his people would be destroyed anyway, and their destroyers in turn under the heel of the new men. Either way, he was to be sacrificed to no purpose whatsoever. All that he would have done or not done was to no purpose but this pointless sacrifice.

Ah, ah — damn! Cuelleman jumped up, darted forward before Bengt could restrain him, and got his hands on Charles's throat. Bengt pulled him off, but with the extra strength born of anger Cuelleman in turn threw him, the bigger man, to the floor, intending to batter his face. That proved to be not well thought out. Bengt only had to turn his head aside and let his brother drive his fist into the naked stone. The crumbling of bones sounded loud in the small, hard room. Cuelleman collapsed, kneeling with his mangled left hand thrust into his belly, forehead pressed to the floor, breathing quickly but otherwise stoically silent.

Which side are you on, Frew? Bengt asked, poking him with the toe of his shoe.

Cuelleman sat up, pulling himself straight, no longer crouching over his mangled hand.

What do you come here for, Frew? Bengt broke in, repeating himself impatiently, stupidly. You're wasting our time.

Cuelleman's eye fell on a laser pen lying on the map table. That would do, together with the clasp knife hidden in an inner pocket which the polite frisking of the old men downstairs had missed. He worked his good hand into his clothing and opened the knife underneath his shirt, and before either Charles or Bengt could turn away he sprang forward, driving the blade into Bengt's neck. Blood spurted out over Cuelleman's arm. It became a frothy pink fountain. Bengt sagged, collapsed. Leaving the knife sticking out, Cuelleman pushed the dead man aside and swept the laser pen off the map table behind him, slashing Charles across the eyes with it. Charles crashed into the table and tried to sit down, but he missed the chair.

Now for the detonator in the embrasure.

It was a double motion switch that required two hands. Clenching his teeth, Cuelleman clamped his frozen hand around the outer ring and twisted the two parts together.

Nothing happened.

Through the bleary, blood-spattered window and the sweat which was running into his eyes Cuelleman could only see the scaffold still standing on its low hill of garbage like an ironic Golgotha.

It's a dud, Bengt, he said. I might have known, if you

were in on it.

Then, sometime later: Where's Sis? There was no reply

Cuelleman waved a hand vaguely toward the ruin beyond the wall of the court house.

He kicked Charles. Was it for real?

Charles scowled, offended. Of course it was for real, he said.

So you bungled it.

Charles sat on his dignity and would not reply to this.

Cuelleman tore a strip from the hem of his shirt and began to wrap his broken hand so that it didn't hurt so much.

They always think it's going to work, he said. But it never does. You should have known that, Charles. You, of all people.

Cuelleman finished wrapping his hand and recovered his knife and the pen.

They're probably going to pump this place full of gas, he said. As soon as they get around to it. If they give you a chance to come out, are you going to come out?

No.

Well, you got some sense anyway.

Cuelleman took a few unsteady steps, opened the door, and went out. In the hallway beyond, the crush was now worse than before. Some of them plucked feebly at his clothes as he pushed through, tearing away his already mutilated shirt finally a few threads at a time. He lost a shoe, too, twisted off when his foot got caught on the stairs. On the floor below he forced his way into a toilet. That, too, was full of people. Standing up on the bodies and then on the sink, he used his remaining shoe to beat out the window, squeezed through, and let himself slide down the glacis onto the pavement below.

Across the plaza they were beginning to tidy up.